Friends of the Wigwam

A Civil War Story

JOHN WILLIAM HUELSKAMP

Original Edits by
C. H. Lundy, M.Ed.
Harvard University

Barrington Group Publications
* Chicago, IL *

ISBN-13: 9780692348826
ISBN-10: 0692348824
LCCN: 2014921976
Barrington Group Publications, Chicago, IL

Praise for Friends of the Wigwam

"John William Huelskamp has an amazing ability for using descriptive words and phrases that form distinctive images and inspire the reader to use all five senses; to capture a scene that matches the action, to listen for the quiet, to feel the muddy slime of the riverbed, or taste the "grass stem" between the lips.

Reading Huelskamp's *Friends of the Wigwam* has given me a new appreciation for the insight and research necessary to create the right balance of historical accuracy, realism, and creative license. *Friends of the Wigwam: A Civil War Story* is an important dramatic reminder of sacrifice, dedication, and courage of the heroes of American history."
- **Richard R. Blake**
  Senior Reviewer, *Midwest Book Review*

"I found this book to be incredibly moving and brilliantly written. I was touched right from the beginning by the intensity of the descriptions and the beauty of the author's writing. Even minor details are fascinating when you read this book. You feel what was felt by the people during that time. Don't miss this one if you love history, historical novels, or stories which are noble and magnificently told."
- **Jean Baldridge Yates**
  Vine Voice

"Although billed as a historical novel, which it is, *Friends of the Wigwam* is based almost entirely on events (including several Civil War battles) that actually occurred and on the lives of historical people. The book combines meticulous research of more than twenty years with vivid and imaginative description. All in all, this is a book I highly recommend."

- **Doug Erlandson**
  Amazon TOP 50 Reviewer

"John William Huelskamp is not only an author, he is a Civil War historian. It is only natural then that *Friends of the Wigwam* be a passionate story of the Civil War with all of its permutations . . . Very strong writing in a must-read novel that could not be published at a better time in our history. Lessons to be learned and not forgotten."

- **Grady Harp**
  Amazon Hall of Fame, TOP 100 Reviewer

"*Friends of the Wigwam* is an outstanding story that preserves and promotes a more vivid understanding of Civil War history. Personally, I have read mostly non-fiction narratives and biographies. Stellar Civil War historical novels are very rare. *Friends of the Wigwam* is one that is refreshing and exciting. If you are a fan of Illinois or Civil War history, you'll love this book!"

- **Krista August**
  Giants in the Park, CWA Nonfiction Book of the Year Award (2011)

It took a stranger passing through town to pull together one of the most important historical dramas of the Civil War. Mr. Huelskamp's research and story has set the record straight for future generations."

- **Harriet Gustason**
  Freeport Journal Standard

"*Friends of the Wigwam* captures the great struggles of the Civil War, its prelude, conclusion and aftermath. This book is a must read for historians of this period in American History."

- **Joseph S. Maresca, Phd.**
  Amazon HALL OF FAME Reviewer

"A consistently compelling read from beginning to end, *Friends of the Wigwam: A Civil War Story* is a deftly written work of fiction that is quite accurately factual in background details . . . Very highly recommended for community library General Fiction collections and for the personal reading lists of Civil War enthusiasts."

- **James A. Cox, Editor-in-Chief**
Midwest Book Review

Acknowledgments

Friends of the Wigwam is the culmination of over thirty years of research and writing. I am indebted to the many people who offered encouragement and advice along the way, including the many professionals and archivists from Northern Illinois museums and historical societies who shared primary source documents and also their love of Civil War history.

Special thanks to Kirby Smith of Barrington, Illinois, who provided me with the core letters and war documents from his ancestor General John E. Smith that are "centerpieces" to this work, and to the late Professor John Y. Simon, noted Ulysses S. Grant editor and scholar, who suggested that I focus my research for the story to include other important Civil War-period personages who lived in the "Union political power corridor" extending from Galena to Chicago.

Similarly, I am deeply indebted to author Peter Cozzens of Alexandria, Virginia, for his encouragement and editorship of my first publication in *Civil War Regiments: A Journal of the American Civil War*, which provided a firm foundation for the larger story found in *Friends of the Wigwam*. Also, my thanks to author Wiley Sword, who many years ago encouraged me to research and document Western Civil War engagements during a very enlightening visit to his home.

The idea of writing a creative historical novel on Northern Illinois history was first suggested by Civil War author Rob Girardi of Chicago and artist Keith Rocco now of Edinburg, Virginia. Both of these individuals have had a very positive impact in bringing Illinois history to the forefront of America. I will always be grateful for their early suggestions and encouragement along the way.

Special thanks to *WGN News* anchor and historian Larry Potash of Lake Forest, Illinois, for his passion, insight, and creativity in bringing the national spotlight to three important characters in my work. His scholarly minidocumentaries of Colonel Putnam, Jennie Hodgers, and Elmer Ellsworth have created national interest in Illinois Civil War history, and for this the people of Illinois will always be grateful. I am also indebted to Dwight Jon Zimmerman, *New York Times* best-selling author of many military and historical works, for his recommendation to include runaway slaves and the Illinois underground railroad in the manuscript.

On a personal note, I would like to thank my wonderful wife, Pat, for always keeping my dreams alive and for the countless hours she has spent reading and enhancing multiple drafts of *Friends of the Wigwam*. A fatherly thanks also to Christy, Tim, and Jeff for their encouragement and suggestions that also contributed to the form and content of the work. For their love, kindness, and understanding during my many years researching, reflecting, and writing, I will always be grateful.

To my parents, siblings, and extended family, I thank all of you for listening with great interest to my storytelling, which began at a very young age, and for your positive encouragement during those memorable times together. You have truly influenced my life's journey as a writer...and the core development of the story contained within these pages.

Introduction

Friends of the Wigwam is a historical novel about key soldiers and citizens who lived during the dramatic years of the American Civil War. Only true-to-life characters have been selected for this novel. Some of these characters will be very familiar to you; others not so. To be sure, though, all are important to the story. They are "actors" who between the years 1857 and 1865 collectively staged a very tragic time in our nation's history. All lived within one hundred miles of my home in Northern Illinois.

The landscape of the events and battles, I trust, will come alive for you as the characters evolve through the storytelling. I have selected actual firsthand documents and correspondences in the story to give you a closer "feel" for the times. Many of these primary source documents are published here for the first time. These entries are italicized, numbered, and noted at the end of the manuscript. It is my hope that these literary treasures will continue to be chronicled by Civil War scholars and enthusiasts for present and future generations.

As most historians agree, an accurate chronology of real events best serves the historical timeline. To this end you will find chapter headers true to the date and place that the historical event occurred and, where noted, the actual time of day.

To conclude, even though the people and events are factual and real, the dialogue between the characters, as in all historical novels, comes from my pen, and, therefore, the interpretation of each character in *Friends of the Wigwam* is my own.

John William Huelskamp
Deer Park, Illinois
May 17, 2015

"In our youths our hearts were touched with fire."

Oliver Wendell Holmes Jr.

Chapter 1

Pecatonica River

Freeport
Northwest Illinois
Summer, 1857

Will and Aaron were the best of friends. They were by most impressions in town…true brothers. Will, older by three years, had the knack and the spunk to take Aaron under his wing at an early age and often protected him in playground fights, usually taking a black eye or a bruise for him. Aaron looked up to the sixteen-year-old as his leader and friend.

Freeport that year was considerably more hot and humid than previous summers. As expected, the townsfolk, young and old, always found time to head to the river. The Pecatonica, named years ago by the local Winnebago Indians, meandered at a slow pace. It looked like more of a flatboat waterway than a vacation spot. And though the air was thick this summer, the breeze that topped the waterway caused it to ripple and brought the desired respite.

Aaron stood close to the water. The afternoon sun caused him to squint as he peered across the Pecatonica. He cupped his hands around his mouth, took in a deep breath, and shouted, "Hey, Will!" Startled, a brown-bellied gray squirrel on a branch above leaped to a higher branch, dangled for a quick moment with his front claws embedded deeply in thick bark, and then righted himself and scrambled out of sight.

Aaron looked for movement across the water. A large twig floated slowly by, but there was no other movement. Again he cupped his hands and increased his pitch. "Hey, Will! Where are you?" Aaron dropped his hands to his sides and peered left to right, but there was only quiet. He then proceeded upriver where he had seen Will last. Squeezing between an old hickory tree and the shoreline, he gripped the bark with both hands so he wouldn't slip into the water. He moved slowly, very slowly, as he peered back over his shoulder.

A shout shattered the calm: "Hey!…Gotcha, Aaron!"

Unlike the startled squirrel, Aaron lost his grip and, with his arms extended like a cross, smacked backward into the water. After quickly rolling to his side in the now-murky current, he righted himself and then squatted with the Pecatonica at his waist. Glaring up at Will, who looked down at him from a stout log high on the riverbank, Aaron slowly rose. Standing knee deep, he placed his hands defiantly on his hips.

Will gripped his chest and gasped for air with arms crossed over his torso. He could not speak. He was laughing too hard.

"Why do you always sneak up on me like some old Potawatomi Injun?"

Will howled and continued to gasp for air. He stood up and then settled down again on the fallen tree stump, forearms resting on his knees.

Aaron looked up, shook his head in disgust, and then forced out a smile. He slogged his way closer to the shore, brown clouds of stirred-up mud swirling around his legs.

Will grinned, reached down to the ground, and plucked a thick piece of river grass out of the damp soil. He stripped it and placed the stem in the tiny space between his two front teeth. Dropping his hands, the stem remained with the grass blade dangling in midair. "Did you think a granddaddy copperhead jumped me and dropped me for dead?" he asked with a curious smile.

"No," Aaron replied. "Shucks, you know there ain't no copperheads around these parts. No poison snakes around here at all! And what took you so damn long to get here from the stable? I left Tutty's Tavern downriver about two hours ago. I could've made another two cents today if I knew you were gonna be late!"

"Oh, hush down there. You don't make a cent an hour! Ol' Tutty won't pay a barboy more than five cents a day! So cut your whining. You just lost a penny with me being late, I reckon. And here…" Will reached into his pocket and pulled out an Indian-head penny. He held it up to the sun, which was at its peak now. The copper twinkled. He smiled and then looked at his wet friend. "Here ya go…Sorry."

A cardinal chirped, and they both looked up to the treetops. It darted through the branches out of sight.

"That's all right, Will. You can keep it," Aaron replied softly. "Friends are supposed to wait for each other. Don't matter how short or how long."

Will smiled and nodded. The grass stem was all chewed. He spit it out and reached for another.

"But what took you so long at the stable?"

Will looked across the Pecatonica as if gazing at a mountain range. He was silent for a moment and then shook his head. "Damndest thing happened today," he said almost in a monotone voice.

"What, Will?…What is it?"

Will sat down tucking his legs up until his knees touched his chin. The river grass he was chewing dangled at an angle. He pulled it out and tossed it in the Pecatonica. It swirled and then floated away.

"I was in the stable as usual, pullin' the feed for a few mares when I heard a whinny from a small colt. I looked up, and there in front of the double door stood a Negro man with shoulders as big as a blacksmith's. I was in the shadows looking out, and I couldn't see clearly at first, but, sure enough, it was a Negro man starin' at me silently. He had straight black hair and a long moustache that went down to his jaw."

"Well, what did he want?" Aaron replied curiously.

"The damndest thing, Aaron—the damndest thing!"

"What? What of it?"

"Next to him stood this little black colt only about six hands high. The man was very strong and was holding him tight so he wouldn't jump away and hurt himself. The little colt would dance and whinny, and the man would, in one quick motion, pull him in. It was the strangest sight!"

"What then?" Aaron exclaimed.

"The man was short on words. He didn't say much more but that he needed a home for the little colt for a while. He asked me how much it was to quarter it at the stable. I told him five cents a day. He then handed me a ten-dollar gold piece, handed me the reins, and left. Before I could say anything, he was gone!"

"Well, jumpin' jiminy, where is this little colt? Let's go see it! Bet it's a beauty!" Aaron looked north to the town.

"Hold on. He's resting now! Best not stir him up. Besides, we can't leave now. We gotta get those cane-pole lines in the river if we expect to catch some big cats for dinner." Will looked around him for the fishing poles. "Where are they at?"

Aaron hesitated and then stood up and pointed with his arm as straight as an arrow. "Over there behind that ol' stump by the ripplin' water! See those water bugs?"

"Can't see 'em," Will replied as he got closer to the stump. "Come on. Where did you put the poles?"

"On the other side. Are you blind?"

"Where?"

"Just look over the stump!"

Will toed his boot tips on the base of the stump facing the river. He then placed his left hand on the center of the stump, squatted, and then reached down to feel for the poles. He looked back to Aaron. "Jeez, Aaron, where in heaven's half acre are they?" He reached further and looked down again.

Aaron made his move. He quickly darted in and then pushed Will head over heels into the Pecatonica. After a deep thump, large ripples rolled. Frogs on the other side of the riverbank jumped for safety. Will emerged a moment later like a wet dog.

"You son of a..." Will screamed. He jumped up, slipped, and fell down again.

Aaron screamed like a howling coyote. He couldn't breathe; he was laughing so hard. He then headed downriver for what he thought would be the race of his life.

Will climbed out. He looked down at his soaked leather boots scuffed by mud and rock. Peering downriver, he pushed off, digging his heels into the shore mud.

But Aaron had the jump on Will. Though just thirteen, he had more speed and quickness than any older challengers in Freeport. Knowing this, he quickly increased his stride, bounding over logs and rocks and brushing past small bushes along the way with Will, fast in his own right, hot on his heels. Aaron knew he could widen the distance and continued his stronger pace until Will was left far behind.

There was always a quiet along the Pecatonica. Even at a full run, Aaron could feel it. The breeze cooled his sweaty brow with gentle bursts. The sun pierced occasionally through the deep shade of swirling cottonwood trees that rose over him. The riverbank was cool, and his motion mixed with nature's wonder had a calming, even mesmerizing, effect on him as he continued downstream. His pace was even and steady now, and he floated into a dreamlike state.

Proceeding a little farther, he suddenly stopped in his tracks like a startled deer, digging his heels in the shore mud in one quick motion.

He did not move. His heart pounded in his head. He could not believe what he saw ahead of him. It was like a mirage, so he remained in place, quiet and steady in his tracks.

Will soon crashed into the silence, still caught up in the chase, water dripping down his face from the fall.

"What's wrong, Aaron? You tired already? What did you think— you could outrun me?"

"Shut up. There's somethin' up there at the bend!"

"What is it?"

"Do you see that flash?—See it? There it is again!"

"Yeah, I do," replied Will as he tried to catch his breath.

"What do you think it is?"

"I don't know."

Both boys hunched forward and remained quiet with anticipation. And there it flashed again.

"Looks like a flicker firefly," Aaron said curiously. "But you only see them in the night."

"Let's move a little closer," Will replied calmly as he gently placed his hand on Aaron's shoulder. He caught his wind, gasped a bit, and then whispered, "It's definitely coming from that crack in the rocks at the bend. Could it be a fire?"

"Fires show smoke. That just can't be," Aaron replied.

They moved forward with caution, side by side. Their wet boots squeaked, startling a bullfrog and causing it to bob. Looking curiously at each other, they faced forward and crept, hunched over like Indians treading on leaves, each step measured by silence and stealth. Both boys then stopped in one motion and stood up straight as soldiers.

"Lookee there. It's a cave, I think!"

"Reckon so," Will replied.

Just upstream and very close to the cave was a massive oak tree with northern moss growing on its trunk about twelve hands high. The tree itself bent over the river like a taut Indian bow curving toward the water, and was just a few steps from the entrance to the cave. Near this strangely curved oak tree and around the dark cave entrance were holly bushes with hundreds of red berries. Several pointed spruce trees completed the odd-looking pattern that secured the cave entrance from the notice of passersby.

"Jumpin' jiminy!" Aaron screamed. He gasped and then swallowed again, "There might be a pirate's treasure in there! Should we go in there? Or should we go get Sheriff Taggart?"

Will lowered his voice and said with a solemn hesitancy, "No. We best check it out ourselves."

He felt strange, even spooked now, as he passed by the old oak tree. Yet he felt a sense of peace as he approached the cave entrance. Aaron was two steps behind. This was indeed a special place, Will thought, but he could not understand why. Pushing back the holly branches that concealed the entrance, he crouched down, and with a crunch of his boot, he stepped inside.

The inside of the cave was about as big as a chicken coop. The walls rose to the ceiling at steep angles and ended in the center where a foot-wide opening allowed the summer sun to shine through at high noon.

"This beam of light is the source of the light flash! But how did it bend outside through the cave entrance?" Aaron scratched his head and then rubbed the sweat off his brow.

Both boys were now totally confused. They wondered how the light could be directed to the spot where they first saw it upriver.

"Maybe it's a reflection off some silver or gold," Will replied. He squinted as he looked to the ceiling and then down again.

"Get down on your knees and help me find what's causing the flash," Aaron beckoned as he took to the cave floor. "We can find this thing!"

Sunlight from the hole in the ceiling cast a dusty glow that widened when it reached the floor. Dust particles seemed to stay steady as they floated, despite the boys' curious movement below.

"Whatever it is, it has to be down here somewhere near the ground," Aaron whispered as he carefully grappled through the loose leaves and twigs on the cave floor. He moved his hands in a circular movement around the perimeter of the light beam so nothing could escape his grasp, and then he felt a sharp pain in his palm.

"I found it! It cut me good!"

"What is it?" Will asked.

"It's a mirror."

"A mirror?"

"Yeah, a mirror, and it cut me good. I'm bleeding like a stuck pig. Give me your kerchief. I've got to wrap it quick!"

Will quickly handed his handkerchief to Aaron who held it in place on his palm.

"Tie it tight," said Aaron calmly. "It got me good, but I'll be all right."

Both boys paused, looked at each other, and then peered through the opening.

"Are you thinking what I'm thinking?" Aaron asked as he clutched his palm.

"What's that?" Will added with a slight hesitation in his voice.

Aaron continued. "This mirror was placed here for a reason. Somebody left it here for someone else to see coming down the river like we did. It was propped on a stone." He lifted the mirror into the sunray. It was oval shaped with a sharp edge all around it. It was about the same size as his now-bloody palm.

"This is a special place," Will replied with conviction. "People, maybe Winnebago Indians, used it as a wigwam or hiding place."

"What's a wigwam?"

"It's a small domed Indian hut made from branches, twigs, and mud. But this place is real special because it's right on the river, and it's hidden. Bet it took a while to dig into this hill."

Aaron nodded his head gently. As he held the mirror in the sunlight, he angled it and directed the reflected light onto the cave walls like a lantern in the night. He spanned the shadows slowly, crisscrossing the beam, combing each inch with a careful eye.

"Look over there!" he said. "It's a tomahawk! And there's a medicine bag with lots of colored beads next to it! You're right. This must be a secret wigwam!"

Will placed one knee on the ground and picked both prizes up gently. He held them in the sunray, which was beginning to dim now as it was approaching midday.

"We found a wigwam," he said. "A secret wigwam. We have to swear as friends that nobody knows about this place. You can't tell anyone. Not Sheriff Taggart. Not your ma or pa. Not anyone. Can you do that?"

Aaron nodded slowly.

Will placed the tomahawk and medicine bag back in the dark space where they found them. "We best leave these things where they are for now," he said calmly. "It's getting late. We have to get going. This will be our secret place," he said with a strong and steady voice.

Aaron extended his wounded hand into the light beam. He winced again as Will grabbed it, but his face could not be seen in the darkness.

"We are friends of the wigwam now," Will announced in a solemn tone.

Aaron nodded. "Friends of the wigwam, now and forever."

Chapter 2

Tutty Baker Tavern

Pecatonica River
Freeport
December, 1857

"Do you want pints or quarts, gentlemen?"

"Bring on just one quart!" replied the taller of the two as they stepped through the tavern door. The wind whistled for a quick moment putting pressure on the door. A few flakes swirled to the floor.

"Well, Elmer Ellsworth of Rockford!" Tutty exclaimed in a robust baritone full of warmth. "And is it young Alfred Smith of Galena?" He continued as he sized him up from head to toe. "It is mighty good to see both of you again. It has been much too long. I hope your families are well. And who, my boys, would like that quart of rum and cider?"

"It is good to see you, too, Tutty! Feel free to pour rum for me. Elmer doesn't drink but plain cider," replied Alfred as he pulled off the long gray coat that hung to his shins. "It is great to be home for Christmas."

Tutty grabbed the coat and shook it strongly. The fire was up. He walked to the mantel and reached for the hook. "And your coat, Elmer?"

"If it is no bother, I will keep it for a spell...until the chill settles."

"Very well, boys, I will warm your drinks."

Tutty's countenance reflected the warmth of the fire. He smiled once again and then turned to step behind the crude split-oak counter that served as a mail station and bar. Several letters were punched onto the nails that were side by side on a hickory post that extended from the bar to the ceiling.

"Aaron, my boy!" Tutty shouted as he turned his head toward a back room, pulled the cork of the rum bottle with his teeth, and then tilted his head in an awkward move as he balanced a quart mug with his meaty hands.

Aaron appeared with his eyes wide open and eager. "Yes, sir, what do you need?" he stated earnestly.

Elmer and Alfred looked at each other and smiled.

"You would make a great West Point cadet from the looks of you. It appears you know about obedience, respect, and stature. You look strong, too," Alfred said with conviction.

Aaron looked over, returned the smile, and glanced at the three neat rows of polished brass buttons on his West Point dress jacket.

"Yes, and if your marching someday is a bit better than those West Pointers," countered Elmer with a smile, "then you could join my Rockford City Greys...all one hundred of them! You could sure show up those boys at the Point. Perhaps even command them some day!" Elmer raised his right eyebrow and continued. "You reckon that's true, my friend?"

"Elmer, you don't know what it's like in the true ranks," replied Alfred quickly and with a wry smile. "The boys at the Point march for fightin'...Your boys march for the ladies!"

Elmer stood up and, with his right palm open, reached over and slapped Alfred's back loudly. He smiled. Looking at Aaron, he asked wryly, "Well, young man, what would you prefer?"

Aaron looked down at his boots and smiled back. He said nothing.

"Aaron," interjected old Tutty, "go pull two irons from the coals. We need to warm these drinks up for these boys. They both still have a chill in their bones." Tutty winked at his two uniformed visitors. "We will get these quarts good for you in short time," he said as he poured the rum ale from the cider spout and walked to the mantel. Hot supper corn mush swung above the embers on a kettle arm. The aroma reminded one of a bakery store in the morning.

"We will warm these up a bit for you," he offered as he signaled Aaron to get the two irons that were buried deep in the red coals.

Aaron bent down to his knees and reached for each iron with a wooden grasper handle. He slowly inserted the round wood cylinder handle on the first iron and pulled it out of the coals. The tip of the iron was as red as the coals. Tutty placed the pewter quart mug on the flat rock floor to the left of the fireplace. Aaron gently pushed the iron into the grog. It hissed and gurgled as he stirred the iron in the liquid. Grabbing the second iron in the same way, he repeated the movements. After resting the handle on the brick wall, he stood up and looked at Tutty.

Tutty smiled and nodded. "Nice work, boy."

Alfred and Elmer nodded in unison, the glow of the crackling coals giving their faces a ruddy hue.

"This grog will take care of your bones. Just give it another minute or two," Tutty said confidently.

Elmer looked across the table at Alfred and winked. He grabbed the lapels of his uniform, pulling one loop off the brass eagle buttons nearest the top. The lapel flapped down. "Tutty, we see your tavern door is still painted scarlet. Is your daughter still looking to be courted?"

"That she is, gentlemen!" Tutty exclaimed. "Are either of you betrothed as yet?"

"Not yet," replied Elmer. "I plan to marry Kitty Spafford someday, but her father wants me to become a lawyer first." He looked at Alfred, pitching his head to the side as he continued. "Perhaps Alfred here would be a great catch as no doubt he will be a general someday, but folks will say your daughter should have nothing to do with military men like us. Praise God, she should be a farmer's wife in Freeport."

"And what military matters are so important that a marriage and family should be put on hold?" asked Tutty as he squatted by the fire. He removed the irons, picked up the rum quarts, and set them down squarely on the table. "What are you two here for on such a night?"

"Well, Tutty, if I may be formal, Alfred came home from his winter break at West Point to do this town a service. He has been kind enough to meet me here to help me raise a drum and drill corps." Elmer looked at Tutty, who was stirring the mush, to see if there was any reaction.

Tutty continued to stir.

"And if I may be so formal," Elmer interjected as he smiled, winking at Alfred, "I will captain a drill-team company, fifty men strong. These boys will be of good moral character and will be of sound mind and body. I am recruiting here in Freeport and Rockford. And if I may say, the search has not been an easy one."

"Are you saying there are no men of character in these parts?"

"No, sir," replied Elmer confidently, "recruiting is tough when the winter rolls in. I will find them before the thaw."

Elmer lifted his mug of warm cider and nodded, turning his head to the fire. The light reflected off his face, revealing a moustache neatly trimmed to each side of his mouth. His curly dark hair fell to the collar. His cap was tilted slightly to the side, exhibiting a certain dash. The collar of his coat was stiff in the military fashion and fit with form and grace. He looked like a leader of men. "Perhaps I should wait 'til spring," he said solemnly as he grasped his mug and drew it closer to his lips. "Perhaps I should wait until spring," he repeated as he swirled the warm cider and watched its settling surface mirror his own reflection.

Boom!

The tavern door opened with a great gust. Wind-swept snow billowed in, breaking the silence and warmth. Tutty stepped back, nearly falling to the floor by the mantel, and then stood to see a heavily clad man framed by the threshold, almost filling it. Elmer and Alfred turned their backs for an instant and then stood to see what was confronting them. Both men automatically reached for their revolvers in their belts.

"What in God's name is going on!" Tutty screamed. "What is the alarm? Who are you?"

"Tutty, it's me, John Sheetz! We met a few months ago. There's a bucket brigade forming! There's a big fire in town! You and your guests here must help fill the line to the river. The winds are picking up fierce. We don't have much time. Bring your buckets!" He exited, slamming the door shut.

"The quarts are on me, boys," Tutty said as he grabbed for his coat. "If we don't beat this thing, there won't be much left of this tavern. Let's get to the bucketline! Aaron, you stay here and tend the tavern!" Tutty opened the door and disappeared into the swirling snow.

Elmer grabbed his great coat off the hook. Both men quickly buttoned themselves to the collar.

"Can I come, too?" Aaron begged.

"No, son, you must stay!" Elmer replied.

The wind howled through the crack in the tavern door causing Alfred to push it almost closed.

"But I can help the bucketline, too!"

"Stay here, son," Elmer replied again. "Someday you will be able to help in these things. Tutty wants you here!"

Alfred pulled the door open, and he and Elmer strode out into the cold. Alfred slammed the door shut so forcefully that the sound echoed off the nearby river shoals. Despite the night and blizzard, they could make out an ominous glow in the distance. They began advancing toward it, the snow crunching loudly beneath their boots.

"Elmer, we will be of better use if we see what the extent of this fire is. Maybe it is not so bad. Let's find Fire Marshal Putnam. He'll tell us where we're needed most. Let's do the double-quick!"

"We must be quick." Elmer exclaimed. "Be careful of the footpaths. They are narrow. Don't risk a fall. I don't want to carry you into Freeport."

The orange backdrop of the fire got bigger as they advanced. Turning a corner around a huge oak tree, they clearly saw the source. The men of the bucket brigade contrasted against the hue, like ghostly silhouettes. There were at least three hundred men posted between the business district and the river. The buckets moved down the line quickly so that there was barely a moment's hesitation between each toss into the growing inferno.

At the front of the line stood Holden Putnam, Freeport's fire marshal. He was a banker by trade but was elected to his position. He stood taller than most men and had eyes that glared fiercely as he shouted commands in the growing fury.

"Form a second line at fifty paces by the stable!" Putnam command-ed. "And get those horses out now!"

"Sir," Elmer asked respectfully, "how many horses are in there?"

"I believe four," Putnam replied.

"I will get them out. The fire is moving too close!"

"Go with caution," Putnam warned, "and get out quick!"

Ellsworth dashed to the door, yanked it open with both hands and disappeared inside. He saw smoke seeping in from the upper wall and loft slats. But the real danger was the flames, and the crackling of timber was getting louder. He had a minute, perhaps two, before the flames would lick the stable's wooden walls with their deadly tongues.

"Elmer, are you OK?" Alfred screamed as he cupped his hands around his mouth. "Ellsworth, are you there?" he repeated.

Suddenly Ellsworth appeared, backing out of the stable, hold-ing with both hands the reins of three frightened horses. Snorting and whinnying, the panic-stricken steeds fought against the reins. But Elmer resolutely led them out. As soon as Alfred saw him, he rushed up and helped pull the horses to safety.

"I could only get three," Ellsworth shouted as he gasped for fresh air. "The other is a small black colt in the last stall. I could not get to him as he pushed away from me! I think I can get him, too."

"It's too dangerous to go back in; the fire's already reached the loft," Putnam lamented. "We will have to shoot him. Hand me a carbine!"

The trapped little colt continued a shrill whinnying as burning clumps of hay from the loft fell on the troughs and the floor, igniting hay. Thick gouts of smoke poured out of the top of the stable door. A somber-faced man from the bucketline rushed up to Putnam, nodded in recognition, and seeing Alfred's uniform, handed the West Pointer a sawed-off smoothbore musket.

Suddenly, Will and Aaron approached the scene, running down the line.

"Don't shoot that little colt, Mr. Putnam. He didn't do nothing," Will shouted above the fury. "We can get him out! I promised the man who left him at the stable that I would take care of him. He gave me a gold coin. Please, Mr. Putnam, let me get him out!"

The colt whinnied again...even louder now. The fire rolled along the floor.

Putnam turned to Alfred.

"Alfred, no doubt you know how to fire a carbine," he said, ignoring the boy's request. "Dispatch that horse. Do it quickly!"

Alfred nodded his head slowly. He grabbed the carbine and raised it to his shoulder, placing the bead on the shadowy target that whinnied in high-pitched terror.

"Stop! I'm going in!" Will screamed. He dashed to the stable door with Aaron on his heels.

The stable was belching smoke through the slats by the eaves. Each grabbed a door handle, and both dashed in.

"Get back, boys! Damn it, get back!" Putnam screamed. "Get out now!"

The whinny of the horse reached a fearful screech as the floor took fire, advancing now to both ends of the stable. Alfred grasped the barrel of the carbine, placing the butt on his boot. He looked to Putnam and Elmer with anticipation. The flames reflected off their faces. The sweat beaded on their brows as they watched what unfolded before them with horror.

"Boys! Are you there?" Putnam shouted with a sense of alarmed urgency.

The whinny of the horse stopped. There was a pause.

"Boys, answer me!" Putnam shouted again.

The back roof of the flaming barn collapsed, sending thousands of embers into the night sky. The firefighters dropped buckets and pulled back from the intense heat.

"Boys, damn it, answer me!" he repeated with concern as he looked at the barn. The flames swirled in a strange way, like a fiery vortex rising into the night sky.

Suddenly, the door burst open and out they came. Will and Aaron had grasped the reins on each side of the bewildered, kicking colt. The intense heat on their backs, they sprinted to Alfred, Elmer, and Putnam. The colt stomped again and then settled down, bowing his head as if thanking his rescuers.

The smoke from the barn continued to drift their way. Both boys coughed deeply. Will bent over forward in an attempt to pull air into his lungs. Aaron's eyes began tearing up as he dropped to his knees to catch his breath again. Elmer quickly grabbed the reins and tied the stout black colt to the branch of a hickory tree near them.

"You boys are damned fools!" Putnam shouted as he shook his head side to side with a look of complete astonishment. "You disobeyed my direct orders and almost killed yourselves!"

"I thought I could make it, Mr. Putnam, and I guess I did. Thanks for letting us go in," replied Will respectfully as he rested his knee to the ground.

"You sure did make it," Elmer replied. "Let's take to the bucketline, boys."

Will and Aaron, after coughing again and then catching their breath, walked over to the little colt, whose sweaty black coat now reflected strange, shadowy images of the terrible inferno.

"Wish I knew this little guy's name," Will said as he placed his hand gently on the colt's dusty mane.

Aaron looked over and nodded but said nothing.

"Let's get to the river and find our buckets," he said softly.

In a moment they reached the swarthy, bobbing row of men; picked up their buckets; and stepped back in line. The bucket brigade had grown to over four hundred men. Will and Aaron looked at each other and smiled. They knew they had come of age.

"Mr. Putnam, the winds are rising, and we are stretched to the end. I fear the entire town will burn." Elmer had a look of solemnity as he waited for a response.

"The fire is moving through the business district. If it moves beyond Stephenson and Chicago Streets, every home in this town will go up. The buckets can't keep up with the winds. The men are getting tired."

Alfred looked at Putnam. "Have you thought of powder, Fire Marshall?"

"What do you mean?"

"I learned at the Point that powder will cordon off the fire if we do it right."

"If you are right, we should do it quickly," Putnam replied with a direct and urgent tone.

"We can set powder kegs at the corners of Bridge, Chicago, and Stephenson Streets. If we act now, we can blow the perimeter buildings that the fire has not reached. The collapse of the buildings may contain the fire within the borders. It is worth a try."

"We will do it, gentlemen. I will go for the kegs." Putnam dashed off into the dark.

The flames rolled upward into the black night. The water from the buckets flashed into a mist that was evaporated by the heat with each ineffective toss. Though it was like sweeping waves back on a beach, the brigade kept its rhythmic motion nonetheless. The men became more silent with each passing moment. It was midnight now.

"That's a pretty old carbine you got there, sir!"

Alfred looked at the stranger who made the remark and then stepped out of the dark. He pulled a shiny new rifle up to his waist, resting the deep-blue barrel on his left forearm as he gripped the case-hardened, colored breech with his right hand.

"And who are you, young man?" Elmer replied.

"T.J. Lockwood, sir. I'm from Buda, just down the river."

"And what is that you're holding, T.J.?"

"It's my new Sharps target rifle," T.J. replied proudly. He raised it confidently with one hand. The reflection of the fire cast a rainbow glow on the breech, which sparkled like oil on water on a summer day. "Never saw a little old musket like yours before. My baby can hit a fly on a barn door at two hundred yards. Something sure to reckon with."

"That's dandy, young man. But we got work to do. I'll watch your Sharps. You grab a bucket and get to the line."

"OK, sir. Keep care of my baby." T.J. handed over his piece and grabbed the bucket rope. With a slight swagger, he smiled and walked to the river.

Within moments Putnam arrived with a two-horse team, drawing a wagon loaded with kegs of gunpowder. "Alfred, we will place them where you see fit. Get into the wagon."

They proceeded down Bridge Street, advancing before the fire could reach them. Alfred directed the powder crew to place a keg at each of the corners at Chicago, Bridge, and Stephenson Streets. The remaining kegs were placed between them. A total of seven kegs formed a U-shaped pattern around the fire. The buildings would go up if they didn't move quickly.

"And what now, Alfred?" Putnam asked curiously as he glared at the fire again.

"We must set off the kegs one by one. We can use a powder trail or rifle, but we must act quickly before the cordon is caught on fire. We must blow the buildings before the fire reaches them."

"I will follow your lead. What is best?"

"We need a rifle in the church belfry. The First Presbyterian has a trapdoor to the tower. Reverend Schofield will open it for us. I will go for him. Now take this Sharps rifle and go to the line. There is a young man named T.J. Send him to the belfry." At this moment Alfred realized he was taking charge. He looked down at his boots. With an embarrassing glance, he handed the Sharps over to Putnam. "Sorry for giving you commands, Mr. Putnam. I am caught up in the moment."

"Your commands are so taken, Alfred. You are saving our city," Putnam replied, placing his hand on Alfred's shoulder. "We will get it done together."

Both parted in haste.

A half hour had now passed since the burning of the stable. The fire was peaking in all its fury. The brigade line faltered. Many of the men were exhausted and sat in secure places. Several leaned on trees by the courthouse. Nobody spoke. Most wondered what morning would bring.

The town had grown to over two thousand folks over the years. It was a jewel of activity year round. And now it could disappear by daylight.

Within moments Reverend Schofield opened the trapdoor to the belfry, and Alfred and T.J. appeared in the bell tower. Their dark shadowy silhouettes stretched before the shiny brass bell, which reflected the rising lisps of fire. Everyone looked up at the belfry with great anticipation and concern.

"Can you see the powder kegs, T.J.?" Alfred pronounced with resolute authority. He pointed toward the distant powder kegs that formed a U-shaped pattern around the buildings down below. "There are seven kegs around those buildings. Mr. Putnam has cleared the streets. You must start at the top of each side of the U and fire progressively right to left. The seventh, and last, keg to be dispatched is the one closest to us. You must load and fire quickly. Do you understand?" Alfred stared directly as he waited for a response.

"Yes, sir, I do."

T.J. pulled the linen cartridge with ball from his cartridge box, dropped the breech of the Sharps, drove in the cartridge, and closed the breech by pulling up the lever. He then reached in for the tiny ignition cap that looked like a miniature brass top hat. He placed it on the nipple cone at the breach. This cap would send the flame through the cone, discharging the weapon. He looked with confidence at Alfred and calmly stated, "I will load and fire on command. I can fire seven rounds, sir, in one minute."

T.J. was sinewy and tall. It gave him the advantage of reaching up over the bulwark of the belfry. The view from the tower was unobstructed. Before him he could see the silhouettes of men in the scattered brigade line. He could even see the river. The fire picked up as the wind whistled through the belfry. It was advancing to the perimeter of the U, and he could clearly see Alfred's plan.

"Are you ready, T.J.?" Alfred asked quietly with anticipation.

"Yes, sir." T.J. leveled his rifle on the buttress.

"Fire!"

The Sharps rifle cracked through the night. Boom! The first keg exploded! Screams from the townsfolk below echoed back as the first building, on the right, collapsed to rubble, the dust rising with the wind.

"Load and fire!" Alfred commanded again.

The Sharps boomed…another hit…this time the left keg.

T.J. responded in rhythm every eight seconds. The carbine's hammer was pulled back, loaded at the breech, capped, aimed, and fired. The motion was steady with no moments of hesitation. Reflections of the fire could be seen by Alfred in T.J.'s calm and determined eyes as he dispatched the powder kegs one by one.

Alfred shouted his command again. Each crack of the Sharps rifle was rewarded with another magnificent explosion that rumbled through the crisp night air.

"Last keg, T.J. Load and fire!"

The Sharps cracked! The last keg exploded. As the bucket brigade huddled in the distance, dazed at the smoke and dust rising over them from the explosions, Putnam, standing in front of the brigade, pointed up to the belfry. There was a pause.

In a moment a resounding "Huzzah! Huzzah! Huzzah!" from the chorus of men rose into the night.

Standing tall in the belfry so all could see, T.J. looked to Alfred with a hint of pride in his smile.

"You almost missed one," Alfred said, grinning as he extended his hand to T.J.

"I guess you can say I almost missed seven," T.J. replied, respectfully patting Alfred's shoulder.

"Let's go see our friends," Alfred replied with a wink and nod as they descended down the belfry stairs.

The echoes from the cheering townspeople could be heard throughout the business district. Folks from the neighboring towns of Cedarville and Woods Grove, who watched the fire from the other side of the Pecatonica, crossed the river and crowded the town, choking off the streets. The noise of the gathering crowd rose above the last crackling of the fire.

As the winds died down, there was a rising excitement in the air. Family, friends, neighbors, and strangers gathered one last time to hug each other before going home to their Christmas hearths. They looked to the morning glow in the eastern sky. Many fell to their knees in thanks and prayer. The town could move past this setback. The business district would begin a long process of rebuilding come morning.

The last embers were smoldering now. The great fire had lost its battle with the citizens of Freeport, and the sparks that lifted slowly into the dawn light landed gently onto the cold waters of the Pecatonica.

Chapter 3

Tremont House Hotel

Southeast Corner of Lake and Dearborn Streets
Chicago, Illinois
One Hundred Miles East of Freeport
December, 1857

"Mr. Couch, would you play a Foster piece for me?"

The piano player in the hotel's parlor had been about to play a tune. Instead, he rose and looked at the nearby open French bay window that separated the lobby from the parlor, where the request had come from. Couch didn't recognize the voice, and the window's thin curtain and cigar-smoke haze in the room prevented the piano player from seeing the speaker's features. But the speaker's silhouette was distinctive enough. Returning to his stool, Couch poised his fingers above the instument's keys.

"Well, hello and welcome, Congressman Washburne. And which song of his meets your fancy?"

"The piece called 'Jeanie with the Light Brown Hair,' which Stephen Foster wrote, oh, maybe three years past. It would be most pleasant if it is agreeable to the rest of your patrons."

Washburne glanced at the hotel patrons in the dimly lit parlor. Oil lamps flickered. He then stepped into the parlor and settled into an overstuffed wing chair that faced the open bay window. After setting his cigar on a side-table ashtray, he raised to his lips the brandy snifter he was holding and inhaled the liquor's heady fumes. Lowering the snifter, his eyes roamed across the parlor, dimly lit by fickering oil lamps. He noticed a young, married couple holding hands in the distant and darkest corner of the parlor. Near them sat an old man with a gray beard that matched his wrinkled suit. He sat upright on the edge of a red leather chair, propping his walking stick in front of him. He nodded, smiled, and raised the cane to note approval. The couple, too absorbed in themselves, did not hear Washburne's request, so the player smiled at the congressman and began the slow, sad melody.

Washburne looked out the bay window. He noticed large snowflakes floating outside. The melody continued to play sweetly through the parlor, occasionally punctuated by the pronounced clop of carriage horses' hooves that struck the frozen cobblestones on Lake Street. He noticed coachmen with tall black top hats bundled in greatcoats dusted with snow. Winter had arrived early again this year. The congressman expected his good friend to arrive at any moment but wondered if he would be delayed.

It had been quite some time since Washburne had been back to his hometown of Galena. His time in Washington was especially lonely this go-around. The congressional sessions took longer because of the increasing rancorous North-South sectional disputes. He missed his wife and children dearly. He took a sip of brandy and picked up his cigar, barely keeping back the tears as the song played its haunting melody. Time seemed to stand still as he stared through the window.

"Well, Congressman, are you counting snowflakes tonight!" announced a man behind him in a raised tenor voice with the hint of a country twang.

Washburne felt the smack of a thick, flat palm across his back, causing his cigar to hit the carpet. The brandy swirled, lipped over a bit, and then settled back to the bottom of his snifter. Washburne bent over quickly, picked up the cigar, and then turned to see who was the cause of this loud intrusion.

"My God, Lincoln, where did you come from?"

"I got a room upstairs, Congressman. Thought you would, too, but when I saw you, I couldn't resist sneaking up on you like an old

Potawatomi Indian. You know, Wash, you've got to watch your back all the time." Lincoln grinned and extended his hand. "Wash, you're about the best friend anyone could have. Sorry to startle you like that."

Washburne looked up at Lincoln. "You know, there is nothing to apologize for. You can knock me over any day." He smiled again, lifted his brandy, and said, "We have a lot to talk about. I will check into the hotel tonight and leave for Freeport and Galena tomorrow."

Washburne looked for the piano player. He was nowhere to be seen. The couple had gone, too.

The old man balanced himself forward on his cane and stood up slowly. He walked over to Washburne and Lincoln, tipped his hat, and extended his shaky hand. "Just wanted to let you know I am not a Democrat. Thought you'd like to know there is at least one Republican here in Chicago!"

Lincoln stood up and grinned. "Do you think I could beat Senator Douglas? The papers here call him the 'little giant.'"

"If your speech is as big as you, I wouldn't expect anything less from you!"

"Thank you, sir. Let me open the front door for the Chicago gentleman who will cast my first vote." Lincoln proceeded to the door and grabbed the knob.

The old man nodded again and stepped into the cold. He wrapped his scarf tightly around his neck and placed his cane tip on the wet boardwalk. "I'm surprised there are any damn Democrats up here at all. It's so damn cold!"

Lincoln turned to the lobby to meet with his young colleague. Washburne had known Lincoln during his congressional years. Both being from Illinois brought them together on many important issues. Illinois folk were often called "Suckers" to the surprise of most. Some say those who migrated to Illinois territory in the early years were suckers because they thought the lands would be open lands, clear for farming. Yet when they got here, they noticed the woods were so thick a squirrel could cross treetop to treetop over the entire state without ever touching the ground. Nonetheless, both Washburne and Lincoln knew the Suckers well and would serve them in any circumstance.

"Shall we have dinner, Congressman?" Lincoln asked as he patted his friend cordially on the back.

Washburne rose, and and they proceeded to the dining area where they were escorted to a table. As they sat down and placed napkins on their laps, the host turned the screw on the table's oil lamp to increase the illumination.

"So, Wash, what brings you here?"

"I have an idea for you that could help you beat Senator Douglas."

"And what might that be?"

"You should challenge him to debates across every county. But, especially, you should force him to come up North so you will have an advantage over him. My constituency and those around Freeport are very strong Republicans. You know, Abraham, south of Springfield those voters would side with southern Democrats. Douglas has roots there already."

"Interesting," pondered Lincoln as he stared directly into the lamplight. He looked as if he saw a vision of the actual debate unfolding in front of him. "I believe you are correct in your strategy, Congressman. But what if he says no to the idea of coming this far north?"

"The 'little giant' believes himself to be invincible in any debate. I have seen him in Washington. His supporters also will not allow him to back down from any debate. I am sure he will do it!"

Lincoln reached around the oil lamp with his large, wide hand and gripped Washburne's. "I have known you to be correct in your assessments on many occasions. And I believe you are duly correct on this one. As the old farmer says to his boys, 'You've hit the nail on the head.' Let's keep hitting it hard."

Washburne smiled at Lincoln and then noticed a man to his right who glared at him from the shadows across the parlor room. The man took one puff of his cigar and then blew it in the direction of Washburne's table as he looked down at the tablecloth in front of him. He shook his head as the cigar smoke swirled to the ceiling.

Washburne looked over again. "Sir, have I offended you?"

The stranger pulled his napkin out of his stiff collar, uncrossed his legs, and then stood up in a methodical manner. He was dressed in tailor-made garments that had a greenish sheen to them. His cravat was tied in the Windsor fashion. Barely five feet five inches tall, he crossed the room erect, like Napoleon, with his right hand tucked deliberately between the loosened buttons of his crimson vest.

"I couldn't help overhearing your conversation, Congressman," he said with a wry smile.

His short stature was even more apparent as he stood before the table. Washburne drew in a deep puff of his cigar, turned his head, and blew the smoke to the right of the intruder, as not to be discourteous.

"And how can I help you, sir?" Washburne asked respectfully.

"I am a Democrat," he said.

Washburne drew a couple more puffs from his cigar.

"And do you hail from this state?"

"No, I hail from three states. I have lived in Connecticut and Wisconsin, and I am now relocating to Chicago. I guess I'm a Sucker now…like both of you."

Lincoln let out a hearty laugh. He stood, towering at least a foot over the stranger.

"Please allow me to be the first to welcome you into the Sucker family," Lincoln said, extending his hand as he winked at Washburne.

The stranger took a step back and kept his cigar firmly in the grasp of his right hand so the shake could not be returned. He looked fleetingly at Lincoln and then stared into Washburne's eyes without smiling.

"I don't shake hands with Republicans, especially from the Sucker State. I am a Douglas man and will vote for him in the next election. I heard your strategy, and it has no chance for success. Whatever you do, Mr. Lincoln, you will fail against the man you call the 'little giant.'"

"And whom do I have the pleasure of addressing, sir?" Lincoln asked in earnest.

"I am John Mason Loomis the third!" the stranger replied as he nodded his head in a cavalier fashion. The light reflected off his half-balding head. He drew another puff from the cigar and blew it toward the table lamp.

He continued. "I am from Windsor, Connecticut. My family's roots go back to colonial times. My ancestors have fought in all the wars and, in fact, were friends of the founding fathers. I myself have spent many years traveling across the seas doing business in China tea." He held his head up.

"And what brings you to the port of Chicago, Mr. Loomis? Are you sure you are following your sextant correctly?" Washburne replied in jest. He looked at Lincoln who placed a hand over his mouth to hide a slight grin.

Loomis looked at the ceiling and perked his thin lips. He then reached over to the ashtray, crushing his cigar in it. "Gentlemen, if you wish to know, I am one who is not tied to just one soil. I am not tied to just one business. I am an adventurer. I am an investor. I own a lumber company in Milwaukee. I also own a new lumber business in Chicago. That's why I am here."

Loomis nodded and turned away, quickly marching back to his table as if on a retreat. He abruptly pulled on his gray beaver top hat, which rested on the seat of a neighboring chair, and grabbed his black wool coat, tossing it in one motion over his left arm. He turned in a quick, catlike motion to Washburne and Lincoln.

"If you truly wish to know, Mr. Congressman and you Mr. Lincoln, I am looking to establish my headquarters somewhere between Milwaukee and Chicago. In the interim, gentlemen, I will be on my white mare riding frequently between both locations. Therefore, one could say, my headquarters will be in my saddle!" With this, he turned quickly without looking at them, entered the lobby, and exited. The front door slammed behind him.

There was a short pause.

Lincoln moved upward in his seat and looked at the oil lamp and then at the congressman. He shook his head slightly back and forth. He cracked a slight smile. "Well, Wash, I think that last comment he made about his saddle sums it all up for Mr. Loomis."

"And how is that, my friend?"

"If what he says is true about his saddle, Mr. Loomis doesn't know his headquarters from his hindquarters!"

Washburne let out a deep laugh. Lincoln grinned. Both stood up in one motion and retired back to the lobby.

Chapter 4

John E. Smith Home

High Street
Galena, Illinois
Grand Mississippi Riverboat Town
Fifty Miles West of Freeport
Christmas Eve, 1857

Thick snowflakes swirled slowly down onto High Street. The peaceful glow of a porch lantern faded into the darkness where a steep cliff dropped off. A hundred feet below, Galena straddled the river for which it was named. Faint echoes of riverboat men resonated through the streets, up the hillside, and over High Street to the lead mines above the Smith home.

Cheers and an occasional distant laugh filled the chilly air this night. Spirits were up because the mercantile year had ended on a very high note. Galena's lead business was booming. The riverboats, which were typically loaded to the gunwales with lead, were now snugly settled onto the riverbank. It was a special time. It was Christmas.

"Adelaide, my dear, could you play a tune for me this fair night?" Washburne beckoned. He sat comfortably in the warm parlor with his legs crossed. He turned and winked at the rest of the Smith family, most of whom were standing by the piano. John E. was not to be seen as yet. He was still gathering wood from the shed, which was cut into the hill out back.

John E. was a good man known for his high integrity. He had one of the finest reputations in Galena. As Galena's only jeweler and watchmaker, he had made quite a fortune since moving from St. Louis a few years back. He was happy to have the entire family together. Alfred was even home this season from West Point and Freeport, where he fought the fire just a week ago. Nearest to the piano was young Ben, quite diminutive at eleven years old, who worked his summers at the Grant & Perkins store, the Grant family being friends with Mr. Smith. Eight-year-old Adelaide, nicknamed "Addie" by her father, was the youngest and was eager to show her talent at the piano.

"I can play 'Silent Night,' Mr. Congressman!"Adelaide replied as she turned to her mother, Mrs. John E. Smith, known as Amy to her friends in Galena.

Mrs. Smith nodded in approval to her daughter, who was tiny for her age but whose confidence always was greater than her years. Adelaide beamed and then nodded back with a quick smile. The others in the room felt the grace of her childlike charisma.

"I will sing for you, too, if you wish, Mr. Congressman. Did you know 'Silent Night' was first written in German, but then the French loved it so much they put it to their own words? Grandfather taught me all the words before he died. He fought with Napoleon and knew German, Swiss, and French!" she stated proudly as she glanced to John E. for acknowledgment.

His eyes welled, and he spoke softly, "Adelaide, my dear, please play and sing the song for all of us. Grandpa would be very proud of you."

"Adelaide, I would be honored to hear you sing and play." Washburne uncrossed his legs and leaned forward with his elbows on his knees. He nodded again and smiled.

Adelaide placed her quaint, little hands to the white and ebony keys. She sat with her back arched in a ladylike fashion. After a brief hesitation, she found her place on the song sheet, which had the French version on the left and the English translation on the right. With a deliberate tone, she began the slow and solemn song, bowing her head, mouthing each slight rhythmical change.

Douce nuit, sainte nuit!
Dans les cieux! L'astre luit.
Le mystère annoncé s'accomplit
Cet enfant sur la paille endormi,
C'est l'amour infini!
C'est l'amour infin.

"Excellent, Adelaide!" Washburne exclaimed with great cheer. "May I have a translation?" He scooted to the edge of the red leather chair, tilting his head to the right so he could hear more intently.

Adelaide turned to the congressman and glanced fleetingly back at her parents. She did not look at her siblings because she was in her moment and felt quite pleased. Tipping her head gracefully, she nodded and smiled at Washburne. Again she postured herself at the keys and continued to play and sing for them.

Silent Night! Holy Night!
All is calm, all is bright
Round yon godly tender pair.
Holy infant with curly hair,
Sleep in heavenly peace,
Sleep in heavenly peace.

"Bravo!" exclaimed Washburne. "I'm sure Grandpa in heaven is very proud of you, as we all are, on this most heavenly night. You have many bright years ahead of you, young lady." He pushed back into his chair and crossed his legs again.

"Would you like some eggnog, Congressman?" Mrs Smith asked. "I am bringing one for John and Alfred. Please stay and share more time with us." Amy met his eyes directly and then blushed, realizing she was pushing a little too much for the situation.

"I would be honored to stay for a while. I hope I am not keeping you up into the night."

"The night is still young, Wash," John E. replied as he turned to Ben and Adelaide. "It is time, my children. You best be off to bed. The morning will come sooner than you think. Thank you, Adelaide, for the great little rendition. Grandpa and Grandmomma are as proud of you as the whole family is."

Alfred stood in the corner as resolute as a vigilant sentry. He was dressed in his stout gray uniform for this special occasion with the congressman who had appointed him to West Point. He was as proud as all West Point cadets were. The parlor lamp where he stood caused his eyes to glisten like the buttons on his waistcoat. There were twenty-one buttons aligned in three vertical rows of seven connected by a smart, black piping. The collar was stiff. His head rested on it as if it was a statue on base marble.

"Alfred," called Washburne with his low, resonant voice, "please join your father and me for an eggnog. I'd like to hear what the latest news is at the Point. But before that, tell me about the fire in Freeport. I heard you were there."

"Yes, Congressman, I was near the bucket brigade. I assisted Fire Marshal Putnam. He asked for my advice on controlling the fire. Elmer Ellsworth was there, too. It was a sight to see. The whole damn town was ablaze, and we had to blow it up. And we *sure as hell did!*" Alfred paused embarrassingly. He glanced down at his feet, fleetingly to his father, and then across the room to Washburne. "Forgive me, sir, for my language!"

"That's absolutely fine, young man. Please continue."

"Well, some kid from Buda named T.J. Lockwood walked up with a Sharps rifle. Now how many kids have a sniper's rifle like that? I took him quickly to the belfry tower of the First Presbyterian Church where we could clearly see the seven powder kegs that we had placed around the fire. The kid told me he could get a bead on anything, and he did it right quick. Elmer said he grabbed onto a tree when *all hell broke loose.* The seven shots that were fired by this kid sounded like a damned artillery duel." Alfred caught himself again. He shook his head sideways and smiled. Washburne and his father did not flinch this time.

"Well, to continue, Congressman, seven powder kegs exploded in less than one minute! The entire town was stunned by the enormity of it all. I could barely speak a word after it was over. We all fell silent, and then Fire Marshal Putnam led the bucket brigade and every man in the town with three loud 'huzzahs.' The huzzahs were so loud they echoed up and around the belfry tower where T.J. and I were. Imagine, in less than one minute, the entire fire was snuffed out. The kid saved the town with his marksmanship. It was a sight to behold."

John E. looked at Washburne.

The congressman lowered his eyebrows and slowly raised his eggnog to his lips. "Well, one does wonder what would have happened to that town. That young man is a hero, truly."

John E. nodded. The congressman paused for a moment, looking into his china glass.

"Alfred, may I be so imposing as to ask you about a few issues that have every legislator in Washington up in arms?"

"Sure, Congressman."

"Do you have friends at West Point who are from the southern states?"

"Yes, sir. We have quite a few at the Point," Alfred replied.

"What do they say about the slavery issue? Do they think it will lead to a war?"

Alfred backed off the parlor wall and walked toward the piano bench. He placed his eggnog on top of the piano and then turned and sat down, looking at his polished black boots that seemed to reflect like mirrors. Pausing, he looked up to Washburne, who was still sitting in the big red mahogany chair. He pondered about his West Point friends spending Christmas in warmer climates as he stared at the parlor lamp on the other side of the room. There was a look of sadness and a sense of solemnity in his gaze.

"Congressman, we will certainly have a fight from them. I pray it does not come soon."

"Have those southern boys heard of Senator Sumner's beating at the Capitol? He was struck over the head with a walking stick and almost killed by a fanatic congressman from the Carolinas."

"Yes, they have heard of it. And they're all quite glad. They think he deserved it for insulting their people. I certainly don't defend it, but it serves my point. I think they will leave the states. It is just my opinion, Congressman." Alfred sat upright, now, spine straight, pleased to be conversing with a man of stature.

"Well, thank you for being candid, Alfred." Washburne raised his glass again and continued. "I have talked to Mr. Lincoln, who will soon make a run for senator against Mr. Douglas. Lincoln told me directly that the talk in Washington is that we will let them keep their slaves as long as they do not secede from the Union. If they do, then responsibility for war is on their shoulders. Let us pray that the South comes to its senses." Washburne paused and then looked at John E.

"John, you have not said a word. What do you think of it?" He crossed his legs and leaned back in his chair.

"If they call it on, we will give them the good fight," John E. replied with conviction. He pulled himself up from his chair in the corner and walked over to the fireplace. He stoked the fire, causing ashes to briefly swirl above the burning wood. He leaned the poker on the brick face and then reached for a case that was centered on top of the mantel. The evergreen swag above it had a blood-red bow that curled downward. The crackle of the fire rose, sending a reflection back into the room. The brass buttons of Alfred's military waistcoat began to burnish. John E. opened the case and carefully pulled out a small revolver.

"Congressman, this handgun was my father's." John E. walked across the room to the red mahogany chair. He handed it to the curious congressman.

"It looks like a French military piece," noted Washburne, who held the brass backstrap toward the fireplace. "I see it is inscribed 'J. B. SMITH.' Is this your father's inscription?"

"Yes, it stands for John Bander Smith. He was from Switzerland. He was an officer on the staff of Napoleon, like Adelaide mentioned before her recital. We are quite proud of Grandfather," John E. replied as he looked to Alfred for endorsement.

Alfred nodded and pushed out his chest proudly. The brass buttons brightly reflected the glow from the fireplace.

"Well, Alfred," replied Washburne, "you have quite a tradition to uphold. Was your grandfather on the winter death march from Russia?"

"Yes, sir, my grandfather was determined to make it back to his family, and he made it all the way. Ten thousand men perished during that winter march. It was the end for Napoleon."

"Your grandfather's conviction is most admirable," Washburne replied in earnest, "And he obviously kept good company." He stood up and held his glass upright. "I would like to make a toast."

Alfred rose quickly from the piano stool. His father stood by the parlor light. Both stood erect, like soldiers at a military round table, with glasses raised. The congressman looked at the fire and then turned to both father and son. With a stoic look of confidence in his eye, he tilted his head to the right and lifted his glass.

"I would like to toast the past, present, and future military success of the Smith family. God forbid, if our country comes to conflict in the coming age, the people of this city, this state, and this country will need your services. You are leaders, all of you. You will get us through the conflagration, and for this, Godspeed and God bless you."

Alfred and his father nodded their heads in appreciation and downed their drinks in unison. The parlor was silent now except for the crackling of the fire. Washburne stood up. He placed his glass on the top of the piano. Grabbing Alfred's right hand with his own, he took his left hand and grabbed Alfred's wrist. "God bless you, Alfred, and Merry Christmas."

He then turned to John E. and embraced him in the same way, proceeding to the front door where he reached for his tall beaver top hat and dark-gray overcoat. He pulled both off the wooden peg in one motion. After cocking the hat on his head smartly, he pushed his arms through each sleeve of his lengthy coat. Grabbing the doorknob, he leaned against the door, opening it with one hard push. A whistle of air entered the parlor. Snowflakes whipped in and up and then descended to the floor.

"These times are cold, gentlemen. There is something in the air, and I fear it will only get worse."

Washburne's facial expression grew more solemn. He lifted his head to speak but held himself back. He stared at the floor for a moment. With an awkward turn through the doorjamb, he looked back toward the parlor. John E. and Alfred looked like dark silhouettes against the wall.

"God bless us all," he said.

Turning back for one last glance, he stepped into the night.

Chapter 5
Grant & Perkins Store

Galena, Illinois
Spring, 1858

"Mr. Grant, there's a Negro man at the counter."

"What's he want, Ben?"

"He said he wants to talk to Mr. Grant or Mr. Perkins."

"Tell him to wait a few minutes. I will be out of the counting room soon."

Ben looked up wide-eyed at the looming black figure in front of him. The man was a dark stranger, who was over six feet tall and dressed smartly in a vested suit with ascot tie. His black wool coat covered a massive chest the size of a cooper's barrel. His hair, straight and long, fell just above his stiff white collar. His defined moustache was as black as his jet-black hair, and it tracked down both sides of his chin as if pulled by weights.

"Mr. Grant will be out shortly," pronounced Ben as he looked quickly down at his dusty boots and then just as quickly excused himself to the counting room.

A moment later, Grant appeared at the counter. "Can I help you, sir?"

"Are you Mr. Grant or Mr. Perkins?" said the stranger in a steady congenial voice.

"I am Ulysses Grant—there is no Mr. Perkins. My brothers and I bought this store from him just a few years ago. What can I do for you?"

"I have a proposition for you," said the stranger in a polished eastern accent.

Grant looked upon him with curiosity. He had never seen a freed black man dressed so well and possessing such an authoritative bearing. "And what is your proposition?"

"I have a colt for sale. Since you and your brothers are in the leather and harness business, I would imagine you could find a buyer for me. I will pay you a percentage that would be suitable to your interests."

Grant scratched the back of his head thoughtfully for a moment before reaching over to a little cigar box behind the counter. He pulled out a cigar and grabbed a match and struck it against the counter's rough-hewn surface. As he placed the tip of the lit match against the cigar in his mouth and inhaled, he silently compared the colt owner's more fashionable attire with his own dusty work clothes. With a friendly smile, Grant said, "Do you mind if I ask you a few gentlemanly questions before I accept your proposition?"

"Certainly, Mr. Grant. I welcome any question you may have. But before you start, I would like to properly introduce myself. My name is Ely Parker."

Grant's expression was impassive as he mentally debated whether he should ask any questions at all. He knew, however, that the townspeople would frown on him bartering with a runaway slave dressed like a riverboat gambler. And even doing business with a freed man could pose problems for some, though most of those folks came up the river from southern ports. He thought back to his days in St. Louis, where there were tensions of this sort. But because it was the right thing to do, he gambled on the answer and asked the question anyway.

"Well, thank you, Mr. Parker," he replied. "I see from your dress and manners that you present yourself as a gentleman, but I must first ask you this: are you a freed man or a runaway?"

Parker stared at Grant, whose last words seemed to hang in the air between them. Grant felt uneasy.

"Mr. Grant, I do not blame you for your very direct question. But you should know that I've heard this same question on many occasions.

Since you are direct, I will be as direct as you. I am not a runaway slave. I am not a freed man. I am an American, like you. I am a Seneca Indian." Parker drew himself up proudly, and Grant, for the first time, noticed the man's strong Roman nose and long, sloping forehead.

There was a brief pause and then Grant smiled, and with a twinkle in his gray eyes, he said, "My apologies, sir. Would you like a cigar?"

Parker smiled, as well, and said, "I will accept your offer only if you accept mine."

"No bargain gained or lost if none ventured," said Grant as he handed over the cigar. "I think I know a gentleman up on High Street that would be interested in your colt. Tell me first, Mr. Parker, about this young colt of yours. But before you do, I would like Ben to hear it…Ben, come out here. I want to introduce you to Mr. Parker."

The boy came to the counter and displaying a congenial smile that had made him a friend to all who met him, extended his hand to Parker.

"Mr. Parker has a colt for sale. Is your father still looking for one?" Grant asked.

Ben's eyes grew wider at the thought of owning a pony.

"Yes," replied Ben. His voice cracked with enthusiasm. "We live way up on High Street, but we could stable him down here by the river. I promise I will take good care of him. I will ride him every day, Mr. Parker!"

"You may call me Ely," said Parker.

Grant nodded. "And where is this young colt?"

"He is on a farm, running in a meadow on the Mississippi, but he was not born in these parts. Two years ago I bought a mare back in my home of upstate New York. After my commission to come here to build the Seaman's Hospital, I first arrived in Chicago by train with my mare. It was about this time last year. When I arrived in Chicago, I noticed she was ready to sire, so I waited. Soon after, the colt was born, and after waiting a few weeks, I decided to ride the mare with my little colt in tow behind me through Freeport to get here to Galena. When I got to Freeport, I had to move faster, so I left him at a stable in Freeport. I gave a young stable boy a ten-dollar gold piece to quarter the colt for a few months. Then I found out when I returned to get him that he survived the big fire in Freeport last December. The stable where he was quartered is just ashes now." Parker paused as Grant raised his eyebrows inquisitively.

"Ben, that was the fire your brother helped snuff out, wasn't it?" Grant asked as he flicked a dangling ash from the tip of his cigar with his forefinger.

"Yes," replied Ben, "that was my brother Alfred from West Point."

Parker looked down at Ben and smiled, his countenance lit up. "You must be very proud of him, son," he said. He paused now and looked out the window at a passing wagon. Turning from the window, he leveled his eyes on Grant, and with a deep conviction in his voice announced, "I do have one condition to the sale of my colt."

"And what is that?" replied Grant.

Parker looked out the window again and then looked back at Grant. "I have given him a name already. The condition of sale is that no one change his name."

"And what have you named him?" replied Grant.

"His name is Black Hawk," replied Parker, looking directly into Grant's eyes to see what his response would be.

"Black Hawk...Interesting...Black Hawk. A horse named Black Hawk." Grant pondered and then looked at Ben. He flicked an ash to the floor. Working the ash into the thick oak panels with his boot, he looked curiously at Parker, "And tell me more about this young colt."

"He stands twelve hands high at twelve months. He is as black as Pennsylvania coal. When he runs, you can see reflections of light sheen off him. He is here for some grand purpose. I do not know what it is." Parker retreated, realizing he was overselling. He now withdrew a bit. He hadn't asked yet for a light for the cigar Grant had given him.

"Well, Ely, you tell a mighty story about a horse we would like to see. You do know that Chief Black Hawk and his warriors kept this town under the fear of siege a couple of decades ago, don't you?"

"I know the story of Black Hawk, the great Sauk chief. And that is why I named my colt in his honor. Black Hawk and his tribe were from

Illinois. He tried to keep the lands. He tried, like Tecumseh, to keep all Indians together as one nation." Parker decided he had said enough, possibly more than enough.

"Ely," said Grant as he reached for a match to light Parker's cigar, "I agree with you. There is always strength in union."

"And what of our deal?" replied Parker, as he lifted his cigar for the long-awaited light.

"What is your proposition?" asked Grant. He struck another match and raised it to Parker's cigar.

"Fifty dollars!" Parker replied with a glint in his eye.

"Fair enough," Grant replied in earnest. "Bring Black Hawk to me. I will find him a good home here." He looked at Ben and winked. "I am quite sure his address will be on High Street."

Parker extended his swarthy, thick hand to Grant and then turned and smiled as he stepped to the front door. "I will bring him to you in two days," Parker said as he leaned on the door, hoisting his lit cigar.

Grant nodded to Parker and then turned to Ben and smiled. He put his arm around the boy and returned to the counting room.

Chapter 6

Lincoln-Douglas Debate

Freeport
August 27, 1858

"Congratulations, Alfred. I see you were awarded another stripe at the Point. Your family must be very proud of you."

"Thank you, Major Ellsworth. It will be an honor to serve once I graduate. Just two more years and I will have a commission. They should give you a commission, too, for saving those horses last winter! Is your coat as hot today as it was in that stable?"

"I didn't much feel the heat during the dash. I was too busy thinking about that screaming horse. Besides, it is you who saved the town by directing that fire from the belfry tower." Elmer raised his sleeve to his dripping brow.

"Well, we could use that bucket brigade today for sure. Mr. Lincoln and the senator will certainly heat things up to a boiling point. Let's move to the trees. Both of them should be here soon."

Elmer and Alfred looked like picture-book soldiers. Each wore smart gray coats of splendor. Their black boots were shin high. Tilted slightly on their crowns, their caps had small brims and were patterned after French kepis with embroidered gold piping and brightly polished matching side buttons.

Elmer had raised his company of one hundred men. They were called the Rockford City Greys, recruited from Northern Illinois, all straitlaced marching cadets who had come to Freeport to demonstrate the pomp and splendor of the art and science of military drill.

There would be a lot of vistors this day. In fact while most of Freeport's citizens were still in their beds, the roads leading to the city were choked with wagons and buggies from towns forty miles distant. The drizzle of summer rain that dropped on the dusty roads earlier in the day made the trip more comfortable for the travelers who were eager to witness the second of seven Lincoln-Douglas debates.

Now eight months after the big fire, Freeport had risen from its ashes in first-class fashion. Along with the precision marches of the Rockford City Greys, bands played patriotic music, and cannon shots heralded in the two greatest stump speakers in the Sucker State. The platform for the grand debate was two blocks north of the Brewster House, Freeport's finest hotel. Here, Senator Douglas, the "little giant," arrived ahead of Lincoln's entourage, spending Thursday night preparing his speech. It was decided that Lincoln would lead off when they took to the speaker's platform.

The gathering swarm of fifteen thousand excited citizens packed the city center like never before. The platform was strategically placed in an open common bordered by a small grove of trees. The Brodhead Brass Band from Wisconsin came down to play one patriotic song after another, the favorite being "The Star-Spangled Banner."

Fire Marshal Putnam was there with his big tin and leather hat. His hand was tired from all the greetings and compliments for snuffing out the fire the previous winter. As he towered above the crowd, he caught sight of Alfred and Elmer and immediately approached the tall shady oak tree.

"Hello, Alfred and Elmer," Putnam said. Then pointing to the new buildings in the town center, he added, "Quite a change from the night in December, no?"

"Quite an improvement, for sure!" replied Alfred.

"I'm impressed that there's no trace of what had happened," said Elmer.

"The townspeople are to be congratulated," Putnam said. "I have to apologize, gentlemen, but I must attend the event. If you pass through Freeport again, come see me." He placed the fire-marshal helmet back on his head and stepped into the crowd. His head towered above the throng of visitors as he got closer to the speaker platform.

The hot noon sun made them uncomfortably warm, and Alfred and Elmer sought relief from the heat by stepping deeper into the shade of the grove and found it beneath the large branches of a stately oak. The wind briefly picked up, causing a cooling breeze to flow across the open field before them. Ladies in hoopskirts who stood at the center of the field, however, didn't feel it. Some of the women in the gathering audience had wigs adorned with red, white, and blue ribbons. Others, mostly from the countryside, had their hair pulled straight back and wore bonnets to shade their faces. The ladies of fashion, carrying lacy parasols to protect them from the sun, also used them as shields to block the vision of their husbands as they discretely cast an admiring eye at nearby soldiers. When the breeze faded, hundreds of hand-held fans were unfolded. The back-and-forth motion was like the fluttering of butterfly wings. Meanwhile the bands continued to play, a pleasant distraction from the rising heat and one that also kept everyone in great spirits.

"Elmer, Congressman Washburne told me in Galena that you are friends now with Mr. Lincoln!" Alfred said enthusiastically.

"Yes, he invited me to study with him at his law practice. He has been very gracious to me. I made his acquaintance at the Tremont House last fall when I was recruiting. He asked me what burning desires I have for my life. I told him I know a little about law but want to know a lot about soldiering. He replied, 'Son, I know a little about soldiering and a lot about law. So it looks like we're destined to be partners.'"

"And did you accept his offer?" asked Alfred enthusiastically.

"I did indeed. I will go to Springfield when the Rockford City Greys are on leave."

"And where did Mr. Lincoln get his military experience?" asked Alfred as he pulled off his small kepi hat and rubbed the sweat from his brow on his left sleeve.

"Well, Mr. Lincoln was a captain of militia in the Black Hawk War. He told me he saw no Indians but saw a hell of a lot of lice. He is about the most humble man I have talked to in his position. He even told me he had problems with the drill. He said as he practiced one day with his small company, he thought he was getting the hang of being a drillmaster as his troops turned on a dime with each barked order. The problem he had was when he marched over a rise and approached a split-rail fence that had a ten-foot-wide opening that could only accommodate about the middle third of his company's line of march. Since his command book was back in his tent, without knowing what the command should be, he began to panic. Several troops turned to look for his next order. Lincoln became more frantic as the split-rail fence got closer and closer."

Elmer paused and smiled. "Well, Lincoln's wit came through for him as it always does in tight situations. He pondered for a quick second and then decided what the best course of action would be for this unexpected emergency since he didn't know what commands to give to get them through the gap in the fence. Lincoln called for his company to halt within three feet of the fence. He then shouted, 'At ease.' After a brief pause, he said calmly, 'Soldiers, we will break for ten minutes...and then reform... on the other side of this fence!' The entire company broke into laughter."

"Sounds like you can teach Mr. Lincoln a few things, too," Alfred said in jest.

"No doubt about it," replied Elmer, wiping his brow with a kerchief.

Ellsworth leaned comfortably next to the shady oak tree with the heel of his boot raised almost to his knee. There was a slight pause in the band play as the crowd's enthusiasm grew. The wind stepped up again, blowing cool air through the grove. A green acorn dropped and popped off the brim of Ellsworth's kepi. The cap tipped over his brow.

"Jeez, the heat is poppin' the acorns already. I wish the little giant would get here soon."

Again, after a slight pause, two acorns dropped directly on the crown of the cap, causing Ellsworth to push forward pulling his cap to his side.

"What in heaven's is causing those acorns to drop?" he exclaimed, as he looked up at the oak's branches.

"For cryin' out loud, Allie. What are you doing up there?"

Perched on a strong bough with one hand on the trunk squatted Allie. She had her fifteenth birthday this month and was sassy as ever. Wearing britches with overall straps and boots tied with strong leather crossed to midknee, she could certainly be mistaken at a glance for a country boy. She was a towhead. Her hair was white as salt. Her bangs were crudely cut perpendicular to her red freckled nose. There were no ribbons in her hair because there wasn't enough to pull back. She grinned at Ellsworth.

"Oh, Elmer, why are y'all dressed up in that fancy uniform? And why are you actin' so stiff and stuffy?"

"I am a Major of the Rockford City Greys, Allie."

"Well, I suppose you think you are really somethin' now? What about last summer down by the Pecatonica?"

Alfred looked up into the tree boughs with other curious bystanders. He smiled and leaned closer toward Elmer to hear his response.

"What are you referring to?" Ellsworth replied nervously.

Allie rolled her eyes and shook her head. She spoke rapidly, "Well, I saw you, Major Elmer, with your pants rolled up to your knees. You was in the Rock River, walkin' the mud dunes with that trap of yours, lookin' for muskrats like you did back in Kenosha!"

Alfred and the others around the shady oak tree howled with laughter, causing Ellsworth to blush in embarrassment. Placing his cap back on his head at a jaunty angle, he hesitated and slowly looked at the sassy teen above him.

"Allie, you are correct. I must admit, though, I am a gentleman and an officer now. When you grow up some day, you will learn to choose your words more wisely so as not to insult even the worst of scoundrels. Can I trust that in the future you will act more becoming as a lady? In fact, you are situated strategically in this tree. Look to the crowd before you. Can you see the truest of ladies adorned with ribbons and bonnets? They are the ones to be most admired. Look hard and long, Allie, and some day you, too, will be a lady of distinction." Ellsworth tilted his head and looked at Allie again.

"Jumpin' jiminy, Elmer, your words are as big as those britches of yours! So being the gentleman that you look like, can I be a lady and be askin' you a couple a questions?"

"Sure, Allie, what is it?"

"Do you think a lady deserves a hand when she puts her foot to the carriage step?"

"Of course, Allie, it's the gentlemanly thing to do."

"Well, those ladies are city folk, and I'm not," she replied in a rebellious tone. She grinned widely and tilted her head to the side like a curious cat. Then, quickly, she lowered her voice in a graceful manner, much like the ribbon-laced ladies before her. Sweetly she said, "Now, dear Major, would you be so kind as to grab my glove and assist me down from this forsaken and dusty old oak tree?"

Alfred chuckled again along with the throng of bystanders who, though facing forward, were close enough to hear the exchange.

Elmer smiled, shaking his head slowly side to side. He looked up at the tree bough. Nodding respectfully, and with a pleasant inflection to his voice, he replied, "Allie, some day you will be some gentleman's happy handful. I must go now. Alfred, let's move closer to the platform. I would rather take the heat over there than here!"

The bands continued to play, echoing through the grove of trees. Then the pitch and tempo picked up quickly. Senator Douglas, the little giant, and his entourage were waving to admirers from the steps of the Brewster House where Douglas had stayed the night before, preparing his speech. Within moments a beautiful coach pulled by two fine horses approached the hotel to escort the little giant to the speaker's platform. Douglas shook hands, turned for a brief moment, and thanked the hotel proprietor for the fine accommodations. He then turned to the street to enter the carriage. Grabbing the coach handle, he placed one foot on the step, but a rousing cheer caused him to step back. He quickly turned to the right to see a throng of people swirling with excitement as the dust rose before them.

"Do you see that!" retorted Douglas. His voice seemed strangely forceful for a man of short stature. "Here we go again!" He repeated, "Here we go again!" Stepping back from the coach, he stood with both hands on his hips.

"Clear the way for Honest Abe!" the leaders of the throng demanded.

One hundred or so cheering citizens of Freeport walked by the Brewster House alongside a large Pennsylvania farm wagon pulled by four workhorses clopping along at a steady gait. The driver was perched on the front left horse, allowing his most notable rider to stand alone on the flatbed with an unobstructed view of the crowd. It was Abraham Lincoln politicking at his best. The wagon continued to close on the Brewster House.

"Always up to fancy tricks, that Lincoln! I can't take this carriage to the platform. The citizens will mock me as some pompous Chicago city slicker," said Douglas as he scratched the back of his head. "He pulled a stunt like this in Ottawa, too. I agreed to have this backwoods stump speaker lead off in Freeport, and he is taking full advantage of the situation now. Must I now walk in this dust to the speaker's platform?" Douglas retorted as he wrung his hands together. He flushed with increasing anger.

The wagon slowly plugged along. Lincoln looked like a giant. He stood six feet four, nearly one foot taller than Douglas, and with the buckboard raising him higher, he stood no less than eleven feet from the ground, top hat and all. His coat sleeves looked too short for his lanky arms. He carried two small leather books in his left hand as he waved with his right hand to his admirers. His overall appearance was dusty. He had no beard. Occasionally he would pull off his top hat, tipping it to those he recognized, exposing rough hair that stuck out in all directions. Above it all he smiled and slowly nodded, showing his appreciation for the growing throng of people. When he approached the Brewster House, where Douglas was standing firm like a statue, he smiled again and tipped his hat to his adversary. He then raised the two leather books in his left hand and pointed to them with his long bony finger.

Douglas stood firm with his hands on his hips and nodded back. "He will make this a contest for sure," he said.

The procession continued by the Brewster House and turned the corner.

"Senator, are you ready to depart for the platform?" the driver asked respectfully, dropping his hand to assist the senator.

Douglas looked up at the driver. "After that episode," replied the little giant, "it is certain I would lose this debate before it even begins. That crowd is cheering dear old 'Honest Abe' from the backwoods of Salem. If I ride in your carriage, my dear sir, I will be the laughing stock before I step on the stage! I will walk to the platform. There will be no carriage or parade for Stephen Douglas today. I will meet this man one for one by foot or by folly!"

The little giant stepped off the porch. He grabbed the lapels on both sides of his shiny black suit coat. Stepping heel to toe in the wagon ruts to keep his balance, he rounded the corner in a huff and disappeared into the crowd.

Chapter 7

Pecatonica River

Freeport
Autumn, 1858

"Well, I sure showed Elmer what it's like to be a river rat."

"Come on, Allie," Will replied. "You can always get the gander on anyone. What did you do? Am I going to hear about it when he comes back from the Point?"

"He ain't at the Point and never will be. He just rights himself in that fancy uniform impressin' all those big-city girls. He needs to get back to the river and have some fun."

"Sounds like you might have a big crush on him, Allie."

Allie looked quickly upriver and then turned to Will. She bent over to pick up a hickory stick that was trapped in a little pool by the bank. Swishing it in a circular motion in the pool, she hesitated and then pulled it up. There was silence now. She looked up at Will again.

"There is only one man that keeps my fancy," she replied as she stood up, holding the stick in her right hand. "I am not much for words about it, Will, but I will draw it for you."

Will looked curiously at Allie as she took the tip of the hickory stick like a wand and started drawing in the wet sand. There were a few leaves in the way, so she pushed them aside with the stick. Looking up at Will, she smiled gently. She still had a slight look of mischief in her bright-blue eyes. Gazing directly back at Will, and without looking at the movement of her hand, she held the stare. Slowly, she pulled the tip through the wet mud, drawing it slowly until the figure was complete.

"Do you know what that symbol is, William Erwin?"

Will looked down and then looked up to catch her inquisitive gaze directly.

"It's a heart."

"That's my heart," she said gently as she bent over again. "I want you to turn your back now 'cause I'm goin' to write the first letter of the first name of the boy who keeps my fancy. Turn your back now."

With a swift motion, she slashed four quick lines in the mud. Throwing the stick in the river, she giggled and headed down the riverbank at a fast pace.

"You can't catch me," she dared. Giggles echoed through the trees.

Will, confused at the commotion, looked down at the heart drawing and noticed a "W" enclosed within. He felt stunned for a moment as he grabbed his trouser suspenders with his thumbs.

"Well, golly, Allie. I didn't know at all. Just wait a minute now!" he yelled.

Allie continued at a quick pace down the river. Will pursued, high-stepping over small bushes and logs just like his river runs with Aaron. This time, though, he felt a tingle of joy in his belly. He always had a thing for Allie, since meeting her during the Lincoln-Douglas debate, but never thought she felt the same. Now he knew for sure.

"Allie, slow down…Allie, where are you?…Allie, don't hide from me!"

After continuing his frantic pace, Will stopped at a bend in the river just north of the hidden wigwam to catch his breath. He leaned against a fine old hickory tree, placing both his hands on his knees. His wavy brown hair was saturated with sweat, making it curl even more. His eyes reflected the water and the autumn skies above in differing shades of blue.

"Boo!" Allie shouted.

Will pushed himself back off the tree. In one quick motion, he swirled around and faced her. "Allie, why do you do these things to me?"

Allie stepped forward from behind the old hickory.

"Do what, Will?"

"I almost fell in the river when you put up that scare!" He shook his head briefly and then looked down at her. There was silence again as they looked at each other.

"Will, come with me. I know of a secret place around the bend. I found it when I was trapping frogs a couple years ago. It has a secret entrance and a mirror that reflects the sun at high noon in summer."

Will dropped his jaw in astonishment. He couldn't believe someone else had found the wigwam. He wondered if Aaron had perhaps let the secret slip to her. Composing himself, he asked as he walked, "Who else knows about this secret place you found?"

Allie stopped and put her hands on her hips. "Well, if it was some lady folk in Freeport, with all the gabbin' they do, then all of Stephenson County would know about it! I saw a flash and found it one day as I was walkin' close to the other side of the Pecatonica. I reckon my curiosity was more than an ol' cat. I stuck my head through the hollies and saw the cave!"

"Interesting," replied Will.

Allie reached for Will's hand, and he gently placed her hand in his palm. With the movement, the wind picked up and blew ripples across the water. Two turtledoves were startled on a sandbar and flickered up before them. Allie turned and hugged Will.

"That's a sign. I just made a wish for us."

"What do you mean?"

"Did you know that turtledoves mate for life? You always see them in pairs, ya know." Allie looked up at Will. Her words were more restrained now. She almost whispered. "The place I'm taking you to is very special. We will be there soon."

Will remained silent as he looked into her blue eyes. Afraid he'd hurt her feelings, he decided to keep his knowledge of the wigwam secret for now. He reasoned it was best to reveal what he knew after making sure it was the same place.

The waters rippled and echoed gently as they gazed at each other. In the moment, he was awakened to the realization that someone very special cared for him for the first time in his life. He felt a little uneasy about it but was excited in a strange but comfortable way.

His heart pounded as they rounded the bend, and he kept his hand firmly in hers all the way to the wigwam.

Chapter 8

Tremont House Hotel

Southeast Corner of Lake and Dearborn Streets
Chicago
May, 1859

Three figures stood like dark silhouettes against the morning light that drove its way into the Tremont House lobby. Smoke trails from a cigar lifted to the ceiling. The room was quiet for the most part. It was too early for the piano player.

Galena friends John E. Smith and Congressman Washburne were there by the window. They had arrived moments before with Fire Marshal Putnam of Freeport. The train ride from the west was only a half-day's ride, yet they boarded the iron horse in the still of the night so they would not be late. The purpose of their trip was to see Mr. Lincoln and discuss his future.

"Do you think the drawbridge is up?" Putnam asked.

"Could be," Washburne replied as he puffed on his morning cigar. "Old Abe is a timely fellow. He will be here in a moment."

"I am looking forward to meeting him, Wash," John E. replied. "I will wait until midnight for the chance."

"Well, we will sure know when he approaches," Putnam added. "Though he lost the senatorial election to the little giant, he still stands taller than most people in this city, and not just physically."

"Rightly so," continued Washburne as he lifted his jaw and puffed out a small cloud of smoke. "I think he's pulling up now."

The door burst open. The noise from the rabble of Chicagoans echoed through the lobby. The three turned quickly to catch the spectacle. Lincoln and Elmer were within plain view inside the carriage.

The Irish driver held his whip up high and in a thick brogue screamed, "If ya want to feel the leather against your noggins, then stay where you are. Move yourself away, or I will move you!"

The crowd pressed against the carriage doors. No one in the carriage could step out.

John E. Smith, Washburne, and Putnam advanced.

"Clear the way!" Putnam yelled, "I am a fire marshal. Clear the way!" He reached out and grabbed a young fellow by the collar nearly lifting him off the ground. "All of you, move yourselves away...Now!"

Like a crowd dispersing after a fistfight, a few of the spectators peeled away, and then the rest fell away, standing across the street to get a follow-up view.

Putnam reached for the door and opened it. He saluted the freed inhabitants.

"Jesus, Mary, and Joseph," the Irishman breathed, "you cleared 'em good. I thought you'd be needin' my whip, sir!"

"These are good people," Putnam replied. "They came to cheer for Mr. Lincoln."

Putnam grabbed the latch on the carriage door and pulled it open with ease.

"Good morning, Mr. Lincoln, and to you, too, Elmer," Putnam interjected as he reached his hand inside the carriage cabin. He looked very pleased, not only to see Elmer again but to see him in the company of Abraham Lincoln.

"Good morning, Old Put!" Lincoln replied. "It's been too long since that hot day with Douglas. I beat him in Freeport, but he got the total win in this Sucker State!" Lincoln slipped out onto the curbside and placed his top hat on with a tap. "Hope things have cooled down in Freeport?"

"We are still keeping the irons hot for you!" Putnam replied, gripping Lincoln's hand again.

John E. and Washburne approached the carriage and extended their hands, too. The carriage door swung shut. The Irishman cracked his whip, and the carriage quickly disappeared around the corner.

"Quite a crowd, Abe," Washburne commented. "Maybe there were a few votes out there that weren't counted in January?" He smiled and nodded.

Lincoln returned the smile and then looked somber. He walked to the windows. His top hat nearly touched the ceiling. Taking a seat, he perched his hat on his knee and calmly stated, "Gentlemen, I now sink out of view and will be forgotten."

Elmer looked at Washburne. Smith and Putnam stood in silence.

Washburne broke the silence. "You will rise above this, Mr. Lincoln. Your friends here have a plan, and we have a year before the next election."

"And what election is that?" Lincoln replied.

"The presidency, sir."

Lincoln paused and then picked up his top hat. He moved it to his other knee. "So, Wash, you're believin' that we can win a platform?"

"I am sure of it," Washburne replied with enthusiasm. "We have a plan!"

"Well, don't stand on my behalf." Lincoln was upbeat again. "Take your seats, gentlemen; light your cigars; and tell me this plan."

One by one the four men drew positions on the leather seats by the window, which still had winter frost in the corners. A cloud of smoke gathered over their heads.

As a lobby attendant approached, Washburn said, "Sir, bring us three of your finest brandies, and two glasses of water for Mr. Lincoln and Colonel Ellsworth. But not right now. Let no one disturb us for the next half hour. Then bring it on. We will make our toast then."

The attendant bowed his head in acknowledgment and respectfully stepped out of the parlor.

Washburne turned back to the others. "Elmer, have you told him your plan?"

"I was holding it as a surprise, Congressman."

"And what have you?" Lincoln asked.

"I have been elected as commandant of the newly formed US Zouave Cadets of Chicago, forty men strong. We will show Chicago our drills on Independence Day! The event will begin in front of this hotel in the morning." Elmer raised his chin and tilted his head smartly.

"Congratulations, Colonel. I am very much looking forward to seeing your militia in action," Lincoln replied with a courteous nod. He then turned his attention to the others.

"And you, Fire Marshal Putnam, what is your plan to put out the Democratic fire in this state?"

"Mr. Lincoln, I suppose those fires will dwindle by themselves if we can keep the Republican fires lit into the night."

"And what do you mean by this," Lincoln replied curiously.

"John E. and I will make sure that the Lincoln platform will be reckoned with."

Lincoln looked at John E. Smith, who confirmed Putnam's confidence as he replied, "Old Put and I will have torch-light parades in Galena and Freeport. We will make sure every town in this corridor will be awakened with the news even late into the night. We will call our night volunteers the 'Wide Awakes'."

Lincoln paused and shifted his top hat to the other knee. He looked at his friends and said, "Well, with all of this noise and commotion into the wee hours of the night, I hope that when the election comes around, the people of Illinois will be awake on voting day!"

The five rolled out a burst of laughter.

"Bring out the cordials!" Washburne interjected. "Let's toast to Illinois and to Mr. Lincoln, our nominee for president in the next election!"

The door opened. A stranger entered the lobby. The five looked at him curiously.

"Well, Mr. Lincoln, do I detect a celebration?" the stranger asked.

"And who, sir, do I have the pleasure of addressing?" replied Lincoln calmly.

"Do you remember John Mason Loomis the third? I am he. We had the pleasure of acquaintance here about a year and a half ago. At that time, I informed you that no one would beat Senator Douglas in the senatorial election. My prediction was correct. You lost, Mr. Lincoln… so why the celebration?" Loomis smiled curtly with his nose upright.

There was dead silence in the parlor. No one could believe the audacity of the insult.

With a condescending smirk, Loomis tilted his head, awaiting a response.

After a short pause, Lincoln placed his broad hands on the arms of his chair and slowly rose, all the while staring directly into the eyes of Loomis, who began to fidget, anticipating a fight.

As Lincoln completed the motion, he raised his right hand with his palm up, smiled, and replied to the insult, "Well, Mr. Loomis, would you like to join us in a toast?"

Loomis was shocked and noticeably relieved. He stepped forward.

Lincoln motioned to the waiter attending, who then reached over and poured another glass of brandy for Loomis. The silence in the room was even more deafening.

"Gentlemen, it is written in the good Bible to turn the other cheek. It does not say that we have to toast our enemies, but this I will do should you decide to join us in the toast, Mr. Loomis."

Loomis nodded and grasped the glass.

Lincoln raised his glass with the others and continued. "And on that note, Mr. Loomis, I would like to share some country wisdom with you." He smiled, nodded gently to those around him, and continued. "Down in Springfield, where I hail from, the smart folk have said, 'If you call a tail a leg, how many legs does a dog have?' Would you say five?…No! The answer is always four! Just because you call a tail a leg… doesn't make it a leg!"

Lincoln grinned. His voice rose slightly as he lifted his glass, almost touching the chandelier and continued, "So with that, dear sir, I would like to toast your Democratic colleagues for your unabated logic and your misguided politics, which have truly helped the Republican Party in the short run. And in the long run, you Democrats will be running full speed…tail between the legs…where that tail should be…to the rear...as our Republican Party takes center stage as a true and honest voice of the people!"

A resounding burst of laughter filled the room, causing Loomis to step back. He did not raise the brandy to his lips. Instead he slapped the glass back on the attendant's tray, turned abruptly, and started for the door. Stepping halfway out the entrance, he turned back and laid a parting shot at the five. "Your Republican Party is full of too many Suckers! I will toast you all when Senator Douglas defeats you again!" The door slammed shut behind him with a boom, echoing to the guest rooms upstairs.

Washburne smiled, nodded to his colleagues, and then raised the brandy glass.

"A toast to Mr. Lincoln...our next president!" he said confidently.

Glasses clinked together.

Chapter 9

Tremont House Hotel

**Southeast Corner of Lake and Dearborn Streets
Chicago
July 4, 1859**

The basement was dark and damp even in July. A dripping noise broke the silence like the slow methodical ticking of a small clock. Elmer awakened from a deep slumber. Wrapped in two wool blankets with his red diary tucked under an arm, he began to sense that the brilliant Lake Michigan morning sun was rising, but rolled uncomfortably to his other side to get just a few more winks before lighting a candle.

As he stared into the darkness, he thought about his men, who were to arrive this day in front of the Tremont House for their first military-drill exhibition. Elmer, because of his prowess with the Rockford City Greys, was recruited and elected as commander by these untested

Chicago boys just slightly over two months before. They, too, were arousing from their slumber, having slept in blankets on the floor of the armory just a few blocks away.

Mr. Couch, the owner of the Tremont House, had kindly allowed Elmer to sleep in the basement for free so that he could make early preparations for his men, the newly named US Zouave Cadets of Chicago.

A crackling noise and a swift furry shuffle broke the silence. Elmer jumped up like a cat. The blankets twisted around his legs, and his red diary clunked onto the floor. Reaching for the candle beside him, he knocked it over with a clank, causing the scurrying noise to increase. The candle separated from the base and rolled away. Reaching out with both hands, he searched the damp floor around his blankets, and within seconds found the candle and placed it back in the holder. He then struck a match on the rocky floor and relit the wick. Shadows of scurrying rats stretched and then faded into the corners of the room.

Elmer rose to his feet, smiled, shook his head, and coughed twice. His toothache had mostly gone away, and the catarrh, which had caused him to cough incessantly during the cold winter days, seemed to only affect him in the morning now. He coughed deeply again.

Stretching his arms behind his back, he walked over to the small table that had his breakfast waiting for him. For months he had subsisted day and night mostly on crackers and water. A one-pound box, which he had paid eleven cents for the previous day, was in a shredded state from the rats who feasted on the crackers during his sleep. Picking it up, he peeked inside, shook it, and then tipped it toward his open hand. Three crackers dropped out.

Well, those four-legged ones have to eat, too! Thank God they left me a few. Placing the crackers one by one in his mouth, he reached for the tall sturdy glass of water on the table. *Glad they weren't strong enough to knock this over.*

He looked back again to the corners of the basement. His nighttime visitors were nowhere to be seen. He caught the reflection of his bright-red diary from the candlelight. Bending over, he picked up his blankets and diary and placed them on the table.

"I will make another entry tonight about our military drill today, dear diary. I don't expect folks would care to know much about this basement right now," he said calmly. Tears welled up in his eyes.

He then grabbed his prized little journal and opened it to the very first page. The entry was written on his twenty-second birthday.

> *April 11, 1859*
> *I do this because it seems very pleasant to be able to look*
> *upon our past lives—such a jumble of strange incidents*
> *that should I ever become anybody or anything, this will*
> *be usefull [sic] as a means of showing how much suffering*
> *and temptation a man may undergo and still keep clear of*
> *despair and vice.*[1]

Elmer closed the diary and placed it gently on the table. His thoughts drifted to days on the Hudson River and the Rock River where he trapped muskrats to support himself. Now he was the colonel of a great Zouave drill team. He remembered the long walks along the Pecatonica River with Allie and the friends of the wigwam...the Freeport fire... and the proud Rockford City Greys.

A creak from the oak floor in the parlor above snapped him back to the present. *Best get ready for my address to the city folk. Best get ready for my men.*

On a hook in the corner was a newly fitted and brightly colored Zouave uniform patterned after the famous French soldiers in the Crimean War. Elmer had learned the movements and tactics of these soldiers from his fencing instructor, Dr. Charles A. DeVilliers, also of Chicago, whom he had met in a gymnasium and befriended. The dash and swiftness of the Zouave movements impressed Elmer greatly... so greatly that he was already a recognized drill master in Rockford. Today, Independence Day, would be another proving ground to the citizens of Chicago.

Reaching over in the dim light, he grabbed the scarlet-red pantaloons, which were baggy to allow quick and graceful movements during drills. Elmer tucked his pants into his boots and then wrapped yellow gaiters at the top of his boots. His shirt of sky blue was then tucked in his pants and complemented with a collarless navy-blue jacket trimmed with gold braid. Reaching over for the last remaining piece of his elaborate uniform, he grabbed a scarlet French kepi, a small cap with gold and orange decorations, about the size of a small frying pan turned upside down. Elmer placed the cap deftly on his head, cocking the cap slightly to the right. He then grabbed the black chin strap attached to the kepi and pulled it over his chin. He leaned down, picked up his blankets and diary, stood straight at attention for a moment, grabbed the candle holder at the base, and walked up the creaking wooden stairs to the Tremont House parlor.

"Colonel Ellsworth! You look grand this fine day. How was your sleep?"

"Very comfortable, Mr. Couch. I am indebted for your kindness," Elmer replied with his usual charm.

"Are you ready for the presentation today? Mayor Haines believes there will be a crowd of twenty thousand folks to see you! Are you nervous?"

"We will do our best, sir. My men have practiced long and hard for this."

"Well, good luck, Colonel. I am betting on the US Zouave Cadets this grand day!"

Elmer gently nodded his head. His kepi remained firmly tilted in place.

The crowd was thick outside, waiting for the approach of Elmer's company, and he could hear the excitement outside. Suddenly, single shouts were heard above the hum of the crowd, and a cheer broke out as his colorfully clad company proceeded north on Dearborn Street to the hotel. When they reached the intersection at Lake Street, they turned east on Lake Street and stopped abruptly in perfect formation in front of the Tremont House. With a curt command from a lieutenant, Elmer's forty-man Zouave Company snapped the butts of their small musketoon rifles to the ground in one motion and then uniformly looked up to the balcony where Abraham Lincoln delivered a grand speech the previous year. The late-morning sun reflected off the shiny barrels of their rifles, causing many of the spectators closest to the men to hold kerchiefs to their eyes. As the Zouaves stood silently like sentries of old, the crowd noise began to subside, broken with an occasional shout or laugh, until it dropped to almost a whisper.

Noticing the silence and considering it his cue, Elmer peeked through the curtains of the parlor window overlooking the street scene and proceeded upstairs, each clunk of his boot steps building his confidence as he rose to the third-floor balcony. As he walked, he stretched his back to ease the ache from sleeping on the basement's damp, hard floor. Placing both hands over his mouth, he coughed deeply to clear his throat. Touching the brim of his cap to make sure it was smartly placed on his dark-brown curls, his deep hazel eyes gazed through the balcony doors that were opened wide for him.

He stepped out onto the balcony.

The crowd looked immense. It remained silent. His heart began pounding faster as he noticed all eyes upon him. Then a sense of calm and grace came over him. He smiled, nodded, and tipped his hat directly toward a small group of admiring ladies who had summer fans opened, covering their mouths as they whispered to each other.

With a strong and confident voice, Elmer began. "Ladies and gentlemen of Chicago, Mayor Haines, council members, and officers of the Fire Brigade!"

He paused for effect.

"We are gathered today to celebrate the heroic deeds of our colonial forefathers! This great Union would not be here today if not for them."

He paused again, his silence causing an even more intent anticipation from the crowd. His eyes turned fiery yet tender as he continued.

"Through them and their great sacrifices on the fields of fire and around lonely hearthstones in homesteads across the colonies, fathers, mothers, children, and grandchildren suffered eight long years for the dream of liberty."

He paused again and spanned the crowd from left to right. He raised his right hand and cocked it at angle, beckoning the crowd to answer.

"Shall we raise a cheer to them now?"

A thunderous roar rolled around the Tremont House, echoing east to Lake Michigan, across the Chicago River, and to the south and west! It continued for two long minutes, the ovation encouraged by Elmer's slow nods and graceful movements as he stood with shoulders erect, turning to each side of the balcony so every individual within view could enjoy his delivery.

When the crowd noise slowly subsided for Elmer's next remarks, cries of startled babies could be heard, and the distant barks of dogs punctuated the forming silence.

In a deep and sonorous voice, he continued.

"My grandfather was just a boy of fifteen when he took up a musket and joined the ranks of the Continental army at Saratoga, America's great first victory in the Revolutionary War. Just a boy. Just a militiaman. And, as we know from the annals of history, like the Greek soldiers of old…a just and dedicated *citizen* soldier. Like all of our grandfathers and forefathers who built this fine country, we must be prepared to defend our rights and liberties, our firesides, and our altars." Elmer paused.

The crowd clapped thunderously. Small Betsy Ross flags fluttered in the hands of children as colorful red, white, and blue ribbons in the bonnets of the ladies curled up with gentle bursts of lakeshore breezes. There was silence again.

"The US Zouave Cadets of Chicago militia inherits that proud tradition!" Elmer nodded and then tipped his hat in salute to his command below, who did not react to the cheers of the crowd.

"And whatever tends to induce a military spirit among the people and render them capable of standing erect against a world in arms, that is surely patriotic, that is surely beneficial to the nation!"

Teenage girls glanced admiringly at the cadets and appeared to swoon.

"My fellow comrades-in-arms—" He continued as he directed his gaze over the cross rail of the balcony and reached out to them with both arms extended. "We are gathered here on Independence Day to demonstrate the Zouave military drill. You are trained for this day! You have practiced over the last ten weeks every day except the Lord's day for four long and strenuous hours…and to heavy your burden to build your skill…with twenty-five-pound knapsacks on your backs!"

The crowd clapped with appreciation. Those closest to the cadets turned directly toward them and nodded, but the cadets kept their chins up and steady as they looked at their colonel. He continued.

"Soldiers, you have excelled and become masters of the military drill…But your *greatest* achievement is your daily devotion to our Golden Resolutions, which have made you strong in body and resolute in character!"

Elmer paused again. The crowd was silent. He continued with his strong, direct tone that with each point rose in intensity yet was calm, deliberate, and with great strength and reach.

"We are bound by our Golden Resolutions: We will not drink! We will not smoke! We will not gamble!"

He paused as he gazed at the throng of citizens on Lake Street.

"And we will not wear our uniforms in any place that would disgrace the honor of the US Zouave Cadets of Chicago!"

As Elmer hit the final point, the cheering again reverberated through the streets and alleys and rolled like a wave to those in the distance at Lakeshore Park. Those citizens at the park wondered what Elmer had said. They could not see the colorful cadets as the distance was a quarter mile away, but soon they would see them in their full grandeur.

As the crowd noise built to a crescendo, the flags continued to flutter like in a red, white, and blue blur. Elmer tipped his hat to the excitement in front of him, turned on his heels with back erect, and disappeared from the balcony. As he turned, the Light Guard eighteen-member military band struck up "Yankee Doodle Dandy." The crowd continued to roar in appreciation.

Within minutes the door of the Tremont House swung open, and Elmer reappeared in full splendor. Smiling and shaking hands with those close by, he gradually made it to the side of his forty-man Zouave contingent and stood in position to direct his command. When the band had finished, the crowd fell silent again.

"US Zouave Cadets of Chicago!" Elmer ordered, "We now represent with honor this great city on the prairie. Give them our cheer and stand ready for drill!"

The forty were positioned to the right of Elmer, faced in rows of eight and five lines deep. Most of them, like Elmer, were slightly shy of medium height. They were muscular with chiseled arms, legs, torsos, and countenances from the long hours of preparation.

At the moment, Elmer smartly pulled his sword from its black leather sheath. Holding the sword hilt at chest level, he began a slow movement, swinging the tip of the sword to the twelve o'clock position. When the tip hit twelve, he quickly snapped the sword upward to chin level with the tip of the sword now two feet over his red kepi cap.

Immediately, a deep guttural cheer from the forty rebounded off the front of the Tremont House as they shouted with pride, doffing their caps and raising them up and down with each shout!

"Hi...Hi...Hi!"

"One—Two—Three—Four—Five—Six—Seven!"

"Tig-a-r...Zouave!"

The Chicagoans were stunned by the shouts, and the cadets then began their first movements with Elmer's crystal-clear commands directing them into action.

The eight rows of five broke quickly and symmetrically apart into ten distinct groups of four, each Zouave facing outward. Muskets swirled like batons and dropped back to their side. With the command of "Fix bayonets!" forty bayonets were pulled and snapped to the muzzles with the greatest precision with rapidity. Elmer's next command caused the deadly weapons to be pressed outward at a forty-five-degree angle, causing the tip of the bayonet to be only inches away from the faces of the closest admirers. The ten squares of four moved in step eastwardly down Lake Street like a deadly animal. The crowd gasped as the Zouaves marched with the thump of their boots. Police barked their own commands to the crowd, methodically clearing hundreds of people in the path of the forty. They pushed hard to clear the way. The Zouaves suddenly stopped when Elmer shouted, "Company halt!"

All waited in anticipation for what the next maneuver would bring. Police continued to clear the crowds to either side of the street, Dearborn Street to Lakeshore Park, a good mile away.

"Company, re…form!" Elmer commanded. The ten squares quickly formed into a single square again. Bayonets snapped in unison in the long leather sheaths at each man's side.

"Present arms!" Musketoons were then raised to waist level at shoulder side.

Elmer in consecutive quick commands shouted, "Ready! March! Quick time! Then double-quick time!" With each command, the forty moved like a marching machine with boots slamming the muddy street with a thud and all eyes and muskets forward. Crowds pressed against the buildings en masse as the pace of Elmer's command quickened.

And then the unexpected happened.

"Prepare to fire!"

In full quickstep each Zouave systematically reached into his powder and cap pouch, pulled out a linen-wrapped cartridge with gunpowder, tore the wrap with his front teeth, poured the powder down the front of the musket barrel, flipped the musket back to normal position, pulled the hammer back to a half-cocked position, reached again into the pouch for a tiny ignition cap that looked like a tiny top hat, placed the cap on the ignition nipple at the breach, and pulled the hammer to full-cock position…all with a twenty-second rapidity. The forty then pointed their minimuskets at a perfect forty-five-degree angle toward the blue skies over Lakeshore Park."

Elmer screamed, "Ready. Aim. Fire!"

Folks nearby cringed and placed their hands over their mouths and ears in anticipation, and the roar of forty muskets boomed! The maneuver silenced the crowd for a moment like the effect of fireworks in the sky, but demands for more drills and movement were shouted as the US Zouave Cadets in quickstep continued to the lake. Within the thirty minutes that had passed, in their demonstrations on the way to the park, the company of forty somersaulted with bayonets in place, fired rounds into the air while lying on their backs, and yelled and screamed Zouave cheers…all in perfect and precise synchrony while the crowd enthusiastically applauded every move. By the time they reached Lakeshore Park, the Zouaves were firing their weapons at a full run and hastily scattering the crowd in front of them.

When the Zouaves reformed in the field, the thousands who had missed Elmer's speech, scary bayonet movements, and firing exercises were treated to even more elaborate drill movements. They slowed to a stop and reformed into ten ranks of four squares again.

The noise settled down, and the crowd could not take their eyes off the handsome young officer who had a charisma that caused his men to move as one. And now they were about to see a parade drill executed with faultless precision, as if the muscle of each Zouave was controlled by one mass of men.

Elmer looked at the Light Guard band, who in their own snappy style had enhanced the spectacle of Zouaves before them. He nodded, and the band struck up Stephen Foster's popular tune "Hard Times Come Again No More." The music, with its folksy military beat, immediately elevated the crowd's spirits even more. Elmer paused and then shouted a curt command that again directed the men and moment as if he were an orchestra conductor.

In perfect harmony the familiar squares beautifully morphed into double crosses and then evolved into perfect pyramid shapes. After delighting the lakeshore crowd with this successful movement, the pyramids then formed into scarlet and blue rotating circles that blended with the flags and patriotic color in the bright afternoon sky. The sunlight reflected off the polished bayonets and musket barrels like dazzling reflecting mirrors. The movements became even more complex as the music provided a pleasant backdrop to each perfect step. The ten circles touched each other in movement and began mixing the four-man groups back again into one. Squares and pyramids appeared again like a massive kaleidoscope on the green.

The crowd shouts and cheers carried up and down the swampy shores of Lake Michigan. Then the music stopped. The forty stood shoulder to shoulder again, five rows of eight, like in front of the Tremont House earlier that morning.

Elmer raised the hilt of his sword to his chin, and the Zouaves responded with a hearty shout.

"Hi...Hi...Hi!"

"One—Two—Three—Four—Five—Six—Seven!"

"Tig-a-r...Zouave!"

Elmer snapped his sword firmly into its black sheath, signaling the end of the military drill.

After a short silence, the citizens responded with increasing shouts of approval and glee. They were stunned by the quick conclusion of the drill, which had lasted just over two hours. Passersby who were close to Elmer vigorously shook his hand as others patted him on the back with gusto. The dashing bayonet exercises, the rapid firing of muskets on the double quickstep, and the final kaleidoscope parade executed with elegance and artful movement would always be remembered and celebrated. Newspapers and folks would report that on this day, the Zouaves had exceeded their expectations.

Elmer turned from the admirers and joined his company again. With a final command, the US Zouave Cadets of Chicago proudly snapped a final salute to the city that would now become their permanent home.

At the close of day, with the celebrations over, the cadets would proudly march back to the armory.

They would sleep on the floor again.

Chapter 10

Light Guard Hall

Armory of the US Zouave Cadets
Garrett Block
Southeast Corner of Randolph and State Streets
Chicago
July 5, 1859
Two Hours Past Midnight

The boys were on the floor comfortably rolled up in their scarlet blankets with their heads on their knapsacks. A few snores quietly echoed across the gymnasium. Elmer lay on his back in the center of his men with his eyes wide open. He could not sleep.

The celebration just hours ago seemed like a dream. And just twenty-four hours ago, he was sound asleep on the cold damp floor of the Tremont House basement. Thinking of his red diary, he thought it best now, while his comrades were sleeping, to jot down the events of the day. Gathering his scarlet blanket, he rolled it tightly with his diary under his right armpit and left the blanket on the floor. Rising slowly, he made his way to the Terpsichorean concert room to the little desk where he signed personal invitations to the visiting ladies and gentlemen who wished to see the cadets sing and play instruments.

The room was quiet, as expected, and he pulled the candle lamp by the entrance of the room and placed it on the writing desk. Placing the diary on the table, he flipped the pages near the middle of the book, held it with his left hand, grabbed a quill, and dipped it into the inkwell.

July 5th 1859
Victory, and thank God a triumph for me. This day has
well nigh (sic) established my reputation…our Boys looked
very handsomely in their new uniforms and equipment and
marched like old veterans…We commenced our movements
first in quick time, then on the run…From that time until
the close of the drill, the crowd was absolutely enthusiastic
applauding every new movement & cheering alternately
the company and myself. An Army Officer…came to me
on his own accord and said he wished to congratulate me,
that he had been in the Army seven years, but he had never
in the Army or out of it seen such drilling as our company
performed that morning since he left the point.[2]

Elmer placed the quill down. Though he was just a few yards from his company, he was overcome with a sense of tearful joy. Resting his elbows on the table, he placed his face in his hands and began to sob a sigh of relief and happiness. He wanted to pray out loud, but he did not wish to wake his men, so he softly whispered in his hands, "I enter the second year of my manhood with my heart filled to overflowing with gratitude for the many and undeserved mercies for which I am indebted to God." Wiping his tears, he stood up, blew out the lamp, grabbed his red diary, and returned to his blanket.

Wrapping his blanket around his shoulders, he rolled comfortably to his side and whispered, "God bless America. God Bless our cadets."

Chapter 11

Pecatonica River

Freeport
Autumn, 1859

The fall season always fell short in Freeport as if squeezed by summer and winter. Despite this, the colors along the Pecatonica were magnificent. The river always maintained its meandering pace, but now it was laced with an assortment of colorful growth. A burst of red maple and yellow birch leaves contrasted with the wall of oak trees still sporting green leaves, awaiting the winter snap to turn. Most birds were gone already. The water was too cold to walk in with bare feet. Catfish and river bass were still thick though. The river level would soon drop, but it would rise again in the spring.

"This is my favorite time of the year," Allie exclaimed. "Have you seen anything as beautiful as this, Jenny?"

Jenny Putnam was the only daughter of Fire Marshal Putnam. A year younger than Allie, they became fast friends when they first met in town just a few weeks earlier. Jenny had never gone to the river without her father, and it was Allie who dared her to come with her to see the secret wigwam that Will, Aaron, and Allie visited frequently.

In contrast to Jenny, who was a member of a prominent Freeport family and whose father was both the fire marshal and an important local banker, Allie was poor and her family was small. She lived with her grandmother Lucy in a tiny one-room cabin in a beautiful clearing close to the river. Jenny was always modest about her wealthy family position. She was, in fact, sometimes embarrassed by it, especially when she was around her new friend, Allie, who walked the river in britches and thick leather boots. Yet neither difference in clothing nor standing in the community could keep either of these newfound friends apart now. They had become soul mates.

"Jenny, did ya hear what I just said?"

"I'm sorry, Allie, I couldn't keep my eyes off the colors. I thought I was dreaming."

"Well, I've been a dreamin' myself about Will lately," Allie responded with a crooked smile that could warm anyone's heart. "I 'spect he and Aaron are at the wigwam now."

"Who is Aaron?"

"I reckon that when you meet him, you'll feel your heart throb a bit. Aaron is younger than Will, but they are like brothers for sure." Pointing downriver, she continued, "Our secret place is just around that bend by the swirlin' water. Perfect place for a muskrat trap! Someday, I will teach you how to catch 'em!"

Jenny blushed. "Well, I don't think I could ever bring one home for supper!"

Allie smiled and winked. "Let's get to the wigwam."

"Yes, we best be moving on," Jenny replied. "My mother wants me home by noon for supper. If she ever knew I was this far down the Pecatonica, I would be in trouble for sure."

Aaron and Will were indeed in the wigwam waiting. Nothing had changed much since they first found the cave just over two years ago. Allie being closest to the Pecatonica visited the wigwam almost every day. She always made sure the tomahawk and beaded bag were in the original place by the south wall. The rock that angled the mirror causing the flicker flash was placed to the side as well. The curved mirror was secured next to it. By doing this, they kept the secret place hidden from any passersby.

As Allie and Jenny rounded the bend, Jenny looked curiously to the bushes onshore.

"Allie, are you sure the place is near here? I can't be late for supper!"

"Stop in your tracks, and cover your eyes right now, Jenny!"

Jenny responded.

"Now turn to the right and open your eyes!"

As she dropped her delicate hands to her side and opened her eyes, she gasped. Directly, not two feet away, stood the boys.

"My goodness. Where did they come from?"

Both boys grinned. In unison they reached behind them to the holly branches that secluded the wigwam and pulled them quickly back, revealing the entrance.

"Come in, friends," replied Will, smiling.

Aaron entered first, followed by Allie and Jenny.

The sun angled directly from the top as it did before. The ray cast a bright late-morning glow through the small particles of dust, revealing a fine spread of pine needles, which had been collected by the friends over the past two years. The matting was as thick as a goose-down pillow.

Jenny turned quickly to the boys as if having an epiphany. "I remember you two from the Lincoln-Douglas debate last year, during that very hot summer day!"

"Sure enough, Jenny. Your father introduced us to you that day," replied Will.

Captivated by Jenny's beauty, Aaron remained quiet and fidgeted a little.

"You were the boys who helped put out the Freeport fire and saved the little colt!" she said excitedly. "The whole town is so grateful to you!"

"Well, we had a lot of help from your father and the bucket brigade. All the boys had a good hand in it," replied Will, smiling again.

"Well, Aaron! Why do you jist sit there like a church mouse!" exclaimed Allie. "Open those smackers of yours and treat Jenny like a lady!"

Aaron blushed and fidgeted more. He quickly turned and nodded to Jenny who, in return, bowed back gracefully and smiled in an effort to suspend the awkward silence. Aaron diverted a question back to Allie in an effort to save himself from the embarrassing moment.

"Do you bring more Indian stories from Grandma Lucy?" he asked.

His green eyes reflected in the beam of light, showing his keen interest. His curly black hair blended like coal into the dark shadow behind him. Jenny felt an instant attraction to him and looked at him when he finished the question. She held his gaze for a moment…and then her eyes quickly darted away.

"Well," Allie replied with a grin, "would you like to hear about Grandma Lucy's first Injun fight?"

"Indian fight?" Will replied with two raised eyebrows.

"I guess you could say so. She told me that years ago, right after the Black Hawk War, a treaty was signed, and the Winnebago Injuns were sent to the other side of the Mississippi. Our Injuns were mainly farmers, like Freeport folk. They were friendly like us, too. Some of them stuck around though 'cause it's hard to leave your homeplace, ya know."

Allie continued. "Grandma Lucy was married to a big man about the size of Abe Lincoln. She is only about five feet tall, though, so he towered way above her. We reckon he was the tallest man in these parts. His name was William Wadham. Well, because Lucy was a kind woman, she always kept a pot of cornmeal mush on the fire hearth for anyone who was comin' by her place. No one would feel the starvin' pangs near her cabin. She fed both Injuns and white folk. One day, seven feathered-up braves, don't know if they were Winnebagos or not, stumbled by the cabin. They was drunk, and they knew about the corn mush. Lucy, thinking they were up to no good, shoved her three little ones under the straw bed. William met the Injun strangers at the door but was grabbed by the throat by the biggest of the seven. Grandma Lucy was as quick as a bear cat! She grabbed her rollin' pin from the breadboard and chased after the big one. She beat him about the knees 'til he buckled to the floor. He got up and hobbled out the cabin door. All of them scattered through the woods. Believe they kept dodgin' trees 'til they got back to their village!"

"She scared off seven Indians with a rolling pin?" Aaron asked curiously. His voice cracked from disbelief.

"Sure as we're sittin' here," replied Allie. "And that's not the end of it. Big William grabbed his rifle from the mantel to see if it was loaded with powder and ball. It was. They waited all night, scared when the next fight would be. They put water buckets around in case the Injuns tried to set the cabin on fire."

Will, Jenny, and Aaron blurted out together, "What happened next!"

Allie picked up the medicine bag that was snuggled against the wall. "The next mornin', Lucy peeked out the gunport in the front door and saw the Injuns lined up on the edge of the woods. The big Injun had a beaded bag just like this one. He walked slowly to the front door of the cabin. His moccasins made no noise. When he got right close, he began talkin' in chopped English. 'Little white fightin' squaw, no shoot me. We sorry. We make no fight. Medicine bag for little white fightin' squaw.' And then the Injuns left and never came back."

There was complete silence in the wigwam. Allie put the bag back on the wall.

"Do you think this is the same bag that he gave to Grandma Lucy?" asked Jenny.

"No. Grandma Lucy still has hers. It does look like this. I reckon this was put here for a good reason," Allie replied confidently. She looked at Will and smiled again.

"Why do you think the bag and tomahawk are here?" Will asked.

"Well, Grandma Lucy has ideas about Injuns in these parts. I 'spect she's right."

Will continued. "What can you tell us, Allie? Does she know about this place?"

"No, she don't, and never will. I did ask her about wigwam stuff after I first saw this place."

Jenny, Will, and Aaron again jumped in together, "What did you ask her?"

"I didn't much want her to know about this place, so I gave her bits and pieces, hopin' she could put it together again. You know like piecin' a broken china plate back together."

The friends leaned in closer.

"Did you ever rightly wonder about these holly bushes and that big oak that covers this place?"

"Never much thought about it," replied Will, "but it sure hides this place nicely year round."

"That's right. Those holly bushes have leaves that are green all year. All evergreens are a symbol of eternal life. Ya know, like you never die. That's what Grandma Lucy says. She says those Injuns did believe that the red berries of the holly bushes stand for love. So the holly branch stands for eternal love. The leaves from that big ol' oak outside are for courage."

"I still don't get what you're getting at," Aaron replied with a look of frustration in his face.

Jenny and Will remained silent.

"Well, if you think of puttin' the china plate together, it all makes sense. And there is a legend about these things that Grandma Lucy told me. So it all makes sense." Allie straightened her back. She looked somber and continued. "Back before any white folk came to the Pecatonica, there were Injun tribes who fought in these parts. She said there were two Injun lovers who walked along this river."

Jenny blushed and glanced at Aaron and then quickly looked down in embarrassment.

Allie paused, smiled, and continued. "Young braves would take off to other tribes to take horses, tomahawks, and other stuff. Sometimes they would just face off without killin' one another. They were still brave when doin' so."

"Like a fistfight?" asked Aaron.

"No, they counted coup. They would ride their horses at each other in an open field, like the knights of old, you know. The riders would carry a coup stick that was skinny as a sapplin' and about ten feet long. When they got right close enough, they would touch the Injuns they were fightin' with the coup stick and, sure as a rabbit, ride their ponies as fast as they could to git back to the other braves that couldn't git the gumption to go with 'em!"

"So they didn't kill each other in the fight?" Will asked.

"No. Just gittin that close and touchin' 'em with those long sticks was brave. Grandma Lucy says they would get feathers for each coup they did get."

"What does this have to do with the wigwam? I still don't get it," Aaron replied, his green eyes peering inquisitively.

"I will tell you the story 'bout this place. An ol' legend has it that the Injun lovers met somewhere 'long this river. After each raid the brave would meet his maiden here. One day as the dusk was settling in, he didn't come back. His lover returned to the Winnebago village to find him wrapped in buffalo hides. He was killed during a coup fight. A Potawatomi touched him with a coup stick and rode back. The Winnebago lover then took his stick and rode his horse to do the same. When he got real close, a Potawatomi broke the Injun code and shot him off his horse with a musket ball. They all took off 'cept the friends who carried him on his horse back to the village."

Allie finished and looked up with a tear in her eye. The silence in the wigwam was deafening. Jenny sniffled on her lacy silk kerchief. The boys said nothing.

"So do you think the tomahawk and medicine bag are theirs?" Jenny replied as she dabbed both eyes.

"Legend has it that the medicine bag was hers, the tomahawk is his, and this place was their secret place on the river!"

"So what about the holly and the oak tree?" Will asked.

"I 'spect the two planted those holly bushes. They rightly loved each other more than one could know. And that big bowed oak...I reckon she put that there for him because of his courage and bravery." Allie paused. "Strange how it bends. It looks kinda sad as it hangs right over the river. Makes a good climbin' tree, though."

Everyone looked at each other and nodded. There was silence again. Nobody knew what to say.

Suddenly, a loud *crack* of a gunshot pierced the air, followed by the sound of the bullet impacting something very close to them. Jenny screamed in fear. The four jumped up, huddled by the entrance, and peered out across the river.

"Who do you think it is, Will?" asked Aaron as he placed his arms snugly around Jenny.

"I don't know. Wait! I see it!"

"What? What?"

Across the river was an old hickory tree that had lost its footing in the river bank soil. A gust of wind had tipped it over into the river during a storm. The top half of the tree had been stripped of its leaves by the current, and over the years the old hickory had become deeply buried in the muck. The massive roots on the bank appeared like a dragon's foot with the tree trunk resembling a submerged leg, giving the impression that a dragon was sleeping in the Pecatonica with one of its feet resting on the opposite shore.

"I see a rifle perched between the toes of the dragon's foot. And it's pointing in our direction," Will whispered as he squinted toward the other side of the Pecatonica.

"Oh my God!" Jenny exclaimed.

"Jenny, now you just settle down a bit. We got to see this thing out," Allie stated calmly. "No sense gittin worked up right now. Could be someone just huntin'."

Allie squeezed out of the cave entrance, walked to the riverbank with both hands on her hips, and glared at the two strangers.

"Come outa there and show your faces! You damn near hit me with that ball!"

The barrel of the rifle was pulled back from its resting spot between two of the center toes of the dragon's foot. It pointed straight up now. There was a tense moment of silence. A rustle could be heard distinctly across the water. Two heads popped up between the toes. Both were covered by wide floppy hats.

"Ma'am, I am very sorry," shouted the tallest one across the river. He raised his rifle over his head, perpendicular to his body so all could see he meant no harm.

Allie cupped both her hands to her mouth and announced directly, "I ain't a ma'am. I'm a miss! Now, come out from behind that tree and reckon with us!"

There was a hush of wind that caused ripples on the slow-moving water. The hats disappeared from view. Another pause, and then two figures appeared on each side of the dragon's foot.

"We are boys from Buda, just down the river. Can we cross?" answered the tall one.

At that point everyone slowly emerged from the cave. Allie looked at Will. Will then glanced at the others. Everyone knew the strangers were now aware of the cave entrance. There was quiet on both sides of the Pecatonica.

Will shouted, "You can come over, but keep your rifle over your head with both hands up!"

The strangers disappeared again behind the dragon's foot. Within a moment the tall one put both hands on two toes of the fallen tree and pulled himself up onto the trunk. He then grabbed the rifle from the other stranger, who lifted it up between the same two toes. From there he started walking with the rifle raised above his hat. He started down the angling shin of the dragon's foot so he could get as far across the river as possible without getting his boots wet. Step by step he proceeded down the trunk, placing each foot carefully in front of the other. Within a few minutes, he was close to the friends. The dragon shin was nearly submerged at that point, only ten feet from the wigwam.

"The river is only about three feet deep from where you are. You can easily walk the rest if you don't care much about your britches and boots getting wet," Will cautioned the tall one. Since he was the oldest and tallest of the friends, he wanted to make sure the strangers knew he could fend for the group.

The tall stranger proceeded into the water and stepped up, slipping slightly, on the muddy shore. He nodded gently under his wide-brimmed hat and then looked at his friend by the dragon's foot.

"My fishin' pole is stuck in the roots, and I can't get to it rightly without fallin' in the river," the other stranger announced in a nervous drawl. He stood short, not much over five feet tall, and wore a hat with a turned-up, wide brim. His eyes and hair were a charcoal black that accented his large nose, and he had a moustache that looked like cat whiskers. He was pudgy, shaped like an egg. His shoulders were sloped and his hips too wide for his body. "Now, hold on! Yep, I got it! I will be there lickety-split!"

"Hold that pole to both sides of you so you can balance," Will instructed.

The pudgy little stranger held the long cane pole over his head with both hands, causing his shirt to rise up and expose his big belly, belly button and all.

"I will be there right quick," he said.

Suddenly, the breeze picked up again, sending a wave of ripples across the river. The cane pole began to wobble.

"You better watch your step!" the tall one cried out.

"I don't much have any steps right now!" he screamed. "Could you get me some chicken feet to make this distance!"

When he was at midriver, the deepest point, he stopped to balance himself. "I can right make it," he said. "I just hope this dragon doesn't wake up soon and send me flyin'."

Everyone chuckled.

The tall stranger looked at the kids, shook his head, and replied, "Well, if he does, you can slay that dragon with your cane pole!"

With that comment, the friends let out a hoot, causing the pudgy one to start laughing, too. As his chuckles rose in pitch, the wind picked up, sending the pole and him headlong into the river. A head soon emerged followed by two hands that slapped the water. One held the hat; the other gripped the cane pole.

"Guess that damn dragon thought I was a flea or something."

Everyone hooted again. Arms and legs flailed as the stranger tried to get closer to the muddy bank.

"Give me that cane. I can get you out," Allie exclaimed. "Take your boots off so you don't lose 'em in the deep mud!"

"Why, miss, I can't rightly do any bendin' right now to get my brogans off! Can't even reach my knees out here! Can you take my pole?"

Allie reached for the tip, now within two feet of the riverbank, and grabbed it firmly. "We can pull you in. Keep your boots on, then!"

The other friends grabbed the pole and pulled hard.

"Now don't let go!" Will shouted.

"Bet my boots and britches, I won't!"

With his hat and pole gripped firmly, he was pulled quickly onto the muddy shore. He rolled over and in one quick motion jumped to his feet like a cat. He put his soaked hat back on his head and pulled it down to his ears.

"I want to thank you kindly, miss. And you, too, miss. And the misters, too," he replied with a smile that grew to a radiant grin. "I suspect you must be wonderin' how I can catch anything with this pole if I keep swimmin' with it 'stead of stayin' on dry ground!"

Chuckles rose from the group.

Allie turned to the tall one. "So why did ya shoot at us? Why were you snoopin' on us?"

"Whoa, hold it, missy. I think you're reading us dead wrong now," replied the pudgy one. He looked down to his muddy boots and britches and then pleaded, "And besides, we haven't made proper introductions."

Allie looked down river, paused, then gently nodded her head. "Well, I am Allie. This is Will, Aaron, and Jenny. They are from Freeport. I live over by the Rock River. We are friends of the wigwam."

The pudgy one walked over and stood erect by his friend, who easily stood a foot taller and was blond and sturdy. He held his rifle with an easy grace. The contrast was striking.

"We are friends from Buda. He fishes, and I hunt," said the tall one.

"And what are your names?' asked Will.

The tall one replied in a steady tone, "His nickname is Trick. It's short for Patrick. His last name is Kane."

"And you?"

"My name is T.J. Lockwood."

There was a pause.

Will and Aaron quickly looked at each other.

"Are you *the* T.J. Lockwood who shot from the belfry tower during the big fire?" exclaimed Will.

The friends glanced at each other as Will asked the question.

"Yes, I am," T.J. answered.

There was a longer pause this time before Allie spoke up. "Well, why in the dickens are you firin' at friends?"

"I was shooting at a squirrel that was hiding in those holly bushes."

"Well, it looks like you missed it good," replied Allie.

T.J. approached the holly-covered entrance to the wigwam. He poked the barrel of his squirrel rifle into the greenery and then reached in and pulled out a dead squirrel by its tail. "Guess we best be off, Trick. Supper will be coming up shortly. We best be getting home."

Trick grabbed his cane pole.

"Don't go!" Aaron begged.

"Will, don't you think we should show T.J. the wigwam? He saved the town two years ago. He would make a good friend."

Will looked at Allie and Jenny. Jenny nodded.

"What about you, Allie?"

"Well, I suppose, but I can't quite see lettin' *him* in," Allie replied as she pointed to Trick.

Trick replied in a beat, "Yeah, I guess I can't save a town with a cane pole from the belfry, but I can sure fish this river better than anyone."

"We go together," T.J. said. "That's the way it's been. That's the way it'll always be."

Will looked at Allie, who nodded reluctantly. He approached T.J. and Trick and extended his hand. "You are friends, and we are friends. You can join us now as friends of the wigwam."

T.J. grasped Will's hand firmly and nodded. Will grabbed Trick's thick hand and turned to Allie, Aaron, and Jenny. "Both of these boys from Buda will make good as friends. We have something to show you now."

Will was first to lift back the holly branches that hid the wigwam. He ducked inside the entrance followed by T.J., Trick, and the rest of the friends.

The boys from Buda would be late for dinner, but it was all good for now.

Chapter 12

Republican National Convention

Chicago
May, 1860

The Wigwam
Southeast Corner of Lake and Market Streets

Black smoked belched up through the cone-like stack one last time as the red engine reeled into Chicago Station. The dark cloud of soot reeled over the passenger cars and descended on the waiting throng of delegates who waved small thirty-four-star-studded flags. It was convention time in the city of the big shoulders. Most of the trains traveled from the east where William H. Seward of New York was expected to take the Republican Party nomination for president of the United States on the first ballot.

"Congressman Washburne! Congressman Washburne!" barked a surly looking character whose head poked above the crowd.

"Yes, sir, how may I help you?" Washburne replied hesitantly. He did not extend his hand because he did not recognize the stranger.

"Don't you remember me? My name is John Hanks, Mr. Congressman." The stranger took off his hat and raised both eyebrows in anticipation of a nod of recognition from Washburne.

"John Hanks…John Hanks…" He looked at the stranger, brow furrowed as he struggled to remember.

The stranger stared back.

"Oh, Mr. Hanks! Why, of course. You are Mr. Lincoln's brother, I should say." Washburne smiled, nodded in recognition, and then extended his hand.

"I am his uncle, mind you!" Hanks shook Washburne's hand and then pulled on his beard, which was a foot long and ran from ear to ear like that of an Amish farmer's.

"My apologies, sir, for my impropriety. Good to see you, Mr. Hanks. Shall we head toward the wigwam now?"

Hanks nodded and pulled his large, broad hat down to his ears. The two proceded to walk down Wacker Street where the growing crowds surged toward the wigwam. Washburne and Hanks stayed close so as not to be separated in the excitement of the gathering. Over one hundred thousand Chicagoans were in the streets and it seemed as if all were gathering around the wigwam.

"What is this wigwam, Mr. Washburne?"

"It is a marvelous new building constructed and named by the Republicans for this convention. It's over on a corner of Lake and Market Streets. It was named to honor the original citizens of this Sucker State, mainly Potawotomi and Winnebagos."

"Will there be Indians there?"

"Only one that I know of, and he's a Seneca Indian from Western New York who lives in Galena now."

"What is his name?"

"He is Ely Parker, a friend and member of the Wide Awakes."

"And what is a Wide Awake?" asked Hanks, who pulled on his beard again as he looked down at Washburne.

"Wide Awakes will stay up all night with torches, cheering on your nephew, Mr. Hanks. They let everyone in town know that Old Abe is vigilant even in the night. Mr. Seward thinks he has things all wrapped up here. The Wide Awakes and the rest of these Suckers around us still have a say in what happens in the wigwam tomorrow night. I hope you will join us there and help the cause."

"I certainly will, Congressman. I am not one for stump speeches, but I will do my best to help my nephew."

"Are you aware, Mr. Hanks, your nephew will stay in Springfield? He will make no speeches at the wigwam."

"Well, sir, I thought he would be. I came all the way from Decatur. I suppose now I should be here in spirit for him." Hanks looked to his feet, stroked his beard again, and then looked at Washburne.

"Good night, Mr. Hanks. It was a pleasure to meet you."

"Good night, Congressman."

Hanks looked at the swelling crowd that created a bottleneck at Market Street. He decided to make his way to the Rush Street Bridge and cross the Chicago River to the less busy north side. He had not booked a hotel room, so after crossing the bridge, he headed east to Green Bay Street for another mile or so. By the time he reached the Catholic Cemetery south of North Avenue, he was clear of the noise and clatter. He entered the cemetery, meandering for a while between the headstones before finding a grassy spot that looked suitable to sleep on. In the distance he could hear waves gently slapping the swampy shore of Lake Michigan. The wind whispered through the boughs of a tall oak nearby. He stretched out on the ground, nodded twice, and then fell into a deep slumber.

In what seemed only minutes, he was awakened by the bright morning sun as it rose steadily above the lake. A distant clatter could be heard building to the west. The wigwam was gathering a crowd even at this early hour.

Hanks rolled to his left and knocked into the headstone that shadowed him. Startled, he rolled back, hitting his crown. He was awake but stiff and chilled. The sun almost blinded him as he looked up at the boughs of a tall oak that rose above the gravestones. He stood up, and faced the rising sun, letting it warm the night's chill out of his bones. Then he brushed off his pants with a quick stroke of his hat, put it on his head, and turned south to the Rush Street Bridge.

"Hurrah for Seward!" cried a young lady standing outside the Wigwam, her bonnet adorned with tiny flags.

Inside the wigwam shouts of delegates rose to the rafters of the magnificent building, which seemed to shake from the multitudes. Ten thousand Republican delegates from all over America, except the South, were packed in the hall. The rafters rose to over fifty feet. Delegates crowded the floor with their friendly constituents.

"Mr. Parker!" shouted Washburne, seeing the familiar face as he entered the visitor's gallery above the delegates.

Ely turned his head and waved Washburne over. Within a minute Washburne was at his side.

"Hello, sir, how was your trip from Galena? Are the Wide Awakes here?"

Parker hesitated for a second and then hugged the congressman. "It's been too long, old friend. Yes, they are here!" he responded as if boasting. "John E. Smith is here, and we picked up Fire Marshal Putnam on the way. Everyone should be here shortly."

"Very good," replied Washburne. "We will give *Mr. Republican Seward* a run for his money. We have placed the Pennsylvanians between the Indiana and Illinois delegations."

There was a hush followed by the distinct retort of a band. The echo faded in the rafters.

"We are here!" Putnam interjected. "It has been a long road, but we are all here."

Washburne and Parker looked at the Galena-Freeport contingent.

John E. Smith raised his pipe and then extended his hand to Parker and Washburne. "Indeed," he said. "We are all here!" He beamed with enthusiasm.

"When will Seward approach the stand?" Parker asked, stroking his goatee.

"Hopefully never," Washburne replied. "He will be nominated by one of his own, as Old Abe will by our Mr. Judd shortly. I think it best that..." A rousing brass band entered the wigwam, drowning out Washburne's voice.

The tune of "Oh, Isn't He a Darling" echoed throughout the wigwam, drawing attention to the New York crowd of delegates pouring through the front door. Pandemonium erupted among the delegates. The flutter of flags flipped and rolled with the undulating crowd of spectators.

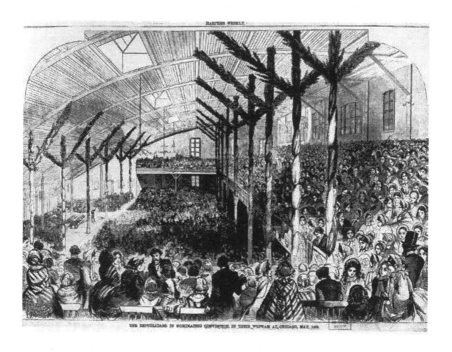

"What a grand entrance!" Washburne shouted to his cronies with his hands cupped to his mouth. "But wait till those New Yorkers take to their seats!" He smiled confidently.

"What do you mean, Congressman?" asked Parker.

"They have no seats," Washburne replied as he tilted his head and looked spryly to the others. "The Pennsylvanians and our Suckers took them all."

The rising shouts from the New York delegation mixed with the cadence of the band. Then the music stopped abruptly, allowing the New York delegates to move as one tight group to the center of the platform where the seats of the delegation were supposed to be.

Suddenly, Mr. Evarts, a short, stout man bellowed out an exclamation that was muffled in the crowd. Within minutes heads twirled every which way; then several of the more prominent leaders of the New York delegates began waving their arms. Muffled shouts could be heard from the floor by those on the platform.

"Watch, now," Washburne continued. "They will disperse like a storm that's lost its fury. When it comes to Mr. Lincoln, we will see a calm before the rising storm."

"Strike one up for the Suckers, Congressman" Putnam replied. "I'm sure they are not finished hearing from us tonight!"

Parker and Smith smiled.

A hush came over the crowd. Below, a stately figure with a large top hat in his hand slowly strode onto the platform.

"That is William M. Evarts," Washburne commented. "He will introduce Mr. Seward as a nominee."

A shout knifed through the silence of the wigwam, followed by another as the crowd waited with anxious anticipation for a long-expected announcement. Mr. Evarts placed his hat to the side of the lectern and then pulled a small piece of paper from his right pocket. Reaching into his left pocket, he pulled out spectacles.

Glancing first to the right and then to the left and then to the center of the massive crowd, he dramatically paused, nodded to the crowd, and then announced in a rising tenor voice, "I, William M. Evarts, am honored to be here on this platform, and on behalf of the proud delegation of New York, and on behalf of these United States, I nominate William H. Seward for president!"

The roar from the crowd spilled over like a cup flowing over. The wigwam seemed to shudder from it all. Flickering flags rippled again like waves. And then it all stopped when Evarts took a step away from the lectern. He turned and waved his top hat, and then the band struck up its cadence again. "Seward for president! Seward for president!" was chanted to an almost deafening level.

After Evarts exited, another figure approached the steps.

Washburne smiled and said, "This is our man, gentlemen—Norman Judd. We will see what befalls the crowd when he introduces Old Abe. I suggest that all of you keep your hats on your heads."

The others glanced at each other, perplexed by Washburne's comment.

Standing taller than Evarts, Judd ascended the stairs, the noise of the crowd diminishing with each step. Judd was without hat and spectacles. He had no paper in his coat pocket. Placing both hands confidently on each side of the lectern, he looked over the crowd who again waited in breathless anticipation.

"Ladies and gentlemen," he shouted, "I desire, on behalf of the delegation from Illinois, to put in the nomination as a candidate for president of the United States—Abraham Lincoln of Illinois!" As he uttered those last words, the roar of the crowd almost drowned them out. Then the clamor abruptly stopped.

Suddenly, thousands of tiny round wood chips rained down on all the delegates from the rafters, like hail dropping from the sky. Shrieks of laughter and shouts of glee mixed with the rising voices and created a new crescendo in the wigwam.

As the chips descended on the convention, Putnam reached down and picked one off the floor. Squinting, he peered at the chip closely and then looked at Washburne, shook his head, and smiled like a giddy child.

"Are you glad now you kept your hats on, gentlemen?" Washburne chuckled. "Take a close look at who's on that wood chip!"

"Why, it's Mr. Lincoln," Parker replied as he passed the small wood engraving over to Smith.

Smith squinted at the chip and exclaimed, "Nice move, Congressman! What else do you have up your sleeve?"

"Well, gentlemen, you should always expect the unexpected from the Wide Awakes!"

Parker, Putnam, and Smith chuckled in unison. The noise from the rafters changed now as hundreds of delegates passed the engravings around to their cronies. Instead of a roar, it was a steady flow of sounds like one could hear in a train station. Not pitched, but steady. Then things changed again.

A rolling laughter mixed with excited shouts echoed by the front entrance of the wigwam. The crowd looked toward the source of the noise.

"My God, it's Old Abe's uncle," Washburne cried out in disbelief.

The laughter and shouts increased as the tall lonely figure crossed in front of the delegates who were closest to the platform. Some of the ladies held their hands to their mouths like schoolgirls.

John Hanks was dressed as he was the day before. No suit, just his country clothes. As the crowd shouted their appreciation, he nodded and beamed with pride. With each step the laughter and excitement continued to build, causing the wooden wigwam to shake.

There was no reason for Uncle John to take the podium. He would make no speeches. He knew he didn't have to. As he did in his hometown of Decatur, Illinois, he proudly carried two ten-foot-long split rails, one in each arm, dragging them through the forum like a plodding horse on the prairie. Attached to the rails, a sign which read:

ABRAHAM LINCOLN
The Rail Candidate
FOR PRESIDENT IN 1860
Two rails from a lot of 3,000
Made in 1830 by Thos. Hanks and Abe Lincoln
Whose father was the first pioneer of Macon County

Washburne turned to his friends. "Gentlemen, this is our night. Old Abe will win this nomination!"

As the midnight hour approached, the Morse telegraph began to click away. A young attendant earnestly transcribed the message from Chicago. He passed it over to Lincoln, who was awaiting the news in Springfield.

Placing his reading glasses on his nose, Lincoln pored over the message. After reading the telegram, he looked at his friends and said with an earnest smile, "Well, there's a little lady down on Eighth Street who'll want to hear the news."

That night Abraham Lincoln was elected the Republican Party nominee for president.

The Wide Awakes would keep the fires lit for sure!

Chapter 13

Wigwam

Pecatonica River
Summer, 1860

Light rain fell gently along the Pecatonica. The rising and falling mist coated everything. Stout meadow grasses mixed with pink prairie roses and purple violets, and goldenrods lined both sides of the river to blend a fragrant and colorful bouquet. The deep-green branches of the holly bushes that hid the wigwam sprouted tiny white flowers now. All was quiet except an occasional chirp of a red cardinal flickering through the boughs.

The friends were inside the wigwam. All except Trick, who stood vigilantly in the rain, holding his cane pole, which he had planted firmly in the riverbank. July was a good time to fish on the Pecatonica.

"You can't right catch a thing in this rain, Trick. Come on inside now!" Allie announced, breaking the silence.

Trick put his finger to his lips. "Keep quiet, Allie, you're gonna scare the big ones away!" His wide hat dripped from accumulated mist. He dropped his finger and smiled.

"Well, I'm gonna go inside then. T.J. sent me out here to git you. You can git as wet as you want, but we ain't gonna start any fires here to dry you off."

"Wait, Allie, I want to show you somethin'. This rain doesn't fall like this but only once in a few years. It sets everything at peace on the river. Take a look around you. If you catch it right, you can see the sparkle on the leaves."

Allie looked curiously at Trick. She thought it strange that her newfound friend could say such beautiful things about the Pecatonica. She paused then and looked up to the boughs overhanging the river. She peered across the river and marveled at the colors, glancing even to the fishing line that Trick had thrown deep into the river. The line caused a perfect V-shaped wake as the gentle water rippled along.

"Look up yonder at the Winnebago oak, Allie. You see how sadly it bends over the river. You showed me that last year. Now look up to the leaves. Do ya see what's a happenin'?"

Allie peered up again. Her eyes followed the trunk. The leaves were a brilliant green.

"Do you see, Allie?" Trick said softly.

"Yes, I do."

"What do you see?"

"Some of the leaves look like they're droppin' tears. It looks like there cryin' right sure. Like maybe that Winnebago warrior is missin' his maiden."

"Thought the same thing," Trick replied as he grasped his cane pole with a swagger. "This was their special place for sure."

Kerplunk. A splash broke the silence. The cane pole bent down with force and then quickly arched back upward again. Trick, with one swift motion, flicked his wrists. "I sunk that hook in 'em good," he said as he grappled with the pole, his heels driving deeper into the mud.

After another quick pull, the fish flapped in a desperate flurry on the surface, turning the water into a churning mix of green and brown. Trick quickly grasped the wobbly pole with his left hand. In a moment he clutched the fishing line with his right and, in one swift motion, jerked the fish onto the riverbank. Fins and tail rolled alternately on the muddy bank. The great fish gyrated in an attempt to fall back to familiar waters. After pausing to catch his breath from the excitement, Trick reached casually down, put his thumb in a gill, and raised his captured river prey.

"Jumpin' jiminy," Aaron cried, "that's gotta be the granddaddy catfish of the Pecatonica. Maybe the biggest in the Sucker State!"

Trick turned to see the entire group of friends behind him. He grinned as always in awkward situations and then laid out a high-pitched chuckle. "Hee, hee…this old cat is a good un," he said. "And we won't right have to eat squirrel tonight for supper, T.J.! No need for your shooter today."

T.J. smiled and nodded. Will and the rest of the friends laughed. They were delighted to see Trick's new trophy.

"You can git back in the wigwam, now," said Allie. "Besides, I got some more stories to tell."

Trick could barely lift the catfish with his right hand, and he raised the catch just slightly above his head. He then grabbed his soaked hat with his left hand and shook it downward with a flap and placed it smartly back on his crown. With slow, deliberate steps of a waddling duck, he paused, took a breath, and then continued across the muddy riverbank to see his friends in the cozy, dry wigwam.

"Good job, Trick," Jenny said as she took her spot along the cave again.

"Nice, Trick," Aaron added as he squatted down beside her.

"Looks like you won't be needing your rifle today, T.J.," Will announced nodding his head to Trick.

"Right sure," T.J. replied, I suspect that cat will hold us over for a couple days. We've had enough squirrel for a good time now."

"Well, why don't you shoot somethin' else?" Allie interjected. She was anxious to tell her Indian stories but kept getting sidetracked. She continued. "You oughta shoot some of those birds that hang by the dragon's foot. Ya know, the ones that hoo and a hoo at you."

"You mean the turtledoves?" replied Trick.

"Yeah, the slow ones that have holes in their heads. I'm sure they taste like chickins," Allie replied. She braced her back with a slight swagger to see how Trick and T.J. would respond.

T.J. sat down against the wall where there was a tall shadow. The cave light now was much dimmer because of the mist. You could still, however, see everyone's movements.

"When I was younger I used to shoot everything that moved." T.J. continued. "I shot lots of birds for sport. I didn't eat any of them 'cause they were too small. Anyway, not many got away." T.J. looked at the friends to catch a reaction, yet all were transfixed on him, so he continued.

"I came home with a turtledove I shot one day, and my pa saw me throw it to the pigs. He ran out of the shed and asked me what I threw into the pen. I told him a turtledove. He at once grabbed my rifle, said nothing, and went into the house. He didn't talk to me for two days." The friends remained silent.

Will cut through the silence. "Why was your father so upset?"

"Well," replied T.J. with a low voice, "I didn't know that turtledoves come in pairs. I mean they mate for life. Like a husband and wife."

Silence again.

"When I shot the one, I killed the other, too, I reckon. I remember that the other one flew away quickly, but it returned and hooed from a tree nearby. It even followed me down the river for a while. Then I didn't see it again. I suspect it never did go back to the place where I shot the other."

Jenny began to sob. Aaron put his arm around her. Allie's posture slipped back to normal. She raised her arm and buried her face in the bend of her elbow.

T.J. continued. "Well, I don't shoot birds anymore. In fact, I only kill what we can eat. I believe God put me on this earth to hunt in this way. I don't kill for killing's sake."

The friends could see that Allie was not her normal self. She began to sniffle with her face buried in her shirt jacket, pulling out little gasps of air. Will stood up and walked to her and placed his arm around her. She looked up. Her tears reflected in the beam of light.

"I didn't think I'd ever sob so," Allie cried as she dried her eyes with her forearm. "But I must tell you somethin'."

The friends looked at her. Jenny held her fancy silk kerchief to her eyes. The boys looked over in dismay. All of the friends were intrigued. There was a hush in the wigwam.

"Gramma Lucy is not my gramma," she said in a reserved tone. "She took a baby girl sixteen years ago from some travelin' folks who adopted the baby and then couldn't afford to feed the young infant. They told me the mother had died soon after the infant was born, and then the father died soon after that. Well, that youngin was me. The folks said my momma told them I was born on Christmas, and I was a gift from God to them."

Allie continued. "Turns out my folks were like those turtledoves. They were happy together when I was born, but they died soon after in separate places somewhere between Ireland and the Rock River. Those nice folks who gave me to Gramma Lucy are nowhere to be found. I guess, as it is, I did get lucky havin' Gramma Lucy to take care of me so."

"Well, Allie," Jenny replied softly, "you are the lucky one. You have us all now as friends and family."

Will stood up. "Friends are family. Doesn't matter where you come from or who you are. Friends are true to the end."

"That's right," exclaimed Aaron as he looked quickly to Jenny for her nod.

T.J. and Trick remained silent as if undisturbed by any of the conversation. The boys from Buda just looked ahead, waiting to see who would speak next.

"All of us here are friends." Will continued. "And to the day I die, we will always be family. We will always be friends of the wigwam."

Allie dried her tears on her sleeve again. "I guess it's best we all head home for supper now. Gramma Lucy will be worried sick if I don't head upriver now. It's a gittin dark."

Will grabbed Allie's hand with his usual tenderness. "Come on, Allie," he said. "I will take you to Lucy."

T.J. picked up his rifle, which was leaning on the cave wall, and Trick pulled up his big catfish from the floor. Neither said a word. As they headed south, both boys turned back for a moment at the first bend, waved, and then continued on the footpath that headed down the Pecatonica.

Aaron and Jenny were the last to leave the wigwam. They ducked their heads under the holly bushes, which were still dripping from the mist. The red and white color of the flower buds contrasted beautifully with the thorny dark-green leaves. A red cardinal darted through the branches without a chirp. The beauty and silence added to the serenity of the moment. Aaron grabbed Jenny's tiny hand.

"Let's go home, Jenny. I will take you back to Freeport."

Chapter 14

John E. Smith Home

Galena
June 14, 1860

The flame in the oil lamp by the piano dipped once, twice, and then vanished.

John E. noticed the flickering from his desk by the window. Placing his quill pen in the inkwell, he reached over and pulled the candle closer to his pages. The glow reflected throughout the parlor, obscuring his view of High Street. Below on Main Street he could hear the assembly of a large crowd. It was the Wide Awakes who were in full support of Lincoln's nomination, and so-called because they championed him in night gatherings, causing such a stir that all of the citizenry would join the clamor on the streets or view the spectacle from their upstairs windows. John E. was proud to be named commander of the Wide Awakes, who carried large wooden axes, promoting Honest Abe and his rural roots, alternating with oil lamp torches that together looked like a moving, roaring mass of fire.

Looking at the parlor window again, with the candle now in its proper place, he thought it best to write Washburne a quick note appraising him of the Galena crowd before stepping outside.

He reached for the quill, drew ink from his inkwell, and began writing in a slow cursive style.

Galena June 14th 1860
Hon E. B. Washburne
Dear Sir & Friend
Mr. Head of Vinegar Hill desires me to enclose two letters
from his Council at LaCrosse, the Contents of which will
inform you of their proceedings there in the matter, Mr.
Head is very anxious to have this matter settled and I know
it is not necessary to urge your attention as you will do all
you can.

Hurrah for Lincoln. Trusting we shall soon see you in
good Health & Spirits for the campaign,
I remain yours,

Respectfully,
John E. Smith
Commander in Chief of the Wide Awakes [3]

Making two horizontal folds on the letter, he folded it once again lengthwise and slipped it snugly into an envelope. Grabbing the quill, he addressed the envelope: "Congressman E. B. Washburne, Washington." After blowing gently on the ink to dry it, he placed the envelope on his desk and dropped the quill back into the inkwell. He pulled his pocket watch out of his vest pocket and held it up to the candlelight. It was midnight. He returned the watch to his vest and stared out the window.

"Father!"

John E. jumped from his chair.

"Father! Father! Do you hear them?" Ben cried out from the top of the stairs.

"Son, come down here!" John E. replied with a stern tone. "You about knocked me out of my chair! Come down here now!"

The heels of Ben's boots clunked as he took slow and cautious steps down the wooden staircase.

"Ben, what are you doing all dressed up at this hour?" John E. said reprovingly.

Ben couldn't hardly get the words out. "Father, it's the Wide Awakes! I can see them from my bedroom upstairs. They are forming down the hill on Main Street!" He gasped for air and then continued. "I can see torches from up there. Open the door. You can hear the echoes!"

"Hold on, son. Get your breath. You are not going down to Main Street tonight. So get back up to your bed!"

"But, Father, I'm fourteen now. You said last week that I should start acting like a man. I want to help Mr. Lincoln, too."

"Can I come, too?" cried a voice from the top of the staircase.

John E. glanced quickly to Ben. "Now, you see. The whole house is awake!"

Ben looked around and smiled. "We are all Wide Awakes, aren't we?" He looked up the stairs to Adelaide. "Can I be a Wide Awake for Mr. Lincoln, just tonight?" he pleaded.

"All right, Ben, we will see how it works out tonight. But, Adelaide, young ladies are not permitted on the streets at night." John E. turned to grab his cloak. Ben had it already in hand. He grabbed the cloak and then looked up the staircase. In a calm, loving tone he said, "Adelaide, some day you will understand these things. The Wide Awake marches are not for ladies. We will see you in the morning."

The shuffle of his little girl's slippers could be heard across the ceiling. Then there was the familiar creak of the bed ropes.

Ben turned to John E. and beamed, "Thank you, Father...I mean, Commander."

John E. pulled his cloak around his shoulders. The June midnight air was crisp. As they approached the rocky stairs that would take them one hundred feet below to Main Street, the strong scent of oil lamps lingered in the air.

They crossed to the handrail. The magnificence before them caused them to stop. Hundreds of torches bobbed down below like signal lamps on a ship bow. Up and down they went. Cries and shouts mingled, the echoes climbing up to High Street and continuing to the lead mine above. Wavelike white banners with Lincoln slogans swirled and snaked as if floating above the crowd.

John E. turned to Ben. "Somewhere down there we will find Mr. Parker and Mr. Grant. Do your best, son, to stay with me as much as you can. If we separate, stay by our friends, and I will find you back here." John E. placed his hand on Ben's shoulder, and they proceeded down the circuitous stairway.

Ben felt truly like a man now. His pride swelled in his breast. The smelly oil lamps and the confused chants kept him on the course of the Wide Awakes. Though he heard his father's cautions, he couldn't care less about anything but his newfound pride. He was, of course, the son of the commander of the Wide Awakes. At the halfway point of the stairs, Ben paused and looked back at their house as his father continued the long march down the stairs.

The young Wide Awake could clearly see the upper level of the Smith home. He looked at the little windows a few feet to the right of his bedroom. There was a white face pressed against the glass.

Ben raised his arm slowly and waved. Adelaide waved back. He turned and continued his trek down the stairs. He paused again to look back, and his sister was gone. Looking at the grand crowd forming in front of him, he knew he had finally come of age.

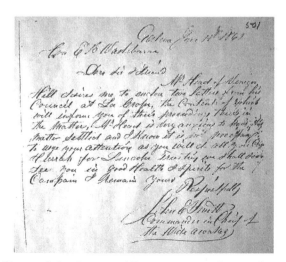

**Copy of the Original June 14, 1860, Letter from
John E. Smith to Elihu Washburne**

Chapter 15

Wigwam

Pecatonica River
Spring, 1861

With the weather now getting warm, the friends could be found by the wigwam most days. The boys were almost fully grown now. Jenny and Allie had blossomed, too.

The news in town was that southern rebels had fired on Ft. Sumter Island off Charleston, South Carolina, and that Abraham Lincoln was preparing for war. The sounds of southern cannons could not be heard in the heartland, and in their youth the friends could only wonder what impact a war would have on them.

As always, the waters of the Pecatonica flowed slowly south. Trick had his fishing line in a deep hole downstream from the wigwam where T.J. crouched with his rifle on one knee and eyes scanning the treetops. Supper was still hours away, and the boys from Buda still had hours to bring in a catch. They were silent as they crouched at the muddy shore.

Aaron and Will were farther up, north of the wigwam, so as not to disturb their vigilant friends. Chuckles occasionally echoed toward the cave as each of them skipped flat stones across the watery plain. As they gripped the gray prairie stones between their forefinger and thumb, the blue veins on their forearms would pop up before each stone was tossed across the swirls.

Jenny and Allie sat on a fallen tree trunk by the Indian oak, which was now leafing out after a cruel winter season. With each passing spring, the Indian oak bowed just a little more toward the water. Though still a strong and healthy tree, the exposed roots were too close to the water. One day it would make its final bow and would be pulled into the murky waters of the Pecatonica, eventually disappearing many miles south of the wigwam.

Allie picked up a twig by the stump, drew a heart in the mud, and scratched a "J" near its center.

"Oh, Jenny, do you still have a hankerin' for Aaron?"

The two sat side by side on the stump, and Allie grinned and raised an eyebrow.

Jenny blushed. In contrast to her britches-clad friend, she sat on the stump in her Freeport finest. The hem of her skirt was laced, and she sat ladylike, poised back with one arm on the tree stump.

"Yes, I do," she replied, "but you shouldn't embarrass me so." She looked down at the heart shape.

Allie placed the tip of the stick inside the heart and added a plus symbol after the "J." She then quickly scribbled an "A," smiled at Jenny, and then gracefully flicked the stick with a whipping noise into the Pecatonica. "Well, when Aaron sees this, he may just give you a kiss in the wigwam. You might call him here quick 'cause the boys from Buda will sure be comin' upriver soon."

Jenny blushed and smiled again.

"Allie, you shouldn't talk so."

Boom! The report of T.J.'s rifle echoed past the wigwam, causing the girls to flinch and Aaron and Will to pause in midmotion.

Everyone knew that dead-eye T.J. had hit his mark again and that the boys from Buda would now be heading to the wigwam with quarry in hand. Aaron and Will began sprinting to the cave. Within minutes all arrived together.

"Howdy, Trick," Allie announced. "I 'spect T.J. got the bead on dinner?"

"Yes, ma'am," Trick replied. "He dropped it on the other side of the river and should be crossin' back about now. He'll be here rightly sure." Trick took a spot on the stump, plopping himself between the girls. Placing one hand on his hip, he held his fishing pole erect. He turned to each of them and smiled and then looked down when something caught his eye.

"Well, jiminy…lookee here! There's a heart in the riverbank. Right sure, and it looks like a T and an A! Allie, I didn't quite think you had the hankers for me. Well, mighty lordy…hee, hee, hee!"

Jenny's jaw dropped and she was at full blush when Allie stood up and turned to face Trick. With hands on her hips, she leaned down until her eyes were level with Trick's. He grinned from ear to ear, his fishing pole in both hands.

"Trick, you better git downriver before I grab you and pull you by your big floppy ears!" she said angrily.

Trick grabbed his wide-brimmed hat and dog-eared the brim on both sides snugly over his ears.

Allie pouted and continued, "You shoulda spent more time in the schoolhouse down the river…'cause you can't right read! That heart has a J and an A in it…not a T! There's a tail on the T that makes it a J! Don't you see it, now? Jenny loves Aaron!"

Trick grinned. "You wanna say that again a li'l louder, Miss Allie, so Aaron can hear it? Hee! Hee! Hee!"

Jenny and Allie turned and looked up the river. Will and Aaron stood just ten feet away in stunned silence.

"I was just joshin' you, Allie. Just to get your gander," replied Trick as he stood up and stepped over the stump.

"Well, I'll have your ears yet, Trick," replied Allie as she jumped up like a cat and stood erect on the stump. "You better git movin' back to Buda, and don't come back!"

Trick grinned. "Well, come on now. It was only a trick! I do apologize to you."

"Well, don't be speakin' to me 'cause I ain't listenin'. You should rightly save your apologies for Jen."

Jenny said nothing. She was embarrassed. She looked at Aaron and then back at Trick.

Aaron then broke the awkward silence. "Trick was only joshin' as he always does, Jenny."

"Why, I do apologize, Miss Jenny," interjected Trick sincerely. "I cross my heart—I will never trick you again." He looked at Jenny. She smiled.

"Hey, friends, have you heard the news?" announced T.J., as he approached the wigwam and dropped the squirrel he had shot onto the ground.

"Hello, old friend, nice hit!" Will replied.

"Looks like you got the bead on him good," Aaron added.

Allie turned to T.J. and said, "Looks like your floppy-eared friend here came up short on his pole. Why, I coulda grabbed a big fat cat in this river with my bare hands!"

T.J. rested the butt of his Sharps rifle on the ground and, placing his hands on its muzzle, leaned on it as if it were a walking stick. He then calmly announced, "We are going to war, my friends. That is the news from Buda."

The group paused, silently absorbing the news.

"Have you heard about Elmer?" he asked.

"You mean Elmer Ellsworth? My river rat friend from Rockford?" Allie replied. "You mean Old Mr. Fancy who wears that red baggy-pants uniform and marches with the boys?"

"Yes, that's him," Jenny replied. "He was with T.J., Aaron, and Will when they saved the horses and put out the fire in Freeport."

"She's right," replied Aaron.

"We wouldn't have had the gander to save the last horse if it wasn't for Elmer," Will added. Aaron nodded.

"That's true," replied T.J. "I saw it all. Fire Marshal Putnam, Jenny's dad, wanted to put that colt out of its misery. Alfred Smith from Galena was home from West Point. He was there and was about to shoot him when Will and Aaron stepped in, but it all started with Elmer Ellsworth savin' the older horses."

"Well, what is Elmer doing now?" asked Jenny. She glanced at Allie who looked solemn.

"The war has been declared by President Lincoln," T.J. said. "Elmer is camped near the White House green. His regiment is eleven hundred strong now, and he is colonel. He went to New York City to look for a regiment and found one. He was the first to muster a Union regiment under the Washington Monument. It's the Eleventh New York Volunteer Infantry, and they are called the New York Fire Zouaves."

Everyone leaned toward him, more focused than before.

"Well, is he just a marchin' around that big White House?" Allie asked.

"No, Allie," Will said. "He is there to help put down the rebellion. His men are carrying bigger muskets now. They march to the drums. They will go to the fight...wherever it is."

"I don't want Elmer killed!" Allie stated. Her voice began to crack a little. "He's my friend and brother. He taught me how to fish and trap muskrats. He should be comin' back home. I don't want him to be hurt!" Her eyes began to tear up.

"Don't worry, dear Allie," Aaron replied. "Elmer is strong, and he has good men. I would not want to be a rebel fighting against him. I am quite sure that Mr. Lincoln and his generals will give him good orders. The war should be over by the time the summer heats up around here. Those rebels will probably give up without a fight when they see old Elmer dressed up and leading his men!"

Allie stared at the heart shape in the mud and then one by one into the eyes of her friends. There was a look of deep sadness in her blue eyes. She smiled softly at Trick. He was forgiven for his prank. The incident was trivial compared to the news of Elmer.

"Do you think I oughta fetch an oak leaf for Elmer? You know that Indian maiden planted this tree for her brave who got shot. Gramma Lucy says the oak leaf stands for courage. Maybe Ol' Elmer can put an oak leaf in his cap for me. Should help, I imagine." Allie looked up, a little confused, and continued. "I could send it in a package by rail to the White House. Jenny, could you rightly help me with the writin'?"

"Sure I will," replied Jenny smiling.

"Well, I 'spect I best climb the tree to get that oak leaf," Allie said in a softer tone now. She stepped up over the trunk again and headed to the Indian oak and began to scale the ruddy trunk.

"Allie, hold on there now," Trick said. "A lady shouldn't be climbin' trees."

"I've been climbin' trees for quite a spell with Elmer. He taught me how to hold on," replied Allie who continued to shimmy up the trunk in her britches.

"Now, Miss Allie, let me do you the favor. After all, I'd like to make things right…so you don't pull on my ears!" said Trick in earnest.

The friends chuckled.

"Well, I accept your apology for Jenny and me. I s'pose I'm a lady now and shouldn't be climbin' so much."

Allie looked at Jenny for approval. Jenny nodded her head gracefully as if approving a gentleman's hand before a waltz.

Trick then broke the silence, stating loudly, "Hee, hee, let me climb this big oak like a cat with claws as big as spikes!" He started toward the tree. "This ol' oak ain't seen the likes of a Buda boy, I 'magine. I s'pose if I git my gut on the grain, it'll be right good." He stopped and turned to the friends, dropping his fishing pole to the ground.

Rubbing his hands like a master about to begin his work, he hugged the tree, pushing his floppy hat back up on his brow so as not to obstruct his view. His legs were curled outward, almost bowed, to each side of the trunk so that his boots could dig into the rough surface. His boots moved quickly and rhythmically, crunching bark off the tree. Trick grinned as he hugged the big oak.

"You gotta move on up if you're gonna make it," shouted T.J.

"Hee, hee." Trick grunted. "Maybe if I move these brogan boots faster, like a chicken on the run, I can set this trunk on fire!"

The boys laughed. Jenny and Allie giggled with glee.

"Tell you what, Trick," T.J. announced, smiling, "we'll give you a boost. We sure don't want that tree to catch fire and fall into the river."

Will, Aaron, and T.J. approached the Indian oak. They locked their hands together in a tight grip to support their portly friend. Trick then placed his boot in their grip as if putting a foot in the stirrup of a saddle.

"You hold on now, Trick," T.J. advised calmly. "We will boost you up about three feet so that you can walk the bow like a cat. Keep your hands and feet to the center."

Trick grabbed the tree. "Heave ho!" he shouted.

He ascended in one motion to his place of security. The bend of the trunk now made it easier to safely reach a branch. He proceeded cautiously over the bowed trunk, placing each hand and boot tip in motion together.

"Well, Allie, hee, hee…it's a might high up in these high places. I can almost see the White House from here!"

Allie laughed.

"I'm gonna git you the biggest oak leaf here for good ol' Elmer," he said nervously, his voice cracking a little. "Gotta hang on now."

Allie cupped her hands around her mouth and replied, "Trick, I'll be patient if you just hang on!"

More chuckles echoed across the gently swirling water.

Trick was squarely over the river now, about twenty feet below the bough. He could see an occasional twig or branch float by at a slow pace, and was confident of his success; so proud now—he was the first of the friends to scale the rugged Indian oak.

"Well, Miss Allie, I can see a good one right above this branch here." Trick squinted at the prized oak leaf before him and then quickly looked up at the branch he would need to grasp firmly to secure the prize. He looked down at the river again.

"Lordy, it's a stretch up here!" he shouted. "I will stand up now and get it."

"Be careful, Trick," Allie warned.

Trick reached up, grabbed the branch, and picked the big oak leaf. Holding the branch, he turned to the friends proudly.

Standing erect like a soldier himself, he announced, "I 'spect ol' Elmer will be proud to wear this oak leaf straight from the river he hunted and fished before he became famous."

The friends clapped.

"Hee, hee." Trick chuckled with glee. "I 'spect comin' down is easy. I best turn around here and git goin' the other way. Yep, I'll just turn around here like this and git my chicken feet movin' again."

Suddenly the branch Trick was holding snapped with a loud crack, like a bolt of lightning had hit the trunk. Down he went. Jenny screamed, and Allie gasped. Trick's large torso was framed by his rapidly gyrating arms and legs. He belly flopped into the water with a loud splash. Alarmed squirrels scurried away in the canopy above.

The friends raced to the riverbank.

In a moment a hat emerged through the water, followed by the familiar flapping of arms, which caused rolling rings in the river. Soon, a head followed the hat, and Trick moved quickly, dog-paddling to a dry stretch of the muddy shoreline.

"Are you OK?" Allie called out with her usual concern.

"Hee, hee, I'm just fine, Miss Allie. I didn't wanna run your patience too thin, so I took the quick way down!"

The friends laughed with relief.

Trick worked his way to the bank with hat and oak leaf in hand and handed the big oak leaf to Allie. "Here you go, Miss Allie. I hope Elmer will wear this proudly for us!"

Allie approached Trick slowly and stood before him reverently. She reached down and grabbed his soaked hat. The friends watched, puzzled.

Standing even closer to him, she shook his hat with two quick flicks of her wrist. Grabbing the hat with both hands now, she lifted her heels like a ballerina. She raised it high above Trick's head and then placed it snugly on him like a crown of glory. Pulling it down to his ears, she looked at the friends and looked back into Trick's pleasant gleaming eyes. Pausing for a quick moment, she looked to the river and then hugged Trick like a brother.

Allie broke the silence. "Thank you, Trick. Elmer *will* wear this proudly."

Trick gently nodded and then bent over awkwardly to pick up his cane fishing pole.

T.J. grabbed his rifle.

The boys from Buda took a few steps together, looked at each other, and then turned again. Raising the pole and rifle up high in concert, they waved and headed back down the river to home.

The sun was about to set. It was suppertime.

Chapter 16
White House Balcony

Washington
May, 1861

"Father, Willie won't give me the periscope!" little Tad Lincoln whined. He was barely tall enough to boost his chin over the balcony rail.

"I will give it to you in a minute!" Willie replied indignantly. "I can't see Elmer yet. There are trees in the way."

"Give me the scope now! It's my turn," little Tad demanded as he pulled on the coattails of Willie.

"Now, boys, let's keep it down, or Mother will be here lickety-split and make us come off the porch. I can see Elmer's regiment now," the president replied confidently as he picked Tad up.

Tad quickly wrapped his legs around his father, hugged him, and rubbed his face on his father's long whiskers. "Your face tickles, Father," he said as he smiled and snuggled himself. Tad could clearly see his pet sheep on the lawn.

"Boys, can you see the red glow down by the Potomac? It moves in a wavelike motion. I am proud to say that Colonel Elmer Ellsworth is at the front of what you see. It is a regiment one thousand men strong. His men will be clear of the trees soon, and you will be able to see them better. They have fancy uniforms with many buttons, red bedrolls strapped on their backs, and red kepis tipped smartly on their heads."

The president smiled. He was very proud of his young law clerk and close friend of the Lincoln family. So close, the boys fondly called him Uncle Elmer. He was a good "uncle" to the boys, often spending hours wrestling and tussling with them during visits to the White House, even catching measles from them in the early days.

"What is a kepi, Father?" Willie asked as he stared upward and over the balcony rail.

"It is a fancy cap that French soldiers wear. Elmer made sure all the men in his regiment got them."

Who are those soldiers he is leading?" Willie asked.

"They are the New York Fire Zouaves. They are also called the Eleventh New York Volunteers."

"What are Fire *Zoooveees*?" Tad asked excitedly as he pulled on his father's whiskers.

"The name is pronounced *Zoo-ahvs*." Lincoln chuckled. "They are firemen who volunteered to put down the rebellion. They will fight for three months and then go home again, boys."

"Why do they have to fight, Father? Don't they save people whose houses are on fire?" asked Willie. He looked perplexed. Turning with the periscope in his hands, he braced his elbows on the balcony rail for a better look at Elmer and his regiment.

"They are all brave men," Lincoln responded. "They have come to Washington to protect the city. Now they are preparing to go over to Alexandria, Virginia, on the other side of the Potomac to help them, too."

Lincoln looked down at Willie and then looked to the bridge. He squinted and continued. "God bless Elmer and his brave men. They are the best we have, my sons." Lincoln then fell silent. He had a somber look. He continued, "Boys, listen carefully, and you can hear the tramp of the Zouaves's boots. They are heading south a few miles to pitch camp so they can cross the river by boat."

Willie cupped his ear with his right hand as he lowered the periscope with his left. Tad mimicked him but kept a firm grip on his father's beard.

Elmer, now a mile south of the White House, marched proudly a distance of ten feet in front of his men. His red kepi was pitched slightly to the right. His goatee formed in wisps around his mouth and was trimmed closely to his face. A scarlet sash was tied snugly around his trim waist. The knotted ends of the sash fell down a foot or so and flowed back and forth as he marched.

Soon, small groups of Washingtonians appeared before the volunteers at broad turns in the roadway, cheering the colorful spectacle before them. At every opportunity Elmer snapped his sword from the shiny black leather scabbard, nodded, and then saluted the bystanders with the tip of the blade point vertical and upward, the hilt of the sword in his hand just inches from his nose.

Feeling the warmth of the crowd on this crisp spring day as he tramped forward, Elmer's mind drifted back to the his early beginnings as colonel of the forty-man Chicago US Zouave Cadets, who toured the many eastern cities less than one year ago. Though he commanded one thousand volunteers now, he felt the same inside.

He was in his element: the beau saviour of women, the proud leader of men.

Chapter 17

Camp Lincoln

Eleventh New York Fire Zouaves
Potomac River
Four Miles South of Washington
Evening of May 23, 1861

Elmer and his Zouaves were ready.

After splitting time during the daylight hours between preparations for an advance against the newly seceded Virginia and a game of baseball with their colonel, they felt as confident as ever. First to be mustered into the Union army, they now camped in a place of honor and would be the first Union regiment to cross the river into Alexandria.

It was dark, and a full moon cast a silvery glow across the Potomac like a steady beam of light that seemed to find its place at Elmer's feet wherever he walked along the riverbank. In the darkness the dark figures of his soldiers seemed to stretch to and fro in front of the fires, masking rank and recognition. Elmer decided to take one last look at Camp Lincoln from the heights above.

He followed a sandy path that crisscrossed up the eastern slope. He brushed a sapling, grabbed it for support, but stumbled over loose soil and rocks that had been scattered by his Zouaves when they descended on the camp weeks before. He looked up. No stars could be seen above the canopy, but as he turned to look down the encampment, it was like magic.

Before him, nestled in a bend of the river, no less than one hundred cone-shaped Sibley tents placed in neat rows glowed like white Halloween jack-o'-lanterns. The moon, still bright, seemed to cast its glowing light in a straight line as if beckoning him to the other side of the river. Another ring of red formed around the moon itself. Elmer thought back to his days in Rockford, where the Indian legends taught that a moon with a red ring about it meant that the tribe would be blessed with a good hunting season. His thoughts drifted to his muskrat trapping on the Rock and Pecatonica Rivers. He thought of Allie in her britches, spry as ever and always looking up to him for strength. Kitty came to mind, and her parents, who gave him a handsome Bible before he left for the East. Chicago seemed very distant to him now as he looked over his new regiment. The US Zouave Cadets of Chicago, with all their glory, were no longer, having disbanded in October 1860. He was grateful, though, that his moment had come, to prove what was to come with dignity and honor.

He must go down to the men now before they rolled up in their scarlet blankets, which rested on common straw. He must let them know what tomorrow would bring. And so he descended the ridge. The moon still shone at his feet.

"Lieutenant Colonel Farnham, call the men to their ranks!" shouted Elmer with the resonating and deep voice the men knew so well. Within a few minutes, with the rustle and clanking of weaponry, the men were formed to perfection. They stood like sentries of old as the swirling and trickling sounds of the Potomac magnified their silence.

A prominent boulder about three feet high and somewhat flat on the surface seemed to be a fitting stump for Elmer's speech. Quickly bounding on top of it, he turned deftly to his men, who stretched in companies about eighty yards to each side. The full moon shone on Elmer's back, making his frontal figure look like a ghostly black silhouette. Raising both of his arms slowly upward with hands near his shoulders, he broke the silence again,

"Boys, yesterday I understood that a movement was to be made against Alexandria. I went to see General Mansfield and told him that I would consider it a personal affront if he would not allow us to have the right of line, which is our due as the first volunteer regiment sworn in for the war. All I can say is prepare yourselves for a nice little sail and, at the end of it, a skirmish. Go to your tents, lie down, and take your rest until two o'clock when the boats will arrive and we go forward to victory or death."

In silence the men shuffled back to their tents, wondering what their first skirmish would bring. After they had departed, Elmer hopped off the boulder and, like his boys, proceeded to his command tent, which was closest to the Potomac. Turning his head slowly to the south as he opened the flap, he noticed the moon reflecting off the bayonet blades already positioned on the thousand-plus rifles stacked and locked in groups of five, ready for the movements to come. Dipping his head, he entered and dropped the tent flap behind him.

All was eerily quiet on the Potomac, and Elmer's thoughts drifted again, but this time to his parents who he loved so dearly. He was their only son now. His little brother, Charley, had died of smallpox in Chicago almost two years before. He remembered the tremendous grief his parents had shown when he brought Charley's coffin by train to the station to meet them in Mechanicville, his boyhood home in New York State. A simple church service and burial along the riverfront followed. He now thought of his own mortality and the promise he made to his mother the last time he saw her at the Astor House in New York City, before the Zouaves departed for Washington.

"I must write them," he whispered softly.

Grabbing the oil lamp and setting it next to his red diary and Bible at the corner of the table, he picked up his quill and dipped the tip in a small rosewood inkwell. He sat down and looked at the pointed peak of his tent, which drew the lamp smoke upward. Placing his wrist near the corner of the paper, he looked up one more time, squinted at the lamp, breathed a sigh, and began to write in a steady motion.

Headquarters 1st Zouaves
Camp Lincoln
Washington D.C.
May 23d 61
My dear Father and Mother,

The Regt is ordered to move across the river tonight. We have no means of knowing what reception we are to meet with. I am inclined to the opinion that our entrance to the City of Alexandria will be hotly contested as I am just informed a large force arrived there today. Should this happen my dear parents it may be my lot to be injured in some manner. Whatever may happen cherish the consideration that I was engaged in the performance of a sacred duty, and tonight thinking over the probabilities of the morrow and the occurrences of the past, I am perfectly content to accept whatever my fortune may be, confident that He who noteth the fall of a sparrow will have some purpose in the fate of one like me.

My darling & ever loved parents, goodbye. God bless, protect, and care for you.

Elmer (⁴)

When he finished the last line, he placed the quill down and stood up. His frock coat and scarlet sash hung on the back of his camp chair. Putting the sash to the side, he grabbed the handsome uniform coat and donned it. Reaching into the small drawer of his camp desk, he grabbed a tiny gold badge about the size of a quarter. It had a Latin inscription that read, "Not for ourselves alone but for country". He pinned the badge above his heart. He then reached for his letter, folded it, and placed it in the inner pocket of his uniform. He wondered what the morning would bring.

Outside, the volunteers lay on their scarlet bed rolls, staring into the darkness, awaiting word from the sentries.

"Tomorrow is our day," Elmer whispered to himself. "God bless the Union. God bless our boys."

Chapter 18

Alexandria, Virginia

Morning
May 24, 1861

The early risers began to gather in the streets at sunrise as Elmer and his men crossed the Potomac and captured the city.

It was a clear day. The sky was especially blue in the early morning hour. The crisp spring air drummed up a slight breeze that quelled the dust of tramping feet. The Zouaves undulated through Alexandria like a large serpent slithering over rocks. The streets in front of the regiment began to narrow, causing the soldiers to extend their ranks over three city blocks. Many bystanders peered down from windows. The soldiers kept their faces forward, even when a young or old detractor flapped a tiny rebel flag, which would then be pulled back from view into the dark contrast of the window.

"Colonel Ellsworth," shouted the orderly sergeant who carried the regimental flag, "do you see that flag ahead?" A massive rebel flag waved gently high atop the roof of a grand hotel a few blocks away.

"I see it, Sergeant. We will halt there for a rest. We will keep in step and take the boys one block forward so the center will rest there."

Over the hotel door was a sign that read, "Marshall House, James Jackson, Proprietor." The flag had a blue field with eleven circled stars representing the Confederate States. At first glance it could be mistaken as a Union flag of the North, but at closer look, it revealed only two horizontal red stripes instead of seven. The two red stripes that bordered the edge balanced the bright-white stripe in the middle. Even though it was red, white, and blue like a Union flag, it was a symbol that flapped defiantly in the face of the White House over the past few months, and now was the Federal army's for the taking.

As the regiment approached the Marshall House, Elmer stepped to the side and allowed his men to continue down the street. He stood on the front steps of the hotel, facing his men as if he was a general reviewing his troops. When a large complement of his troops had passed by, he called a halt so that the main contingent was approximately centered in front of the hotel. The rebel flag continued to whirl and snap as the dust lingered below and settled on the boots of the Zouaves.

The Marshall House, Alexandria, Virginia, 1861

"Private Brownell, step forward!" Elmer commanded.

"Yes, Colonel, I am at your service."

"Private, assemble Lieutenant Winser, Mr. House, and Reverend Dodge. I would like them to assist us in cutting down that flag!"

"Yes, sir."

Elmer stood like a statue on the porch, motionless as he awaited the contingent. Soon the three appeared with Brownell on the front porch and proceeded to quickly duck inside with Ellsworth in the lead.

Hearing the commotion about the hotel, a man suddenly appeared in the lobby.

"Who put that flag up?" Elmer demanded.

"I don't know; I am a border here," the stranger replied nervously.

Posting corporals at the front door and at the bottom of two turning flights of stairs, Elmer proceeded with the chosen four to the attic of the Marshall House.

The Zouaves outside waited in anticipation.

"Well, look at the bastard flag that mocks us all," shouted one of the soldiers.

Another Zouave shouted to a bystander near the porch, "Can you tell us where Jeff Davis is? We're lookin' for him."

And another in the ranks, "Yes, we're bound to hang his scalp in the White House before we go back!"

The soldiers laughed and looked up at the roof.

"Look!" shouted another in glee. "I can see the colonel pulling it through the attic window!"

"By jiminy, he's got it off now and waves it back and forth."

Another loud "huzzah" from the soldiers echoed through streets, arousing the early morning slumber of the Alexandrians. Then the flag disappeared from view.

Inside the attic Elmer turned to Winser. "Like takin' candy from a baby, Lieutenant. Thank you for the use of your bowie knife. Let's take this trophy to the men."

Winser smiled and handed Elmer's revolver back to him.

A moment later the clunks of their military boots on the steps sounded like a deep clatter as Private Brownell led the procession with Elmer carrying the large rebel banner wrapped around his shoulders. Behind him was Edward House, the *New York Tribune* correspondent, and Lieutenant Winser. The four descended the several oak stairs that connected the landings and could distinctly hear the loud resounding cheers from the troops outside as if a major battle had been won. The four looked at each other with pride and smiled in anticipation of the rousing ovation that they would receive when they broke outside to the front porch—just a few more steps to glory. The contingent had captured the regiment's first rebel flag!

As they reached the bottom of the last set of stairs, their view of the parlor was obstructed by the narrow stairway passage. Elmer, now in the lead, was the first to turn the corner. Standing before him was the hotel owner, James Jackson, holding a double-barreled shotgun leveled at the gold badge over Ellsworth's heart. A clank was heard as Brownell lunged forward to spoil the shotgun's aim with his musket barrel.

But Jackson managed to pull on one of the triggers just as Brownell's musket made contact. A terrible *boom* echoed through the house!

The shotgun blast hurled Elmer back. In his recoil he clutched his chest with the flag gripped tightly around his shoulders, dropped to his knees on the stairway, then fell face forward on the landing with a horrible thud. The silent but determined Jackson turned to deliver the second shot at Private Brownell, but it was deflected, missing Brownell and hitting the panels of a bedroom door. The loyal private delivered his own musket load directly into Jackson's face, and the hotel owner fell onto the blood-spattered landing beside Elmer. Brownell, in a rage, repeatedly drove his bayonet deep into the proprietor's body.

Jackson's wife appeared and screamed hysterically at the sight. Her heart-felt outcries continued for a few more minutes. The grieving turned to sobs...then silence.

A throng of red-shirted Zouaves rushed inside to see what was happening. They were stopped upon seeing Brownell, who stood with blood on his bayonet. He had never killed a man before. His voice quivered, but with determination he announced, "That son of a bitch killed our colonel. We will make these rebels pay for this!"

The soldiers stared at the sight in the room in a stunned silence.

Both bodies lay facedown on the blood-spattered rebel flag. War had come to the regiment—but not in a way they had expected.

Across the Potomac the Lincoln boys had left the White House balcony and were getting ready for lunch. Lincoln was with Secretaries Nicolay and Hay, awaiting word on the success of the troop movements in Alexandria.

Lincoln with periscope in hand raised it to his eye, held it for a moment, and then turned to both secretaries. "Gentleman, we will be greeted with some great success today! The rebel flag that flew defiantly in our faces for many months has been struck down by our volunteers. It no longer waves freely over Alexandria! I would like to see it when it returns to Washington, a true war trophy from our noble efforts to secure the Union."

Nicolay and Hay smiled and nodded.

There was a sudden pause.

The balcony door opened with a gentle creak, followed by the sound of footsteps.

"Father," Mrs. Lincoln quietly announced as she entered the room with Willie and Tad close to her side.

The boys smiled and nodded to the secretaries, who smiled back.

"Yes, Mother," replied Lincoln calmly.

"The strangest thing arrived in this package today!"

Mary Todd Lincoln opened the top of the box, looked inside, and cocked her head to the side with a confused look. "Well, I thought perhaps the three of you would know what this is all about. Our boys are as baffled as I am." The boys nodded as she made the remark.

Lincoln looked at his wife with a deep inquisitive look. "What is it, Mother?" he replied.

"It is a package for Colonel Elmer Ellsworth." She squinted this time. "It is from 'Friends of the Wigwam' in Illinois."

"What did they send to Elmer?"

"It's an oak leaf."

Chapter 19

Wigwam

Pecatonica River
Summer, 1861

The sun had risen to a place midpoint in the sky.

The blue above the treetops now budding with luster made the river look serene again. Breaking the silence were Jenny, Allie, Aaron, and Will who sat on the riverbank swirling their feet in the flowing water. The green waters were low but still cold from the late winter thaw. As summer progressed, the waters would get warmer and deeper as they rolled gently south.

Aaron looked down at Jenny's dainty white feet. Her lacy dress was pulled up just enough to expose her ankles. Allie's britches were rolled up to her knees; she was ready to pounce in the Pecatonica.

"Will, I betcha I can beat ya to that sandbar over there," Allie challenged as she stepped into the river. Raising her eyebrows, she lifted her chin, placed her hands on her hips, and then pointed to a sandbar in the distance about a hundred yards downstream.

"Will, are ya hearin' me?" she said. Her voice echoed to the other side of the river, causing a startled bullfrog to plunge into the river.

"Now, come on, Allie, why do you have to do this to me? We are sitting here having just a grand old time, and you want to make a contest out of everything!" Will shook his head, smiled, and looked down at his feet. He cocked his head and looked back up at her.

"Well, if you're not gonna run with me, then maybe I should run with someone else!" she said, looking at Will. She cocked her head and repeated the challenge. "I suppose you think you can git to that sandbar one lickety-split ahead of me!"

Will glanced at Jenny and Aaron who smiled and gently nodded in approval. Will then rose up and stepped into the Pecatonica.

Allie continued. "I wanna give you a head start, seein' as though you're not used to river runnin'. So I'm gonna give you ten steps ahead of me to make sure I have somethin' to run for."

Will took ten steps ahead of her, deeper into the swirling water.

"When I say go, you best get runnin' hard cuz I'm gonna beat you by ten steps before you make it to the finish!"

Will turned nervously toward the sandbar. He stopped smiling. The thought of a sweetheart, or any woman, beating him in a race did not settle well with him. Even Aaron now had a look of concern.

Checking to make sure the race would be fair, Will took another look back again to see if Allie had moved up on him. She hadn't. Looking at him with a wide confident grin on her face, she pointed and motioned him to go forward.

"You ready?" she asked as she crouched into a racing position.

Will, with a short nod, mimicked Allie's stance. Small beads of sweat formed on his brow as he prepared for what he considered the run of his life. He knew he could always outrun Aaron, and in his mind he was running for more than just himself. Certainly the townsfolk would chuckle if word leaked out that he lost. So the race with Allie was a race for every man in Freeport.

"Go!" shouted Allie.

Will buried his feet deeply into the sand, then dashed toward the sandbar with his eyes fixed on the finish line. Each stride kicked up a violent spray of water reflecting radiant colors, like miniature rainbows. Tiny frogs along the muddy bank jumped for safety as the serenity of the river was broken by the unnatural sound of feet storming through the water.

Will had learned years ago to never look back during a footrace, knowing that if you looked over one shoulder, you could be passed on the other side. A turning head could also cause a rhythmic running motion to slow down. So he fixated his eyes on the sandbar, each arm rising in rythmic motion as he closed on the finish line. When he was just ten paces away, he realized a win was quickly going in his favor. Even so, he would not look back, so as he neared the finish line, he increased his high-stepping, furiously pulling his feet upward with wide arcs of water rainbowing as they fell to the river. He thought, *Just two more steps...Just two more steps.*

Within seconds, he fell across the dry sand at the finish line. Panting deeply, he picked himself up, gasping for breath. The waters of the Pecatonica settled back to its meandering flowing ways. Sand toads popped around him as he looked back at the friends.

And there stood Allie, firmly planted on the bank, with her hands on her hips and grinning widely. Hoots and gleeful hollers echoed across the expanse of the river. He suddenly realized that he had been duped by his sweetheart.

Allie placed her hands on her mouth as she bent forward and giggled and gasped for air.

Will smiled and waved back. He realized Allie had challenged him to demonstrate his manhood. She wanted him to show focus, strength, and purpose in achieving a goal, even a small goal, like racing to a sandbar. The race caused his love for Allie to run deeper than the shallow waters he crossed. He stood up now and took a bow as if he was on the stage of an opera house. Allie, Jenny, and Aaron clapped and shouted gleefully as Will stepped slowly back in the swirling waters of the Pecatonica.

"Build a fire!" Will shouted as he returned to the riverbank by the wigwam. "You owe me dry clothes, my sweet!"

The girls giggled and nodded in response.

Shuffling through the water, Will detected a faint but distinct echo downriver. He heard it again. It sounded like someone was shouting "friends" repeatedly. Stopping midriver, he put his hands to his knees and peered to the distance. His muscular legs were planted firmly, and the water waked in two wide V shapes.

"Do you hear that shout?" Will yelled with his hands now cupped around his mouth.

"I can't hear anything," Aaron replied.

"Me neither," Allie and Jenny replied in unison.

Will signaled. "There it is again. I see someone is coming our way. He's on this side of the river. Allie and Jenny, you best get into the wigwam. Aaron and I will meet whoever it is down the river a bit." With this warning, Will high-stepped it back to the shore.

Jenny rushed into the wigwam. Allie waited outside, peering around the holly bushes that hid the entrance.

Will and Aaron were only yards from the wigwam when they heard the distinctive shout echo just a stone's throw away.

"Friends!"

"Why, that's Trick comin' up the river," Allie interjected as she walked up to Will and Aaron.

Jenny peeked out of the wigwam and slowly advanced to Aaron's side.

Suddenly, Trick emerged through the high grasses and brush. He was not his normal jolly self. Sweat had matted his hair under his hat, which was soaked through the brim. He panted heavily. When he reached them, he dropped to his right knee, put his hands over his face, and wept loudly.

"What is with you, Trick?" Allie asked with a look of alarm. "You look as if ya lost a good friend. Why are you cryin' so?"

Trick wept even louder as he buried his eyes in his forearm. His body shook sadly as each friend put a hand to his shoulder.

Only Allie had the gumption to speak, so she asked again, "My Lord, Trick, don't tell me T.J. is hurt. Is somethin' wrong with our dear friend T.J.?" Allie reached down and removed the wide-brimmed hat.

Trick looked up at her with tears streaming down both cheeks.

Allie placed her gentle hand on his cheek. "Trick," she said kindly, "is T.J. safe and sound? Please, Trick, tell us!"

Trick drooped his head and then looked up at the friends. "Dear, Allie, oh dear, Allie," Trick replied with tears welling in his dark-brown eyes. "T.J. is fine. He is huntin' somewhere. I couldn't find him, so I headed upriver to find all of you!"

Trick hesitated and gasped once more, and his voice cracked, "Oh dear, Allie, I have bad news for you." He hesitated, looked down, and said in a soft, very soft, apologetic tone, "Elmer is dead."

Trick's words exploded like a crack of lightning in a dark sky. The friends gasped in horror in unison, and then there was an awkward pause. The swirling motion in the river looked as if it was in slow motion to Allie. The chirps of the birds and the croaks of the frogs fell silent to her ears. Everything looked different...as if she were cast into a dream.

"Why do you say that, Trick? How do you know?" Will asked directly.

"Yeah, Elmer is in Washington. There were no battles fought there!" Aaron added.

"It's true, Allie. It's in those papers," Trick replied. "He was killed a takin' a flag off the roof of a hotel in Virginia somewhere near Washington. The whole country is in mourning for him. Mr. Lincoln is 'specially so! Elmer was like a son to him. The papers say Lincoln called Elmer the greatest little man he ever met! The Lincoln boys even called him Uncle Elmer."

Allie looked at the sky and then put her tiny hands over her face. Her blond hair fell down on both sides. She sobbed gently at first but then, in a frustrating flash, cried loudly. Her voice resonated on the river with each rising and deliberate word. "Oh, Elmer...my Elmer!...Why did ya have to put on that fancy ol' uniform? I knew it would git ya killt someday!" She looked over at Will.

Will approached her and placed his arms around her gently as if cradling a newborn. Allie began to weep uncontrollably in the security of Will's loving embrace. He, too, wondered how it could be possible that their mentor and friend, a hero, could vanish so quickly. Elmer was like big brother to Allie, and now that brother was gone forever. Allie buried her face into Will's shoulder. Her gasps slowly subsided as Will patted her back gently.

As she stood there, the rest of the friends approached her delicately and formed a circle around her. Nobody said a word. The trickling water continued to swirl. A red cardinal and a turtledove flickered above them through the boughs of the Indian oak tree.

Allie pulled her head up from Will's shirt and looked into his tearful eyes. She gazed at the waters of the Pecatonica and then up at the sky, which was still a brilliant blue. She sniffled, looked to the Indian oak, and lowered her voice as she said solemnly, "Elmer, I met you on the river, and now you've crossed over the River Jordan. I'm sure you'll be the best frogsticker and muskrat trapper those angels will ever know."

She continued. "When I cross over that river, I will see you again, but I plan on stayin' on this one as long as I can. You were like a brother to me. I will love you always."

Will smiled, kissed her on the cheek, and hugged her tightly.

Allie looked up and noticed white clouds drifting away in the distant blue sky. She placed her thumbs in the pockets of her britches and smiled, "Well, Elmer, I hope you liked the oak leaf we sent ya. Guess it don't matter anymore. You were brave, and we will always be proud of you." Her eyes connected in fleeting glances with all the friends as she composed herself with one last sniffle, which she wiped away on her forearm.

Everyone made gentle gestures to Allie and then departed in silence.

Aaron turned back toward Freeport, walking hand in hand with Jenny, who stepped gracefully over the exposed roots on the riverbank. Trick wandered a few paces downriver before stopping to stare at a swirling pool of water and then into the gray spaces beneath the submerged rocks and logs that angled into the water. When he reached a distant turn on the riverbank, he looked back at the wigwam and waved. He looked like a distant shadow now. Allie and Will returned the wave. Turning again downriver, he pulled his floppy hat down to his ears and continued home to find T.J.

Chapter 20
Galena

August, 1861

"Papa, Papa!" Ben shouted as he started up the zigzag stairs rising to the Smith home on High Street. His shiny black brogan boots shuffled on each stair as he rose above town in a furious effort to make it quickly to the door stoop. A long horn blast from a river barge on the Fever River below echoed upward to the lead mines above the house. The sound seemed to spur young Ben along.

Now fourteen, he could feel his muscles burning in his calves and thighs as he rushed up the wooden staircase that hugged the steep rocky slope. At the halfway point, he stopped and looked down at the letter in his hand that was addressed to his father, John E. Smith. After catching his breath, he resumed his climb.

"Ben! Ben! What's the emergency?" John E. shouted from above.

Ben decided to save his reply until he reached the top of the stairs. He looked back toward town and the river where the barges were lined up, loaded with cargo.

One barge blared its horn, making the sense of alarm more urgent to John E. "Ben! Is someone hurt?" he asked as his son neared.

"No, Father! I have a letter for you," Ben breathlessly exclaimed when he reached the top. Gasping as he handed the letter to his father, he said, "Father, it's a letter from Congressman Washburne."

John E. took the beautifully scripted envelope from Ben. He pinched the corner of the envelope open just enough to place in a thumb, pulling it along the length to create an opening. Tilting his head to the side, he reached for his spectacles in the front pocket of his waistcoat. Glancing at Ben, he pulled out the letter from the envelope. He unfolded it and began reading. When he finished, he smiled and nodded thoughtfully.

"Father, what is it? What does the letter say?" Ben asked.

"Well, son, I will let you read it yourself."

Just then little Adelaide arrived. She had seen Ben from her bedroom and had come to investigate.

"Father…Ben, what is it?" she asked.

"Read aloud the letter, Ben, and then we will go see Mother," John E. replied.

Ben held the letter firmly and began reading in a slow, steady tone.

H. of R.
July 23, 1861
My Dear Colonel:
I have this morning called on the Secretary of War and got
him to telegraph that he will accept a regiment from you,
if ready for marching orders in 15 days. You should give
immediate notice and I have no doubt you can get up a

regiment in that time. Write to J. R. Howlett...to get up a company. He will want to be adjutant and I should be glad if he could.

The disaster of Sunday does not seem to be quite so bad this morning but bad enough.

I write in haste to go into the mail today.

Yours, etc.

E. B. Washburne [5]

When Ben finished reading the correspondence, he looked up at his father with pride.

"What does this mean?" Adelaide asked.

"It means Father will be a commander of a regiment one thousand men strong! He will be a colonel and fight the rebels down south!" Ben's voice rose to a higher pitch. "He will whip those rebels for sure!"

Adelaide looked confused and somewhat stunned by Ben's remark.

"Now hold on, Ben, let's not get ahead of things," his father said as he led the children back to the house. "I must raise a regiment first, and then we'll head south...but only for a short time. We'll be back in good order once this rebellion is put down quickly. Not to worry, Adelaide. Let's go see Mother. She will want to know the news from our good congressman."

John E. placed his hand on Adelaide's head. She looked up proudly, grabbed his hand, and kissed it. Then she frowned pensively, looked him in the eyes, and asked in a low voice that was almost a whisper, "Pappa, if you go down south, will you come home again?"

John E. lifted his hand and gently stroked her curls as they stepped onto the door stoop, which creaked as they approached the front door. "Adelaide, your mother expects that I will always come home. I will not disappoint either of you. I love you so."

Ben placed the letter back in the envelope as if repacking a gift in its wrapping. When they reached the front door, he grasped the doorknob with his right hand and pulled it open. The door creaked loudly.

"Mother, come quickly!"

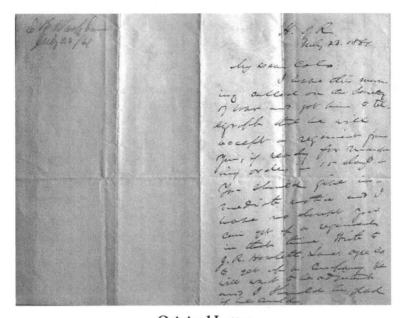

Original Letter
From Congressman Elihu Washburne to Colonel John E. Smith

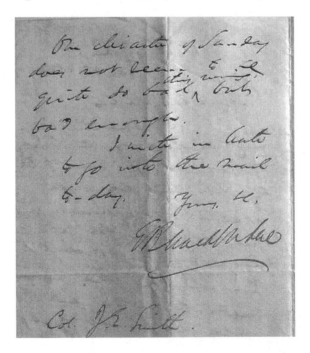

Chapter 21

Pecatonica River

Freeport
Early Autumn, 1861

As always, wild plums and blackberries were thick along the Pecatonica this time of year. Turkeys darted in and out of the dense thickets on the shoreline farther downstream, competing with red and gray foxes that also feasted on the wild fruit, which would soon fall to the frost.

The friends had arrived late morning and sat on the riverbank with their feet in the cool, swirling water, waiting for T.J. and Trick to pick a bounty on their way up the river from Buda. The misty fog that covered the water earlier in the morning had lifted now, and sunbeams filtered through gaps in the dense canopy of the Indian oak tree.

"We gotcha a nice bunch here!" Trick called out as he pulled his haversack from his side to the front. "Lots of berries for pies, too! Jenny's mom and Gramma Lucy will be busy tonight for sure. Best bring back pies to us tomorrow, Allie. I 'spect you will have your sleeves rolled up this evening rolling dough and scatterin' flour all over the floor!" Trick smiled.

"Trick, you best shut your smackers," Allie quickly replied, "or you won't get nothin' tomorrow! Now, can you pass that haversack around like a gentleman?"

The friends chuckled. Allie smiled, too.

Suddenly, a high pitched "hatchoooo!" echoed out of the wigwam.

The friends jumped to their feet and turned to face the entrance. T.J. grabbed his rifle, which was leaning on the Indian oak. They looked at each other with wide-eyed alarm.

"Who's in there?" Will demanded. "Come out! We have a gun."

There was silence.

"Come out! We have a gun!" Will repeated.

They heard the sound of shuffling feet inside the wigwam, and then two small hands appeared, pushing the holly bushes that obscured the entrance. A head then popped through.

"Goodness, gracious," Allie said with alarm, "It's a Negro boy!" Allie looked at Will and continued. "Let me talk to him. He looks too scared." Taking a few careful steps, she stopped a short distance from the wigwam entrance. She turned to T.J. and said slowly, "T.J., put your rifle back on the Injun oak tree." Turning back to the boy, she said calmly, "Come out. We won't hurt ya."

The branches moved again, and the intruder stepped out. He stood just over five feet tall and was dressed in butternut-colored britches with no shirt, just straps over his shoulders. His boots were muddy, shoddy leather with split seams. His big toe protruded from his left boot. As he inched closer to the friends, he trembled. In his hands he raised the wigwam tomahawk at an angle in front of him with the blade up over his curly black hair.

"Please don't shoot! Please don't shoot!" he said. "Li'l Joe be good!"

He looked at Allie and then rested the head of the tomahawk on the ground. He dropped to his knees and looked at all the friends, his dark almond-shaped eyes welling up as he placed his face in his hands.

"Please don't shoot! Li'l Joe be good," he repeated slowly, yet quieter this time. His trembling then became a pronounced shaking.

Allie quickly rushed to him. "You'll be safe now," she said calmly. "We ain't gonna hurt you. We are friends of the wigwam. You can trust us." She then grabbed the boy by his elbows and gently lifted him up. Looking directly into his eyes, she smiled and then hugged him until the boy's trembling faded away. In a moment the friends were beside them, and Trick placed his right hand on the boy's shoulder.

"We'll all take care of ya," Allie said calmly.

The boy nodded his head and smiled. He picked up the tomahawk and handed it to Allie as a turtledove's call broke the silence and echoed downriver.

"Whoo-da-loo, hoo, hoo!"

It was repeated again, this time closer to the wigwam.

"Crazy, that ain't no turtledove," Trick said. "Turtledoves do three 'hoos.' They go 'whoo-da-loo, hoo, hoo, hoo!' Listen again."

Another call with two "hoos" clearly sounded, this time close by the bend in the river where Trick and T.J. turned before returning home.

"Hush, everyone," Will said. "T.J., grab your rifle."

T.J. darted over to Indian oak and retrieved it.

The friends remained motionless peering at the bend just forty yards away. The loud snap of a branch cracked through the silence, followed by a tail smacking on the water by an alarmed beaver.

Motioning urgently, Will said, "Quick! Everyone get inside the wigwam. Bring the boy!"

Allie grabbed the tomahawk, and they all dashed through the holly barrier. Allie placed the tomahawk by the medicine bag and sat down next to the boy. She extended her hand to him. He grabbed it and smiled.

Will peered through the holly and looked downriver. A moment later a dark figure of a man with a noticeable limp rounded the bend. He wore a large brown slouch hat that flapped to each side and also forward, casting a shadow on his face. After a few more steps, he raised a large fife to his lips as his haversack swung loosely by his side. Soon a "whoo-da-loo, hoo, hoo" broke the silence again. He stopped and placed the fife in his haversack. He then squatted on the riverbank, raised his hand to his right ear, and peered inquisitively through the mist that was rising upriver. A deep-red cardinal tweeted and disappeared quickly. Feeling secure, he dropped the haversack and turned, taking deliberate steps to the wigwam entrance.

"T.J., grab your rifle and follow me quickly! The rest of you stay here!" Will whispered as he grabbed the tomahawk from the wall and pushed through the holly bushes.

In a flash both boys formed on each side of the intruder. Will raised the tomahawk with both hands. T.J. pointed his rifle directly at the man's shadowy face, causing the slouch hat to fall.

"Raise your hands!" Will commanded.

The stranger stepped back and raised his hands high.

In a moment the friends pushed outside, all except Allie who firmly gripped the boy's hand inside the wigwam.

As Jenny and Trick stood behind Will and T.J., they stared at the stranger in silence. Before them was a black man, medium height, about twenty years old. The man nodded his head as he smiled.

"Who are you? Why are you here?" Will demanded.

There was a slight hesitation as the stranger looked at both Will and T.J.

"Gentlemen, my name is Richard Blue. I am a free black. I was born in Ohio, and I now run the farm of Judge James Rayburn from Bloomington. And you, sirs, whom do I have the pleasure of acquaintance? Are you from Missouri?"

Will and T.J. turned to each other with perplexed looks. The stranger was a gentleman who could speak more polished than anyone they had ever heard in town.

"No, sir," Will replied, "we are from Freeport."

"And what are your names?"

"This is T.J. Lockwood, and I am William Erwin."

"I am looking for a young Negro boy. Have you seen him?"

"Yes," Will replied cautiously. He did not want to reveal where the boy was until he knew more about the stranger.

"And where did you find him?"

Suddenly, Allie pushed through the holly branches and confronted the stranger. Placing her hands on her hips she said, "Why do ya want to know where the boy is?"

"Miss, it is a pleasure meeting you, too. I see you know about the cave. Is the boy in there still?

The branches pushed away again, and the boy came through. He ran to the stranger and hugged him around the waist.

"Li'l Joe, we will be safe now," the stranger said. "These nice people are not slave catchers. They are not from Missouri."

The friends were quiet. No one knew what to say, except Allie.

"Was that you blowin' the fife downriver?"

"Yes, miss. Thank you for asking," he replied kindly.

"Well, ya don't know that turtledoves around these part have three 'hoos' not two! They go 'hoo-da-loo, hoo, hoo, hoo.' "

"Well, thank you for noticing," the stranger replied as he nodded to the friends. "I am aware of that fact and am impressed with your knowledge of such a wonderful bird. I changed the bird call so that Li'l Joe would know it was me. It is our signal. I was gathering food for us."

"Well do ya know that those doves are married for life?"

"Yes, I do. It's a wonderful thing."

"Well, you have some reckonin' to do," Allie said with more conviction. "Li'l Joe was in our secret wigwam. It's no secret no more since ya both know now."

"Well, thank you. I assure you we will keep your place secret for all of our interests and will gladly answer any other questions you may have during our time together. Would it be in your kind graces to place those weapons aside? Would you like berries and plums from my haversack? Can we eat in the cave so I can tell you about our journey here? You may call me Blue. That is my preference."

"Sure, Blue," Will replied with relief. "Come on, friends. We're anxious to hear how you found us."

Soon everyone returned and sat around the light beam again with Li'l Joe nearest to the light. It was noon now, and the sunbeam was almost vertical. Blue took his haversack, opened it, and held it in the light. The deep-purple plums and succulent blackberries were passed around as if in an Indian ritual. The savory fruit silenced everyone as the haversack was passed around a second and third time.

Li'l Joe smiled at each of the friends, exposing an innocent countenance that quickly drew them closer to him. Blue nodded at Li'l Joe and then asked, "Li'l Joe, can I tell our new friends about your journey and our story?" The boy, his grin growing wider, nodded.

"I promise I will not beleaguer you with too many details," Blue said. "I will be brief."

Blue looked up at the sunbeam and then at the friends, pausing to make good eye contact with each of them.

"Li'l Joe is a runaway slave born in Ray County, Missouri. He was a farmhand since childhood. His father, Conrad, was a slave on the same plantation. Both with the last name Arbuckle. The foreman of the plantation was a cruel man. He beat both father and son every time he had the opportunity. Li'l Joe always cried out 'Li'l Joe be good' as he was being beaten by the hickory stick. He called out, pleading to his father until the foreman called it off. Conrad decided one day that they had had enough of the beatings and waited for the next full moon so they could escape under the cover of night. That is what most runaways do, so as not to be found in daylight and returned to their masters by the slave catchers. So about a month ago, they both escaped and traveled for a week following the Missouri River east to the Mississippi River at St. Louis. On the other side of the river is Alton, Illinois, where the people accept and take care of runaways. These people, you may know, are called abolitionists. They hide them in their homes to keep them safe. So now you know why I asked if you were from Missouri. I thought with your rifle, you were slave catchers from there."

"How did they both cross the Mississippi River to Alton?" Aaron asked.

Li'l Joe's eyes began to well up, and he placed his face in his hands.

"Do you want me to continue, Li'l Joe?" Blue asked.

Li'l Joe hesitated, looked at the friends, and then nodded slowly.

"Well, when Conrad and Li'l Joe got to St. Louis, they prepared to cross the Mississippi River into Illinois, our free state. They secured a rowboat under cover of night, but it was not a full moon. It was pitch black. They could see the lights on the shore at Alton, and then decided to set forth. The distance at that point is about a half-mile wide."

"What happened next?" Allie asked. "Why is Li'l Joe so sad right now?"

"Well, about one hundred yards from the Illinois shore, a steamer transport came within a few feet of their rowboat and swamped it. It flipped over, and father and son slipped into the dark water. Conrad immediately grabbed Li'l Joe and paddled him to the overturned rowboat. It took him a long time to get Li'l Joe to the boat, but he succeeded, and Li'l Joe grabbed onto the bow. His father then grabbed onto the stern and paddled his feet, rapidly pushing the rowboat closer and closer to safety. As they neared the shore, a second steamer groaned by, and another big wave lapped over them. Li'l Joe held on tightly to the bow, caught his breath, and then looked behind him. His father had slipped away into the darkness."

Li'l Joe began to sob. Allie's, Jenny's, and the boy's eyes welled up as they tried to hold back their tears.

"Did they ever find his father?" Jenny asked as she dabbed her eyes with a kerchief.

"We don't know what became of him," Blue replied. "The last words he said to Li'l Joe were, 'If we can get to Illinois, look for the soldiers in blue. Look for the boys in blue. They will help us get free!'"

"So how did Li'l Joe find you?" Will asked.

Blue raised his haversack to offer more fruit. "You must tell nobody from this day forward what I am about to tell you. And I promise as an oath to God to never reveal this cave, your wigwam, to anyone. Are we clear on our promises to each other?"

"Yes, Blue, and we have an oath as friends of the wigwam," replied Aaron. "Will and I were the first to find this special place." Aaron then reached into the dark shadows on the cave wall and picked up the glass mirror positioning it in the light. "I cut my palm with this mirror the day we found the wigwam four years ago. After binding up the wound, Will and I shook hands in this light and became the first secret friends of the wigwam. All of the friends here have also placed their hands in the light. We recite a verse from the Good Book, too. Do you and Li'l Joe wish to join us as friends?"

Blue looked over at Li'l Joe. They both nodded and smiled.

Aaron and Will then shuffled to the center of the wigwam. Each of the friends followed suit, placing their right hand with their palms facing up into the glowing light. The scar on Aaron's palm was still prominent.

Will looked across the light to Allie and smiled, "Allie, will you please recite the Bible verse to us that Gramma Lucy taught you?"

"Yes, please, dear friends, let's be puttin' our hands together," she replied. "Let's bow our heads so I can rightly say the verse."

She glanced at everyone, paused for a moment, and then continued in a soft, solemn tone. "As the good Lord says, I will not forget you. I have carved you on the palm of my hand." She then raised her head and smiled.

Blue then broke the silence, "Thank you, friends…Li'l Joe and I will keep our solemn oath to never reveal this place. Do you agree, Li'l Joe?"

Li'l Joe quickly nodded.

"Well, then," Blue continued in earnest, "there are secret pathways called underground railroads that enable runaway slaves to have freedom. I am one of many who travels with runaway slaves in order to get them north to Canada. We have secret stops along the way. Do you understand?"

"Yes, we do," replied Trick and T.J. in unison.

"Good. I assist runaways on their journey. I first met Li'l Joe in Princeton at Reverend Lovejoy's house. He asked me to take Li'l Joe under cover of night to Oscar Taylor's house in Freeport. So Li'l Joe and I departed in the dead of night from Princeton about a week ago. We followed the rivers, as we always do. Last night, in the light of the moon, I noticed faint footprints in the mud that lead to this wigwam. That is how we arrived here. We only travel at night. We rest during the day. Do you know where the Oscar Taylor house is?"

"Yes. It's just one hour away from here by foot," Will replied. "We can take you there tonight for sure. Allie and Jenny will go home before nightfall. T.J. and Trick best be getting home, too. Aaron and I will stay here with you until darkness, and then we will lead the way."

"OK," Blue replied. "When we get close to the Taylor house, you must lie back, and we will make it there by ourselves."

The friends nodded in agreement.

"Well, Jenny, Trick, and T.J., we best be headin' home now," Allie said as she walked over to Li'l Joe. "You best keep movin' with Blue. You are a friend of the wigwam now, and we have carved you in the palm of our hands, like the Good Book says." Hugging Li'l Joe first and then Blue, she turned to Jenny and smiled. Jenny then did the same.

"Now you stay safe, Li'l Joe, ya hear?" said Trick with a wide grin. "S'pose some day when this is all over, we can come back to the wigwam and catch some big fish."

Li'l Joe smiled.

Blue extended his hand to T.J. and then Trick and thanked them both.

Will looked at the friends. "You best be headed home. Aaron and I will make sure Li'l Joe and Blue get safely to Mr. Taylor's house," he said.

Within a moment, Jenny and Allie began their walk upriver. Trick and T.J. then began their trek downriver. When all of them reached their respective bends in the river, each turned around for a final wave to the wigwam friends…before fading into the shadows.

Chapter 22

Freeport

**Saengerbund Ball
Brewster House
December, 1861**

The quiet hint of violins echoed through the parlor to the steps in front of the Brewster House. Final preparations were in the making. A large chandelier with two hundred or so burning candles hung above the ballroom floor. Musicians pinched the strings of their instruments causing a discordant pitch. The ballroom was ready for the most prominent citizens of Northern Illinois society. Freezing temperatures and howling winds could not keep them from the dance. By nightfall the ballroom would be filled, spilling out to an overcrowded vestibule.

"Well, if it isn't Captain and Mrs. Cowan! It's is so good to see you here!" Mrs. Putnam exclaimed with her usual enthusiasm.

"You may call me Heather," Mrs Cowan replied, nodding as if touched by royalty.

"And please call me Leonora," she said as she extended her gloved hand to the Cowans. "And who is this fine and lovely young lady with you?"

"This is my dear daughter, Mary," Heather replied. "She has been waiting for this moment for many months now. Perhaps a young officer will take her hand tonight."

Mary giggled nervously. "Please call me Molly," she replied respectfully.

"Molly it is, then," Leonora replied as she looked at the debutante. "Well, Molly, don't be shy because there are several officers in nice blue uniforms on the floor already. But you best do a quickstep. Our Freeport ladies are in a gush about them."

The sixteen-year-old blushed again and looked down at her hoop gown. In preparation for this special event, her first venture into a ballroom, she had practiced the waltz steps with her father, Captain Cowan, dancing for hours on the hickory floor in front of the fireplace in their modest home in Warren, Illinois. Though tired from the long carriage ride, she quickly perked up at the sight of the glowing chandelier that cast marvelous patterns across the ceiling.

"I love your gown. It is just beautiful!" said a soft and charming voice behind her.

Startled, Molly turned to face another young woman about her age and replied, "Oh! Well, thank you." Looking at her ball dress, Molly smiled and said, "Your gown is more beautiful than mine. And what is your name?"

"You have just met my mother. I am sorry. With the crowd and all, I had difficulty getting to you. My name is Jenny Putnam. I live here in Freeport."

"So you are the other debutante tonight?" asked Molly.

"Yes, it is just the two of us. And you are Mary, I believe?"

"Yes, you may call me Molly though."

"Molly...Molly...oh, I like the name! I know many by the name of Mary, but no Molly, so I guess you are the one and only Molly for me." Jenny suddenly felt she had made an awkward comment and felt a quick pang of embarrassment for overstepping the formality of the moment.

Molly nodded and replied, "I live on the Apple River between Galena and here. I have friends from Apple River, but no one in Freeport. So you, Jenny, are my one and only Freeport friend."

Both girls smiled, nodded to each other, and then looked to the soldiers in blue on the other side of the dance floor.

Jenny continued. "Well, my father has always told me that distance has no boundaries for true friends. Some friends are gold, others are silver. The gold shines brighter than silver from afar."

The orchestra struck up again. The noise of the crowd turned to a hush as the strands of the violins took over. The Saengerbund Ball was beginning.

"Is your father an officer?" Molly inquired. The violins started the slow waltz cadence.

"No, Molly, he is the fire marshal here. He has been talking to friends about raising a regiment, but it may take some time. Is your father in the Union army?"

"Yes, he's here tonight. He's a captain in the Forty-Fifth Illinois Infantry. He's recruiting new members this month with Colonel John E. Smith."

"John E. Smith! I know Mr. Smith!" Jenny replied excitedly. "He is a very good friend of my father's. They were in the Wide Awake Society and helped Abe Lincoln get elected!" Jenny's excited voice and hand gyrations caused a stern-looking woman with silver locks to raise her longette to her eyes and stare disapprovingly at the debutant. Chastened, Jenny composed herself, holding her hands next to her satin gown.

"Do you have an escort tonight?" Jenny asked.

"No, but I believe Alfred, the colonel's son, will ask for my hand in a waltz. He sure looks handsome in his gray West Point uniform. Do you see him over there?" Molly pointed across the room to a gathering of officers. "He is the youngest one. He is standing between my father and Colonel Smith. He will dance with me unless he asks you first."

Jenny blushed and quickly replied with a respectful smile, "Well, he may ask me to dance, but my heart is with another. His name is Aaron Dunbar."

"Is he in the Union army?"

"No, but he's thinking about enlisting someday soon. He had a friend sign up already, and he's itching for a fight, too."

"Is he here tonight?"

"No, I am sorry to say, he isn't, although I'd like him to be. He couldn't afford an ascot and suit for the occasion, though he's more handsome than any here in a uniform." She looked quickly at Molly. "Of course, except your Alfred."

Molly smiled. Her eyes glowed happily. The music began to rise and roll like the waves in an ocean.

Molly looked once again at the group of officers where her father stood. "Do you know Alfred Smith helped save Freeport a few years back?"

Jenny tilted her head inquisitively. "How did he do it?"

Molly replied proudly, "He was in the church belfry and directed a young man with a rifle to shoot at gunpowder barrels, which snuffed out the fire. It was pure military genius. I guess he was the general that day."

Jenny, knowing that her father directed the whole town rescue, did not speak for fear of ruining a relationship with her newfound friend. She knew that in time Molly would learn about Fire Marshal Putnam. And she would someday learn about Elmer, Will, and Aaron, who saved the horses…and perhaps T.J., who was with Alfred…and the three hundred men in the bucket brigade who fought the fire furiously for hours. Jenny paused for a moment and looked up. The music seemed to swirl like smoke drifting upward and into the chandeliers. The candles twinkled brighter.

"Yes, Molly," Jenny replied, "I have heard of Alfred. I did not know he was Colonel Smith's son. It does not surprise me, though, that he would have the courage. Colonel Smith is a brave man, too."

"Do you know who the young man was with Alfred on the church belfry that night?" Molly asked as she kept her gaze on the group of officers.

"Yes, he's a friend of mine. He's from the town of Buda."

Molly looked back at Jenny. Her curiosity piqued. "Buda is pretty far from Freeport. How do you know him?"

Jenny looked at Molly and said, "Aaron, my beloved, and I met the rifleman on the Pecatonica River a few years back. His name is Thomas J. Lockwood. We call him T.J. for short. He always walks the river with his friend Trick, who is also our friend. Maybe you will meet them someday."

"I would be honored," Molly replied. "Truly honored."

Jenny was happy to discover through their conversation that Molly, resplendent in her evening gown, had great character to go with her charm. She seemed wholesome to her with not one arrogant bone in her body. Perhaps one day, Jenny thought, just perhaps one day she would share the secret place of the wigwam and invite her in with the other friends. Jenny felt a sense of peace as the orchestra's waltz tune flowed in perfect cadence to its conclusion.

A silence descended on the ballroom, punctuated by some laughter from a group of cigar-smoking men on the far side of the room. As the musicians set their instruments on their laps, the orchestra leader stepped forward.

"Ladies and gentlemen," he announced. "I welcome you to our annual Christmas Saengerbund Ball and hope that this evening finds you both warm and happy. As is customary at events like this, we will open the dance with a special schottische for the lovely ladies here tonight, the most beautiful ladies in this part of our dear country. I would especially like to welcome our two debutantes, Miss Mary Cowan and Miss Jenny Putnam."

There was a short pause and then silence.

"Her name is Molly!" someone among the cigar-smoking men shouted.

A ripple of laughter filled the ballroom.

The orchestra leader smiled goodnaturedly and said, "My apology to Miss Putnam," he said, bowing to her.

The crowd's laughter lit up the room again.

"It is Molly *Cowan*!" shouted a score of men from the shadows.

The conductor bowed again. "My apology to Miss Cowan."

A few ladies near the orchestra shook their heads.

"As I stand corrected, the important dance of this evening is the dance of the debutantes. And it is also very special because it is a pre-nuptial dance that will someday lead to a dance with their betrothed. So without further adieu, I would like Fire Marshal Putnam and Captain Cowan to join their beautiful daughters on the dance floor so we can commence this special evening."

Captain Cowan and Fire Marshal Putnam crossed the room to the middle of the dance floor. They nodded to their wives first and then to other ladies in the room. The two debutants walked up in concert. Molly's gown was a crimson color that contrasted smartly with her father's deep-blue uniform. His red sash that covered a sword belt in battle was secured snugly around his waist and was a perfect match to her gown. He placed his left palm upward, and Molly placed her palm gently in his hand.

Jenny followed in step. Fire Marshal Putnam stood six feet two in his black suit. His vest and ascot were a powder blue that matched Jenny's gown as well. Both couples were ready. The "Palmyra Schottische" struck up with its early and slow rhythmical cadence. The others waited for the third pass that would permit their entrance to the floor.

Molly and the captain and Jenny and her father all moved in perfect rhythm as the graceful music echoed as if coming from the ceiling and walls. Soon it turned to the Bohemian country dance sequence. The two father-daughter couples lifted their heads, smiling widely as the dance progression moved to two short runs and a hop followed by four turning hop steps. With their fathers in sync, the debutants moved across the floor...*step, step, step, hop...step, step, step, hop...step, hop, step, hop, step, hop, step, hop....*

With the third pass around the orchestra complete, the other couples converged onto the dance floor. The spectacle of swirling color on the floor enhanced the crystal chandelier above them. Within minutes the debutantes were approached by suitors, and Captain Cowan and Fire Marshal Putnam returned to the corner of the room with the other officers.

Captain Cowan reached to the bar table and collected two glasses of whisky. Handing one of the glasses to Putnam, he raised his glass for a toast. "I would like to toast our beloved daughters," announced Cowan. "That they find peace and happiness and are someday betrothed to men of goodwill and good standing in this great county."

Putnam raised his glass. "Thank you, Captain. And to you, sir, hoping that this war brings you safely back home so that you will spend your days in the company not of soldiers but of many, many grandchildren!"

"God bless us all!" Alfred announced as he emerged in his gray uniform from the shadows. He looked at his father as he raised his glass.

As the waltz continued, both Molly and Jenny stole nods of approval from their fathers who beamed proudly in the shadows. The joy of the first dance was being realized by both young debutantes. No dreams of it anymore. They were women of society now.

Alfred was waiting for the right moment to approach Molly when the waltz ended abruptly.

There was a short pause as suitors bowed to the debutantes and returned to their places on the sides of the ballroom. The orchestra shuffled its music sheets in preparation for the next waltz.

During this brief interlude, an older officer on the opposite side of the ballroom from where Alfred stood approached Molly. He nodded and then bowed to her as he grasped her delicate little hands. Lifting his chin in a stoic arrogance, he placed his right hand around her waist and then raised his right grip as if a grand master. The boldness of the move caused a stunned silence.

The colonel was fully decked in his dark-blue wool uniform. He had eagles on his dress epaulettes. The red sash around his waist had tassels that hung down like tapestry cords, swinging to and fro as Molly, with a nervous smile, looked toward Alfred and her father for rescue. Her new dance partner was more than middle-aged and had gray lamb-chop sideburns that extended from each side of his face, around his jaw, and back up, connecting the stream of hair to his moustache, which was overgrown like a sheepdog. His brown eyes were beady, and the chandelier reflected off his mostly bald head. Finally, he was a short man, about five feet five inches tall, which meant he was able to look at Molly square in the eye.

"My God," said Alfred's father, Colonel Smith. "That's Old Hindquarters out there! Do you remember? He walked to our table at the Tremont House and insulted Abe Lincoln?"

"For cryin' out loud! That obnoxious," Putnam paused as he held back an expletive, "*colonel* has the audacity to steal the floor and ruin this fine evening. I will go to him when the music stops!"

The waltz ended, and the old colonel bowed to the startled Molly, turned, and walked away.

"There's no need to go to him, Mr. Putnam. He is coming to us," Alfred replied.

As the diminutive colonel approached the men, everyone, including the orchestra, paused to see what reaction would greet the old colonel who approached the circle of officers as if nothing untoward had happened.

"Hello, gentlemen," he announced arrogantly. "Do you remember me?"

Though Putnam and the officers knew who he was, they remained silent so as not to extend one measure of courtesy.

"I am Colonel John Loomis the third...of the Twenty-Sixth Illinois Infantry. I see, Colonel, that you are doing your duty, but you, sir—Is it Mr. Putnam?—have not found the time to serve your country?"

Putnam seethed in silence, not trusting himself to speak.

"Colonel," replied Colonel Smith, "what is the reason for your introduction? What do you want?"

"Nothing, Colonel, but to say that I am recruiting soldiers in Freeport this week; then I'm heading north and then east to Waukegan. Perhaps Mr. Putnam here would like to join the ranks of my regiment. I could offer you a captain's position."

"Mr. Putnam will not serve with Democrats…especially little ones," said Captain Cowan. "And if you ever approach my daughter to dance, you best clear it with me or—"

"Or what, Captain? Will you court-martial me on a ballroom floor?" Loomis replied sarcastically. He looked at Alfred. "I see you are in a West Point uniform. And by the stripes on your sleeves, you will graduate this spring. Perhaps, young man, I could give you a captaincy along with Mr. Putnam." Loomis looked at Putnam who glared back at the arrogant officer. He smirked at Putnam.

The silence became awkward to those who were in earshot of the exchange. The orchestra quickly struck up a tune, and dancers took to the floor.

As the melodious strains of a waltz again filled the room, Molly and Jenny found themselves enjoying the attention of younger dance partners. Molly looked at Alfred, beckoning his approach with a curious nod. He caught the look, smiled, and nodded back.

Turning his attention back to Colonel Loomis, Alfred replied, "No, sir, I have plans of my own,"

"And what are those plans, young man?" asked Colonel Loomis.

"My plan is to be a colonel, like you, of a Negro infantry regiment," Alfred said, proudly puffing out his chest.

"A Negro regiment!" Loomis replied with a bombastic tone that broke the civility a second time. "Well, my boy, you best go buy a thousand shovels for your boys because they'll never see the front. They'll be digging ditches for the regular army!" Loomis smiled wryly, expecting a supportive chuckle that never happened.

Colonel Smith reached over to confront the arrogant little colonel directly, but Putnam interceded and pounced on Loomis, grabbing him by the back of the collar. He lifted Loomis off the floor in one swift motion and then dropped him on his butt like a rag doll.

The orchestra stopped, and the crowd watched in stunned silence.

Putnam lifted Loomis again by his collar and hustled him across the floor, holding him so his feet were dangling an inch above the floor. The red-faced colonel looked like a puppet ballerina tiptoeing with Putnam as his marionette. Putnam carried Loomis out the ballroom and through the front parlor. The silent patrons of the ball heard a rustle and the solid creak of the old oak door followed by a resounding boom as the door slammed shut.

Now outside, Putnam carried Loomis, arms flailing, across the street where there was a large snow mound mixed with street mud. He then tossed the cursing Loomis headfirst into the snowbank. Turning away, he returned to the front stoop of the Brewster House. He opened the door, paused, turned to face the colonel, and shouted, "You will not recruit our men from Freeport, you coward. You can go to Waukegan, or you can go to hell!"

He slammed the big oak door shut behind him, its resonating boom echoing through the ballroom. The crowd waited in silence as Putnam reappeared. A split-second later, the ballroom erupted in cheers that echoed off the rafters. Nodding to the orchestra leader and then to those gathered around him, he took a graceful bow. Leonora Putnam approached him, and he gently took her hand, leading her to the center of the floor. Grasping her around her waist, he stood erect as the music touched off again. The couples advanced to the floor again.

Molly was with Alfred now, her hand on his shoulder, his hand on her waist. She looked once again to the chandelier above and knew as long as she was in Alfred's arms, she would not fall back.

The lights seemed to burn brighter as the long dark shadows on the walls rose and fell with the night.

Chapter 23

Shiloh

Forty-Fifth Illinois Infantry
Washburne Lead Mine Regiment
Colonel John E. Smith Commanding
April 6, 1862

The rustle in the ravine sounded like swarms of squirrels wrestling in the leaves. Dogwoods were in full blossom, but there were no birds or wildlife to be seen. The men of the Forty-Fifth Illinois Volunteer Infantry were positioning themselves on the southern-most slope of the ravine where a rebel advance was anticipated.

As the Yankees peered over the lip of the ravine, they saw a beautiful field of knee-high Tennessee grasses mixed with wildflowers. The field continued in a gentle slope for another hundred yards until it topped out on another ridge, a natural defense that obscured any rebel movement. All was quiet for now.

Many reclined peacefully on the slope of the shadowy ravine, which felt cave-like in its perceived security. Some sat on the slope, boot heels dug into the dense leaves at awkward angles, arms outstretched. A few rested on their backs with packs for pillows and muskets to their side.

All of them had been bloodied. Led by their colonel, John E. Smith, they had fought for Brigadier General Ulysses S. Grant and had beat the rebels in the battles of Forts Henry and Donelson. But the victories had been costly. Almost half of the original volunteers who so gladly marched off to war the previous year were dead of wounds or sickness. A few, lucky to be alive, went home maimed for life.

No longer raw recruits, the veterans silently stared across the open, silent field. As they waited for battle, many thought of home, calling up memories of loved ones far north in Illinois.

"Attention, Forty-Fifth!" Captain Cowan shouted, breaking their reverie. The troopers jumped up in response and stood in anticipation of the next order.

"Colonel Smith wishes that I read this pronouncement to you from Congressman Washburne!" He had a folded yellow-tarnished letter in one hand. Standing at the base of the ravine, he looked up at the soldiers, who returned his gaze in respectful silence.

After putting on his reading spectacles, he stated in a firm, steady tone, "I take the liberty of reading this correspondence to you. It reads..."

> *Sir:*
> *I have the honor to acknowledge the receipt of the*
> *proceedings of a meeting of the officers of your regiment...*
> *every promise made by persons connected with the*
> *Regiment in regard to arms has been fully redeemed...I*
> *am proud to know that all go into the hands of brave and*
> *true soldiers, who will vindicate the honor of the National*
> *Flag and give additional luster to the glory of our own*
> *beloved State.*
>
> *To have my name connected with such a Regiment is a*
> *distinguished, though I fear, an undeserved compliment. For*
> *it, I desire to tender to the officers and soldiers, one and all,*
> *my sincere and profound acknowledgement and to assure*
> *them of the deep and heartfelt interest I shall ever take in*
> *all that concerns them. Whether amid the clash of arms, or*
> *in the beautiful walks of life, under all circumstances and at*

all times, they can command my best services and my most
earnest efforts in their behalf.
   I have the honor, to be, very
                    Truly, your friend & servant,
                       E. B. Washburne [6]

Captain Cowan looked up at the soldiers as he took off his spectacles. "Thank you, gentlemen," he said. "You may go back to your positions."

As the captain turned away, the silence was broken by the startled shouts of soldiers all along the line. They saw hundreds of rabbits suddenly bounding across the field toward them. Seconds later they reached the lip of the ravine and scurried down the slope, dashing between the legs of many of the men as they did so. Scores more followed with all disappearing in the woods behind the troops.

"For God's sake, men! The rebels are comin'!" shouted Cowan. "Hunker down, and prepare to fire!" The regiment dropped to the ground and readied their weapons.

"Jumpin' jiminy!" shouted a private near Cowan. "Those rabbits can sure run fast. And those followin' ain't too slow either!"

Seeing approaching movement in the distant tree line, one sharp-eyed soldier shouted, "Those aren't rebs in the field! Those are our boys comin' at a fast pace. And they don't have their muskets! They are runnin' as if they've seen the devil himself!"

"Get your heads up, boys!" cried another. "Before these boys run right through us!"

Within seconds five blue-clad soldiers rushed through their lines, panting like dogs in the summer heat. They were followed by a hundred more panic-stricken soldiers. They didn't stop until they reached the bottom of the ravine, where they huddled like sheep.

Suddenly the panicked troops heard a shout from within the nearby tree line, "Who is in command here?" It was quickly followed by another authoritative voice that shouted, "What regiment are you with, soldier?"

Then two Union officers on horseback emerged from the woods. Colonel John E. Smith was on his magnificent war-horse, Black Hawk, the pony rescued by Will and Aaron during the Freeport fire, now fully grown at seventeen hands high, his coal-black coat shining. The other rider was General McClernand, commanding officer of the First Division of the Union army of Tennessee.

"I will say only once more, what regiment are you with?" McClernand shouted angrily.

"We are with the Fifty-Third Ohio, sir!" responded a soldier nearest to the general.

"And who is in command here?" he shouted back.

"He is over there, General, behind that tree!" replied a private who was shaking noticeably.

McClernand and Smith turned their horses and looked in the direction the private was pointing. In the shadows forty paces away, a colonel was emerging from behind a large tree.

"Colonel, step forward!" McClernand demanded.

The colonel shook visibly as he stepped forward, finally stopping several paces from McClernand and Smith.

"Where is your sword, Colonel?" McClernand said.

The colonel looked at the ground and then looked up at McClernand, "Sir, I do not know. I suspect it is in the hands of the rebels now."

"Stand tall, sir! Stand at attention! What is your regiment, and what is your name?" McClernand replied forcefully.

"I am Colonel Jesse Appler of the Fifty-Third Ohio. I am with Sherman's Fifth Division," the colonel replied nervously. "We have been routed by the rebels and need your support, sir!"

"We do not support cowards, Colonel!" McClernand barked back, causing Appler to take two steps backward. "You take your men down the ravine to the right of the Lead Mine Regiment. I want you to order your men to lie down and cover themselves with leaves and branches. Maybe that way you can come out of this scrape with your lives. Go back to your tree, Colonel, and lead your men from there!"

The disgraced colonel of the Fifty-Third looked stunned.

Then a private of the Fifty-Third Ohio broke the silence. "General, we are soldiers, not rabbits, and we won't hide in no rabbit holler! Give us a chance, sir. Let us help the Forty-Fifth and get our gander back. Please, sir."

General McClernand looked at Colonel John E. Smith. Black Hawk snorted. Smith nodded to McClernand and then looked down from his mount to those of the Fifty-Third around him and announced in a calm, steady voice, "Soldiers of the Fifty-Third Ohio, we are all men in blue. If you stay…you fight! You may join our lines now!"

As he gave his orders, Colonel John E. Smith looked like an icon in the saddle. His dark-navy-blue uniform contrasted smartly with Black Hawk's stunning coat, and his commanding presence set the men at ease now.

Within moments the soldiers of the Fifty-Third Ohio climbed up the slope of the ravine. The disgraced Colonel Appler watched as his men worked their way into the ranks of the Lead Mine Regiment. He looked back at McClernand and Smith and then quickly vanished into the woods.

"Let him go to the rear," McClernand stated matter-of-factly. "He will find his discharge there soon enough."

Smith nodded and rode off to give orders to his augmented command. When he reached the center of the line, he reined Black Hawk to a halt. Black Hawk, sensing the tension among the men, briefly pranced before coming to a stop. Smith looked up the slope at his captain.

"Captain Cowan! Can you see the rebels?" he asked.

"Sir, they are not on that ridge yet," Cowan replied, pointing at the field. "If they are there, they are keeping low on the other side of the ridge. It will take the rebs one hundred paces to get to us through that field."

A number of soldiers, especially the younger ones, looked at their colonel with anticipation. During the pause, the line kept deathly quiet in hopes of hearing something of the enemy—the clank of a sword, the snap of a bayonet, or the tramping of feet on the Tennessee soil.

Suddenly they saw flashes of sunlight glimmering off the barrels of a hundred muskets. The gray rebel line surged up over the ridge. As with all great storms, there was a pause, anticipation, and then a momentary crack that broke the silence. A cannon retort rifled across the gray sky and ricocheted through the trees above and behind the blue line. A second round exploded directly above the line, sending limbs and crushing blows to the men below. Alarming cries from the ravine alerted the rebels on the ridge that Yankees were in the woods and awaiting a clash in their front.

"Captain Cowan!" Colonel Smith commanded, "you will remain with the men under the protection of this ridge. I will advance with Black Hawk onto the field and draw their fire when they are at sixty paces from our line. When I wave my hat, you will emerge from the woods and return fire with a massed volley. We will then push them back to Dixie!" Colonel Smith nodded at Cowan and smiled.

"Yes, sir, it will be done," Cowan replied confidently.

The colonel reined in Black Hawk who felt the *zip* of a sniper's shot near his pointed ears. The steed flinched again as Smith rode to the end of the line. Looking up the slope from the bottom of the ravine, Colonel Smith nodded to his youthful comrades giving them the assurance they needed as they waited for the battle to begin. When he reached the end of the formation, he guided Black Hawk to the left until he was front and center of the troops at the bottom of the ravine.

Spurring Black Hawk gently into a walk, he spoke with a rising tone to the restless troops as he moved down the line. "Boys, we are ready now for another big fight. The rebels are on that ridge, and they know we are here. We will hold our line and push them back. This day will be our day as it was at Fort Henry and Donelson. Keep your cool. Remember your wives and your sweethearts." The colonel's voice then rose to a grand pitch. "Boys! We are fighting today for your families, for Congressman Washburne, for Grant, for Lincoln, and for the glory of the Forty-Fifth Illinois and the Fifty-Third Ohio! When Captain Cowan gives the command, we will take the field and get 'em on the run...and send them home to Dixie!"

As he screamed "Dixie," he pulled off his kepi with his right hand, circling the hat in the air as he kept Black Hawk tightly reined in with his left. Black Hawk tipped his head as if bowing in thanks.

The Lead Mine Regiment and the Fifty-Third Ohio boys let out a resounding roar of "Huzzah! Huzzah! Huzzah!" that echoed across the field.

The Confederates remained silent.

Black Hawk and Smith faced the steep incline of the ravine. Placing his hat back on his crown, he bent forward, placing his charcoal-and-white beard near Black Hawk's neck. He then spurred his prized war-horse up the slope, high-stepping between the band of soldiers. The veins on Black Hawk's neck popped out like those on a prizefighter's biceps. To the soldiers at the top of the ravine, Black Hawk at seventeen hands high appeared like the massive Trojan horse of legend as he ascended up the slope. The way was now clear. Black Hawk and Colonel Smith punched through the woods into the open field.

The Confederates on the far ridge watched with curiousity as the lone Yankee horse and rider appeared before them.

Immediately, Black Hawk began prancing to and fro as if daring the rebels to shoot him. Within seconds, like angry buzzing bees, Colonel Smith heard the sound of bullets flying by. He continued a constant zigzag movement as the rebel line rose up from the hill and began their advance.

The Confederates formed in two parade-like lines at the crest, the columns stretching nearly seventy yards. Seeing the formation and knowing the impending consequences, Captain Cowan rose from his knees and commanded, "Fix bayonets!"

Immediately, a clanking of metal on metal was heard up and down the line. He then shouted, "You will emerge from this position on my command only. We will fire a volley and then attack on the double-quick with bayonets! Let no man falter in his duty! Do you understand?"

"Yes, sir!" the soldiers replied.

Black Hawk continued to prance at a rapid pace back and forth and to and fro in front of the tree line. Smith remained calm as sniper bullets continued to zip by. Then Black Hawk reared on his hind legs, whinnying in pain.

Smith looked down at his left trouser leg. It was spattered with blood. He looked at Black Hawk's flank and saw blood oozing from a wound. Black Hawk reared up again in pain as Smith pulled on the reins to keep control. Black Hawk's hooves pounded violently into the razor grass.

"Woah, boy. Woah," said Smith soothingly, as he placed his soft beard against Black Hawk's ear. "You'll be OK, boy."

Sniper rounds continued to zip around them.

Smith noticed the wound was not spouting. The minié ball had struck his prized war-horse in the shoulder but had not penetrated an artery. Smith knew that Black Hawk, though injured, could stand firm in the conquest at hand. The flow, however, continued to soak Smith's trousers, staining the light-blue piping.

The Confederates were getting closer. In another minute the command would be given to charge the Union lines. The boys in butternut and gray moved confidently forward, halting sixty paces from the tree line where the Union troops were. They capped the firing cones on their muskets; pulled the hammers back to full cock; and rested their weapons on their shoulders, pointing the long arms at the woods.

Colonel Smith then spurred Black Hawk to a run parallel between the Yankee and Confederate lines. Blood streamed down Black Hawk's flank in pulsing waves of red. The movement of horse and rider caused a moment of confusion in the Confederate ranks, and they hesitated, awaiting the command to fire.

Finally the rebel colonel raised his sword high, stepped to the front of his command, and shouted, "Fire!" A volley was released in all its explosive fury. The lead balls shattered the deep-green foliage above the Union troops who hugged the sloping ground. Leaves dropped on them like swirling snow in a greenish winter flurry.

The moment had arrived. Colonel Smith pulled off his hat and waved it furiously so Captain Cowan could give the command.

Within seconds the entire Yankee line leaped up and emerged from the woods like a mighty blue tidal wave. Stunned by the magnitude of over six hundred men appearing before them like a vision, the rebel line stood mesmerized, and they hesitated again. Captain Cowan shouted, "Fire!" A blinding blast followed from the Yankee volley that hit the stunned Confederates. Clouds of smoke belched forth like incendiary hell. Half of the Confederate line dropped to the field dead or wounded.

The remaining rebels nervously grabbed at their cartridge boxes in a frantic effort to reload their muskets.

Black Hawk raced back and forth again, galloping like a demon in the wind, nostrils flared, his mane and tail flowing like black waves as Smith spurred him to the center. Smith reined his mount to face the rebel line and spurred Black Hawk to join in the attack. The black war-horse reared dramatically, forelegs batting at the air like a boxer's arms, and then rushed headlong toward the rebel line. Smith whirled his sword over his head, beckoning the blue ranks to follow. The Yankees followed in quickstep, screaming "huzzah!" as they charged headlong with Black Hawk into the rebel lines.

The alarmed Confederates attempted a few shots, but the minié balls were fired in haste and too high to have any effect. They turned on their heels and headed at a full run back up the slope.

Black Hawk and Smith trampled and cut their way through the gray-clad warriors. Screams intermixed with a clash of bayonets as blue- and gray-clad soldiers grappled at close quarters. Soon the field was steeped in red blood.

"Surrender, you damned rebels, or we will cut you all down!" screamed Captain Cowan. Similar shouts were echoed down the line.

Black Hawk continued his pursuit up the ridge, galloping around and through the remaining Confederates like a sheepdog encircling them and containing any movement of further retreat. "Put down your muskets, and you will be spared!" Smith ordered.

The exhausted rebels dropped their muskets, raised their hands, turned, and headed to the Union lines. Smith dismounted and led Black Hawk by the reins as they escorted the captured troops. Other Confederates fed into the procession, surrounding the two as if to secure protection from another Yankee onslaught. The procession continued to the center of the field where the Lead Mine Regiment and Fifty-Third Ohio now stood in a grand arc before the Confederates.

As the contingent neared, a color sergeant lifted the regimental flag of the Forty-Fifth. The national colors was also raised. A stout but muffled command was heard somewhere down the line followed by "Huzzah! Huzzah! Huzzah!" The victory on this field was complete.

Cowan snapped his sword in his black leather scabbard and stepped proudly out of the ranks. "Colonel, we sure gave 'em hell today!" Cowan announced loud enough for the men nearest them to hear.

"Good work, Captain! We have lived to see another day. Go bind the wounds and get all these men back to the ravine. I am sure this won't be the end of it." Smith saluted Cowan and then took off his hat and waved it to the blue line, receiving joyful hoots and hollers in return. Placing his hat to his crown again, he bent over and whispered in Black Hawk's ear. He touched the still-streaming wound with his left hand. Gently reining his young battle horse back toward the ravine so to minimize the pain of his wound, Smith proceeded at a slow gait.

The Confederate sniper who had wounded Black Hawk was still in a comfortable perch in the trees beyond the field. He now had one last chance to bag a Yankee officer. As he leveled his Whitworth target rifle and closed his left eye, he could see the dreamy silhouette of a horse and rider moving slowly and rhythmically through the smoky battlefield to the woods where the conflict had started. He took a deliberate deep breath and placed his forefinger on the set trigger of the long rifle. Placing the bead from the front site on his prey, he peered once more through the dust of the field to get a clear shot. Blinking once to clear his vision, he blinked once more, and the dark shadow of horse and rider disappeared into the trees.

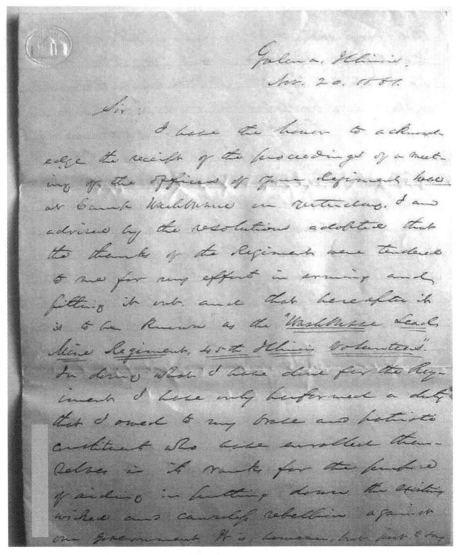

Original Letter
From Congressman Elihu Washburne to Colonel John E. Smith

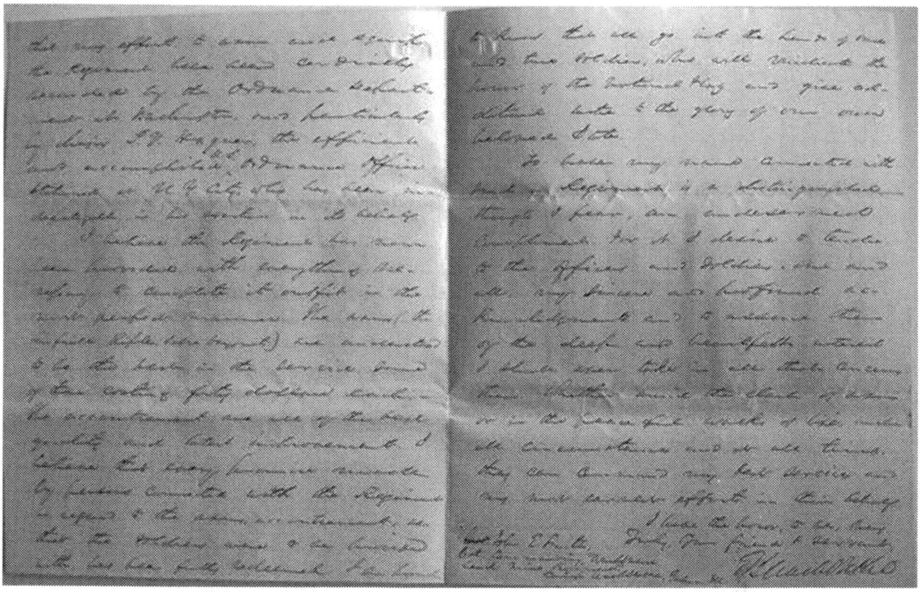

Chapter 24

Camp Near Shiloh

May 3, 1862

Captain Cowan picked up his pen.

It was near midnight now. A flicker of light from a wax candle kept his tent cozy as he prepared to close out the day. He sat in his folding tent chair, which he had positioned by his cot at the back of the tent so as to obtain some sense of privacy as he prepared to write. The candle was embedded in the rifle port of a bayonet that was implanted firmly in the middle of his tent deep in the Tennessee soil. The candle, as centered, cast a perfect glow for his nightly writing projects.

He looked at his own shadow on the tent wall as he dipped his pen in a rosewood ink bottle that his wife, Harriett, had given him the day he headed south with the Forty-Fifth Lead Mine Regiment. It was time to write home again. His thoughts returned to Freeport and his dance with Molly at the Saengerbund Christmas Ball. He thought he should write to the whole family this time: his wife, Harriet; his youngest daughter, Phine; his little boy, Georgie; and, of course, Molly.

Scratching his head with both hands, he then pulled his spectacles from his side pocket. Placing them securely on the bridge of his nose, he looked at the tent ceiling in contemplation. Shifting the blank sheet of paper at an angle on his folding field desk, he put pen to paper.

My dear little Phine:
I am in a great hurry now, I have been writing all day since
I got up. I have to make out pay rolls for the company...
descriptive rolls for all the men that are sick and wounded,
and I have at the same time to attend to company drills,
inspection and all business of the kind and now, since Lt.
Baugher is wounded, I have every bit of the writing to do.

I only weigh about 140 pounds. I lost thirty pounds in
weight in about ten days when I was sick but I believe I
am going to be tough as ever now. We are expecting to be
attacked where we are now; our men are ordered to be ready
all the time, I have just inspected the guns of the company
and furnished cartridges to all, so as to be ready.

George:
Be a good boy 'till I come home. I have a lot of nice
things in my trunk which I intend to give you and Phine
and Molly, which I have picked up on the different battle
fields.

Molly:
I wish you would try to have George learn to read this
summer if he shows any disposition to do it. I don't think it
is best to crowd him too much but if he gets started at it he
will like it better. I feel a great solicitude for all your health
and education.

Harriet:
You need not be uneasy about me...I have never felt
better, and if the bullets don't catch me I think I shall be able
to stand it all right...I have a presentiment that I am not to
be hurt in battle, though ever so much exposed and am not
afraid at all.

It is not worth while to begin to write adventures
now; I will tell them when the War is over. When I can
sit in the corner and spin yarns that will probably not be

believed though ever so true…I don't look upon it to be so
awful to die on the field of battle—those who were wounded
and died soon seemed to care for nothing other than the
safety of their comrades and victory; their last words being
invariably cheering their brother soldiers and telling them
never to give up…

Yours,
L. H. Cowan
Field Shiloh, Tenn.
May 3, 1862 [7]

Cowan laid the pen on the corner of his desk. He could write no more. Grabbing the letter, he placed it on his cot so the ink could dry. Turning back, he bent forward and folded both arms on the desk. He let out a long sigh, buried his face in his sleeves, and nodded off to sleep.

The candle's flame continued to flicker.

Chapter 25

Washburne Home

Washington, DC
Late Spring, 1862

Thousands of Union volunteers continued to pour into Washington for another staging effort to crush the rebellion. Tents were pitched everywhere including the White House lawn, the Washington Monument green, and other public spaces. The shouts of excited sergeants directing marching drills filled the air from dawn to dusk.

Washburne could be found most days stepping through muddy, manured streets or through clouds of dust when the roadways were baked dry. Every day he made routine visits to influential businessmen and politicians around the Capitol Plaza. He was acutely aware of the struggles and privations of his home district's troops and wanted to help them as best he could.

The congressman thought often and fondly about Colonel John E. Smith. Though he had not seen him for months, he had heard of his bravery at Shiloh from letters from Galena and also Union officers who offered up toasts to him at Washington's Willard hotel bar.

As he gazed out from a second-floor window of his small frame house, he could see the Capitol dome still under construction even though the southern states had clearly seceded from the Union. He felt agonized by the thought of it all, and was intrigued, even awed, by Lincoln's mandate to keep the dome moving to completion despite the war.

He picked up his quill, poked it in a small rosewood inkwell, pulled a crisp sheet of linen paper out of his desk, and positioned the paper at its center. He looked out the window at the dome again, thought back to Galena and the boys, and then began to write.

> *House of Representatives*
> *June 20, 1862*
> *Mr. President,*
> *Before the hopper of Brigadier Generals is entirely ground out, I want you to put in one name more, that of the brave and noble John E. Smith, Colonel of the Washburne Leadmine Regiment, 45th Illinois Volunteers. John E. is one of our old friends, and I will undertake to say that there is no regiment in the Service that has done harder and better service than the brave Leadminers. When at Cairo on their way to the Seat of war, they numbered one thousand. The regiment was at Henry and at Donelson, and at Pittsburgh landing (Shiloh) fought with superhuman courage, coming out of that battle with only two hundred forty men fit for service. Between two and three hundred were killed and wounded at that battle...*
>
> *The Forty-fifth Illinois, being the last to fall back, only escaped being surrounded and captured by boldly cutting their way through the closing circle of the enemy's lines and joining the division, under the daring lead of Colonel and Major Smith, of that regiment.*
>
> *It already appears that Col. Smith and Major Smith of the Forty-fifth Illinois, signally distinguished themselves by their exemplary constancy and indomitable courage.*
>
> *We have been entirely overlooked in the northwestern corner of our State. We are so much isolated up there from the other portions of the State; we have never been considered of any account except to spend our money and pile up the majorities. Your friends in*

*Stephenson and Jo Daviess that fought for you in 1858,
in that Senatorial District with desperation never
equaled in the State since you and I have been in politics,
would feel deeply grateful for a recognition by the
appointment of Colonel Smith.*
      I am

*Very Truly
E. B. Washburne* [8]

Washburne laid down his quill. He reached over to a brandy snifter that he kept on his desk and poured a splash into a crystal shot glass. He looked again at the Capitol building. It was dusk. The afternoon shadows lifted now from the grass-laden, mostly muddy field before it, trampled daily by laborers and soldiers. Soon, a vermillion sun seemed to balance itself on top of the dome, hesitate, then descend into a blue-gray sky causing translucent rays to beam through the white columns. He paused for a moment, raised the glass to his lips, then gently placed it down. *The sun will rise again on the Capitol dome tomorrow,* he reflected, *and will always shine brightly on the union of our states.*

It was getting dark now, so he took a last sip, and retired to the small sofa bed by his desk.

Chapter 26

Wigwam

Pecatonica River
Summer, 1862

"Where's Will?" Trick shouted as he passed under the arch of the old Indian oak. T.J., as always, was close by his side.

"He's in town!" Allie replied abruptly. "He's doin' his chores and won't be along right yet. And why haven't ya caught any channel cat yet? Does your cane pole need someone else to hold it?"

"Allie, come on now, you are always getting your digs in me! Can we just be friends today without ya knockin' me around with your words?"

T.J. smiled and looked at Allie, Jenny, and Aaron, who were sitting in the shadows. Aaron shook his head. Jenny giggled.

"Well, Trick, do ya think friends should help friends?" Allie raised her chin and put her hands on her hips, waiting for a response.

"Well, rightly so, Allie. What are you a wantin' me to do?"

"Well, last time I asked you to climb up that tree. Do ya remember?"

"Yes, I do, Allie," Trick replied as he pulled off his wide-brimmed, sweat-stained hat. He rubbed his brow with his sleeve. His cane fishing pole was fixed by his side like a soldier's musket. He continued, "I was fixin' to make it there and back on that Injun oak bow, but got a little wet, you see! I did get the oak leaf for Elmer though!"

"I 'spect that leaf never made it to him," Allie said as she turned away and looked upriver where she and Elmer used to walk. For a moment she felt a tinge of sadness but then caught herself and looked back at Trick. After forcing a smile, she continued. "Well, Mr. Trick, my dear friend, would you mind a climbin' up that Injun oak and tyin' a swingin' rope up there?"

Trick scratched his head and looked at T.J. He then looked at the rest of the friends, shrugged his shoulders, and said, "Sure! I will do anythin' for my wigwam friends."

Handing his cane pole over to T.J., Trick reached down and pulled his britches over his portly belly. "I think I best tighten' up my britches again. I think my brogans will hold like chicken feet this time 'cause the bark on that ol' oak looks akin to climbin' now."

As Trick looked down and pulled his belt tighter, Allie grinned at T.J. and then turned quickly back to the others. She placed her right forefinger on her lips to silence everyone for the moment.

"Well, where's that rope, Allie? These ol' chicken feet are ready!"

"I placed it on the other side of the tree," replied Allie.

Trick nodded, pulled his britches, once again, over the roll of his belly, and waddled confidently to the base of the tree. He looked down at the large roots that secured the oak into the bank but could not see the rope.

"Allie, I'm lookin' where ya told me, but I can't see it. Can ya show me where it is?"

"Sure, Trick," She sauntered to the base of the tree, turned to the friends, and winked.

"I suppose it slipped into the sand down there," Aaron said.

Trick stooped over, peering into the deep water below the Indian oak, his hands on his knees. He looked at T.J., shook his head in disappointment, and then looked at the other friends.

"Oh, there it is!" Allie cried out as she approached him from behind.

"I don't rightly see it!" Trick replied.

"Right there—get closer!" Allie pointed to the water at the base of the tree.

Trick craned his neck and peered deeper into the river. It only took a slight nudge from Allie.

Like a house of cards collapsing, Trick plunged headlong into the Pecatonica River. In a moment he bobbed up like a cork and flapped his arms wildly. The smacking of his arms on the water and the giggles and hoots from the shore echoed down the river.

"Allie, I'm a-gonna git you for this one!" he shouted as he flapped his arms, pulling himself closer to the shore. In a moment he was back by the roots of the old oak.

Allie raced inside the wigwam, laughing all the way. Aaron and Jenny looked at each other and continued to laugh. T.J. shook his head and chuckled as Trick clambered onto the riverbank and jumped to his feet. He disappeared into the wigwam.

"No, no, Trick. No...no," Allie giggled loudly.

Trick emerged from the wigwam with Allie in his arms like a groom carrying his bride. Allie kicked and screamed with a nervous laugh.

"Jenny, Jenny, help me!" Allie cried out as Trick carried her to the water hole.

Jenny jumped up in her petticoat and raced over to cut off Trick before he could toss her into the water. Aaron followed, chuckling all the way.

"Jenny, Aaron, help!" Allie giggled helplessly.

Trick continued his march to the riverbank.

"Come on now, Trick. It was just a joke," Jenny implored. "Put her down. She didn't mean a thing!"

Trick looked at the others with a glint in his eye and smiled. He stood one foot from the drop zone.

Allie extended her hand in one last desperate motion, and Jenny grabbed it.

"OK, you two," Trick warned, "you best let go of her hand, Jenny, or that nice petticoat of yours will end up like a dishrag!"

"No, I'm not letting go," Jenny replied. "Come on now, Trick. It was just a joke!"

Aaron grabbed Jenny's hand. He started to pull all of them back from the river. Jenny with both arms outstretched held on firmly.

"Ya best let go!" screamed Trick lightheartedly. He looked at T.J., who smiled and nodded at his good friend.

"Ya best let go, or I'll take you all into the hole!" he warned again.

Aaron began to pull harder. The girls giggled and screamed.

Trick flexed his muscles, squatted, and leaned toward the river, and like dominoes falling in formation, everyone plunged into the water.

As they emerged, the shouts and hoots echoed again.

"Trick, I'm gonna slap you silly!" Jenny cried out as she gasped for air and slapped the water to pull herself up.

"Hee, hee," Trick shouted back with glee, "your momma's gonna slap ol' Aaron when she sees he couldn't keep you outa this river!"

Aaron waved his arms, grabbed Jenny's hand, and moved to the shore. He gasped for a breath and said, "You got us good, Trick. You got no qualms with me."

"Hee, hee...I suppose Allie won't be a pushin' me, britches and all, in no rivers again!"

Allie dog-paddled over to Trick. She placed her hands securely on his shoulders. "You got me good, Trick. Now, be a good friend and git me back to the wigwam. We best light a fire and git these clothes dry, or we'll be dealin', I 'spect, with Fire Marshal Putnam. That petticoat cost a fine penny, I'm sure!"

After a few more gasps and giggles, the friends moved to the muddy shore. Sand toads hopped away before them. T.J., standing like a sentry on the bank, reached out to each of his friends and pulled them onto the bank with ease.

Suddenly a huge crack of twigs broke the silence just a short distance away, followed by the shout, "Yee hah! Yee hah!"

"That's Will!" Aaron exclaimed.

Within a moment, Will approached the friends, excited and gasping for air. He looked at Allie directly in the eyes, bent over with hands on knees, and then looked up and squinted. "I've got great news, boys!" he said. He looked over and pointed to Jenny. "Jenny, your father is raising a regiment. We're going down south to fight the rebs!"

The friends looked at each other, stunned by Will's announcement.

"There's a meeting this Sunday, where we all can join," he said. "I suspect we will all be officers when it's over. Jenny, your father will be the colonel of a thousand men strong. Men from Jo Daviess, Rockford, Stephenson, and other counties are joining as fast as they can. If we don't join now, the war will be over!"

"Stop!" Allie cried out. Tears welled in her eyes. "You ain't gonna fight no rebels. You put on that fancy blue uniform, and it gits you killed, like Elmer!

The friends fell silent. T.J. broke the awkward pause. He raised his rifle above his head. "Well, I'm not gonna miss this war. Elmer would want us to go. And I 'spect we will."

"Please don't go! Please don't go!" Allie begged. Her hands began to shake noticeably.

Will reached down, grabbed them, and pulled her closer to his bosom.

"Allie, it is our duty to go," he said calmly. "If we don't fight this war, who else will?"

Allie began to sob. Soon Jenny's eyes welled up. She placed her face in her hands and cried, too. Aaron put his arms around her as well.

The friends moved slowly into the wigwam. T.J. struck up a fire that cast strange shadows on the wall. Allie looked down at the medicine bag and tomahawk resting on the wall and stared at the fire. As tears slowly streaked down her cheeks, she looked at each of the friends and then stared back at the crackling fire. Looking up at the light in the cave ceiling, she recited an old Irish adage that Gramma Lucy had taught her, "Here's to good-byes—may they never be spoken. And here's to friendships—may they never be broken."

The friends peered into the flames and wondered what tomorrow would bring.

Chapter 27

Captain Cowan Home

Warren, Illinois
Near the Apple River
July, 1862

The dark hickory floor creaked as Harriet Cowan prepared morning bread for the family. Her children in the cabin loft peeked out from beneath their bed covers and then retreated, pulling the covers back over their shaggy heads. The cock-a-doodle-doo of a rooster shattered the silence. Morning was here.

"Time for chores, children!"

"No, Ma!" little Georgie replied as he wiggled himself deeper into the mattress. The bed ropes groaned from the movement.

"Georgie, put your boots on. It's a beautiful day. I need you to get four eggs from the chicken coop." Harriet reached over and grabbed her husband's favorite hat, lifting it up to the loft. "Here, Georgie, take your father's hat with you, and come back quickly. The embers are up in the fireplace."

George pushed up from the bed. Rolling to his right, he reached down and grabbed the tie strings of his boots. Continuing his roll, he dropped his shins over the sideboard; sat up; and pulled his boots up, lacing them snugly.

"What about the girls, Ma? Why don't they get up first? Ever since that big ball in Freeport last Christmas, Molly thinks she's a fairy princess or something!"

"Georgie, just go get the eggs!" Molly said, her voice muffled by her the covers.

Harriet looked at the loft again, placed her hands on her hips and stomped her foot on the floor. "Molly and Phine will be cooking, scrubbing, and cleaning today! Fairy princesses they are not!"

The girls wiggled themselves deeper under the covers. George stomped his boots in a deliberate, step-by-step march out the front door. His exit was followed by a squeak and a thud from the large oak door.

Molly thought back to the Saengerbund Ball at Christmastime in Freeport, where she first met Jenny Putnam and danced all evening with Alfred Smith—the graceful gowns and the continuous waltzes and dancing partners that swirled gently across the ballroom floor. She thought again of Alfred in his West Point uniform with shiny buttons that reflected light from the grand old chandeliers. She remembered how he looked at her with each magic turn, holding the small of her back firmly in his right hand.

Her memory then shifted to her father. The thought of him, and then a sharp twinge of sadness caused her to spring from the covers, sit up, and quickly head down the loft ladder to her mother.

"Mother, I fear for Father," she said.

Phine, hearing Molly's remark, bounced up from the bed and looked down from the loft rail. She said nothing.

The door creaked open, and George sauntered in with the eggs in a hat. He looked concerned.

"What's wrong, Georgie?" Harriet beckoned as she approached him.

George handed the hat filled with fresh eggs over to his mother, looking down at his feet as he completed the motion.

"The postmaster is coming down the lane," he replied softly.

"So what!" Phine replied in giddy tone.

George looked up at Phine and then at Molly and his mother. "Last time I heard of the postmaster coming out all the way to someone's house was when Lieutenant Sheetz was killed."

"Oh my God!" screamed Molly as she raced to the door and pulled it open. In a flash Phine climbed from the loft, and they all moved out the door, standing in a huddle on the doorstep. Molly and Phine sniffled and hugged their mother. George separated himself from the three and headed up the lane.

About fifty yards down the lane, the postmaster extended his right hand to shake hands with George, pulling a letter from a leather delivery pouch. His voice was strong, and his pronouncement carried itself to within earshot of the front stoop.

"Hello, George!" he announced. "I have a letter for Molly here. It is from her father! But I bet it's for all of you!"

"Gracious God!" Harriet sighed as she looked at her smiling and relieved daughters. "Thank you, sir," she called out respectfully to the postmaster. "Georgie, bring that to us now!"

George shook hands with the postmaster again, turned toward the house, and kicked up dust as he ran back to the house with the letter. Arriving at the door stoop, he bolted by the girls and headed to the kitchen table.

"I'll open this!" he exclaimed with glee.

"No, Georgie, it's addressed to me!" Molly replied.

"Give the letter to Molly," added Harriet. "It's addressed to her. Phine got the last one. The next one will be addressed to you."

"All right," replied George, grinning as he extended his hand with the precious letter. "Oh, here you go 'cause I can't read like you anyway. But someday I will. You wait and see!"

Harriet, Phine, and George circled around Molly as she pulled a chair to the table. The embers in the fireplace began to lose their luster, but breakfast could wait. Molly reached over for a table knife that was neatly wrapped with a fork and spoon in a linen napkin. She pulled the fold of the napkin causing the utensils to clang on the surface of the table. Gently holding the envelope with her left hand, she slipped the blade of the knife through the crease at one end and carefully cut it open, exposing the edge of the letter. After pulling the letter out, she unfolded it so all could see.

"Wow, this is a long letter!" she announced with a smile. "Should I read the whole thing now, or should we wait?"

"Come on!" Phine and George replied in unison.

Molly glanced at her mother, smiled, and then proudly read her father's letter

> *Jackson, Tenn. June 21, 1862*
> *My Dear Molly,*
> *Your letter of the 13th I received today; I am much pleased*
> *with it too—I just read it to Capt. Healy, one of my best*
> *friends, he says it is a very nice letter. I am glad to learn*
> *that you are all so well and enjoying yourselves…I am glad*
> *you are getting along in your studies, also…You must not be*
> *discouraged at the size and number of books you will have to*
> *master…for you are yet young and when you grow old you*
> *will look back upon the time spent in study as being the most*
> *happy of your life.*
>
> *…friend Null today says there is great preparation*
> *being made for the 4th of July Celebration. I am glad that*
> *the patriotic people of Warren are mindful of their ancient*
> *Patriotic practice and do not let it die out…*
>
> *Wish you could see our army on parade, it is*
> *magnificent. I do not wonder that Xerxes cried when*
> *he looked upon this great army with which he invaded*
> *Greece. The display of a great army is so great, so*
> *magnificent that it is almost sufficient to overwhelm ones*
> *soul to look and reflect upon it. I believe it is the general*
> *opinion that the profession of a soldier hardens the heart*
> *and dulls the sympathies. No opinion can be further from*
> *the correct one. I have seen more real kindness shown*
> *among the officers and soldiers since I have been in the*
> *army than I ever saw in all my life before. I would not*
> *wish for you to see a battle fought by two armies but*
> *wish you could see the armies just as they look when*

they go to battle, nothing could be more magnificent. There you could see what it is to be a man. You could see in the countenances of the officers on whom rest the responsibilities of the plans of the battle, all the anxiety and care that it is possible to conceive of. While they sit as firm as iron on their impatient horses watching every movement of the enemy, they encourage and advise the subordinate officers on whom lies the more inordinate responsibility of executing the orders. There you could see the anxious looks of the soldiers as they stand firmly in their places, glancing their eyes along their own lines now to the right, now to the left, and then again to their officers, all the while grasping their guns firmly and wishing for the beginning of the contest—anxious to show to their comrades and to the world their manhood.

Now to think that these men feel savage or barbarious at such a time is another error that people are apt to get into, for at this very time, when a man feels that he would almost be glad to die in battle and would not feel danger, this is the very time that he feels the most generous and kindly impulses of which his nature is capable. I have seen many an eye full of tears and the heart too full to allow a word to be uttered, when the sense of danger did no more enter the mind than if there was no such thing in existence.

People are apt to think too that because soldiers fare roughly that they don't care for the sick and the suffering. It is not because we do not feel for our sick, that we do not make more fuss over a dying soldier. We are willing to help one another when we can, but when an order comes we must go and leave them in comfortable circumstances or not. I have seen hundreds of men tire out and lie down when we have been on marches, some faint and cannot walk, they must be left behind. We don't leave or pass such men with

*light hearts, but our business and duty requires that we
should, compels us to leave them and we do it and feel at the
same time infinitely more tenderly about it than many who
make a great fuss about barbarism of the army.*

*I could write about hundreds of incidents of this and
like incidents which would bring tears to the eyes of any
man who had a heart in him. Many a time may be seen
men turning and going away and saying nothing, but the
hanging head, the constrained and harried step, and a great
many other signs show plainly enough the commotions of
their heart.*

Write to me soon...

In all kindness,
Your Father, L. H. Cowan [9]

Molly read the last paragraph slowly as if it would keep the words of
her father from ending. When she finished, she did not look up. Folding
the letter gently at the seams, she tucked it back in the envelope where
it had been secured on its long road north. Placing it on the table, she
turned and walked toward the door. Phine and George followed in silence. The door squeaked open, and the familiar thud echoed across the
room again as the three stepped outside.

Harriet turned to the table, picked up the envelope, and held it to
her lips and kissed it gently. A tear slipped down her cheek and spot-
ted the ink, but it did not run. She then placed the letter on the mantel
above the fireplace where the other letter was kept when it arrived after
the battle of Shiloh.

Looking back to the table, she reached over to her husband's hat,
which held the eggs George had collected. She reached into the crown
and deftly grabbed three of the four with her right hand. Grabbing the
heavy lead pan with her left, she stooped down to the fireplace.

The embers had died out.

Chapter 28

Freeport

August, 1862

The silhouettes of three riders could be seen in the distance as they moved slowly, almost deliberately, down Chicago Street. The two on the right were dressed in dark-blue coats. They rode light-colored horses. The rider on the left was short on the saddle and wore a white waistcoat. His big black mount towered above the other two horses.

As they got closer to the town center, their images got larger and more defined. Within moments they crossed Washington, Jackson, and Spring Streets, following the sound of the town band, which alternated a continuous play of "Yankee Doodle Dandy" and "Rally 'Round the Flag."

A large crowd had gathered again on the green near the Brewster House, where the Lincoln-Douglas debates had occurred during the same sweltering month four years earlier. Like before, Allie was up in the boughs of the large oak at the edge of the shady grove that offered the best shade and a good view of the activity around her. She swung her small feet to the commanding beat of the music.

"Jenny, come on up here now! I can see the riders a comin'! You best git up here before the boys take your spot!"

Jenny looked up at Allie and replied, "Allie, if I tear this petticoat, my mother would not speak to me again. Besides, my father says ladies don't climb trees."

"Well, you can tell your father the fire marshal or any of them fancy boys that this lady does!" she shouted back with a smirk and a smile. She continued to peer through the branches at the approaching riders.

A familiar voice intruded. "Allie, well, by jiminy, how'd you git up there?"

Allie almost slipped from the tree. The distraction caught her by surprise, and she chimed back in her usual fashion, "Like I always do, Trick. I climbed it. Somethin' you just can't seem to do. Not here, not there, not even on the Injun oak tree by our wigwam!"

"Well, you best slide over 'cause the boys with their chicken feet will be here soon! I will best wait for them so they can hike me up to that little branch over there!"

"There ain't no little branch that could hold you, Trick!" Allie responded. She paused again. Her countenance lost its glow, and she turned solemn. "Is Will comin' up from the river, too?"

"You can bet on it, Allie. He will be one of the first to join Fire Marshal Putnam's regiment!" Trick replied as he pulled off his wide-brimmed hat and grabbed his belt. He pulled the loop up and over his wide belly with one hand and rubbed his sweaty brow on his sleeve. Allie remained silent as the strains of "Yankee Doodle" carried across the grove.

The riders were on the green now and turned in a deliberate motion to the oak tree.

"The riders are a comin' this way. And look at them dandy mounts! Why, I never seen such a thing!" he said excitedly. Then, pointing at the large black horse, he said, "That big one is the biggest I ever seen!"

It was Black Hawk he pointed to. Ben Smith, the short rider in the white waistcoat was sixteen years old now and still small for his age. He pulled on his reins when he reached the shade of the oak tree, sitting in his saddle as straight as a cavalry officer.

"Good day, ladies and gentlemen," announced the officer on a white horse as he and his companion pulled up beside Ben. "My name is Colonel John E. Smith. I am from Galena. This is my son, Ben."

On the nearby speaker's platform, the band paused in its playing. An anticipatory hush came over the crowd.

"I would also like to introduce you to Captain Ely Parker, who is on my staff. He is an engineer from New York State. Some of you may know him from his building projects in Galena."

Captain Parker nodded gracefully to those around him. His dark skin had gotten even darker from exposure since that hot August five years ago when he brought Black Hawk to Galena. The many months of outdoor work on the Fever and Mississippi Rivers had caused deep lines to form on his Indian countenance. He still sported his long moustache and chin whiskers.

"Has anyone seen Fire Marshal Putnam today?" Colonel Smith asked.

"Well, this is his daughter!" said Trick enthusiastically.

"Well, young lady," Smith replied with a smile," you must be very proud of your father for raising a new regiment."

"She don't know what these boys are gittin into!" came a bold reply from the boughs. The crowd looked up at Allie and then back at the general. A few ladies gasped and put their hands to their mouths.

"Well, hello, young lady. What is your name?" replied Colonel Smith with a glint in his eye.

"My name is Allie. I'm from the Rock River."

"Well, I haven't had the pleasure to meet many young ladies who look down on me from treetops, but, nonetheless, it is certainly a pleasure to make your acquaintance," replied Smith gallantly. "And if I may ask, what do you know of the war we are having with the rebels?"

Allie crossed her legs and placed her hand on the trunk as she replied directly, "Well, Colonel, with all a respectin' due, my best friend, who wore one of those fancy uniforms with them shiny new buttons, stood right where you are now. He was with Alfred Smith who saved the town from a burnin' down 'bout five years ago. But I suppose that Smith ain't no relation to you!"

Allie waited for a response from the handsome colonel, erect in his saddle. With none forthcoming, she continued. "Well, they left after the Lincoln debate, and I never seen either of them again. I don't know where Alfred is now, but I suppose he is down south somewhere. Elmer Ellsworth became a fancy colonel back east. He got kilt by a rebel, and Mr. Lincoln cried, they say, when he heard the news. See, he was like a big brother to the Lincoln boys. He was a big brother to me, too, especially when we walked the Rock River huntin' muskrats and frogs. I wish he never put that fancy uniform on. I can still see Elmer and Alfred standin' right there." She then pointed to a shady spot on the ground at the feet of the riders.

Shocked by her words, the crowd was stone-cold silent. Allie realized that the whirlwind of her words had been heard and hit the mark.

"Miss Allie, I thank you for your honesty," Colonel Smith replied in a fatherly tone. "I want to first tell you that Alfred is safe. I know this to be true because he is my son and I received a letter from him just yesterday. He has just recently taken command of an honorable black regiment. He is training his men to arm themselves and fight for freedom, like many of us who have volunteered to save the Union. Ben and I pray every day for his safe return to Galena."

The listeners around the large oak turned their attention to Allie.

"Well, why don't *he* command that regiment? He is a Negro," replied Allie as she pointed to Captain Parker. "Why don't *he* do it, so Alfred can come home?"

Parker rose up in his saddle as straight as an arrow. The leather saddle and his boots creaked. He smiled and looked directly at Allie as the band struck up "Rally 'Round the Flag" again.

"Young lady, I am quite pleased to meet you. I see that you are not afraid to speak your mind even in the company of men. Perhaps we should all be as direct on matters of war and matters of death. I am a Seneca Indian. I am not a black man, although the plight of the Negro and Indian to me is the same. There are people across this land who say the Negroes who have toiled in the fields down south and Indians who have roamed freely in their territories are not free to live with white Americans. I fight for the union of the states so that we all will be free someday. Your friend Colonel Ellsworth was killed pulling down a rebel flag in Alexandria, Virginia. His action defined our purpose. You are very special to have had such a patriot as your friend. We hope there are others among you who will become patriots, too, for our noble cause. God bless all of you, and God bless the Union."

His comments complete, Parker smiled and tipped his hat to Allie like a Virginia gentleman. Allie nodded back, and the band struck up "Yankee Doodle Dandy" again.

Colonel Smith looked over at Black Hawk and said, "Ben, would you please hold Black Hawk's reins for a moment? Captain Parker and I must go to the reviewing stand with Fire Marshal Putnam."

"Yes, Father," replied Ben as he nodded respectfully.

Smith and Parker pulled off their wide-brimmed black campaign hats. Extending their hats to the sky, they dropped them simultaneously to their breasts. Placing the hats back on their crowns, they tipped the brim, turned from the trees, and spurred their mounts back to the reviewing stand.

"What are those spots on the captain's horse?" Trick asked as he pointed to the rump of Parker's horse.

"That's an Appaloosa," Ben replied. "It's an Indian war pony."

"Wow, by jiminy, I never seen such beauties. Where did you git this big black one?" Trick reached for Black Hawk's reins. Black Hawk snorted and stomped, causing Trick to pull back in alarm.

"That's all right," Ben said soothingly, stroking Black Hawk's neck. Then, looking at Trick, he said, "You can pet him on the snout there."

Trick stepped closer and rubbed Black Hawk's nose and glanced at his large fidgety eyes. He moved his hands along Black Hawk's mane, rubbing Black Hawk on the chest. He noticed a long scar. "How'd he get that?" Trick asked, pointing to it.

Allie, Jenny, and those around them looked at Ben with interest.

"My father rode him at Shiloh," Ben proudly replied. "He was shot by a sniper during the battle, but that didn't stop him at all. My father rode him down the length of the field and damn near captured the whole rebel army!" Ben, realizing he was getting caught up in the moment, paused with some embarrassment and then continued. "Well sorry for the 'd' word, but I know Black Hawk did help round up a hundred rebels, and our Illinois boys stood their ground."

Trick stepped closer to Black Hawk's side. He gently stroked the scar with his right hand. Black Hawk snorted again as if comforted by the movement.

"Will he ever go back to battle?"

"Yes, he will," Ben responded enthusiastically. "My father is giving him to Fire Marshal Putnam today as a gift for raising the Freeport men. That is why I am holding him here for now. We want it to be a surprise for him, just like when Captain Parker brought him to our family in Galena when he was just a pony four years ago. Black Hawk was the little pony that a couple Freeport boys saved from the fire! We've been riding him ever since. He's as good as they get. He's a good Indian stallion and loves to jump creeks and swim the rivers."

"Did you say he was the little black pony from the Freeport fire?"

"Yes. My brother, Alfred, said Captain Parker gave a gold coin to a stable boy to board him for a while in Freeport, and about Christmastime the fire broke out, and Black Hawk was rescued by two boys. I don't know who they are though."

"Hee, hee…you kiddin' me? Why, those would be my good friends Will and Aaron who rescued Black Hawk. And my other friend T.J. was the boy who shot the powder kegs on top of the belfry to put out the fire!" Trick grinned.

"Well," said the surprised Ben, "now I know why my father wishes to give his prized war-horse to Fire Marshal Putnam. Wow. And Alfred was in the tower with T.J., too! We are so proud of you boys," replied Ben. He felt a sense of brotherhood with Trick now and continued to talk about the horses.

As they talked, Allie slipped unnoticed down the oak tree and walked over to Jenny. She grabbed both of Jenny's hands and looked into her eyes. "Let's go to the wigwam, Jenny," she said. "I don't want to be here when Will, Aaron, and T.J. arrive."

"But my mother is expecting me here, Allie," replied Jenny. "Besides, I want to be here when Colonel Smith gives Black Hawk to my father."

Allie looked at Jenny once more and then turned away, making her way through the crowd and to the Pecatonica River.

"Allie, wait for us!" cried Jenny, puzzled. "Colonel Smith said Alfred is OK...that's good news for Molly Cowan! Molly may even be here today. I'd like you to meet her. She's taken a liking to Alfred. Please let's go find her together! Allie, come back, now. Did you hear what I said? Alfred is all right! He's still alive! The boys, if they join the regiment, will only be in for just a little while!"

But Allie didn't respond. Instead she kept walking.

Jenny started to cup her hands around her mouth so her shouts would carry farther, but she stopped when an older lady nearby glared at her. Looking one last time for Allie, who had disappeared into the crowd, she grasped the front of her petticoat so as not to catch it on the tips of her fancy shoes from Paris and hurried back to the shady oak.

The rousing song "Battle Cry of Freedom" carried through the afternoon air and rose grandly as the volunteer boys from Freeport and the neighboring towns joined the chorus. Townspeople also joined in. Children waved tiny flags as women smiled and nodded to the boys as they peeked from behind their fans. The patriotic crescendo rose over the crowded square, across the nearby field, and over the yellow grasses that lined the Pecatonica, as if chasing Allie, beckoning her to return to town.

But Allie kept her pace and did not turn back.

Chapter 29

Freeport

One Week Later
August, 1862

The boys stood tall under the big oak tree at the shady grove.

A week had passed by swiftly. Will was the tallest, just about six feet now. His sandy-blond hair contrasted smartly under his new blue kepi. On the top of the crown was a "93" that was fastened smartly within the curl of a large brass bugle pin. He and the others were officially mustered into Fire Marshal Putnam's new Union regiment. They were soldiers now, privates in the Ninety-Third Illinois Volunteer Infantry.

Aaron, as always, was by Will's side. His green eyes shifted nervously. T.J. Lockwood was next in line but without his trusty rifle. He felt almost naked without it. He looked at the treetop as a squirrel scurried across a limb and leaped to the safety of its nest. Beside him was Trick, still short, stout, and slovenly even in his new uniform. Somehow it just didn't hang well on him. His belly hung over the oval "US" brass belt plate that kept his britches from falling to his ankles. His pants were too long and flopped in rolls over his black military boots. When he walked, the pants dragged at his heels. The uniform caused him to sweat profusely as he always did on hot summer days, but the sweat stains blended into the blue. His hat was not like the others. He had chosen a black wide-brimmed felt campaign hat similar to the white hat he always wore on the river. This hat, though, stood taller at the crown, almost like a big chimney stack. On the front were the same pins, the number "93," and the bugle like the others had. Though awkward in appearance, he, too, was a soldier in Mr. Lincoln's army. He felt a sense of pride deep in his broad and bulging chest. He grinned at his friends and then looked towards the Pecatonica River. He wished he had his cane pole in a deep hole just one last time.

"Boys, do ya see who's coming out of the trees?" he exclaimed in excitement. "Well, by jiminy, it's Allie and Jenny comin' toward us from the wigwam!"

Will stood erect and peered over Trick, holding him on the shoulders as if using him for a brace. Aaron moved up quickly to his side.

T.J. squinted. "Looks like they got somethin' in their hands," he said slowly. "Well, we'll be seein' soon what they'll be bringin' this way."

There was music in the air, causing the boys to look to the rickety wooden reviewing stand where they had enlisted the week before. A marching band was planted in chairs on it playing "Rally 'Round the Flag." It was Fire Marshal Putnam's signal to come join the ranks before leaving town. Now colonel of the Ninety-Third Illinois Volunteer Infantry, he proudly reined in Black Hawk, who spurred forward and lunged in from the noise and excitement of the gathering crowd.

In the distance the friends could see the gathering of blue-clad recruits advancing around the reviewing stand. All of them were thinking it was time to join their regiment, yet they did not move because the girls were coming to see them one last time. Rousing lyrics filled the August air as Jenny and Allie walked through the high grass toward the shady oak. In a moment both girls arrived solemn and silent.

"Well, ladies, I 'spect you're a comin' here to wish us a farewell and give us a good kiss!" shouted Trick who grinned ear to ear.

"Trick, why don't ya keep those smackers quiet right now," Allie replied in a huff. "Jenny and I came here to see our sweethearts, not you!"

A chastened Trick looked down at his shiny new boots, then scooted quickly over to the oak tree where T.J. stood, ramrod-straight as a sentry. There was silence as the girls walked up to Will and Aaron. Then Jenny spoke softly.

"We have something for you."

"What is it?" Will and Aaron asked simultaneously.

Allie moved closer to Will. She gazed into his sky-blue eyes, admiring how handsome he looked in his smart blue-clad uniform. She could see that his brass buttons on his waistcoat flickered brilliantly even in the shade.

"Will, I don't want you to go to this war," she said softly, "and Jenny don't want Aaron to go neither." She stopped to see what reaction she would get.

Both Will and Aaron remained silent.

"Well, if ya must go with good Colonel Putnam, ya got to promise us you'll stay away from harm's way. Do ya promise?" she pleaded softly.

Again there was silence. Jenny blushed and then added, "Well, we brought you some branches from the wigwam. We want you to keep them with you for good luck."

"The leaves from the Injun oak stand for courage. Remember we picked one for Elmer?" replied Jenny as she smiled gently. "The holly branch stands for eternal love. Its berries are red...and the leaves are deep, dark, and forever green!"

The silence was awkward again.

"Give us your kepis," Jenny said softly.

Will looked at Aaron this time, caught his glance, and then reached for his kepi. Aaron followed in fashion. Both boys delivered them to the girls.

Jenny handed a sprig of holly and an oak leaf to Allie who quickly pulled back the stiff leather crown strap of the kepi. She placed the sprig and the leaf to the left of the brim and secured it smartly.

"Bend down, Will," she said softly.

When he had done so, she said in a voice loud enough for the friends to hear, "This oak is for courage on the field of battle. The holly represents my heart!" She put his kepi on his head, embraced him tightly, and then kissed Will on the lips for a moment that seemed to last an eternity.

Will pulled gently away as the music struck up again in the distance. He held her small hands and gazed at her as if in a dream. Allie pulled him closely to her again and placed her lips near his left ear. "I will love you always, Will," she whispered softly so no one could hear. "You best keep this holly close to your heart when you lie down your head at night. I will be with you always."

As she finished, the cadence of the marching band struck up to a faster beat. The band played "The Girl I Left Behind Me" now, and a pistol shot echoed in the distance. It was Captain Taggart, the former sheriff of Freeport, calling all the boys to muster. Allie's eyes welled up as she looked once more at Will. A single tear trickled down her cheek. It hovered for a moment at her jaw and then dropped to the dust.

Aaron turned to Jenny who was flustered at the thought of kissing Aaron in front of the others. He bent forward as Will had, and Jenny placed the cap gently on his head. She kissed Aaron on the cheek, blushed again, and looked down at the ground.

Aaron spoke gently, "Thank you, Jenny. I will treasure these gifts 'til I come home again."

Another pistol shot rang through the air.

"Well, we best be moving along," Will said quickly.

"Wait!" Allie shouted as she pounced quickly to the oak tree where Trick and T.J. were standing silently.

"T.J., where's your rifle?" she asked.

"Left it home, missy," he replied. "Won't do much good shootin' squirrels down south. They are givin' us Enfields muskets, which arc better."

"So I 'spect you'll be shootin' a lot of turtledoves down south!" Allie replied softly.

"No, Allie, we'll be shootin' men!" He twisted his head in a curious way. His kepi tipped on his head. He balanced it back into position with both hands.

Allie said. "Well, ya told us in the wigwam that when you shoot one dove, you might as well kill the other 'cause those birds are married for life. You'll be shootin' wives and sweethearts if you shoot those boys!"

The silence was interrupted by another pistol shot. The band now played "Yankee Doodle Dandy" at a fast and furious pace, causing the crowd of blue around the reviewing stand to form into a semblance of a regiment. Colonel Putnam moved to and fro as if herding the remaining recruits into a military formation.

Allie reached to Jenny. "Give me the oak leaves," she said softly. Plucking two out of Jenny's hand, she asked T.J. to bend down so she could reach his kepi. She pulled his crown strap back and placed the leaf snugly in place and then kissed him on the cheek.

She then turned to Trick, who blushed and started shuffling his boots in the dust. As they were about the same height, he didn't have to bend down. His large black campaign hat had no band on it, just the "93" pin and the bugle badge. He pulled off his hat, exposing his sweaty brow.

"Allie, I'll place the leaf in here," Trick said as he pulled back the sweatband inside his hat. "This'll keep it rightly from the sun and rain." He looked down at the dusty road again. She hesitated a moment, as if to turn away, and then kissed Trick on one cheek…then the other. She said nothing and then turned back to Will.

"Best be off now!" Will announced, his voice choked with emotion.

Allie grabbed his hand, wanting to delay the moment of parting as long as possible. Will kept his grip as long as he could, then let go just before they were to join the ranks of soldiers. The four boys then blended into the dark-blue mass.

Allie and Jenny watched the spectacle grandly march by. Shouts and exclamations by officers punctured the air. The several recruited companies now formed as the marching band moved to the front of the blue ranks. Colonel Putnam rode Black Hawk to the front of the volunteers as Taggart took to the ground, marching to the front on the left side of the Freeport company.

Putnam then shouted out the order to march. With that, the boys followed in step while the band played, not walking in military-drill step, but more of a saunter as if in a Fourth of July parade. When they reached Galena Street, the crowd grew into a throng as children and old folks waved tiny flags and even handed baked bread to the boys. The spectacle caused all the volunteers to feel a sense of pride as the excitement welled up in their breasts.

Jenny and Allie ran as fast as they could to get beyond the crowd to the other side, where the road led to Rockford. They got to the intersection of Broadway and State and positioned themselves under the shade of a small cherry tree.

The band was approaching, followed by the undulating blue mass.

As they got within earshot, Allie cupped her hands over her mouth. She looked to and fro, trying to get a familiar glimpse of the boys. She could see no one. The block of men continued down State Street.

"Friends of the wigwam! We love you!" she shouted.

A few strangers in the back ranks turned, smiled, and waved, but none of the friends could be seen.

The band struck up the familiar camp-break song "To the Girl I Left Behind Me," causing more unfamiliar faces in the ranks to glance at the girls.

As the rousing song diminished with the blue ranks vanishing in the distance, Allie turned to Jenny and then back to the departing soldiers.

"What's wrong, Allie? You look like you're thinking about things," Jenny said.

"I am a prayin' that the good Lord takes care of the boys with that promise he made in the Bible. Remember our verse from the Good Book. The verse we pray anytime we welcome a new friend of the wigwam. Li'l Joe and Blue were the last."

"Yes, I do, Allie. It is a special verse."

Allie looked, again, down State Street and then turned to Jenny and grabbed her hand. The music had stopped; only rising dust remained. In a sad, solemn tone, she looked to the distant clouds and said, "I will not forget you. I have carved you on the palm of my hand."

Chapter 30

Camp of the Forty-Fifth Illinois

Lead Mine Regiment
September 2, 1862

Captain Cowan braced his back against the corner of a cotton bale. The sun had crossed to midpoint in the sky. The smell of confined soldiers filled the air. There was a pause in the action, which caused anxiety to fill the air like a penetrating stench. Cowan thought this a time to quickly write home again.

After settling against the bale, he balanced his cherry lap desk on his knees. As he lifted the dusty cover, a cannon shot roared in the distance, causing him to flinch. The small desk flipped to the ground, exposing linen sheets of paper, his pen, and the rosewood inkwell that the children had given him months ago. He righted it again, this time securing it between his knees in anticipation of the next distant shot. Securing the cover again, he dipped the tip of his pen in the well, which he held in his left hand, and then looked up to the sky, in which danced puffy white clouds. He thought of Harriet and the children, who often took long family walks, and how Harriet would direct their attention to the sky, instructing them to use their imagination to see the shapes of sheep or other figures in the clouds. Another cannon report cracked in the distance, causing him to jump again. Dipping his pen quickly in the inkwell, he hurried to write his message.

Toones Station, Tenn.
Sept. 2, 1862
2 p.m.
Dear Harriet,
We are five companies of the 45th Regt. cut off from communication with Jackson both by telegraph and Railroad... The news is heard from every quarter, we don't know what will become of us... We are well fortified with cotton bales, two hundred ten fighting men. We can hold the place against any number of infantry that can be sent against us, but if they get us with artillery, they will surely clean us out...

We are under the command of Col. Maltby and every man feels like sustaining the reputation of the Regiment for fighting, achieved at Fort Donaldson [sic] and Shiloh. There is but little doubt but we will have to fight in all probability ten times our number but the number makes no difference, we intend to fight. No force can scare us to surrender. A bloodless victory will never be gained over our regiment, not any part of it...

Say to the new soldiers to come ahead, we need their help as we ever will—everything looks gloomy but we are not discouraged. If we die here we will die like soldiers, if I do not live to write you again...

The worst thing that we have to contend with is the feeling of anxiety, when we can hear the fight going with such odds against us, but cannot be with them. Do the best you can with the children, tell them they will be my last care. If they will be good, God will supply their necessities. I hope they will be honest, speak the truth on all occasions and put their trust in Him. You need not think from this advice that I am scared. I am not and never felt better in my life, but I don't intend to run nor hide in a fight and am fully aware what might happen.

I came here Saturday, left the things you sent me at Jackson.

Will probably never see them again.

As ever,
L. H. Cowen [10]

Suddenly, a cannonball exploded nearby. Cowan's lap desk pitched, and the inkwell fell by his boots. The black ink quickly disappeared into the red Tennessee soil.

Chapter 31

Camp of the Ninety-Third Illinois

Western Tennessee
Autumn, 1862

The swirling smoke of hundreds of campfires filled the valley.

General Grant's army had pushed deeper south. Union regiments from the upper Midwest and the thousands of soldiers that complemented them moved together like a small vibrant city on the march.

The soldiers rested now after many hours of drilling in the hot southern sun. The buzz of talk was punctured by the staccato notes of a bugle announcing evening mess call. Time for their ration of salt pork, hardtack biscuits, and coffee.

"Sure would like to trade this hish and hash for some of that good ol' hog and hominy," Trick said as a thick chunk of salt pork skewered on his long bayonet dripped fat on their small campfire. "This pork ain't from a pig. I betcha it comes from some other critter...maybe an ol' black bear or somethin'."

T.J. smiled and looked at Will and Aaron. The four friends of the wigwam were still together. The journey south had been uneventful thus far. The constant drilling had made them very hungry today.

Trick rolled the salt pork closer to the flame, inspecting every inch with a chef's critical eye. A drop of fat caused the fire to flare with a hiss.

"Trick, the way you're looking at that piece on that toad-sticker of yours makes me believe you wouldn't trade it for all the tea in China," said Will. The boys chuckled.

"Well, a soldier's got to eat," Trick replied with his usual grin. He pulled the piece close to his lips and hesitated a moment as another drip landed on his waistcoat. Rubbing it away with his left hand, he proceeded to open his mouth, exposing his teeth like two long rows of piano keys. He bit down. Suddenly howling in pain, he dropped the food-laden bayonet, which landed on the log he was using as a seat, and began hopping around, hands over his mouth. The boys laughed loudly. Soldiers from nearby campsites craned their necks and looked at them in curiosity.

"By jiminy, that sucker is hot!" screamed Trick as he continued to hop around the fire.

"You damn fool!" someone shouted.

"What's the alarm?" came another.

"Quit kickin' up the dust, or we'll tie you down!"

Trick sat down beside the bayonet, holding his mouth with his left hand.

"You all right, Trick?" Aaron asked in amusement.

"Yeah, did you burn your smackers?" laughed Will. "Why didn't you just use your tinplate to cool it down?"

"I 'spected to place it on my cracker, but couldn't find it," Trick replied, ruefully.

"Well, why didn't you use your plate over there?" Will countered.

Trick stood up and wiped the fat from his hands onto his blue trousers. "'Cause I'm savin' it for a contest!" he replied.

"What are you talkin' about?" T.J. asked. "You gonna use it for a target? Why, you can't hit nothing with that ol' forty-two Springfield. That ol' pumpkin slinger couldn't hit that plate at ten paces! There are boys here with target rifles that would win with a blindfold on."

"Well, friends, I reckon I can take a few pennies from those loud-mouths over there right now. In fact, I gotta keep my plate clean so the contest will be a good one."

"What are you talking about, Trick?" replied Will.

Trick stood up again slowly and pointed toward the shadowy figures from where the shouts had come. "I 'spect I'll be takin' a few pennies from those boys when we finish our mess. I gotta damn good beetle down here that can race faster than any Yankee beetle ever could!" Trick looked back at the friends for a response.

Will, Aaron, and T.J. looked at each other in puzzlement and then turned to Trick.

"Bet you're wondering how I can beat them with a little ol' beetle?"

"Yes!" they replied.

Trick reached into his trousers and pulled out a small tin cap box about the size of a silver dollar. The lid of the round box had several holes punched in it.

"I punched these holes so she can breathe. You know with all the heat down here, and all the marchin', I gotta have her rested well in my haversack. She's a beauty." Trick's face had a childish glow as he gently twisted the lid of the cap box. It was the type of look that you can see on the faces of children as they open gifts on Christmas morn. He cupped his left hand and then turned over the tin. A brown beetle crawled to the center of his palm.

"Ain't she pretty?" exclaimed Trick gleefully.

Will pulled off his cap and scratched his head. Aaron looked at T.J. and smiled. T.J. remained silent.

"Her name is Dixie!" announced Trick with pride.

"And what do you plan to do with her?" Will asked.

T.J. and Aaron looked at Trick who was crouching by the fire now.

"I'll bet those Fifth Iowa boys over there in that hollow that good ol' Dixie can beat any beetle south of the Mason-Dixon Line. I will take their pennies to prove it. You just wait an' see!"

"And how do you plan to set up this race?" Aaron replied skeptically.

"Yeah, how's it done?" added Will.

"Well, follow me, and I'll show ya how to win a few pennies!"

Trick stood up, placed Dixie back in the cap box, and closed the lid gently. He then pulled open his cartridge box so all could see the contents.

"Heavens, Trick, where are your rounds? What the hell are those damn beetles doing in there?" asked Will with concern.

"Hee, hee, not a worry. The forty rounds are in my sack. Gotta make room for Dixie's friends. Right thing to do." Trick chuckled again as he pulled the flap quickly back over to contain the brown beetles within. "Now, come on, let's win some cash from those Iowa boys."

Trick picked up his plate and balanced it on a large rock closest to the flames. He strolled over to the camp of the Iowa regiment. The friends followed.

"What do you Suckers want?" shouted a soldier from the Fifth Iowa Volunteer Infantry.

"You boys in for some gamblin'?" Trick replied confidently.

"Can't play no cards in this camp. Captain's orders."

"How 'bout some racin'? Captain said anythin' about gamblin' on a race?" Trick countered.

"You damn fool. We got no horses around here, and besides the whole thing would stir up a fix. What the hell are you talkin' about?" Several of the Iowa soldiers stood up as if bracing themselves for a fight. Other Iowans from neighboring campsites approached, forming a large contingent around the fire. Their curious faces reflected the firelight.

"Hold on, fellas," said Trick grinning. He reached for his cartridge box and pulled open the flap so all could see the contents. The Iowa soldiers looked at each other in confusion. Trick quickly snapped the flap back. Reaching slowly into his trouser pocket, he pulled out the small round tin and unscrewed it, exposing his champion beetle so all could see.

There was a hush, followed by a chuckle, and then a chorus of laughter from the Iowa camp. The laughter quickly abated as Trick raised his tin.

"Boys! I got the fastest damn beetle south of the Mason-Dixon Line! And I'm a bettin' I can beat any of these beetles from my forty-dead-men box or any beetle you can gander up from your own!" Trick looked for a response.

The soldiers remained quiet and curious still, so Trick continued, "You just bring your mess plates with ya. Wash it clean so your beetle don't trip or slip on the grease, and I'll be racin' you!"

He held up the tin box again. "My ol' beetle, Dixie, is the same as those others in here! Same kinfolk an' all!" He held up the cartridge box again and continued his instruction. "Our plates are all the same size, too! We will place our crawlers at the center of the plate. The first to run to the edge wins! That'll be five pennies to get in if ya think you can beat ol' Dixie here!"

"You're on!" shouted three Iowans in unison. There was a flurry around the closest fires as soldiers hurried to get their tin plates. Within a few minutes, no less than fifty Iowans lined up with plates and pennies in hand.

"Now, you boys, place your pennies in my friend's cap here, and we will get this race movin' rightly so," instructed Trick again as he pointed to T.J.

T.J. pulled off his kepi and extended it to the contestants. Coins clinked into its blue wool recess.

"You all grab a beetle now from here, get on your haunches, squat, and place your lil crawler in the center." Trick handed the cartridge box to Aaron who opened the flap, exposing the beetles.

The soldiers reached in one by one until only a few beetles were left. They continued with Trick's instruction and formed in a great circle so the rules could be followed under the closest eye. Unbeknownst to the boys, a captain of the Fifth Iowa approached and stepped into the circle of men.

"What the hell is going on here?" he demanded.

The soldiers looked at the officer in silence.

"Speak up, or face a court-martial, I tell you!" he continued.

Trick walked up, his tin box in hand.

"Private, what is your name, and what regiment are you with?" said the captain in earnest.

"Sir, my name is Patrick Kane. I am with the Ninety-Third Illinois."

"And why are you in our camp?"

"Sir, if it be all right now, I can rightly say why," Trick replied with a slow drawl.

"Speak up, private! Tell me why you are here."

"Well, sir, me and my messmates were a hunkerin' to see if we had the fastest beetle south of the Mason-Dixon, and we got to ganderin' about and came this way as it be the closest now to the Ninety-Third camp. We meant no harm, sir, and are glad you came our way. See, we need an officer to make sure we get things right, ya know." Trick looked down at his charcoal-scarred boots.

"You are talking like a damn fool, private! I could have you court-martialed for gamblin' in my camp. Your Colonel Putnam would strap you to a barrel if he knew what you were doing here!"

Trick looked up at the captain. "Well, sir, I 'spect he might do just that on account of the bettin' an' all," he said. "But I 'spect if he knew the winner is givin' half of the winnin's to his commandin' officer, then I 'spect he might give the nod for these crawlers to race now." Trick grinned and waited in silence.

The captain looked at his men, a few smiled and nodded.

"Well, private, since some of these winnings are dedicated to a good cause, then I believe we should proceed. What are the rules, and what would you like me to do to make things right?" the captain said calmly.

Trick opened up his tin. "Well, Captain, this ol' beetle—her name is Dixie—an I'm a bettin' she can beat her kinfolk in a plate race. Your boys all have beetle kin in their hands. When you say go, the boys will place them beetles in the center of their plates. Now, the winner has gotta raise his right hand at the moment the beetle jumps over the rim of the plate. The lucky one walks with the all the winning's, save what is your take."

"Well, Private, where is your plate?" replied the captain.

"Oh, jeez, I best be gettin' it!" cried Trick. He handed the tin with Dixie to the captain and then rushed out of the circle and back to the camp of the Ninety-Third Illinois. The Iowa soldiers laughed as Trick's trousers slipped, exposing the top of his buttocks. Trick pulled them up with both hands and continued at a rapid pace. A couple of minutes later, he returned to the Iowa camp with his two hands grasping his oval US belt buckle, his tin dinner plate tucked under his left arm. Stepping quickly to the center of the circle of soldiers, he squatted and dropped his plate below the feet of the captain.

"Now, Captain, can you give the go and raise your hand for me when ol' Dixie or some other beetle hits the finish line first?"

"Certainly, Private. Glad to help. I wish you luck, but reckon you'll be out of luck with all my company around you. Are you ready, Private Kane?"

Trick slowly twisted the box lid and gently picked up Dixie between his thumb and forefinger. He held her an inch above the center of the plate as did the Iowans who squatted with their beetles in hand. All contestants were silent and staring at the center of their plates.

"Dixie is ready, Captain. Give the go!" announced Trick.

"Go!" shouted the captain.

The hush of the men was replaced by shouts and screams. The Iowa and Illinois boys shouted, "Go! Go! Go!" as their beetles moved circuitously on their mess plates, making little progress to the edges.

"For criminy" screamed an Iowan. "Get movin', you little critter. This ain't no mountain you have to climb!"

"Get your little feet a moving!" screamed another.

The captain, seeing Dixie scurry and leap off the edge of his mess plate, shot up his hand like a saber jab to the sky, silencing everyone. The curious captain looked to the front, around him, and then left and right. His hand was the only one extended.

"Damn it," said a frustrated Iowa boy.

"Can't believe this. My beetle just went in circles, too," said another.

"Mine just tucked herself in for a long nap," followed another yet again.

Soon a chorus of grumbling could be heard from the Iowa soldiers as the stunned captain shook his head and Trick picked up Dixie and carefully placed her back in his cap box. Standing up and raising his fist like a triumphant gladiator, he left his plate on the ground.

After saluting the captain, Trick said, "Well, Captain, ol' Dixie here did her dance again like a true champ! We boys from the Sucker State thank you and your Iowa boys for the winnings!" Reaching into T.J.'s blue kepi, he grabbed a handful of pennies out of courtesy and handed them to the Iowa captain. Smiling a broad grin, he clicked his heels and then reached down to the ground for his mess plate, which he rapidly placed under his armpit again. In the silence of the Iowa camp, he turned toward the Ninety-Third encampment, grinning all the way until the silence was broken by Will.

"Trick, now how's it possible that Dixie wins that race every time?"

Aaron added, "Yeah, how can you beat a whole company like that? That's a lot of odds to beat. That captain there thought for sure he'd have half those winnings until he shot his hand up like so!"

Trick reached over and grabbed the kepi full of pennies and shook it. He looked at the others and said, "We are friends of the wigwam, right?"

Will, Aaron, and T.J. nodded.

Trick smiled, nodded, tilted his head to the side and said, "Well, then, I will tell y'all the simple secret...Ol' Dixie, like us friends, don't rightly like to have her feet to the fire."

His grin was even wider now as he giggled. "Hee, hee...the secret is leavin' your plate on a hot rock 'til the contest begins. That heat sure makes ol' Dixie move all those little feet fast to get off that tin!"

The boys looked at each other, chuckled, and shook their heads in amusement. A moment later they were pensively staring into the fire, the lighthearted mood now a memory. They wondered what Jenny and Allie were up to.

Chapter 32

Wigwam

Pecatonica River
Autumn, 1862

There was a hush on the river.

The childish echoes that once rose above the deep pools were gone. The boys were not there anymore. A quiet network of red and yellow leaves dropped from the Injun oak jarred by a short gust of autumn breeze. The leaves fell to the water, mixing with other greenery coming from miles up north. The colored network swirled around the deep pool that Trick had plunked his cane pole in. As if waiting for the right moment to move on, the leaves continued silently downriver as if pulled by a mysterious force.

Allie stood on the riverbank in front of the wigwam. She thought of the great times the friends had had over the years. From her first meeting with Jenny, Will, and Aaron...and then the boys from Buda, T.J. and Trick, who always announced themselves in a raucous manner. She remembered Trick falling off the Injun oak, her pushing him in the river, their frolicking and laughter that once was common here. She also thought of Elmer.

She looked to the other side of the river at the dragon-footed tree, where T.J. and Trick once popped up their curious heads as they peered across the river with rifles and fishing poles in hand. She smiled and shook her head in silence. She wondered how far south the boys were.

She looked up at the Injun oak tree and dazzled at the array of color. She felt a sense of peace now. A tender voice broke the silence.

"Allie, is that you?"

"Yes, dear friend, it is me," replied Allie as she stepped from the wigwam entrance to get a better view.

"I have the clothes and hat for you," replied Jenny, holding a smartly folded bundle with a large broad-brimmed hat on top. She placed the bundle under her arms and then entered the wigwam with Allie holding back the thick holly branch that disguised the entrance.

"Did ya bring the shears, too?" asked Allie as she gently reached for the bundle.

"Yes."

"Did your mom see you pull 'em from the sewin' room?"

"No," Jenny replied as she reached into the bundle and pulled out the fancy cutting shears. "I hid them in the bundle, so she couldn't see them."

"Well, I rolled this ol' stump in here, so we best get it over and done with."

Allie bent over and slowly positioned herself so that the light from the roof of the wigwam shone squarely on her golden locks, which now reached her shoulders. She could see her shadow on the wall above the medicine bag still tucked in its place. Jenny stood behind her and raised the shears, casting a distorted shadow that rose to the ceiling.

"Are you sure you want me to do it?" Jenny asked softly.

"Yes, Jenny, it has to be done today."

There was a slight, awkward hesitation, and then Jenny squeezed the shears. With each deliberate clip, golden locks dropped. Allie squinted as if she was wincing from pain. But the pain was all internal and tied to her convictions. She caught herself and straightened her back so Jenny could get a better grip.

Jenny remained silent.

"Well, Jenny, I 'spect if Gramma Lucy can fight off those Injuns, I reckon I can fight those rebels, too!"

Jenny did not respond.

"Jenny, did ya hear what I said?" said Allie, sharply. The shadow of the cutting shears reflected upward as Jenny stepped back, pointing the sharp blades to the ceiling.

Jenny stepped over to Allie's side and put her hand on her shoulder.

"Allie, lady folk are better off taking care of things at home. You best leave the fighting down south to the men. And besides, even though I cut your hair, I suspect the recruiting officer will size you up and send you home. I am only cutting your hair because I know it will grow back. If you go down south, you may never come back!" Jenny caught herself. She was not a woman of words and felt that she had overstepped her boundaries. Allie was her friend, and she wondered now if she had hurt her feelings. She looked down at Allie and caught her glance. There was a twinkle in Allie's eyes.

"Don't see much good about stayin' up here while the boys are down there," said Allie slowly. "I just keep thinkin' about Will, and it breaks my heart. I don't know where he is or what he's doin'. I fear for him. I don't want my sweetheart taken away like Elmer."

Both fell silent.

"Allie, you do what you have to do. If you can fool those recruiting officers, I will know because you won't be here at the wigwam this Sunday. You know I can't take that trip to Belvidere with you. Have you told Gramma Lucy that you're going south?"

"Yes, and I swore her to secrecy like a friend of the wigwam."

"Well, let me finish this up for you, Allie, so you can be on your way."

"Make sure ya keep my ears, Jenny," replied Allie in a quirky way. "I'm gonna need them to hear those rebel guns when they are a comin'."

"You best stay away from those muskets, Allie. You must be careful. You promise?"

Allie nodded gently as the shears rose up, again casting strange shadows on the walls. Allie's sandy-blonde strands of hair dropped to the dirt floor of the wigwam as both girls remained silent, as if a special ritual was at hand.

"I am finished," Jenny said awkwardly. "Now pick up that hat and see how it fits on your head!"

Allie stood up and immediately ran her fingers over her cropped head. She smiled. Staring at the beam of light for a moment, her eyes darted to and fro. She then picked up the wigwam's mirror and looked at her reflection and nodded gently. "Thank you, Jenny. I best be goin' now."

"Well, get these clothes on, and don't forget your hat," replied Jenny in a motherly way. "I'll walk with you up to the river bend. I'll be waiting outside."

The holly branch brushed noisily across the wigwam entrance as Jenny pushed her way outside. She waited. It seemed like an eternity. Visions of the quiet grandeur of the riverbank clouded her mind. She thought of the boys and how they frolicked outside the wigwam. She could feel her angst growing as she realized that Allie was *truly* leaving. She gambled, though, on the thought that Allie's ruse would *not* work. *How could it*, she thought. Allie was only five feet three...and a woman. She shook her head at the thought, and then tears began to well in her eyes. If Allie could pull it off, she may never see her again.

A rush of wind caused more leaves to fall from the Injun oak tree. The breeze seemed to whisper, gently mixing with the Jenny's quiet sobs. She placed her face in her hands and turned away from the wigwam so Allie would not see her.

She felt an assuring hand on her shoulder and turned around.

"Now, Jenny, you best not cry about me. I will write you."

"You're the last to go, Allie!" sobbed Jenny. "If you go, there won't be anyone here anymore. I fear that you and the boys may never come back!" Her gasps broke up her verbal yearnings. Tears flowed down both her cheeks...then she started to giggle a bit as she looked at Allie with her floppy hat, which was now oversized and dropped down to her ears. She looked like a circus rider with her baggy pantaloons rolled over and cuffed at the ankles, forming a tight fit over her mud-splattered boots.

Jenny giggled again. They both smiled.

"I hope your mother has no need for the colonel's hat and clothes," chimed in Allie as they started upriver toward the bend. She continued. " I 'spect he won't be needin' 'em for a while now that he's wearin' that fancy blue uniform. I'll be sendin' them back to you once I get my new blue suit."

Jenny nodded.

As they walked the half mile to the bend, a breeze picked up again, sending more leaves downward. The blend of hickory, oak, and willow leaves cascaded into the water and carpeted the river. It was noon now, and Allie wanted to make it to Belvidere by midafternoon. She needed to hurry along.

"Good-bye, my dear friend," said Allie with a smile. "You will keep my secret won't you?"

Jenny began to sob again. "Yes, Allie, you are my best of friends. I will love you always." Remembering what Allie had said when the boys marched off to war, Jenny straightened up and calmly said, "I will not forget you. I have carved you on the palm of my hand."

The girls hugged. They didn't know what to say to each other. Allie started to say something, but hesitated. In the awkward silence, only the trickling waters of the Pecatonica could be heard. She then took a deep breath, turned, and began a slow deliberate walk upriver. When she reached a large, majestic willow tree near the river bend, she stopped and turned back to get another glimpse of Jenny. The willow's brilliant, yellow branches swayed gently with the breeze, framing Allie in a wonderful way. After pausing for a quick moment, Allie slowly raised her hand.

Jenny waved back, hoping that this beautiful memory of Allie would not be her last.

Chapter 33

Recruiting Station

Ninety-Fifth Illinois Volunteer Infantry
Belvidere, Illinois
Next Day

The trip to the recruiting station was uneventful for Allie.

As she walked up from the Rock River, she could hear a band play-ing in the distance. The tunes were strikingly familiar, like the rousing songs played in Freeport when the boys enlisted. She could hear "Rally 'Round the Flag" followed by "Yankee Doodle Dandy." She wondered if her disguise would bring her success. Pulling her hat down smartly across her forehead, she adjusted her pants; placed her right palm into her shirt between the middle buttons in a Napoleonic pose; and then walked forward in an irregular military gait, stepping to the music as if she were the "little corporal" himself. Arriving at the town square, she settled into the crowd of onlookers who were roused by the beat of the drums and swayed by the patriotic air of the moment. She looked in-tensely at the rousing spectacle, until her silence was broken by a boom-ing voice that rose above the gaiety. It was directed at her.

"Son, can I help you find your way to the recruiting officer?" asked a straightlaced lieutenant with a full beard.

Startled and taken aback, Allie coughed, cleared her throat, and replied cautiously, "And who are you, sir?"

"My name is Henry Bush. I am an officer with Company G of the Ninety-Fifth Illinois Infantry. My brother, Elliott, is the captain of the company, and he is recruiting over at the general store. Have you come here to enlist?" The lieutenant stared directly into Allie's eyes. She did not flinch.

"Yes, sir, I'd be rightly honored to be in your company!"

Allie then pushed her hand closer into her shirt and continued. "And I have buddies that are lickin' the rebs with the Ninety-Third Illinois from Freeport. I had to keep good watch on my Gramma Lucy 'cause she ain't no spring chicken anymore. But she sent me along now, so I can lick a few rebs for her, too!"

Lieutenant Bush raised his eyebrows slightly.

Allie realized she was rambling, so she stopped and waited for the officer's reply. "Yankee Doodle Dandy" kicked up again, breaking the silence.

"Well, let me introduce you to Captain Bush, young man."

"Yes, sir," replied Allie nervously.

"Follow me," added the lieutenant.

As they approached a general store, they could see a thick gathering of excitable young men forming around the entrance. Allie began to feel uncomfortable at the thought of joining this band of men. She hesitated for a moment but then pushed forward into the crowd. Being the smallest, she snaked her way ahead of the lieutenant and managed to fall to the very front of the gathering of volunteers.

On the opposite wall from the door was a counter that extended the width of the entire store. Behind it was an array of farm implements and general store merchandise arranged so that customers could get a better look at the wares. In front of the counter was a large wooden desk with an officer sitting behind it and facing the front door. He, too, had a large trimmed beard like his brother's. Allie saw that he was the older of the two. In his right hand, he held a large quill pen. He placed a rosewood inkwell close by his left hand so he could, without hesitation, scribble on the large piece of linen that lay flat before him on his desk. As the noise of the crowd died down, he stood up.

"Gentlemen, my name is Captain Elliott Bush. I command Company G of the proud Ninety-Fifth Illinois Regiment." He looked at the faces in the crowd and continued. "Over a year has passed since the rebels fired on Fort Sumter, and our brave comrades from Illinois are now pushing south to victory. You are called today to help finish the fight!"

The men cheered in a chorus of excitement.

The band kept its patriotic beat in the distance.

"Every man will be paid a bounty of three hundred dollars to enlist. If you wish, the money can be given to your loved ones who will support themselves while you are defending the cause for the Union. Please form a line, and step up to my table."

Allie could feel the angst. Her stomach felt like it was rising to her throat. She began to gasp a bit as she stepped forward, now only third in line. She was wedged between two tall men and could not see over the shoulders in front of her.

Suddenly, she was in front of the captain. He did not notice her as he looked at his inkwell. He then looked up at her. There was silence in the room as all the men awaited the captain's words.

"Son!" shouted the captain. "Go home! You are too young to fight!"

The jolt of his announcement almost knocked Allie back to the floor. She stood even more erect now.

Lowering her voice and positioning short deliberate sentences, she replied, "Captain, sir, I am of age!"

"How old are you?"

"I am nineteen years old!"

"Can you prove it?"

"Yes, sir, but those that can prove my age...are a fightin' down south already."

"And what regiment are they fighting with, young man?"

"The Ninety-Third Illinois from Freeport. Colonel Putnam, our fire marshal can vouch for me. I swear as crooked as the Pecatonica River is. And I swear on the Good Book over there!" Allie pointed to the Bible that lay prominently on the counter.

"You are too short, son! How tall are you?" shouted the captain.

"I am five feet three and can fight as good as any wildcat around these parts!" Allie's excitement was getting to her. Her voice rose a little, and she thought her feminine voice was revealed. She lowered her chin and waited again for the next insult.

"Well, son, the musket you will carry is almost as tall as you!" said the captain in a slightly condescending tone.

The crowd of soldiers chuckled as the throng continued to peer through the doors and windows, waiting for Allie's response.

"With all due respect, sir, five feet three is, I reckon, a good fightin' height. Well, good ol' Napoleon was only five feet six, and he was the general of the army. I'm gonna be only a private, so I reckon that all those officers in between should rightly be between five feet six and me. In fact, I 'spect a good captain in this army should be shored down a bit to about five feet four!"

The soldiers chuckled.

The captain was not amused. "What is your name, young man?" he asked. He picked up the quill and dipped it in the inkwell.

"My name is Allie...I mean, sir," she choked slightly, grabbing her throat. "I am, sir—" She could not think straight.

"I repeat...what is your name, young man?" the captain replied sternly.

Allie quickly looked to the dry goods counter on the wall nearby and noticed a tiny sign by the clerk's window. It said "CASHIER". Without flinching, she announced, "Pardon, sir, my name is Al...Albert Cashier. Albert D. Cashier is my name."

"Thank you, Private Cashier," replied Captain Bush calmly now. "Welcome to the Ninety-Fifth Illinois. Sign here. You will get your orders tomorrow."

Allie grabbed the quill awkwardly and scribbled an "x" next to her name. It was her official mark. After signing, she handed the pen back to the captain and extended her hand. The captain shook it and smiled.

Turning toward the rest of the volunteers, she quickly moved through the gathering and stepped outside. The band had stopped playing, and the sun was setting now. She smiled as she thought of Jenny. They had pulled it off.

Allie would be heading south to join the boys.

Chapter 34

General John E. Smith Headquarters

Eighth Division, Sixteenth Army Corps
Near Memphis Tennessee
March 10, 1863

General John E. Smith sat erect on his handsome white mount. The horse craned its neck, snorted, and high-stepped as if eager to join the impending ceremony. Smith thought of his beloved Black Hawk, who he had presented to Colonel Putnam as a gift for raising his regiment. He wondered if Putnam was advancing south. He smiled at the thought of seeing his Shiloh war-horse, shiny coat and all.

"Gentlemen, prepare for dress parade," announced Smith in a soft deliberate voice. His adjutant and the other mounted officers around him snapped a quick salute and stood erect in their saddles waiting for the command to depart to the columns of blue in the distance.

Smith's Eighth Division was assembled in a beautiful valley of lush spring meadows trampled by the feet of over six thousand soldiers. It was high noon, the temperature cool and crisp.

"Officers of the Eighth Division!" announced Smith. "This morning, you received from our adjutant general a short proclamation from my May tenth address to our soldiers-in-arms. Smith looked into the eyes of each of his officers and continued. "It is our duty to keep to our course and put down this rebellion. The sooner it is over, the sooner we can return to our wives and sweethearts. I expect you will deliver this message with your usual zeal and conviction. When you have delivered the proclamation to your men, prepare for the dress parade, and execute your formations with the skill that each of you has demonstrated on the field of battle and in our camps. Proceed now." Smith saluted again.

The riders dispersed. The sound of hooves rumbled away.

"Gentlemen, let's we see how the Lead Mine Regiment is holding up?" Smith announced, "It's been almost two years since Shiloh!" He flipped his reins across his white mount's shoulders and trotted the short distance to his old Forty-Fifth Regiment. His staff followed in step.

When they arrived at the camp of the old Lead Mine Regiment, the recently promoted Colonel Maltby was shouting at his men with his exaggerated style. He was an odd-looking officer but was highly respected by the men. As the newest commander of the regiment, he felt proud of what they had accomplished and was looking forward to doing great things with General Smith.

Maltby, seeing General Smith and staff approaching, shouted commands to his captains, and the regiment quickly aligned into perfect formation of ten companies. He then pulled out the proclamation from his frock coat and looked across at the legion of blue standing silently before him.

"General Smith has requested that I read this proclamation from him. May all listen up!"

> *Fellow Soldiers!*
> *We are called upon to co-operate with our brave*
> *Companions in Arms, whose proud lot it is to precede us...*
> *Most of you, by your prowess on many a well contested*
> *field, have already proven your devotedness to the noble*
> *cause for which we battle: the restoration of the Union*
> *and the perpetuity of the institutions bequeathed us by our*
> *forefathers. Those among you, who have not had as yet, that*
> *opportunity, I feel, will emulate the valorous deeds of your*

> *veteran Comrades and prove to the world that the trust of*
> *the Federal Government in its Citizen-Soldiery is, indeed,*
> *well founded, and the honor of the national flag is safe in*
> *your hands... The South, despite the spirit of our century,*
> *despite history which has ever branded with failure the*
> *attempt to harmonize together two antagonistic principles:*
> *freedom and servitude, has dared to declare it her purpose to*
> *rear up a Confederacy whose cornerstone shall be slavery...*
>
>   *Hence it became logically necessary to issue a counter*
> *Proclamation, emancipating slavery: for, the corner-stone*
> *once shattered and broken, the whole fabric must topple to*
> *the ground...*

Maltby paused, and then raising his voice deliberately between each deep breath, he continued.

> *Forward! Then, fellow soldiers! And...reassured of the*
> *justice and sacredness of our cause let not our efforts cease*
> *until the Union be restored in its full integrity and our*
> *glorious banner will wave triumphant over a land forever*
> *reclaimed from treason, and restored to its former glory,*
> *peace, and prosperity.*
>
>   *Jno E. Smith*
>   *Brig Genl* [11]

Maltby looked at Smith.

Smith nodded and then snapped a salute, holding it for a brief moment. Turning on his white mount, he advanced to a small knoll in the distance where he could review his troops.

A moment later, the undulating blue mass moved in rhythmical sequence like waves hitting the shores of a distant ocean. The beloved general was pleased with what he saw. He knew his men would do their best again when the next battle was waged. Gazing across the fields in a slow sweep like a Roman general of old, Smith kept his back straight in the saddle, holding the reins loosely on the saddle horn. His white mount did not move.

From the distance, the men could plainly see him on the hill. He looked like a statue. Each regiment kept its tight formation, and the thud of boots echoed across the valley.

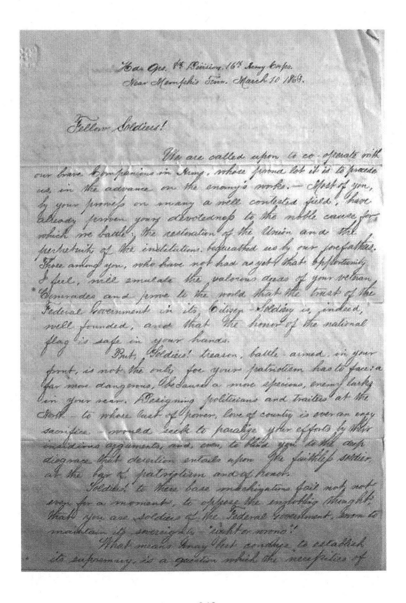

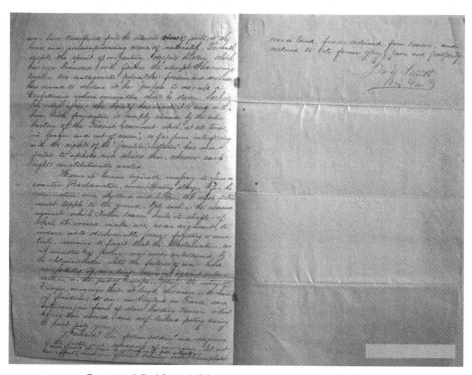

Original Soldier Address by General John E. Smith

Chapter 35

Captain Cowan Home

Warren, Illinois
Near the Apple River
Spring, 1863

A flutter of turtledoves broke the silence.

Georgie looked up. He could see a rider coming down the lane toward the cabin. *It's the postmaster,* he thought. He squinted his eyes to get a better look. In a flash he hurried to the door stoop, kicking up dust all along the way. His loyal labrador pup followed close on his heels. Squirrels in the yard scurried quickly to the treetops as another trove of turtledoves rose up, circled over the cabin, and then departed for good.

"Mother, Mother, the postmaster is coming!" announced Georgie as he bounded through the front door, his dusty boots clomping on the hard oak floor.

Harriet looked up, set down a black cauldron she was cleaning for supper, wiped her hands on her apron, and proceeded, with anxiety, to the front door. Thoughts of her husband ran like quick snapshots in her mind. She felt sick to her stomach and held her breath for what today would bring...a rude intruder to the calm she felt just moments before.

The slow clop of hooves moved closer to the entrance of the clapboard cabin. She looked at Molly, Phine, and Georgie, who were huddled by the table. She could not breathe.

"Hello, Mrs. Cowan," announced the postmaster when he appeared at the door. "Looks like we can expect some sunshine now." He smiled cordially.

Harriet still could not speak. She stared down at the handful of letters in a fleeting attempt to see if the letters were from her husband. If they were, she could expect he was still alive. If the letter was from General Smith, she would expect the worst. She continued her agonizing gaze at the pile of letters.

The postmaster broke the silence for her. "I have three letters from the good captain," he said. "I suppose the Forty-Fifth has been campaigning a bit, and these were delayed. Damn lucky we get any of these with the boys now down deep in rebel territory!" Realizing he cursed, he caught himself and looked at the children apologetically.

Harriet shrugged and then breathed a deep sigh of relief. She extended her hand to the postmaster and smiled. "Thank you, sir, for making the trip out here. You didn't have to inconvenience yourself."

"No problem, ma'am. Your husband is helping us more than I could. All of us in the Apple River Valley are very grateful to him and the boys. Let me know when you're back in town what these letters all say. I am sure there is some good news in there!" He beamed again, nodded at the children, and smiled once more as if to confirm what he had said. Tipping his hat with his free hand, he turned to his horse, mounted him, and trotted back down the lane.

"Can I read one?" exclaimed Georgie as he rushed to his mother's side.

"Let's all sit by the table, children. Georgie, you may read the first one."

There was a silence mixed with excitement and relief. The children sat quietly as Harriett pulled a knife out of a cupboard drawer and placed it at a small gap at the corner of the first letter. She pushed it slowly as if performing a surgical incision. The contents were a timeless gift to the family, and she did not want to miss the cut and damage the letter in any way.

"Here, Georgie, be careful now. Tell us what your father is doing."

Georgie reached for the letter. His face beamed with excitement. He felt proud now that he could read just like his sisters. Holding the letter at eye level, he looked at the girls and then began to read in slow deliberation.

> *Jackson Tenn.*
> *Oct. 1st 1862*
> *My Dear Children:*
> *I am tonight (it is now night) together with one of my best friends, Capt. Duer of Galena, here in the hall of the court house. There is a great commotion out in the streets and in the lot surrounding the court house, among the soldiers; they are singing, playing the violin, dancing, playing cards, talking…to while away the time.*

Georgie stopped for a moment and looked up. "I know Captain Duer," he said. "He gave me a penny once when Father and I were in Galena."

"Just read the letter!" shouted the girls in unison.

Georgie continued.

> *Most of them are very merry but there is once in a while one who is not…some are thinking seriously of home, families, or friends and wishing for the war to end so they can return to them. But—how many, many of those poor fellows are doomed never to enjoy that privilege…hundreds of them will not live to see their homes and friends again and hundreds more will return to them maimed or crippled from wounds or disease…from which they will never recover.*

Georgie looked up again. Tears welled up in his bright-blue eyes. Harriet lifted her apron to her face and began to sob gently. The girls moved closer to her side.

*It makes me feel very sad to look over the fields, covered
with brave and generous men, devoting their lives to their
country. Most people think that the army is made up of
coarse, hard hearted thoughtless men who never saw or
thought of anything nice…but whosoever thinks that way is
badly mistaken…*

*I have a great many good friends here in the army and
amongst the citizens too. If I needed anything here I could
get it in a moment; there was a man, a Secesh (rebel) citizen
too, told me today that if I needed any money I could have
it of him. I told him it's queer that he should talk to me so
when I came here to kill Secesh. He said he knew that but
still he knew if I told him anything he could depend on it…*

Georgie looked up again at the girls. They looked perplexed.
Harriet nodded to Georgie. "Continue," she said calmly.

*So you see how well it is to tell the truth at all times
even to your enemies. They respect us if we tell the truth
and try to do our duty. I hope that you will always
be honorable toward everyone, even those who misuse
you; and never do anything that will place you in
circumstances which will make you tell lies. Always speak
the truth frankly, even though it may seem to be a bad
policy at the time, for I tell you it is always best and comes
out right all the time.*

I remain your Father and Friend
L. H. Cowan [12]

There was silence in the cabin except for a quick snap from the fireplace. Harriet sighed and looked down at the second letter. She opened
it like before, in a delicate and deliberate way.

"Molly, would you like to read the second letter? It is addressed to
you."

"Yes, Mother," she replied softly as she reached for the prized piece of paper. She did not smile or look at the others before beginning.

> *Oxford, Miss, Dec. 10, 1862*
> *Dear Molly*
> *It is now 8 p.m. I had not thought of writing...I am in a*
> *bad mood to write too for I have heard that our much loved*
> *and good brother Chris is dead.*

Harriet dropped the knife and third letter to the floor while she raced over to the fireplace and placed both hands on the mantel as she wept and gasped for air. Georgie jumped from the table and held her waist. Molly looked at Phine, who placed her face in her hands. She could not look up.

Undaunted, Molly continued in order to finish the letter quickly. She thought if she could end it, maybe it would wipe out the news that was stabbing their hearts. Maybe this letter about Uncle Chris's death was some sort of a rude joke written by her father. She continued.

> *I cannot tell how I feel, and I will not try, but if it were not*
> *for you, George, and Phine, I feel as though I would rather*
> *die than not myself.*

Molly's voice quivered. She sniffled and then continued.

> *...he was a good boy in every way, honest, tender, generous,*
> *sincere, moral, and industrious. There was never so good a*
> *boy in that county. I almost break my heart to think of his*
> *condition while sick. I know how his feelings were actuated.*
> *I think I can imagine something of his anguish. He was so*
> *young and tender, dying alone, no one to console him...*
> *I am in a poor mood to write Molly, you can imagine*
> *my condition better than I can tell you. All I can do is to do*

as I always have...brace up against this trouble and try to
do my duty...
    Good night to you all and each,
    I am still your father

                        Most affectionately,
                        L. H. Cowan [13]

Georgie's lab barked outside the door in three short yelps. The family looked to the door.

Harriet broke the silence as she sobbed, her apron still to her face. "Someone let her in," she said. Her eyes were red and swollen.

The pup scrambled into the gathering, wagging her tail furiously. She jumped on Molly and continued her happy intrusion to the solemn moment. Phine sniffled and then followed it with a giggle as the lab's tail thumped against the table.

"Callie, cut that out! We'll send you back outside again if you don't settle down!" warned Georgie.

The dog continued to swirl on the floor, thumping everyone with her wiggling back haunches and tail. The girls chuckled. The family felt better now.

"Phine, it's your turn now. Do you want to read the last letter?" asked Harriett. The letter was already opened with care. She handed the contents to Phine who began to read in earnest, too.

Camp on Tallahatchin, Miss.
9 p.m., Jan. 4, 1863
My Dear Ones:
The last letter I received from any of you was dated the first
of December. It seems like a long time—though I know there
is a good reason for it. We are a long way from River and
railroad communications and the railroad has been cut off so
that mails could not reach us...
    We have been living on half rations now for two weeks.
We have had corn on the ear issued to us for rations instead

*of bread, and only about two ears to the man…we have
foraged through the country for meat still it is very hard to
find any, and when we get it, it is poor and thin. We have
not had…salt enough to season it. Yet our soldiers make very
light of it, particularly the old Regiment…*

*I was elected Lt. Col. of our Regiment on the 18th of
last month…I must acknowledge that I am a little proud of
it, for the officers of the Regiment voted me into the position
without my asking or expecting it…also Gen. Grant gave
me a fine recommendation…Am not near so fat as I was in
the summer.*

Affectionately,
L. H. Cowan [14]

As Phine read the last words, the family looked at each other with a
sense of shared calm and grace. They felt happier now. The lab pup had
settled and was silent now, curled and slumbered by the fireplace.

Chapter 36

Steamer Jesse K. Bell

Tallahatchie River
North of Vicksburg
April 2, 1863

Black Hawk snorted!

He did not like his confinement on the deck of the *Jesse K. Bell*. Occasionally, a thump would rock the boat as the slow-moving paddles in the rear banged into the hidden tree stumps below the waterline. One of the smokestacks had been knocked down by low-hanging trees just days before, but it was righted again, causing steam to whistle through the crack like hissing demons. Occasionally, a snake would fall onto the deck from the cypress moss-covered branches that loomed over the river above and writhe and twist in an attempt to escape to the cloudy water. After a quick succession of shouts, though, the butt of a musket would drop on its head—a boot then finished the job, shuffling the dead intruder into the murky Tallahatchie. Six hundred soldiers in blue stood on the decks of the proud *Jesse K. Bell*, herded like cattle on a cargo train.

"These damn gallinippers are swarmin' so much, I can barely see!" complained Trick as he held his musket close to his left shoulder. With his black, broad-brimmed hat, he swatted at the mosquitoes, hoping for some relief. "Wish we were back on the Pecatonica. I 'spect the leaves are buddin' now by the wigwam."

T.J., who was typically calm in tough situations, interjected with a sharp tone, "If we keep this up, sure 'nough someone's gonna end up a mossback and skedaddle off this boat and make it back home north for sure! It's been twelve days on this damn boat, and I'm getting sick of the wanderin' about!" After finishing his remark, he smiled in an awkward way and then cast a glance at Aaron and Will, both of whom were calming Black Hawk down at the bow of the steamer.

Will held the reins and stroked Black Hawk's snout while Aaron calmly rubbed his mane, gingerly touching the deep battle scar that Black Hawk had received at Shiloh.

T.J. looked downriver again to the tangled green mass before him. He stood comfortably, like a sentry. Resting his chin on the back of his hands, which cupped the muzzle of his Sharps sniper rifle, his mind wandered. He thought back to the cold winter night in Freeport when he first met Fire Marshal Putnam, who shouted swift commands during the raging fire. He remembered how Putnam ordered him to the belfry with Colonel John E. Smith's son Alfred. His mind's eye flashed back to the quick succession of rifle shots that blew up the powder kegs and snuffed out the fire. He said in a monotone voice, "Colonel Putnam says that the Ninety-Third, all of us, will land right soon. It'll be fine right sure. We can set our fires and cook our hominy and pork on some dry ground. We can sleep in the leaves—"

A loud rifle crack broke the silence! Every soldier flinched. A scream of pain was heard from someone on the starboard side. Black Hawk twisted as if writhing in pain too, whinnying in a furious way, knocking several soldiers into the river. After rising on his hind legs, his front hooves jabbed into the air, punching down the deck rails and scattering them to pieces.

"Whoa, Black Hawk! Whoa, boy!" Will shouted as he pulled at the reins in an attempt to settle the situation.

The agonizing scream again chilled the air, causing Black Hawk to twist and buck even more. After kicking the deck rails again, he pulled and freed his reins; twisted; turned once more; and then fell, curled in a contorted way, submerging sideways into the Tallahatchie. He disapeared for a moment then rose blasting water from his nostrils.

After a few strong strides, Black Hawk kept pace with the bow of the steamer. Feeling the need for footing, he turned toward shore with his head bobbing in a rhythmic motion. There was an opening cut into the thick mass of vines at the shore. Black Hawk shifted toward it, pounding furiously in the brown water, making what appeared to be progress in an almost futile motion. He continued at his loud but slow pace.

"What the hell is going on here?" shouted Putnam as he rapidly approached the bow.

"It's Chester Tracy of K Company!" replied a panicked soldier who squatted over the writhing soldier. "He's been shot in the side, Colonel!"

"And where did the shot come from?" Putnam demanded.

"Over there, sir." The soldier pointed to a white mansion that could be seen on a slight rise in the distance about a hundred yards from shore.

Putnam looked at the house and then turned to Will and Aaron. "Will...I mean, Corporal Erwin, tell the captain of this ship to head to shore where that house is. Tell him to dock this boat by the gap in the cane breaks. We will go see who's responsible for this action."

The wounded Tracy lay on the deck, holding his bloody right side. He gasped once...then again before falling unconscious as the *Jesse K. Bell* blew a whistle, her paddle wheel rhythmically turning in the dark waters.

Black Hawk approached the muddy shore and began floating in a circuitous wake near the cane breaks. He snorted as he looked, first fleetingly, to the boat and then to the shore as waves of blue soldiers moved down to the overcrowded lower deck. Bayonets, canteens, and belts clanked and rattled in the movement. Anticipation was rising by the moment. A shore landing was imminent.

Within moments the steamer was a rod's reach of the shoreline. A thick oak gangplank kicked up a splash as it settled into the shore muck. Black Hawk, with determined force, snorted again. He continued to high-step, causing clouds of river sand to swirl. Blowing out steamy muck through his nostrils, he popped up by the plank.

"Captain Taggart!" Putnam shouted.

"Yes, sir!" replied Taggart coming to attention near the plank.

"Do you remember the boys who helped us during the Freeport fire?"

"Yes, sir, I do. Erwin, Dunbar, and Lockwood."

"They will be the shore party. I will meet you at that white house. " Putnam pointed through the gap in the cane breaks, turned toward the shore, and continued down the plank. Grabbing Black Hawk's reins, he advanced to the gap and tied them to a cypress trunk. He then pulled out his field officer's sword from its black leather scabbard and stepped through the gap.

Captain Taggart turned and shouted over the rattle of disembarking men, "Erwin, Dunbar, and Lockwood! Report for duty!"

Will, Aaron, and T.J. stepped forward. Trick followed behind them about ten paces. "Gentlemen," Captain Taggart said, "the colonel has ordered us to meet him by that white house. Follow me!"

Trick moved closer to the deck rail and looked at the silent figures in blue marching ashore. Quickly, he grabbed his musket and walked down the gangplank in his waddling gait, walking through the cane break but stopping at the edge of a clearing. He peered through leafy spaces so as not be be seen, and watched with concern as his friends advanced to the white house.

Colonel Putnam was the first to approach the mansion, which was situated on a small knoll. Cotton fields extended for a hundred yards in all directions from the house with the exception of the neatly trimmed Kentucky bluegrass lawn that bordered the mansion and extended for about one hundred feet from the front door.

When Captain Taggart and the boys caught up with Putnam, they saw a movement at the windows. Soon a shadowy figure could be seen moving to the front door. The door then creaked open, revealing a middle-aged man with dark hair. He was dressed in a black wool coat and brown pants.

"Welcome, Colonel, to my home," the owner said in a polished southern drawl. "Would you and your soldiers like to come inside for a nice cup of chicory or tea?"

Putnam stepped forward. "We are not here for coffee or tea, sir. We are here to arrest the sniper who wounded one of our soldiers!"

"And what battle, sir, was he wounded in?"

"Sir, you know what we are here for," replied Putnam directly. "Give up the sniper who shot into our steamer, or you will be arrested, sir. Do you understand me?

The man began to fidget noticeably. Then the mistress of the house emerged on the front porch dressed in a modest, country plantation dress.

"What is going on, my fair colonel?" she stated calmly.

"Madam, your husband here is holding a rebel insurgent who wounded one of my men a few minutes ago!" Putnam pointed the tip of his sword to the Tallahatchie. He looked back at the couple with a glare in his eyes.

"Why, sir, we have no guns that could reach that distance. Just squirrel guns, you know." The woman looked nervously at her husband and then furtively at an upstairs window.

Putnam saw this and said, "The shot came from that window, madam, didn't it?" Pointing his sword at the plantation owner, he said, "Was it you, sir, that fired the shot?"

"No, it was not him!" replied his wife, who quickly raced to her husband's side.

"Who was it, then, ma'am?" demanded Putnam with rising anger.

"Please! Please!" she begged. "Go leave us alone!"

"I ask you again: who shot at the steamer?"

"Please, leave us alone!" she begged, this time clutching her husband's coat.

"*Who was it*, ma'am?" Putnam said, his voice dripping with menace.

The woman's shoulders sagged. Her knees began to buckle. Her husband braced her from a fall. Bursting into tears, she cried, "It was my son. It was my son, you damned Yankees! You killed two of his brothers at Shiloh, and he wanted to even the score. I only wish he had a second clear shot!"

There was silence.

The man hastily pulled his wife to the door stoop. He looked back with horror in his eyes. The door opened, and the woman quickly disappeared inside.

"Well, sir," Putnam replied in a calm voice, "I suppose your son is fifty rods away from this place, so we will take you with us in his stead. We are just one day's distance from Greenwood. I would like to personally introduce you to our corps commander, General McPherson. He will decide your fate!"

The man was silent. He did not know how to reply.

Putnam looked back up at the window where the shot was fired, walked over to the man, and grabbed him by the nape of his neck. His black coat lifted up so that his white sleeves showed through to the elbows. Putnam and the man turned to the Tallahatchie River. After taking a few strides, Putnam turned to Taggart and the boys. "Return to the steamer!" he commanded.

A hollow scream soon echoed through the house followed by loud sobbing.

The friends looked at each other, frozen in the moment. The plantation owner's wife emerged again through the front door. She rushed to the side of the house where the boys were.

"Boys, you look kind. Please don't take my husband away." In the pause that followed, she looked directly into each of their eyes, one by one, as if waiting for a sign or an answer that would allow her husband to return.

"Please, please, I beg you! Return my husband! You Yankees have killed two of my boys already. Please don't take my husband away. Please don't take my husband away!" She slowly dropped to her knees as she sobbed and repeated it again.

The boys remained silent, stunned by it all. Captain Taggart looked over at the madam, now hunched over in grief by the foot of her door stoop. He turned to the boys. "Return to the boat." he commanded, less sternly than before.

As the captain disappeared into the cut of the cane breaks, the boys quickly caught up with Trick who had anxiously waited for the three. Now together, they all turned back to the mansion for one last glance. The woman was silent now and nowhere to be seen.

The whistle of the *Jesse K. Bell* suddenly punctuated the air with a loud, sustained shriek!

The friends moved quickly through the canes, carefully stepping up the narrow plank which still stuck in the mucky shore. When they reached the lower deck they returned to the bow of the steamer. Will grabbed Black Hawk's reigns and walked him slowly through the mass of men on the starboard side of the lower deck. The soldiers took every caution not to spook the great Shiloh war horse, stroking his mane at every opportunity.

When the regiment appeared settled on the decks, the steamer captain called out, "Raise the gangplank!" Soon the paddlewheel began to churn slowly in reverse, causing the brown water to foam up again.

As the *Jesse K. Bell* slowly rumbled away from the shore, the boys looked in the distance to the white mansion. In the silence around him, Trick glanced over at the friends. "That poor woman is all alone now," he said softly. An awkward silence followed.

Will looked over at the friends, paused, and then replied with confidence, "I figure good ole' General McPherson will return her husband to her soon. He is a fair and kind general, I hear. And Colonel Put says we are just a day away from Greenwood. I 'spect that ole' man will be back lickety split." He smiled.

The soldiers within earshot of Will looked at each other and nodded. The boys felt better now.

Within a moment, the boilers roared, causing clouds of steam to hiss, rise up, and then drift gently down onto the Tallahatchie. The engine driving the paddlewheel kicked in with a thud and grinded again into a steady rhythm. With her bow pointing south now, all was clear, and the shrill whistle of the *Jesse K. Bell* shrieked across the skies once more.

The Yankees were here to stay.

Chapter 37

Admiral Porter's Flagship

USS *Benton*
Mouth of Yazoo River
Eight Miles Northwest of Vicksburg
Early April, 1863

Major General Grant looked to the west. From the upper deck of the ironclad river gunboat *Benton*, he watched the swirling muddy Yazoo River flow southward to the mighty Mississippi River just two hundred rods away. Strange patterns of rolling waves rose up, chopping at the starboard side of the flagship as if trying to coax it out.

The *Benton* was anchored off the muddy red shore. It looked to most, at first glance, like an alligator, nose and eyes above the waterline, resting in the sun or waiting to pounce on prey. With a full battery of twenty-one guns pointed out of window ports and protected by thick, sloping iron plates, she was a formidable warship for any enemy that challenged her. The twelve guns mounted securely on the starboard and aft could be deployed in minutes. Three more guns were mounted at the bow to engage any contender head on. The ironclad was complemented by two massive smokestacks that rose nearly twenty feet in the air, releasing steam in a whoosh from the growling engines below. Today, the *Benton* and its flotilla of steam rams and floating batteries rested at the mouth of the Yazoo on the eastern shore, hidden by dense forests. The rebel sentries in Vicksburg, even from the highest lookout at Fort Hill, could not see them.

Grant reached into his breast pocket and pulled out his watch and chain. It was four o'clock, and the sun would set in about three hours. Reaching into his sack coat, he pulled out a thick brown cigar, bit off the tip, and spat the brown piece onto the deck. He looked across the river again as he put the cigar into his mouth but didn't light it. The water continued to quietly lap at the side of the gunboat.

"Good afternoon, General!"

Grant turned to face the shore. He noticed the two figures in dark blue approaching the vessel. They boarded the gangplank leading to the *Benton's* lower deck and continued to the stern. A moment later they stood before Grant.

"Sorry we are late," said Rear Admiral David Dixon Porter respectfully.

"It was I, General, who held up Admiral Porter," said his companion, Major General of Volunteers William T. Sherman. "As you know, our esteemed admiral has never been late for any occasion.

Grant nodded again. "Thank you, General, for the clarification."

Grant's looked at Porter and Sherman. "Are both of you ready for our biggest challenge, the taking of Vicksburg?" he said with calm deliberation.

"Well, sir, our army has failed to take Vicksburg five times," replied Sherman in an animated way, waving his arms as he spoke. "In the last five months, I failed at Chickasaw Bluffs. The army also had low water at Duckport Canal, too much swampland with the Lake Providence move, blasting the levee to open Yazoo Pass also did not work, and Steele's Bayou Expedition failed too!"

Porter quickly interjected, "I thank you, again, General Sherman, for rescuing me at Steele's Bayou."

Unlike Sherman, Porter's jet-black hair, dark eyes, and prominent nose remained unmoved when he spoke. He was not animated like Sherman, and when he spoke, he spoke with a tone of authority and conviction. Formidable on the deck of any ship, he stood tall in his navy frock coat with eighteen anchors buttons lined up in two rows, extending from his waistline to under his beard. The eight stripes and a star on each sleeve prominently marked him as the highest ranking officer of the flotilla.

Porter continued. "You spoke, Sherman, of your failure at Chickasaw Bluffs. Well, mine at Steele's Bayou would have meant disaster for both the navy and army."

Sherman and Grant looked at each other and remained silent.

Porter continued. "I took my eleven vessels into those winding waterways of stumps, vines, and endless bayous. The rebels noted my movements and at Rolling Fork, as you know, bottled me up damn good. Had you not had your night march on the nineteenth, we would not be standing here today on this deck."

"I will serve my fellow officers, sir, in any way I can," Sherman replied with a glint in his eyes. Porter's compliments were not given freely to anyone, and Sherman knew now that even with his own failure, he and Porter together had gained success.

"By the way, General" added Porter, "how did you make your night march in those swamps? I have heard a rumor, but I want to know for sure."

Sherman replied, "Well, Admiral, one clever sergeant passed out candles to his group and ordered them to place them in the barrels of their muskets. Once lit, the small procession was noted by the entire corps, and it caught on quickly. Within minutes we had thousands who lit the way. It was magnificent to see."

Porter raised up his chin, then nodded.

"Gentlemen," Grant said, "the reason I have called you here is to get your read on a bold plan that I will now propose." He grabbed a match, struck it on the steam stack, and proceeded to puff his cigar until an orange ember glowed. He continued. "I have spoken to Admiral Porter about the initial plan, and now our strategy is complete. The navy and army will move together as we have before to capture fortress Vicksburg." Grant took another puff and pointed to the Yazoo.

"On April sixteenth, Porter will run the gauntlet of the Vicksburg batteries at nighttime. He will take the *Benton* and another eleven gunboats and rams and proceed south of Vicksburg to a point of crossing at Hard Times Landing. The navy will ferry supplies and soldiers across the Mississippi below Vicksburg where we will then advance on the city from the south. I will have General McClernand open a road for the men on the west side of the Mississippi River from Millikens Bend to a point on the river where Admiral Porter's flotilla will be waiting to cross him along with the rest of the army. Colonel Grierson and one thousand troopers in his cavalry command will also create a diversionary move to cut railroad and communication lines to the east of Vicksburg. You, Sherman, will create a feint at Haines Bluff and will then proceed down the west side of the Mississippi to join the entire army at the point of crossing. We will unite the entire command south of Vicksburg this way. We will then be able to strike General Pemberton or General Johnston east of the city. This will give us our best shot at victory."

Grant puffed his cigar once more then flicked it into the Yazoo. "Do you have any questions, gentlemen?" he asked.

"General, will we be abandoning our supply line?" Sherman asked.

"The men will carry rations of hard bread, coffee, and salt until we land. The country will furnish the balance until our line is firmly established."

Both Sherman and Porter nodded. Sherman extended his hand to Porter. "Admiral, I will wait for you below Vicksburg and will join you after your success."

"And how do you propose to do that?" replied Porter.

"I will row out to you when you run the gauntlet. I will meet you on this deck to celebrate it!" Sherman's eyes beamed.

Porter turned to Grant and then looked back at Sherman. He stroked his beard once and then replied, "The thought of rowing to me is crazy, but so was doing a night march through the bayou. You rescued me once. Maybe this time, I will be rescuing you!" Porter smiled, nodded, and shook Sherman's hand.

Sherman returned the grip and looked at Grant. "Good luck, Admiral," he said confidently. "Godspeed. I will see you downriver."

Chapter 38

Union Steam Ram Lafayette

Ninety-Third Illinois River Crossing
Bruinsburg, Mississippi
Fifty-Five Miles South of Vicksburg
May 1, 1863

Engines groaned. Smokestacks belched both white and black clouds of smoke into the clear blue sky as ironclad steamers, side-wheelers, and gunboats traveled back and forth off the Bruinsburg shore.

The Ninety-Third Illinois took to the river again after marching for what seemed endless miles through mossy forests and cane breaks. They arrived at the shore and then tramped up the gangplank to the deck of the ironclad *Lafayette*. Standing prominently on the foredeck at the bow in full uniform and cap was a young sailor who stood vigilantly as he watched the muddy waters to the east. Aaron, Will, T.J., and Trick moved quickly to where he stood. The point of the bow took whip splashes from the constant wave motion caused by the weight of the flotilla moving to and fro.

"You boys don't look like those white-gloved boys from the East Coast," observed the sailor dryly. He stared ahead at the east bank of the river, which was less than a mile away.

"We're with the Union Army of the Tennessee...Illinois boys," Will replied.

"Well, it looks like you're all gonna be in a fix shortly. You can hear guns in the distance from the other side now." He paused and then gave a short signal to another seaman.

"Did the *Lafayette* run the batteries with Admiral Porter?" Aaron asked.

"She sure did. We were second in line, right behind the *Benton*. This old lady took lots of hits. You can see the dents in her iron," he said proudly. After peering again to the east, he raised his arm, and the *Lafayette* nosed into the river. Now under way, the sailor turned his attention to the soldiers. He used his hands to describe the movements of the flotilla that made it through the Vicksburg fortress batteries.

"This old girl is as tough as they come!" he said. "We got some solid broadsides at the town as we passed one by one, and we all made it save one, the *Henry Clay*, but she was beached."

A ram followed by a side-wheeler and then followed by another ironclad crisscrossed the waters like a busy New York harbor. The mixture of steam and coal smoke belched upward, catching the upward draft, which swirled against the clear noon sky and stood like a beacon to the mission at hand. Porter's navy continued the crossing. By the end of the day, twenty thousand Yankee soldiers would step on Mississippi soil.

"Do you see that gunboat comin' with a bone in her teeth, kickin' up all that foam?" the sailor asked as he pointed to the north. "You see... you see...the one with double stacks?"

The boys nodded.

"Well, by jiminy, that is the *Benton*! She's the pride of our fleet! And you won't believe this, but your General Sherman rowed out to her right after we passed the Vicksburg batteries! We were right behind the *Benton* in line and about sunk him and his bogtrotter crew. We thought maybe they were rebels attacking from the western shore. That son of a bitch almost got himself shot by us. Thank God our lookout recognized the grizzly old fool!"

Will stepped forward and replied, "That Sherman may be crazy, but he saved your navy at Rolling Fork. He saved ol' Porter with that candlelight march, didn't he?"

The boys nodded and smiled in unison. Aaron and Trick raised their muskets. T.J. lifted the butt of his Sharps rifle slightly off the toe of his boot.

"You know, when it comes down to it," T.J. said, "it's this type of iron that finishes the fight!" He lifted his rifle perpendicular over his head.

The sailor seemed humbled by the remarks. He looked again at the eastern shore, which was fast approaching, and replied, "It will be Union iron on land and sea that finishes this war. Godspeed to all of you. You beetle crunchers best take care of yourselves, and don't be no gophers when the lead starts flying."

Trick pulled up his cartridge belt, which had slipped almost down to his knees, and patted his shiny black leather cartridge box. "These forty cartridges are ready and awaitin' for a big fight up yonder!" He pointed to the shore. The sounds of cannonading could be heard in the distance as the engines cranked down.

T.J. patted his box, too. "Forty dead men," he said.

With a jolt and a jerk, the *Lafayette* reached the opposite shore and came to a stop. The oak gangplank was dropped into the red mud. The soldiers moved quickly to the shore, advancing into the tall cane breaks that rose to the height of fifteen feet. When Trick got to the opening in the canes, he stepped quickly to the side so as not to get trampled by the blue horde. He looked at the bow of the *Lafayette*. The sailor was still there, staring motionless at the movements of the soldiers with both hands on his hips.

Trick waved his musket in order to get the sailor's attention. He then raised it as high as he could and saluted him with his right hand.

Seeing Trick, the sailor came to attention and replied with the snap of a smart salute.

Trick held his salute as long as he could. He then turned to join the others, slipped on the mud, and nearly dropped his musket before entering the ranks.

The sailor remained silently at attention, right hand in salute, waiting until the last soldier disappeared into the cane breaks.

Chapter 39

Ninety-Third Illinois Volunteers

On Mississippi Soil
Next Day

The dust rose from the marching Union troops in thick clouds. The four friends of the wigwam stayed close, as if protecting each other in some way from what lay ahead. The road extended east for the most part, cutting like a channel into a jungle of vines and cypress trees. Though the sun was hidden by the tangled density, occasionally a small break in the canopy caused a ray to descend on the column of blue-clad soldiers. The relentless tramping of boots kicked up red clay dust, causing a continuous chorus of coughing.

Will, Aaron, Trick, and T.J. felt closer now than ever before. Will was still the leader of the group, tall and strong, his blue kepi firmly fixed on his brow and contrasting smartly with his sandy-blond hair. Aaron, always straight as an arrow, was still quick in mind and movements. T.J., even taller now, was as lean as a rail and still the quiet one. Towering above the group, he was always steady in his movements and had the eye of an eagle. His buddy from Buda, Trick, as always, was quick to engage anyone with a handshake and a grin. He had lost a few pounds since his enlistment but still relished the thought of each meal, whether it was plain hardtack, dandy funk, bully soup, hog and hominy, or just hish and hash. His uniform continued to be in disorder, his oval US belt buckle often dangling below his belly button, and his boots were the dustiest of all. But it didn't matter to him much. He was with his friends, marching in a grand conquest, the memories of which he knew he would relish for a lifetime.

"We best get out of this damn tree tunnel soon, lest we all turn to sacred dust from the chokin' and spittin'," Trick announced. "We keep this up for too much longer, and I 'spect we'll have a few mossbacks runnin' back home."

"I don't 'spect anyone is gonna turn back now," Will replied as he gasped for air and then coughed. "Grant's entire army will be over here soon, and we're all in for a good fix."

Trick turned to Will and nodded, pulling his pants up with his right hand as he shouldered his musket on his left. "Sure wish we coulda helped General Smith yesterday. I heard from a teamster this morn that he whipped those rebels and took a lot of prisoners up ahead of us."

"Well, I am sure we'll all be joining him soon," Aaron replied as he wiped red dust from his brow onto his sleeve.

Just then, the entire column came to a quick and intruding halt, causing a domino effect in the tight quarters. The boys jammed into each other. The clang of canteens and the shuffle of feet announced the intrusion up ahead.

"Whoa to us Suckers!" Trick cried out. "Do you see what I see? By God, it's a sight!"

The boys looked ahead into a clearing. The tunnel of greenery that was the forest ended before a field containing a glorious white mansion. Standing tall and defiant, the white bastion to southern aristocracy was trimmed with an array of roses and other flora that cast their fragrant smell to the boys. They were stunned by the magnificence that spread before them.

Corinthian columns from the base of the mansion rose twenty feet and supported a roof with an extended cupola on the top. These columns stood like silent sentries, spaced eight to a side, creating a balance pleasing to every eye on the dusty red footpath. Protruding from the roof were six chimneys, which kept the spacious rooms warm during the dead of winter. Between the columns windows continued around the house like a cavalcade of glass.

"Bet Lincoln's White House ain't as big as this one," Trick said.

The friends nodded.

"No house this big back home," added T.J. as he placed his mouth on his sleeve and coughed twice. "Good spot to clear our throats!"

"Wonder who owns this place," Aaron said.

Suddenly, there was the sound of hooves thundering from the other side of the house. Three riders rounded the corner of the house in a quick gait. Colonel Putnam on Black Hawk was in the lead. They advanced to the halted column of soldiers. Black Hawk, as always a bundle of nervous energy, danced a bit when the colonel reined him to a stop, causing the soldiers nearest him to back away. Black Hawk's eyes had a fury about them, almost wide-eyed. Putnam, well familiar with his war-horse's habits, kept Black Hawk on a short rein.

"Boys, we have to keep moving," Putnam said. "There are rebels all over this country. We missed General Smith's big fight yesterday, and it is not my intention to miss another one!" He pulled back on Black Hawk's reins, causing the horse to rear up, stabbing the air with his forelegs.

"Colonel!" Will shouted from the front ranks. "The men were wondering what this mansion is called. We'd like to write it down in our journals."

"There will be plenty of things to write down when this campaign is over!" replied Putnam. "Lots of dead rebels and lots of Yankee victories!"

Putnam pulled on Black Hawk's reins again, keeping him steady as the war-horse impatiently stomped the red dust. Realizing that he failed to answer the simple question, he pointed at the mansion. "Boys, that's the Windsor Mansion. It was built from the sweat of Negroes who toiled this infernal red soil for the white man for many, many years. It is the slave who put these columns up, and it will be this war that brings them down. I have been informed that many Negroes, now freed by

Mr. Lincoln's proclamation, will soon be coming our way to the boats." Putnam peered down the road that led directly south from the mansion.

"Captains," announced Putnam, again reining in the excited Black Hawk, "form your men and march this road south for about two miles where you will find an intersecting road that only goes west. Continue south where you will find a rise about a mile farther. Take your men up the hill and rest them in the shade of the trees there. I will join you with further orders when I get there." Saluting the men, he bent forward and galloped Black Hawk around the mansion with the other two riders following closely.

The Ninety-Third Illinois captains formed their men in perfect rank and file. The road was wider now, which helped the formations, and the sun rose high. As they marched, the clouds of dust rose again but moved to the heavens unobstructed by the trees. The choking was replaced by soldier banter.

The column of tired men moved on as Colonel Putnam instructed. Within an hour they had reached the intersection that he referred to and then continued south to a rising ridge that stood a distance from the eastern edge of the Mississippi River floodplain. They pulled off their caps, hats, and accoutrements and rested in the shade of the trees that climbed upward from the ridge. Sure enough, there was a church in the distance, slightly to the south, with a spiral pointing to the clear blue sky. Within minutes the thundering sound of horse hooves could be heard again. Rising from the ridge before them was Colonel Putnam on his black stead.

"Boys," Putnam announced excitedly, "hold down your weapons. There is a false reconnaissance that a column of rebels is advancing up this road. Do you see the rabble around the church down there?" He dismounted Black Hawk, giving the reins to an orderly sergeant. Pulling out his field glasses, Putnam peered into the lenses to get a closer look. "Aha!" he continued. "Those are Negroes, hundreds of them, heading up the road now that our army has cleared it. I see women, children, and old men mostly with packs on their backs, a few goats and an old mule, too."

The soldiers remained silent as Putnam revealed what he saw. The tone of his voice changing to one of pity, he said, "Why, that line of poor contrabands has got to be over a half-mile long!" He put down the field glasses and walked over to the soldiers, some of whom were lying flat on their backs with exhaustion.

"Private Lockwood!" shouted Putnam.

T.J., who was standing deep in the blue ranks, reached for his rifle and stepped to the front. "Yes, Colonel," he replied respectfully. "I am here."

"T.J.," Putnam caught himself. "I mean, Private Lockwood, do you still recall what you did during the Freeport fire?"

"Yes, sir, that was the winter of fifty-seven, almost six years ago."

"Is that in your hands the rifle you used to set off the powder kegs from the belfry tower?"

"It's a different Sharps, sir! It's a sniper's rifle. Captain Taggart convinced the quartermaster to issue me this beauty instead of a musket after I won a shooter's contest."

Colonel Putnam nodded, and then pointing to the church in the distance, he said, "I want to get a read on the distance to that church from here to know for sure how long that line of Negroes is for my report. Do you think you can hit that bell in the belfry down there so I can determine the distance?"

"Sure...will try, sir. My leaf sight is steady, and the windage should be good with all this dust rising straight up. I will try to get a bead on it."

"Come forward then, son, and let's see what you can do." Putnam smiled confidently. He patted T.J. on the back and continued. "I have a wager for you. If you can hit that church bell once from here, the regiment will have supper in the town of Ingraham tomorrow. It is about twenty miles from here, and my scouts report there is a barn full of hams, lots of them...enough for the entire regiment."

Putnam looked at the men and raised his eyebrow as he scratched his jet-black beard.

"If you hit it twice," he said wryly, "we will swim in the clear waters at Hankinson's Ferry the following morning!"

All of the men, even the most tired stragglers, stood up now and looked at the Bethel Church in the distance.

"Come on, T.J., you can do it!" shouted a random member of the Ninety-Third.

"You are better than Davey Crockett!" cried out another.

"Do it for the good ol' Sucker State!" yelled out yet another.

There was silence now on the ridge line. Sweaty brows were wiped clean as everyone peered in the distance. All ears waited in the quiet as T.J. faced the church.

Putnam pulled up his binoculars again and nodded at T.J.

T.J. moved to a spot just in front of the men. He grabbed the visor of his kepi and spun it around so that the brim could not obstruct his aim. Still snugged within the hatband was the oak leaf that Allie had given the boys for courage. It had dried up and crumbled a bit, but it was still visible.

The breechblock dropped back from the Sharps as T.J. pushed forward the lever that protected the trigger when closed. Reaching into his cartridge box, he pulled out a linen-covered cartridge round, placing it securely in the barrel breech with the conical lead ball facing forward. He pulled the lever upward, securing the round for the final step. He then placed a small ignition cap that looked like a tiny top hat on the cone at the breech above the block where the cartridge was secured. The Sharps was now ready to deliver its load.

"Sir, I am ready now," T.J. announced with calm determination.

"Proceed, Private Lockwood," Putnam replied.

T.J. wiped his brow with his left sleeve. Reaching down, he looked to the leaf sight on the breech of the barrel and adjusted it to four hundred yards. There was no wind.

The double-set trigger clicked once as T.J. rested the Sharps on a sturdy low branch of a small oak tree. He took in a deep breath and placed the bead at the tip of the rifle on the belfry target. The movement of figures around the church did not disturb him. He breathed in and out and then pulled the hammer back to full cock.

Taking in one last deep breath, T.J. steadied his rifle, pulled the trigger.

The report of the rifle was followed a second later by the sound of a single peal from the belfry bell, causing the surprised gathering around the church to scatter in all directions.

On the ridge the boys cheered and immediately pounced on T.J., slapping his back in appreciation. His prized Sharps rifle dropped to the ground with a thud.

"Boys, hold back!" Putnam announced, "Give way. He has one more wager to go!"

The throng of blue moved back as T.J. reached down and picked up his Sharps. He did not grin, but he smiled slightly, the corners of his lips barely rising.

"Sir, the distance is four hundred yards to that church," T.J. replied as he stood straight with his hand now on its muzzle. The butt of the gun rested between his boots.

"My God," Putnam beamed. "That was the best shot I ever saw. I will include your action in my report tonight. That is the best news. The sad news is that line of Negroes is about a half-mile long. We will meet them soon and share what rations we have."

A moment passed, and then Putnam looked down to his knee-high riding boots. He held his field glasses to his side.

"Well, Private Lockwood, do you wish to try for my other wager… the swim in the river at Harkinson's Ferry?" Before he could finish the question, several soldiers chimed in words of encouragement for a second shot and the prize.

T.J. looked at his friends, who stood motionless as everyone waited. "No, sir," he replied calmly in a low, steady tone. "I don't want to scare those poor folk again, and sure 'nough, these rivers down here are chock-full of copperhead snakes. I 'spose my luck would run out if I got bit by one."

"Yeah, Colonel," Trick added. "We'd rather swim in the Pecatonica. There ain't no copperheads back home in Freeport."

"You're right, Private Kane," Putnam replied. "The copperheads in our state don't hang around rivers. They hang around the newspaper offices in the big cities. They have two legs, talk like the devil, slander Old Abe, and would like to see the Union and our cause crumble like dust!"

"Those folks are worse than snakes," Trick replied.

Putnam nodded. He walked over to Black Hawk and mounted him.

The blue lines formed in good order again, and the soldiers descended from the ridge to share their rations.

Chapter 40

General John E. Smith
Headquarters

Big Black River
Near Hankinson's Ferry
May 5, 1863

The canvas cot squeaked as Smith reached to pull the lamp closer to his small stack of linen writing paper. The soldiers were deep in slumber now. It was close to midnight. With no orders to give to adjutants or other subordinates, it was a quiet yet unsettling time of night, and because of it, his mind quickly drifted back to Galena.

He missed his family deeply. He tried to think good thoughts. He thought of Black Hawk, too, and the hot August day when Ely Parker, the Indian-engineer-now-Yankee adjutant, and Grant, Galena-store-clerk-now-commanding-general, were all smiles in their loose-fitting shirts with sleeves rolled up. He thought of his young son, Ben, who walked with Parker and Grant to the front porch of the Smith home with Black Hawk, and the laughter and joy when he shook Parker's hand and bought the young colt. His mind, though, quickly shifted to the memories of his family's tears and their solemn stares as he marched the Forty-Fifth Illinois Lead Mine Regiment out of town a few years later. Clouded with mixed emotions, he also thought of son Alfred, who was now in the army and sick, and his whereabouts were unknown.

Rubbing his temples in a circular motion with the fingertips of both hands, he tried to clear the confused thoughts. He sat down on his portable camp chair, which was positioned in front of his field desk. Reaching for a piece of writing paper, he picked up his pen and dipped the tip twice into the little rosewood inkwell. The lamplight dimmed and then flickered.

> *Head Qrs 1st Brig 3d Div 17 A.C.*
> *Camp in the Field Big Black River May 5th/63*
> *My Dear Aimee*
> *I suppose before you get this you will have heard that we have had another Battle at Thompsons Hill near Port Gibson. I thank God I have escaped injury although it was well contested. Yet my Brigade lost very little, about 6 killed & 30 wounded. None in the 45th regiment. I am very anxious to hear from you but I am afraid it will be some time before I get a letter. We shall have a hot time of it now for about a month as we are moving to the rear of Vicksburgh [sic]. The weather is very hot and my clothes I have not had an opportunity to get washed since I left you. I wish now I had left all my baggage at home. We have passed through a lovely country since leaving Milliken's Bend, flowers of all kinds and hedges for miles composed of Roses. It seems to me I have never seen the Queen of flowers in greater perfection. Genl Thomas, Adjt Genl of the US is here organizing Negro Regiments to be officered by whites… The army is in good health and spirits. As for myself I am well and my knee nearly so altho [sic] being in the Saddle constantly makes it very painful at times. I may say without vanity that I was complimented on the Field with the manner I handled my Brigade… Trusting that you are all in good health. May God have you in his Keeping now & ever.*
>
>

Your Husband,
Jno E S [15]
>

The general felt tired. He put down his pen. It was after midnight now. He stood up from his camp chair. It was just two steps to his bed, so the move to slumber was an easy one. Keeping his uniform and boots on, he sat on the cot rolled once and fell silently to sleep.

Nearby was Captain Cowan, who had since been elected lieutenant-colonel of the Forty-Fifth Lead Mine Regiment. Colonel Maltby was still sick, so he became the unit's new commanding officer, a fact that gave him great pride. Cowan lay motionless in his camp cot with his hands and arms braced behind his neck like a pillow. He stared upward at the moon, which seemed to eerily dart between the oak tree that served as his shelter. His lamp still flickered below his cot. After a few deep sighs, he pulled out his right arm and reached into his vest pocket for his watch. The hands of the watch showed that it was already morning.

In the darkness under the tree, his thoughts drifted back home to Apple Valley, Harriett, Molly, Phine, and Georgie. He wondered what tomorrow would bring and if he would have time to write them. Suddenly, he sat up, slipped his boots off the cot, stood up, and stretched. He reached for his camp desk, placed it on his lap, and turned up the flame in his oil lamp.

> *Black River, Miss, May 6, 1863*
> *Dear Harriet:*
> *We have had a hard time since I returned to the Regiment—*
> *almost incessant labor and marching through scorching sun;*
> *rain and mud; and we have slept without tents ever since*
> *we left Millikens Bend, La. The 25th of Apr. Thanks to God*
> *and my constitution, I have been well all the time. We have*
> *been on short rations…and drinking too much stagnant*
> *water in this hot country is very unwholesome…*
>
> *I have no more time to write. My love to you all—tell*
> *the children to be good…and go to school and learn as fast*
> *as they can; give my compliments to all our friends. I will*
> *write better and more elaborately as soon as I can…*

I am going to come home as soon as we take Vicksburg.
                                                    As ever,
                                              L. H. Cowan [16]

Like his general, the good captain settled himself on his camp cot and fell quickly into a deep sleep.

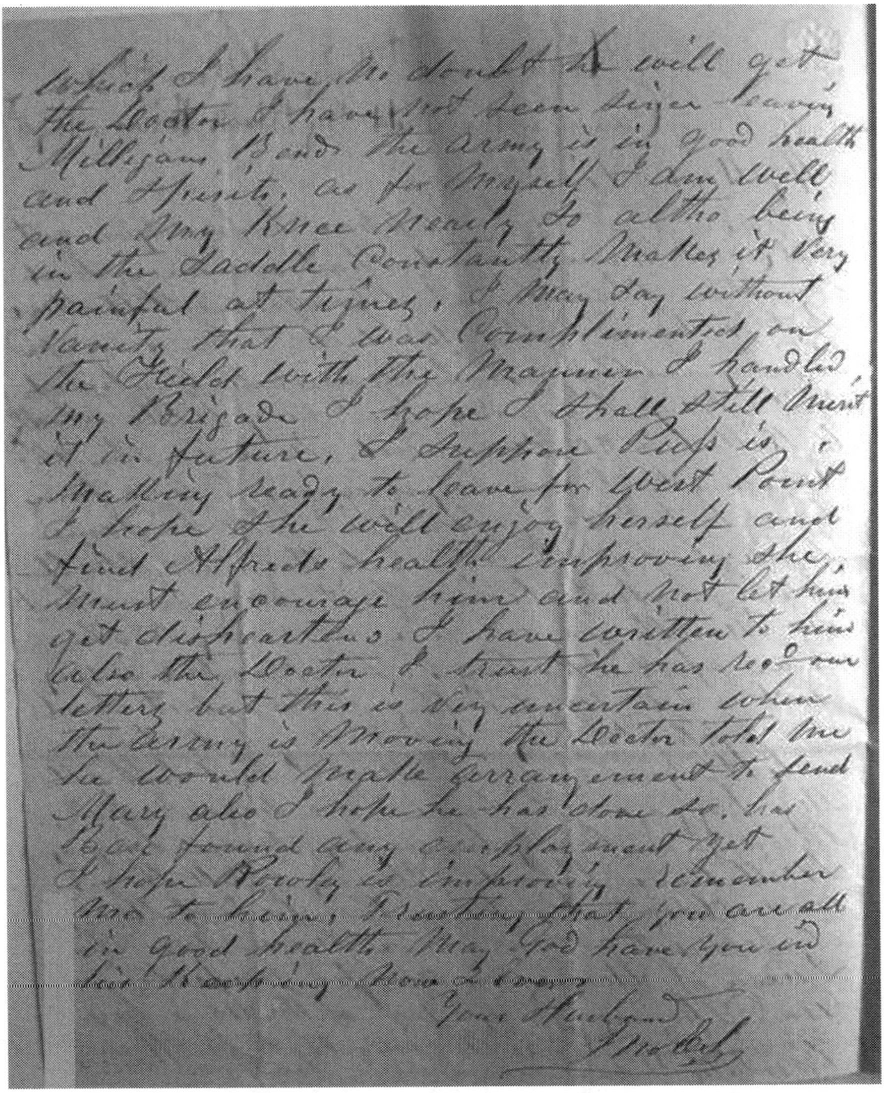

which I have no doubt he will get
the Doctor I have not seen since leaving
Milligans Band the army is in good health
and spirits, as for myself I am well
and my knee nearly so altho being
in the saddle constantly makes it very
painful at times, I may say without
vanity that I was complimented on
the field with the manner I handled
my Brigade I hope I shall still merit
it in future, I suppose Puss is
making ready to leave for West Point
I hope she will enjoy herself and
find Alfreds health improving she
must encourage him and not let him
get disheartened I have written to him
also the Doctor I trust he has recd our
letters but this is very uncertain when
the army is moving the Doctor told me
he would make arrangement to send
Mary also I hope he has done so. has
Bean found any employment yet
I hope Rooley is improving remember
me to him, Trusting that you are all
in good health may God have you in
his keeping now & ever
Your Husband
[illegible]

Original Letter from John E. Smith to His Wife, Aimee

Chapter 41

Champion Hill

Twenty-Two Miles East of Vicksburg
May 16, 1863

As with all great deceits of mankind, the meeting of the deadly armies commenced with a quiet and a magnificence.

The Mississippi countryside was resplendent with magnolias, and the skies were clear. The Ninety-Third Illinois rested with their colonel on a small rise. The clock ticked past noon.

In the distance a quiet rattle of muskets could be heard followed by the intermittent thud of cannon fire. The friends looked resplendent in their dark-blue uniforms. Hats and kepis were tilted smartly on their brows, the now-dried oak leaves that Allie had given them for courage stuck prominently in the hatbands. The oval US and eagle belt plates that held up their trousers and cartridge boxes were secured tightly so as not to encumber their contribution to the grand spectacle on the hill before them. Curiously, the hill was named Champion Hill after the Champion family whose house stood on its own rise just a half mile to the east, but, as if by fate, it was already named for a single victor.

"Do ya think we're gonna see the elephant this time, T.J.?" Trick asked nervously as he stared across the valley to Champion Hill. He grabbed his belt buckle and pulled it tighter.

"Well, since we've been damn lucky in a way, I'm sure the Ninety-Third will see it soon with all it's a thunderin'," replied T.J., who seemed unraveled by it all.

Will smiled and looked at Aaron and then at the other two friends of the wigwam. "I guess seeing the elephant doesn't include bees does it?"

"Don't see any beehives around here, but if we do, make sure to stay clear," Aaron warned.

"Now, what are ya'll talkin' about?" Trick said loudly. He looked at T.J., who shrugged his shoulders.

"Didn't you hear what happened to the Forty-Fifth Lead Mine Regiment?" Will replied. He pulled off his kepi and wiped his brow. The day was getting hotter by the minute. He continued. "Sergeant Crummer told me that two days ago at the battle of Jackson, the veteran Forty-Fifth, who had seen the elephant in over ten big battles, was lined up in battle formation. With the first rebel volley, minié balls went crashing through the beehives behind them, and those bees attacked the Forty-Fifth with a terrible ferocity. He said, and these are his exact words, that men can stand up and be shot all day with deadly muskets, but when a swarm of bees pounces upon a company of men in concert, it's beyond human nature to stand it, and so two or three companies retired from the field...and were reformed in a particular locality so as to avoid those southern bees. They had no rebel yell, but their charge on us was a successful one!"

"Well, hee hee," Trick chuckled. "I guess seein' the elephant is no worse than gittin a few bee stings!"

The friends smiled. There was a sense of nervous calm now as they continued to wait on the ridge.

Suddenly, a *zip* and a *thud* broke the anticipation and silence. A soldier dropped before the front rank and rolled, writhing like a snake. He kicked and reached for the air as he grabbed his throat, which gurgled with red foam. And then another *zip*, and another unfortunate dropped.

"Hold your positions! Let no man move forward," shouted Captain Taggart. "There is a sniper on that hill who we will deal with."

Putnam, sitting erect in his saddle, suddenly appeared in front of them. Another sniper ball droned by as a rapid sequence of cannonading thundered in the distance.

"Private Lockwood, step forward!" Putnam called out.

T.J. stepped forward as Putnam pulled out his field glasses. Black Hawk was fidgety and stomped around the first wounded soldier who continued to writhe in pain on the ground. The other was farther down the line. The boys could clearly see him holding his stomach in complete agony as he lay on his back, stomping the ground with his heels. Suddenly, he straightened out like a corpse, shouted "Momma" one last time, and then went silent. Black Hawk continued to kick up the red dust as Putnam reined him back.

"Private, I can see the sniper in the trees on that ridge before us, the one this side of that big hill. He looks like a dark silhouette about ten feet above that battery." He handed the glasses to T.J. as another sniper round zipped near the rank and file, landing with a thud in the ground in front of Black Hawk. Dust kicked up again.

"He's tryin' to get a bead on you, Colonel," T.J. said. "You best keep movin'."

"Take him out! I cannot afford to lose any of my men to that shooter."

"Sure enough," answered T.J. as he leveled his rifle and placed his sights on the irregular clump in the distant treetop before him. In a slow and distant tone of voice, he said deliberately, "I hope he's like us, Trick—no sweethearts, no loved one to worry about. Hope he's just a lone turtledove who has no one to hoot about."

He clicked the hammer back, took a breath, waited one second, and then pulled the trigger. The rifle cracked, causing many around him to flinch. They looked at the tree, and the rebel sniper dropped like a rag doll, falling onto a cannon barrel below. The body collapsed into a grotesque inverted V shape and then flipped down between the wheels.

A chorus of cheers from the line of blue caused an echo to clearly flow to the high hill before them.

The random comrade who first fell prey to the rebel sniper was silent now. His last agonies revealed by his final death grip on his throat. His eyes were dull, gray, and fixed wide open like a dead fish. Trick, seeing him lying motionless, quickly walked over to him, knelt down, and gently rubbed his palm across the fallen soldier's eyelids to close them. The soldier looked at peace now, sleeping. "You kin rest now," Trick said calmly. "You best be gettin' to heaven right quick. Colonel Put will find you a good restin' place here with the other boys in blue."

T.J. returned to the ranks, receiving pats on his shoulder and back. He smiled, feeling only a twinge of sorrow for what he had done. "An eye for an eye," he muttered. "The score is settled now. Hunter and prey are together with their maker."

"T.J., you dropped that rebel easier than a squirrel on the Pecatonica," announced Will excitedly as he looked at Trick and Aaron. Both nodded.

"Attention, Company! Shoulder arms!" shouted Captain Taggart, breaking the silence. "Left face! Forward march!" The company began to move quickly.

"Where are we goin' now, captain?" Trick asked nervously.

"Private Kane, keep your mouth shut," Taggart snapped back. "The regiment has been ordered off this hill and to the south side of this road."

Trick unabashed continued, "Well, cryin' out loud, Captain! That's just a big ol' mass of vines over there! We can't move through there! There are copperheads there for sure. Can't we take another road?"

"Kane, fall to the rear!" Taggart shouted. "I will deal with you there!"

Trick looked at his friends with some alarm, moved to the outside line of the ranks, and disappeared to the rear.

The five hundred officers and men of the Ninety-Third proceeded as ordered into the thick mass of tangled woods. Slipping and cursing, they moved forward, wondering, each one of them, how this movement could help the fight on the big hill ahead of them. Within a half hour, the order was countermanded, however, and the regiment moved out of the jumbled greenery and across the road to an open field. The deadly, obtrusive sounds of the "elephant" were bellowing stronger now over the hilltop. The noise seemed to be getting closer.

Captain Taggart sensing the tension in his men tried to ease it. "Let's open the ball," he said. Looking down the ranks, he smiled confidently and continued in a calm voice. "We will do all right today, boys. Just keep steady and listen to my commands." He pulled out his field officer's sword from its black leather scabbard and pointed it upward, wrist and elbow locked.

A soldier shouted from the rear of the ranks, "Cap'n, hope that cheese knife of yours can whip ol' Jeff Davis himself!"

The entire company hooted and howled. Will, Aaron, and T.J. instinctively turned quickly and peered to the rear ranks of the company.

T.J. smiled and shook his head. "Sounded like Trick, didn't it?"

Will and Aaron nodded and then looked back at the captain.

The quiet tension increased. Many shuffled their boots. The wait was too much. The silence made it worse.

Suddenly, from the rear, a general on horseback thundered up at full gallop. "For God's sake, put this brigade into the fight!" he screamed as his horse galloped around them.

Rapid-fire commands were shouted through the ranks, and the blue lines lurched forward again, this time directly toward the hill.

Will, Aaron, and T.J. stayed close together in the front of the column. Trick was lost somewhere in the rear. The regiment moved forward like a large beast crashing through a thicket. Cannon puffs blinked on distant hills. The boys were now just two hundred yards from seeing battle for the first time—"seeing the elephant" as the veterans called it—as the clanging of accoutrements and the confident shouts of officers provided some foolish comfort to it all.

As the hill loomed larger before them, scores of retreating blue coats, some carrying wounded comrades, cut swiftly through the advancing columns. All of them had distant stares. No one spoke. The boys in blue moved to the base of the hill and started a quick rush to the crest, stepping over mangled corpses from the early advances.

Trick was the last of the friends to see the bodies. He felt sick, almost vomited, but caught himself. Straggling a bit behind the blue mass in front of him, which rose rapidly up the hill, he pulled up his belt to prevent his pants from slipping.

When at the top of the hill, the last command shouted was, "Double-quick, march!" The blue horde then crashed down the other side of the slope into the deadly contest where the Confederates met them in a blast of fury. The red flame of hundreds of muskets returned the fire as rows of soldiers on each side fell forward in death and agony.

Trick leveled his rifle and pulled the trigger, sending a ball through the smoke in front of him. He reached again for another cartridge in his cartridge box and bit the linen to expose the gunpowder. Quickly, he poured the powder down the barrel, pulled out his ramrod, dropped the minié ball down, and then rammed the missile down to finally seat it. He pushed back his black hat, lifted his musket, pulled the hammer to the half-trigger position, placed on a percussion cap, cocked the hammer completely, aimed at a gray figure just thirty feet away, and then squeezed the trigger.

He could not hear his shot. The constant roar deafened him. Sheets of flame from thousands of muskets crossed in the air from both sides of the contest. Men shifted back and forth on the red Mississippi soil, clanking metal to metal, arms flailing with bayonets finding their way into the bellies of the unfortunates.

In the stunning silence in his mind, things seemed to move in slow motion. The rhythm of his firing took hold of him, and he continued to fire round after round into the cloud of smoke before him. He did not know where the friends were, and he did not care at the moment to meet up with them. The urgency of those around him locked his knees and kept him in place. Then there was a movement to his left.

"They are flanking us!" screamed one of the soldiers above the din of fire.

Trick turned his head quickly to his left where before him now stood a hundred rebel muskets. He reached quickly to his cartridge box. His peripheral vision then caught a blazing wave of fire from rebel muskets, which rolled over him with force, knocking him with a thud to the ground. Stunned, he reached to his belly. He felt a hole near his hip. Oblivious to his wound, the roar of the battle continued.

He lay on the ground, holding his left hip. Silent dreams rose up. His thoughts were peaceful now. As he looked to the sky, he could see no blue, only the gray clouds of smoke passing by. He blinked.

Soon the face of a gray-clad soldier appeared before him. The rebel had piercing blue eyes. His face was covered in black soot and powder. Trick blinked again, but the face remained. The rebel looked kind, Trick thought, like someone he knew from his hometown in Buda. Then, in a quick movement, Trick felt a hand on his shoulder. The rebel reached down and gently pulled off his cartridge belt. He felt no pain from the move. The Confederate infantryman looked into Trick's eyes again, nodded, and then disappeared into the swirling white smoke.

Trick's mind drifted back to the Pecatonica, the river, and the wigwam where his friends once gathered. He envisioned a patchwork of colored leaves swirling around his favorite fishing hole and then slipping slowly downriver. He could hear the girls' giggles and the hearty laughs of the boys that always filled the air after a good prank. He wondered now if he would ever live to see any of them again. He looked up again. He felt a strange peace about him now, a sense of harmony as he lay among the damp leaves. Then out of the peace, a voice called out to him.

"Trick! Patrick Kane!"

Yes, he thought, that is definitely someone calling for me.

He blinked. There was that familiar voice again.

Craning his neck to the left and then to the right, he noticed the fighting had moved away from him. A rebel battery blazed from a distant hill, and a random round zipped above him, causing him to flinch.

"Trick! Patrick Kane of the Ninety-Third! Are you here?"

Trick was sure now—it was T.J.!

"T.J., over here! Over here, T.J.!"

He rose his hand to signal where he was. He could see T.J. thrashing and tripping like a drunkard in the distance.

"I can't see you, Trick! Call out for me again!"

"Over here! Over here! T.J.!"

T.J. was just twenty feet away now, and Trick could not move. So he pushed his right hand up and waved it as furiously as he could in order to gain T.J.'s attention. The clouds of smoke were lifting now, so he was hoping T.J. could see and find him.

Surely and suddenly, he could feel a grip on his hand. A drop of blood fell on his face.

"Help me, Trick! Please help me! I can't see! Everything is black!"

Trick looked up from his prone position with horror. T.J.'s eyes were missing, both shot out by a musket ball, exposing oozing clots of blood, dirt, and soot in the sockets. He looked like a monster.

Trick quickly composed himself, looked away, and took a deep breath. He knew that for his friend's sake, he could not panic. He did not think of his own wound anymore and thought only about how he could help T.J. Softly he said, "T.J., you are safe now. I'll be a takin' good care of ya."

Tears welled up in Trick's eyes as he looked at T.J. and tried to turn on his side. "You can lie right here with me for a moment! We'll git outa here real soon. We'll get through this together. Lie down, T.J....Rest here with me," he implored.

T.J. responded, gripping leaves with both hands as he squatted and then crumpled to the ground in silence.

Trick squirmed and winced from his wound. A flash of red suddenly caught his peripheral vision. He turned and noticed a young Yankee about a rod's distance away resting at the base of a tree. The soldier had his musket across his lap and was silent. He had a red kerchief wrapped around his neck.

Pulling with both hands, Trick managed to drag himself across the distance, grunting with each movement. It seemed like an eternity. As he got closer, he called out to his comrade in blue, hoping to rouse him from his sleep. Crawling closer, he shouted, "By jiminy, can you grab my hand and help me?"

The resting Yankee did not look up.

Moving closer, Trick grabbed the young lad in blue. The pull caused the young lad to pivot and fall to the side of the tree.

The boy was dead.

"My God," gasped Trick. *That young boy could not be sixteen,* he thought, as he unknotted the red kerchief and placed it in his teeth. After taking a few deep breaths, he crawled back, wincing in pain with each methodical move.

"Here ya go, ol' friend," comforted Trick as he reached for T.J., "now, just bow your head a bit, and I'm gonna tie this around your eyes." T.J.

bent forward. Trick lifted the kerchief and gently placed it over his eyes, quickly tying a knot behind his head.

"Trick, where are you hit?" T.J. asked calmly.

"In my belly a little above my left hip. Don't hurt much, 'less I move." Trick gasped as he tried to sit up.

"Sounds like the armies are movin' away from this spot. Let's get to the rear," replied T.J.

"I can't walk, T.J. It hurts a handful when I try."

"I can lift you, ol' friend. You can be my eyes."

Trick sat up. A sharp pain shot up from his hip, settling in his right shoulder. He watched as T.J. rose up before him and extended his hand back down to assist him up. T.J. grasped both of Trick's hands, pulled him up, and then hunched him over. He was now positioned on T.J.'s stout shoulders. As T.J. settled him in, Trick cried out in pain from the move.

"Best go back to that Champion house we passed this morning," T.J. said calmly after taking a deep breath.

"Sounds good," Trick replied. "Go to the right. I'll make sure we get there. Just feel for loose rocks, and I'll help you with the stumps and all. We'll make it back for sure."

The two boys from Buda stepped out of the chaos, proceeding as one person, one human form, best friends who had now given up themselves to the gods of war; never giving in to resting on the bloody battlefield, where buzzards would soon descend in flocks, waiting for the living to pass to eternity before feasting on flesh. Their breaths of determination helped them to carry each other in a different way, step by step, stumble by stumble, and yet still remaining in balance.

"Trick, remember that three-legged race we won in Buda?"

"Yes, I do."

"Tell me about it. It will ease my pain as we walk together, my friend."

Trick tightened the kerchief on T.J.'s head again and replied, "That fourth of July was a dandy. Remember, we were just about ten years old, I reckon, when Mister Mayor announced that a nickel would be given to both winners…And you know who won, crossing the finish line first with a leg tied to each other? That was us, T.J.! We sure made a good match in that race!"

T.J. stopped momentarily and shifted Trick's weight again over his belt so as not to lose him. The movement caused Trick to grunt and catch his breath.

"Keep going, T.J. I can hold onto your shoulders a little more tightly. Put me down if you are feelin' like a mule with me."

T.J. turned his neck to listen more closely as the groans from the wounded began to rise up around them. The battle, though, seemed to be fading away as if moving into the distance.

"I see a house on a hill, T.J., not much farther to go. Just about the distance between the wigwam and my fishin' hole."

"Thanks," replied T.J. with a heavy breath. "Keep on with the story."

"Well, as we know, what's true back then is as true right now. You were like a beanstalk, and I was about the size of a plump farm dog standing on his hind legs!" T.J. chuckled.

"And what the townsfolk didn't know is that we practiced for two weeks before that race. And when we lined up for that race with the bands playin' and all, you could see the young uns and old folks chucklin' at the sight of us! A beanstalk whose left leg was tied to the right leg of, well…me! And what a sight we were!" Trick grunted and winced. His eyes began to tear up a bit from the story. He wiped his eyes with his right sleeve while holding T.J. firmly with his left arm.

"And when the pepperbox pistol fired once, we took off like we were one…like a white-tailed deer jumpin' in the woods. With each step we shouted to each other *one-two, one-two, one-two* to keep our feet in step, never looking back, and finishing the race…the strangest-looking pair to ever win that race in Buda! In fact, those chucklers and doubters who felt sorry for us immediately cheered and ran over to us! We were town heroes that summer, for sure! The *one-two* shouts we practiced a long time. Remember, T.J.?"

T.J. smiled.

"Hey, T.J., I can see the white house on the hill. You can put me down now."

T.J. groaned and outwardly sighed, not from the burden on his back, but with the remembrance of the famous Buda race and his lifelong friendship with Trick.

The Battle of Champion Hill had ended.

As the last wisps of gun smoke drifted away, the dead could still be seen clinging to the places where they gave up their spirits. Mangled bodies lay in clumps at the base of the hill. Trick tried not to look at them. The sun was descending now, and the boys worked their way up the hill to the Champion homestead. The echoes of cannons were lost now to distant hills, and the pitiful cries of wounded soldiers were no longer.

They could hear no calls for water.

No forlorn cries for Mother.

Chapter 42

Champion House

May 17, 1863

Night had fallen upon the house.

In the dining room just off the front parlor was a large table that could seat the whole Champion family with ease at Christmastime. In fact it served as the centerpiece of gatherings for many happy occasions. The battle had changed its purpose now, and the table felt the brunt of an army surgeon's saw that quickly, cut, cracked, and separated mangled limbs from the wounded soldiers. Forty hours had passed since the first shots were fired. The battered legs and arms, testimonials to the terrible destruction, were tossed through a window into the darkness and landed, one by one, on a gruesome, tangled heap.

Because amputation could not mend their wounds, Trick and T.J. were spared that treatment. Instead they lay on cots outside under a large oak tree. It had rained briefly in the morning, but their clothes were dry now. The Third Brigade's surgeon had passed through early in the morning during the rainfall and looked at the boys' wounds. He said T.J. would live, never to see again, but Trick, with his gut wound, would not make it through the month. That realization hit both of them hard. Yet despite their grief, they were thankful that they were still together, a comfort in what they saw as Trick's final days.

The big oak tree where they lay was cordoned off by the surgeons for soldiers with gut wounds, a sort of departure point, a dying place for these mortally wounded unfortunates. About fifty were gathered there around the tree with Trick, all waiting for judgment day. Many clutched their Bibles, and a few read loudly into the night. Under the tree, bayonets, which once proudly snapped onto the muzzles of shiny muskets, were now used as cradles for bright vigil candles, casting strange shadows in the branches above. The toad-stickers, as they were jokingly called on the march, were spiked point down into the ground by each cot, the sleeve of the bayonet now facing upward so a candle could be placed where the musket muzzle had been. And as the lights flickered in the night, the groans and moans subsided with each hour. Some of the men slept for the night, others for eternity.

"T.J., you OK?" Trick grunted as he turned in his cot.

"Just fine, Trick. Can't see nothin', but from the chirpin' out there, I 'spect we're deep into the night.

"I don't wanna die yet," Trick sobbed as he held his left sleeve to his face to wipe his tears. "I never wanted to hurt nobody. I just wanna fish on the Pecatonica."

"We'll be back soon. You jist wait and see. There ain't nothin' gonna keep us from goin' home, you see."

Trick sobbed louder now. "I don't wanna go home in a box, T.J.. I wanna catch one last cat in the river. Wish to see the girls and the wigwam one last time."

Suddenly, a soldier appeared at the foot of their cots. But, because of the darkness, Trick could not make out the soldier's features. Instead of moving on, the soldier stayed where he was. Alarmed, Trick shouted, "Who are you, and what do ya want, soldier? Show your face in the light, or I will draw this toad-sticker on you!"

The soldier hesitated for a moment and then replied, "Bet you coulda used that ol' sticker on the Pecatonica last summer!"

The voice sounded oddly familiar. T.J. sat up in his cot and cocked his head, trying to place it.

"Step up so we can see you!" Trick grabbed the bayonet vigil light and raised it as the soldier slowly advanced. He gasped in surprise when the soldier's face came in view.

"Who is it, Trick?" asked T.J..

An astonished Trick stared at the soldier, unable to speak. He could not believe his eyes. For a moment he wondered if his wound was causing him to hallucinate.

"Trick, who is it? Tell me!"

Trick thrust the bayonet back into the ground.

"It's Allie, T.J.! For cryin' jiminy, it's Allie!" He turned and sat up as best he could, managing a smile despite the pain from his wound.

T.J. grinned ear to ear and sat up in anticipation of a kiss and a hug.

"Shh! Keep your jabbers quiet!" Allie whispered as she placed her forefinger on her lips. "You'll wake up the whole Union army if ya keep it up!"

The boys were happy to hear her drawl again. She walked between the cots and sat next to Trick, placing a hand on the knee of each boy. She then became somber as she looked at T.J.

"Allie, where'd ya git that uniform? Did ya steal it?"

"Shh! My name ain't Allie. It's Albert…Albert Cashier!" Allie said. Trick noticed her long hair was gone and that she did look like a man… sort of.

"Right after you boys joined the Ninety-Third, I reckoned I could fight the rebs, too, so I joined the Ninety-Fifth in Rockford. Jenny cut my hair. I borrowed Colonel Putnam's hat, and I mustered in. That's jist about everythin'."

Trick scratched his head and replied, "So they think you are a man? You mustered in as a man?"

"Rightly so," Allie replied softly as she held her forefinger to her lips again. "Now, where are ya'll hit?"

"T.J. lost his eyes. The surgeon says I'm a gonner 'cause I got hit in the gut," replied Trick sadly.

Tears welled up in Allie's eyes. Her thoughts drifted quickly to the joyful days on the Pecatonica when she first met T.J., squirrel rifle in hand, and Trick with his cane pole. She remembered how they grinned at her when they first met, and the frolicking on the riverbank and in the wigwam. A tear escaped the corner of her eye, and she quickly wiped it away so Trick could not see.

"You boys will make it home soon. Best not be thinkin' of bad things. It only makes it worse." Allie walked away from the cots in toward the direction of the Champion house where a small oak tree stood. The limbs of the sapling were closer to the ground and within reaching distance.

"Where ya goin', Allie?"

Allie turned around quickly and defiantly stared at Trick, her hands on her hips.

Trick quickly added, "I mean where ya goin', Private Albert Cashier?"

Allie did not reply. A few minutes later she returned to their cots. As she sat down on the edge of T.J.'s cot, Trick saw that she was carrying something.

"Friends, now I want ya to do somethin' that you might think is odd, but I want ya to promise me you'll do it...every mornin'."

Both boys replied in unison, "We promise!"

Allie pulled out a bottle from her knapsack. She continued. "Gramma Lucy once cured a Winnebago Injun who got in a fix with a Potawatomi brave. The wound in his gut was an ugly thing, and no doc in the county would help the poor soul. Well, he made his way to Gramma Lucy's cabin, and she nursed him with some Irish whiskey. She poured a shot of it every day on the wound, and sure 'nough, it fixed him up!"

The boys cocked their heads.

"Now, take off that kerchief, T.J., and, Trick, you pull up your shirt."

The boys responded. They settled back on their cots, grunted, and exposed their wounds.

"Now, this is gonna hurt a bit, but you gotta keep doin' it every mornin'. T.J., I'm a dousin' your stitches first." She poured a shot of the whiskey, distributing it on both suture lines.

T.J. crossed his arms and pulled upward, gasping, but he did not scream.

She then turned to Trick, drew another shot in the glass, and poured it in his wound.

Trick kicked his feet, turned on his side, and coughed deeply, almost gagging from the pain.

"Looks like that rebel ball cut ya good, Trick, but at least it moved on. Ya won't be takin' that lead back to Buda! If it a hurts too much, drink a little nip before ya pour. If ya run out soon, make sure ya git the good stuff, ya hear!"

The boys rolled around, grimacing, which caused their cots to squeak. They settled down in a few minutes, but both sweated profusely from Allie's medicine.

"Got somethin' else for ya." She reached into her knapsack again and pulled out oak leaves that she picked from the Champion house sapling. She grabbed Trick's black hat and T.J.'s kepi, placing a small green oak leaf where the crumbled brown ones had been.

"Trick, do you remember the time you climbed the Injun oak and... slipped and fell in the river?"

"Sure do, Allie—Albert." Trick grinned. "I fell off that ol' oak and hit that river like an elephant. Didn't hurt much. Us friends all had a good ol' laugh about it!"

"Do you remember what I said to you, Trick?" Allie placed her hands on both of their shoulders. "Remember when you were movin' up that Injun oak, and I said, 'I'll be patient if ya just hang on'? Well, I'll always be patient—you friends just hang on now!"

The boys nodded, feeling much better than before.

The cot creaked again. It was time for Allie to return to her camp. She thought a good-bye kiss would help them but couldn't, even with the shadow of darkness. It was too risky. She did not want to reveal herself in the slightest, so she walked a few feet away and turned to the boys for one last look and waved.

"Have ya seen Will and Aaron?" she asked.

"Saw them right before the charge, but reckon they made it and are near Vicksburg now," T.J. replied.

Trick nodded. "They ain't on this hill, that's for sure."

Allie's smile was awkward now. Tears welled again in her eyes. She quickly wiped them with her sleeve so none of the other soldiers would see. Looking back at the friends one last time, she turned slowly to the west and then vanished into the darkness.

Chapter 43
Vicksburg

The rebels felt safer now.

The battered Confederate army under General Pemberton had re-treated in haste and rested behind the Vicksburg entrenchments, which snaked deep and far around the town. The fortifications weaved from their highest point, at two hundred feet, through ravines, cane breaks, brush, and trees and continued for seven circuitous miles. One hundred twenty-eight pieces of artillery extended along this line; thirty-six were heavy siege guns. The most famous of these Confederate guns, "Whistling Dick," threw large shells two feet long that screamed with fury across the skies and caused ghastly destruction as they bounced through columns of men, ripping off limbs, decapitating heads, and roaring to rest in the rear of the rank and file.

At key points along the line, the rebel engineers had constructed nine important forts, redans, or redoubts, as they were called, which served as the strongest gathering points for defensive action. These points, conversely, were gathering points for attacks by the Yankees since the breaching of any one of these points could cause a major weakening of the defenses and an eventual collapse of the rebel defenders. In that scenario thousands of Yankee troops would pour through the gap in the line like water through a dam break. Because of the importance of these forts to the overall defense of the line, all were constructed tall, typically twenty feet high. Behind them shooting platforms were placed for the rebel defenders to stand or kneel on. In the front of the forts on the attacking side was a deadly ditch about eight to ten feet deep and as much in length. The attackers then would have to cross this dry-moat depression before climbing up the wall of the fort. From the base of the depression at the wall, the attacking columns would have to jump, scratch, and crawl about five feet up out of the deadly ditch and then continue at an angle to the top of the fort for about another thirty feet. If they could do this and live, they would be eye to eye with the defenders.

The rebels were set. It was up to the Yankees, now, to make the next move.

Chapter 44

Stockade Redan

May 19, 1863
Three in the Afternoon

Allie's regiment was ready.

Captain Bush, who had enlisted her in Rockford, had given a few brave men special orders to lead the charge on the Confederate works. Allie and her comrades had constructed a crude but sturdy ladder that she would use to climb the outer wall of Stockade Redan. Since she was the shortest in the company and limber as a cat, she had volunteered to go over the top first.

She stood in formation with the rest of the Ninety-Fifth Illinois about five hundred yards from the fort. The charge of the Ninety-Fifth would be supported by the rest of Ransom's Brigade, which included the Eleventh and Seventy-Second Illinois and the neighboring state regiments the Fourteenth and Seventeenth Wisconsin. Allie and the Ninety-Fifth would take the lead.

Nearly half the distance before her was a ravine where the north fork of the Glass Bayou Creek flowed. Just to her right, a Confederate abatis was constructed that extended for about three hundred yards. The abatis consisted of large wooden poles that looked like huge spears buried into the ground side by side at a forty-five-degree angle with the sharp points facing the enemy. The sight was unsettling to her, and she looked away from it up into the skies above.

In the distance flew an American bald eagle that circled high above the Confederate works. Allie stared, and the wind rose up and softly cooled her countenance. *That bird is magnificent,* she thought as it soared effortlessly in the bright blue sky.

"Private Cashier!" shouted Captain Bush. "Face forward. We are about to make the advance!"

Allie pointed to the sky as best she could. She almost lost grip of the ladder.

"Cap'n," she replied, excitedly raising her voice to almost feminine glee, "take a look-see. I reckon that's an eagle up there!"

Bush looked to the north with the others in G Company.

"That's the eagle of the Eighth!" shouted an excited soldier from the back of the ranks. "His name is 'Old Abe,' and I 'spect he's up there scoutin' a few things for General Grant and the boys! The Eighth Wisconsin mustered him in when they joined up. It's their mascot, ya know, but I guess it's the whole army's now!"

"Well, I doubt if he can speak to the generals," replied Captain Bush, "but I do reckon that Old Abe will be a strange sight for those damn rebels in the works!" Bush looked down at his vest pocket and pulled out his watch. It was four o'clock, time to make the charge.

The rebels inside Stockade Redan were from the Seventh, Thirty-Sixth, and Thirty-Seventh Mississippi Volunteers. With their backs facing Vicksburg, they would stand firm to the man. Many had family in the town. They could clearly see the Yankee movements. The rebel guns glistened. Cannonballs were stacked in pyramids and ready.

"Well, do tell!" announced a reb as he chewed on his clay tobacco pipe. "There's an eagle up there flyin' above us!"

"Ya think that's an omen or somethin'?" asked an alarmed soldier.

"If it is, we need our sniper to kill it!"

"Too high! If it swoops low, we'll take it out with canister, like buckshot from a rifle!"

Some of the rebels watched Old Abe as he continued his lazy circling. Just then one soldier, keeping an eye on the Union line, shouted, "Colonel, the yanks are comin' sir! Their lines are formin' in columns!"

The Union troops advanced in an undulating blue mass, continuing in all of its magnificence for about two hundred yards. Both national and regimental banners flapped in the wind as if dancing on parade. The silver gleam of the bayonets made the Yankee soldiers look even more formidable. There was a silence now in the fort. The *thud, thud, thud* of tramping boots in formation could clearly be heard until the Yanks stopped at the river.

"Colonel, looks like they are a regroupin' or something," said a rebel soldier. "Can ya tell who they are with your field glasses?"

The colonel rested his elbows firmly on the cotton bale in front of him. The heat plus his nerves caused streaks of sweat to dribble from his brow into his beard. His butternut-gray forage cap showed bands of sweat, too.

"Looks like they're Illinois and Wisconsin boys," he replied. "Yep, it's the Ninety-Fifth Illinois formin' in the lead." He stood up for a moment, stretched, and then went back to his position. He looked even more intently now and continued. "Well, boys, it looks like that Ninety-Fifth is the stormin' party. They got about twenty of the blue bellies holdin' a stormin' ladder. They will be the first to cross the crick bed."

"Should we pull up the canister, sir?" asked an artillery captain who stood nearby.

"No, Captain," the colonel replied. "Let's let them cross the river. Alternate solid shot with fused hollow shot, and see if we can break them up at one hundred yards. Carry on, Captain."

Within moments the rebel Napoleon cannons were swabbed, loaded, and primed.

The Ninety-Fifth surged in irregular formation across the creek bed and started up to the redan. The distance now was almost one hundred yards from the rebel defenders.

"Colonel, I will site the first round on the storming party with the ladder. The color-bearers are on each side. I will take them out, too."

"Very good, Captain."

The captain stepped to the rear of the three batteries under his command. A Yankee sniper's deadly shot zipped by his ear. He did not flinch.

"Gentlemen, let the ball begin," he said confidently. "Let's give those damn Yankees a mouthful of lead."

The colonel braced himself on the cotton bale again with field glasses ready. He looked at the captain and nodded.

"Fire!" shouted the captain. And a volley of three shots roared into the Union ranks.

The rebel line watched silently, their vision temporarily obscured by the thick gunpowder smoke. When it had cleared, they saw that the blue mass of soldiers of the Ninety-Fifth was now a mangled heap of humanity. The lucky survivors picked themselves up from the ground and then sprinted as fast as they could to the rear, crossing the creek bed where the other regiments stood.

"Well lordy, lordy!" shouted a rebel. "Look at those blue bellies scatter so!"

"Colonel, what do you see?" asked the rebel captain.

"Captain, you hit your mark. That ladder is scattered in pieces now. The flags are flying no more. The attack has been routed. Best regards to your command. We need them to be just as good when the Yankee boys come again."

The rebel colonel then looked up.

The smoke had cleared now. Old Abe was nowhere in sight.

Chapter 45

Mt. Ararat

East of the Camps of the Ninety-Third and Ninety-Fifth Illinois Regiments
Between Engagements

From the mountain they could see the glow of campfires in the distance, thousands arrayed like stars in a twinkling panorama of light.

Will grabbed Allie's hand and squeezed it gently. They were safe from the fighting for now, and the sense of longing pulled them closer to each other. Cool breezes swirled around the mountain and brought them comfort. They moved closer to each other and embraced. The stars above seemed to twinkle more than ever now. They were silent. Their hearts beat stronger. Midnight had passed.

"We best git back now, Will," Allie said softly. She moved closer to Will and kissed him again.

He looked distraught as he rubbed his hand through his sandy-blond locks. Allie noticed the two stripes on his sleeve.

"Will, are you a corporal now?" she exclaimed with glee.

"Yes, I'm a corporal, but there's talk about camp that I will be a color sergeant. Some day I will carry the National Flag for the entire regiment," he said proudly.

Allie was stunned. She did not know what to say.

"Oh, my love, why will ya do it? Don't ya know what it means? You could git shot, like Elmer. He grabbed a flag from that hotel in Virginny and got killed by a shotgun to the heart! Trick and T.J. are all shot up, and they weren't even near the color-bearers at Champion Hill. I saw two git kilt yesterday when we attacked the Stockade!" Allie's voice shook. She grabbed Will by the sleeve and pulled him toward her and continued, "Now, look here, my love. Look at me! The charge yesterday was terrible. We lost sixty-one good boys. All went down from the cannon fire in less than a minute. The flag bearers were in the thick of it. It was—" Allie started to cry uncontrollably and put her face in her sleeve.

Will held her and stroked her hair gently. "My love, it is my duty to lead the men. Colonel Putnam may promote me soon and some other boys from Princeton. We are all in this together. None of us will let the Ninety-Third colors ever hit the ground. These colors will never be captured. It is our duty through thick and thin to keep them to the front. The whole regiment is counting on us."

"You're gonna end up like Trick and T.J., even worse," Allie replied softly, "and I jist wanna be sure you'll be headin' home."

"I will be careful, Allie. I promise."

"Did ya hear about Molly Cowan's father?" asked Allie.

"No, what did you hear?"

"Gotta letter from Jenny yesterday. She said her father, sure 'nough, is the colonel of the Forty-Fifth Lead Mine Regiment from Galena. Guess now he's gonna have to lead from the front, too, like Old Put, Jenny's father."

"What happened to Colonel Smith? Did he get killed?" Will asked, worried.

"No, he got promoted. He's hangin' with the biggest blue boys. He's a brigadier general now."

Will smiled and nodded his head. He grabbed Allie's hand. They headed down the mountain.

The campfires in the distance had been snuffed out. It was far past midnight, and the morning light would soon fade out the stars.

Chapter 46
Grant's Headquarters

May 21, 1863

"Can you see the forts, son?"

Young Fred Grant perched his elbows on a barrel of hardtack, raised his father's field glasses, and squinted. He panned to the right. "I can see a fort on a big hill," he exclaimed.

"That's Fort Hill. That's the biggest one. Look a little left. There are others."

"Yes, Father, I see one or two there."

"Look way down to the left. Do you see the railroad tracks?"

Fred turned to the left and adjusted his elbows. "Yes, and I see a big fort there, too."

"That is the Railroad Redoubt. General McClernand will attack there tomorrow."

Grant approached his son and placed his arm on his shoulder. Fred, his oldest, now a teenager, had been with him since the beginning of the Vicksburg campaign. The vantage point on the high hill was a good one. Grant would do battle again tomorrow.

"I have invited Ben's father up here early, Fred, to have a little chat with us. His beard is longer, and a lot more gray is there, but I'm sure you will recognize him. Please make sure to tell him about Ben and where you saw him last. A soldier's life can be very lonely, especially when you think about family."

"Yes, Father, I will tell him everything I know."

The shuffle of horse hooves could clearly be heard nearby. In a moment General John E. Smith and his staff appeared. Smith pulled off his riding gloves, slapped the dust off his sleeves, pulled off his hat, and wiped his brow with his wrist. "Damn hot down here!" he exclaimed.

"Sure is!" replied Fred who grinned ear to ear at the sight of Smith.

Smith looked quickly at Fred and his father and smiled, slightly embarrassed by the remark. "Sorry, Fred," he apologized. "I did not know you were here."

Grant pulled two cigars from his frock coat, nodded, and said, "If you think it's hot now, just wait 'til tomorrow. That's when we will bring hell to those rebel forts!"

Smith nodded and then said, "Well, Fred, how are things back home in Galena?"

"Things are great, Mr. Smith…I mean…General Smith," replied Fred.

"You may still call me Mr. Smith. That is who I am. Continue please."

"Well, our family is just fine. I did see Ben and Adelaide the week before I came downriver." Fred smiled.

"And how are they?" he asked.

"Well, I saw them chasing each other down those stairs that lead up to your house on High Street. By jiminy, both were moving pretty fast, and I thought if one of them fell it would be all over." Fred shook his head and raised his eyebrows a bit and continued. Well, when they made it down, Ben actually tripped and fell in front of a horse on Main Street!"

"Did he get hurt?"Smith asked with excited concern.

"No, but the horse got so spooked that it took off in a big gallop, causing a lot of whoop and hollering!"

Both Grant and Smith chuckled heartily at the thought.

"When you get home to Galena, tell Ben and Adelaide to walk down those stairs…and run up them if they wish." Smith tipped his hat to Fred.

Fred nodded, scratched his head, and then looked up inquisitively. "Oh, I remember!"

"Remember what?" Smith replied.

"Ben and Adelaide asked me to find out about Black Hawk. Is he still with the army?"

Grant struck a match. He lit Smith's cigar and then his own. Smith took a deep puff. "Great cigar, General," he replied. He turned back to Fred.

"Black Hawk rides with Colonel Putnam and the Ninety-Third Illinois from Freeport. When Putnam was recruiting, I thought it a nice gesture to give him a good war-horse for his efforts. In fact, Ben rode him to Freeport with me and Captain Parker that day."

"Is Black Hawk near here?" asked Fred excitedly.

"Yes, son, he is. He is with Boomer's Brigade just south of the Jackson Road. I am quite sure that old black beauty is anxious for an-other fight. Despite getting shot at Shiloh, when he hears the troop movements, his ears perk up, and he is ready to ride into the thickest of the fights."

"Father, I would like to see him," Fred replied respectfully.

"When the time is right, you will."

Grant took another puff from his cigar and wiped the sweat off his brow with the back of his hand. He looked back at Fred and continued. "Now, son, the other generals will be coming shortly. I would like to talk to General Smith for a spell before they arrive."

"Yes, Father, I will see you back down the hill. Good to see you, General Smith!"

"Thank you, Fred. It is always good to see you, too." Smith shook Fred's hand and placed his other arm around him for a moment.

When Fred stepped away, Smith looked at Grant and pulled another drag from the cigar. "You have a fine son there, General. He looks you in the eye and has a firm handshake. You must be very proud of him."

Grant nodded, lifted his cigar, and replied, "And how is Alfred? We know what Ben and Adelaide are up to!" Both men smiled.

"Well, Alfred has been sick. He is doing better now. He finished up his teaching at West Point and will soon command a Negro regiment."

"Very fine, John. You must be proud of him, too. We should try to move him to us. He would be better out here than with the eastern armies."

Smith nodded.

"And how about his pretty little girlfriend?" asked Grant.

Smith gave an embarrassed cough. "Well, Ulyss, now that's out of my department, you know, but she and Alfred still write to each other. Guess there's something there."

"Is she the girl from Warren by the Apple River?"

"Yes, she is the daughter of Major Cowan who now commands the Lead Mine Regiment."

Grant drew another puff from his cigar and looked to the rebel fortifications. "Small world, small world, John. Yes, indeed, it is a small world." He continued to peer into the distance.

The shuffling around them magnified. There were lots of horses coming up the hill. Within minutes three generals and their staffs dismounted, the generals straightening their frock coats, beating off the dust, and stepping forward with spurs and scabbards clanging.

Seeing that they were army-corp commanders of higher rank, General Smith politely bowed his head to Grant and proceeded down the hill. As he passed the arriving generals, he saluted and said, "We'll give 'em hell tomorrow!" The three smiled and returned his salute.

When the three corps commanders, Major Generals John McClernand, William Tecumseh Sherman, and James McPherson, arrived, Grant walked over to a small walnut box on a hardtack barrel, pulled out a handful of cigars, and passed one to each of them.

"Gentlemen, we have big work to do tomorrow! Do you have any questions before I proceed?" The three shook their heads.

"I will take little of your time, then," Grant replied. He pointed at the line of Confederate entrenchments. "Gentlemen, we have failed to take those works. The Ninety-Fifth Illinois made a gallant rush on the Stockade Redan two days ago and got bloodied. We lost sixty-one men in less than fifteen minutes. The other supporting regiments had heavy losses, too."

McPherson nodded. His eyes twinkled in a kindly way. "I am sorry, sir. Those were the men of Ransom's Brigade. They were taken out, as you said, in quick time by the rebels. We have reformed the brigade though, sir, and they are ready for another try."

"Very good, General," replied Grant. He looked back at the fortifications and said, "We will, tomorrow, make a coordinated attack on all fronts. You, Sherman, will attack from the north. General McPherson, from the center, and you, General McClernand, will attack from the south. Is that clear, gentlemen?"

The generals nodded.

"At what time shall we attack, sir?" asked Sherman.

"The attack will commence at ten in the morning. I will order our batteries to begin enfilading the town and the works a few hours before the attack. General Porter will shell the town from the riverboats. When the cannonading stops shortly before ten, you will charge the works."

Grant pulled out a match again and struck it on the barrel. "See if those rebel snipers can get three generals on this matchstick from this distance!" He smiled at Sherman and McPherson who stepped forward for a light. Both of them chuckled. McClernand stepped back, una-mused, and placed his cigar in his pocket.

"Dismissed, gentlemen," Grant said calmly.

McClernand saluted the three and returned to his horse. An orderly handed him the reigns. As he was about to mount, Grant called out to him, "Don't be late tomorrow, like you were at Champion Hill. We need your army this time."

McClernand put his foot in the left stirrup, rose up and settled him-self in his saddle. He turned to Grant, tipped his hat in a slow deliberate manner to acknowlege the remark, then cantered away to the railroad redoubt.

Chapter 47
The Charge

True to Grant's plan, by ten o'clock in the morning, the Yankee cannons had finished wreaking havoc on the Confederate fortifications. There was an eerie silence now on both sides interrupted by an occasional zip of a sniper's bullet.

Then it began again…as if a giant was stirring from his sleep.

Thirty-five thousand Yankees under Generals Sherman, McPherson, and McClernand advanced in tandem. The Forty-Fifth, Ninety-Third, and Ninety-Fifth Illinois Regiments were held in a reserve with other regiments to direct the knockout blow. They were prepared and in line, but none of the line officers knew what time their regiments would be ordered to advance. The sun was high and hot, and many of the soldiers fainted from sunstroke as they waited for the appointed hour.

By noon, Grant from his vantage point could see Union flags in every sector planted in the soil at varying intervals on the outside of the ramparts. The banners flapped in the wind or silently hung limp, daring Yankee color-bearers to push them forward again or rebel defenders to jump over the ramparts to claim them as war trophies. The clock continued to tick past twelve. No one, blue or gray, would take the dare.

❧

Third Louisiana Redan
Attack of the Forty-Fifth Illinois Infantry
Three in the Afternoon

Major Cowan, now acting commander, advanced to the front of the Washburne Lead Mine Regiment. They would take the lead position in the next charge.

He pulled out his small diary from his left pant pocket as it was blocking the movement of his sword scabbard. He pulled open the lapel of his frock coat to place it in his left inside pocket by his heart. In doing so, the diary flipped open to its last entry. He decided to glance through it once more as it was his most recent entry written just one week ago. The men around him did not know it was a diary. They took no notice. They figured he was reviewing last minute orders from General Smith. All were silent as the sniper bullets whizzed by.

> *May 15th—2 a.m.*
> *Alone by my campfire, surrounded by thousands of sleeping soldiers, noble, brave, and generous, all of whom lay down with hearts full of gratitude for the result of yesterday's fight, and many of whom now in their sleep, in dreams converse with those of whom they love, forgetting for the time all the toils, dangers and sufferings in this sweet spiritual visit...I am so full of conflicting thoughts, emotions, and cares to sleep, anxious for the future, grateful for the past. Thankful that so many of us are able to stand the hardships of our hard marches and so favored as to escape wounds or death on the battle field... Hardly know whether it is Lute Cowan as went to war or if it is some new being in some other world. But from my fidgety anxiety and multitude of cares, I guess it is the same old Lute.* [17]

He closed the diary, placing it slowly in his breast pocket next to his heart. *Lute Cowan! Lute Cowan! What a childish nickname for me! And if only my old friends could see me now...a commander...standing at the head of a regiment. I must not fail them...my family...anyone!*

Cowan looked up at the thick fortifications. White smoke from thousands of muskets rose up obscuring the sun. The sound of the cannonading picked up. The fury of fire echoed across the rebel forts. Sweat dropped from his brow. Cowan felt uneasy, yet he kept his composure. It was three o'clock now—the appointed hour had come—and he turned and approached the men of the Forty-Fifth.

"Fix bayonets!" he shouted as he pulled his sword from his scabbard. "Sergeant Taylor, bring up the colors. We will march up this road, and when we see the works, we will form at about two hundred yards from the redan. Hold off until I give the direct order to advance. We will then take the fort! Are there any questions?"

The ranks remained silent.

Cowan turned and began to move on the road out of the safety of his position.

"Let every man stand to his post!

"Forward, Forty-Fifth! Double-quick!"

The column of blue surged forward, moving almost at a dead run down the road. Cowan kept the lead, quickly turning with each third stride to see if they were in good order.

Then, as if the sky had fallen about them, the roar of rebel rifles flashed before the cavalcade of blue, sending scores to the ground.

Cowan, leading the charge, fell suddenly to the ground.

He felt numb. Lying on his back, he tucked his bloody right hand under his left armpit. He lifted his head and looked down at his hip. He was stunned and silent.

A rebel musket ball had hit his sword scabbard and deflected through his hand and then through his hip, continuing on a deadly path deep into his body. He could not move.

I must secure the bleeding with both hands, or it is over!

Grunting loudly as swirls of white smoke drifted by, he reached down to his hip with his good hand. Within seconds blood oozed between his fingers and then spurted forth like an interrupted pulsing fountain of red.

My artery is cut. I will not bleed to death if I can just hold on. Harriett and the kids will wait for me. I must see them one more time!

Holding his wound with frail determination, his thoughts drifted in a strange way.

He felt a peace as he looked to the swirling and rising smoke above him. His eyes darted back and forth until he locked them on a gap of blue. It was crystal clear, a robin's-egg color, and bluer than the skies he could ever recall.

My beloved Harriett, Molly, Phine, and Georgie. They will wait for me, and all will be fine.

Another minute passed.

The pain in his hip began to fade away. His good hand, numb from the constant pressure, began to relax.

Around him were the muffled voices of men. The beautiful blue sky was blocked now by unrecognizable faces and indistinguishable silhouettes.

He felt a sensation of being carried away.

With the movement came a forceful rapidity of heartbeats that pounded in his ears as if trying to escape through his head.

The beats got louder, yet he felt no panic.

He felt an infinite peace.

The streaming blood from his hip had stopped flowing.

The pounding in his head ceased, too.

Just silence now.

Cowan was dead.

Stockade Redan
Attack of the Ninety-Fifth Illinois Infantry
Same Day
Three in the Afternoon

The storming party was ready to attack Stockade Redan again. The ladders were secured up front with the color-bearers. This time, however, Allie took to the rear. She was one of the only survivors in the attack on the nineteenth, so Captain Bush placed her in the back ranks as a reward for doing her duty. She felt uneasy as the Yankee lines formed for the assault, as the southern guns seemed to get more massed and more accurate by the hour.

This attack would be different for the 95th. This time the generals prepared ten regiments for a massed assault. To the left of the 95th were the 72nd Illinois and the 17th and 14th Wisconsin. To the right were the 11th Illinois, 8th Missouri, 116th and 113th Illinois, 6th Missouri, and 13th US Infantry. The playing field, they thought, had been leveled.

"Fix bayonets!" Captain Bush commanded. The clang and snap of the bayonets against the rifle barrels echoed across the line. The order was repeated across ten regiments, and in a moment the undulating blue mass of men moved forward.

Unfazed by the blue spectacle in front of them, rebel artillery began to fire. Twelve-pound cannonballs with timed fuses exploded over the Union lines, causing shrapnel to rain down upon the soldiers lake a hail storm from hell. In concert, rounds of solid shot tore through the ranks like deadly bowling balls, tearing off limbs, punching through bellies, and decapitating heads.

Allie could not stand the destruction. Her heart beat rapidly as she firmly grasped her musket. Then the dreaded order "double-quick" was shouted by Captain Bush. *How can this all be happening? My God, how can this be happening!* A solid shot decapitated a soldier just ten feet in front of her. *That's the boy from Rockford who lent me his canteen just moments ago when I was thirsty!* She felt a mist of blood on her face as another soldier was shot. Her eyes widened with terror. She stepped up her pace along with the others. *I'll never make it.* Another soldier dropped in front of her, then another! The screams got louder but were drowned out by the Luciferian roar of the cannons that continuously hurled canister rounds into the Union troops' ranks. The ditch at the base of the fort was only forty yards from the crest ahead. *I think I can make it.* Three men dropped before her like rag dolls hitting the ground. One looked back at her, stunned, in terror. *I must get moving.* She increased her pace. The crest ahead had soldiers lying behind it. *They're not dead, just protecting themselves. Good, I think I can make it.* She took a deep breath, sprinted, and dove behind the safety of the crest, musket at her side.

Enemy fire swept over her head in a continuous hum, only inches away. She buried her face in the red soil and wanted the noise and insanity of it all to stop. It didn't. She thought she heard a command to charge the fort, but she was wrong. *Where are the friends? God, please make sure they are alive somewhere.* Another explosion caused the ground to shake in front of her. She inched back a foot. A soldier next to her had an expression of alarm. His eyes were wide, yet he did not blink. Allie reached over to nudge him. His cap fell off. His forehead had been shattered by a ball. Her stomach rebelled with dry heaves. *What do I do now? What do I do now? God, help us! God, please help us*! She curled into a fetal position with her hands cupping her ears. She looked back at the field she had crossed. Behind her were at least five hundred soldiers grossly mangled or contorted in death. She closed her eyes. *Please don't order us to charge! Please, God, make this all stop!* She pushed harder on her ears in a vain attempt to eliminate the noise; concussions of cannon fire continued to shake the ground around her. She trembled. *Please, God, make it stop! Please, God, make it stop! Please, God, make it stop!* She continued her silent pleas.

The colors of the regiment rose up for the charge. She saw one color-bearer drop and then another. The flag hit the ground a third time, and then it disappeared over the crest to the ditch below the rebel ramparts. The roar from the fort was incessant now. The constant fire from the Confederate musket barrels caused the cotton bales to catch fire. *I must get to the ditch. I must get to the ditch.* She saw the colors move forward. She lifted her head to follow and blacked out.

Railroad Redoubt
Attack of the Ninety-Third Illinois Infantry
Same Day
Four Thirty in the Afternoon

True to Grant's request, General McClernand was not late when he executed the attacks in the morning. He even reported to Grant that his attacks had established a foothold inside the forts around the Railroad Redoubt. Demanding reinforcements to secure the breach in the Confederate lines, Colonel Putnam and the Ninety-Third and the brother regiments of the Third Brigade were sent by Grant to support him.

Half of the Ninety-Third boys were sunburnt from being under the sun for four long hours. Some had fainted. Some had died from heat-stroke. With muskets in hand, they wondered where they were heading and what nightfall would bring.

Black Hawk pranced in front of the soldiers. He seemed anxious to move to the front. Colonel Putnam reined him back. Another loud shot from Whistling Dick, the Confederate large mortar that launched hundred-pound lead balls, shrieked across the late afternoon skies. Putnam cautiously moved a few yards closer to the point of attack. He slipped from his saddle and tied Black Hawk's reins snugly to an oak sapling. Black Hawk whinnied and stomped his feet as if to protest.

"There will be another battle for you to fight, my boy," said Putnam softly. "I will return shortly."

Black Hawk snorted and pulled back from the sapling to free himself. Unable to do so, he then settled down after briefly stomping his front hooves as if in frustration.

"Boys, we will advance down this small rise, cross the ravine for a distance, and rest on the back side of that intervening hill. We will catch our breaths and then charge the fort. The Ninety-Third will take the advance position. Colonel Boomer has placed us first. We will do our best to be the first in the fort. The Tenth and Fifth Iowa Regiments, and the Twenty-Sixth Missouri will support us and follow us in. Do you understand?"

Will and Aaron looked at each other and then at the fort in the distance. They could see several Yankee flags driven deeply in the rampart and their color-bearers hugging the slope from the morning charge.

"Damn," Will exclaimed, "looks like those boys have nowhere to go. Can't go up and over. Can't go down. Looks like they need some relief, if they haven't already died of sunstroke. Don't see them moving at all."

"I guess we'll soon be marching to our graves, Will," replied Aaron solemnly.

Suddenly, Putnam appeared again. "Corporal Erwin, front forward with the colors!"

Aaron looked at Will, who snapped up the flag, saluted Putnam, and proceeded forward.

"Will!" shouted Aaron, causing Will to look back. "Good luck, friend," he said. "We will see you in the fort...or in heaven."

Will smiled and gently nodded. He continued forward until he was by Putnam's side.

"Captains, form your men for the charge," Putnam commanded. A few moments passed, and when he saw the men were ready, he shouted, "Fix bayonets!" Metallic clinks echoed down the line. The deadly toad-stickers were ready now, and the soldiers moved into the ravine.

Boom! Boom! Pow! Zip! came a shower of lead from shot, shell, and musket balls. The march, which commenced like a parade, moved from common step to quickstep to double quickstep to charge as the Ninety-Third, with Will in the lead, charged forward. The hail of lead continued to rain down on them.

Ascending close to the top of a rise in front of the Railroad Redoubt, Putnam commanded, "Lie flat, men. Lie prone!"

Seconds passed when Aaron, panting heavily, fell next to Will and Putnam. "For Christ's sake, Will, this ain't fighting. This is a slaughterhouse!" he said.

"Keep your head down, Aaron!" Putnam warned.

Suddenly, two colonels also dropped close to the ground near Putnam and the boys. One was the Commanding Colonel Boomer, the other was Colonel Dean of the Twenty-Sixth Missouri. Boomer took off his kepi and wiped his brow. Dean slid his sword back in his black leather scabbard. "Guess I won't be needin' this right yet," he said.

"Colonel Putnam, do you know how far it is from this position to the forts?" asked Colonel Boomer.

"About two hundred yards, sir."

"That's a long damn distance!" added Dean.

"We have orders, gentlemen," Boomer replied, his black moustache still drooping with sweat. "We will do our duty. We must help those boys on the ramparts."

"Are they alive, sir? They could be dead by now," replied Dean in earnest.

Boomer took off his kepi, turned it around, and placed it on the ground so as not to attract snipers to the shiny brass insignia pinned on the front. He took a deep breath and lifted his head for a better view of the situation.

"What do you see, sir?" asked Dean.

Suddenly, there was the ugly sound of a large egg cracking. It happened in a split second. A deadly ball penetrated Boomer's head, scattering gray matter all around him.

"My God!" Dean screamed. "Let's fall back. Let's fall back!"

Putnam grabbed the panic-stricken colonel and held him down. "Colonel, keep your composure! Do you hear me?"

Dean shook uncontrollably and tried to wipe off Boomer's blood from his frock coat sleeve. To no avail, it was stained for good. Then, gaining control of himself, he nodded sheepishly at Putnam.

Putnam turned around and looked at the ravine where they had crossed. Will and Aaron looked back, too.

"My God, Colonel, there are a good fifty of the Ninety-Third dead or wounded back there," Aaron said.

"Lost about forty good men from my Twenty-Sixth, too," Dean added.

Soon there was a gasp from the mortally wounded Boomer followed by a guttural gurgle . Everyone looked away. A minute later the dying man's face twisted in a rictus of death, and then there was silence.

The rebel musketry lessened to a spattering of skirmish-like rattles in the distance. The sun would soon be setting. The boys of the proud Ironsides Brigade, as they were called after their victory at Champion Hill just six days before, now hugged the Mississippi soil, hoping and praying in silence that Colonel Putnam, now the senior commander on the field, would take the brigade to the rear.

Putnam looked at Boomer's body. He thought about what Boomer's last words were and made his decision.

"Captains, ready your men for the charge. We must do our duty!" The conviction in his voice seemed real. The sound of metal clanked along the line as canteens banged against rifle barrels as the men lay prostrate on the ground in preparation for the charge.

Putnam turned to Will. "Are you ready, son?" he asked.

Will nodded and gripped Old Glory tightly. He looked at Aaron who had a distant stare in his eyes.

"All right, then, let's get it done," Putnam said. He looked behind him at the soldiers who were still alive in the ravine. Some begged for water. Some called out to their mothers for comfort. His gaze became more resolute now.

"Attention, brigade!" he called out in a strong clear tone.

Waving his sword so that all could see him, he rolled over on one knee, braced himself up with the weapon, stood up, and screamed, "Charge!"

Chapter 48

Shirley House

**Camp of the Forty-Fifth Lead Mine Regiment
Near Third Louisiana Redan—Fort Hell
June 25, 1863
Two in the Afternoon**

The Yankee attacks had failed all along the line. Over a month now had passed. The siege, however, continued with the Union lines encircling Vicksburg like a large anaconda snake squeezing the life out of the soldiers and citizens.

Three hundred yards east of the Third Louisiana Redan, where Cowan was killed, the Forty-Fifth Illinois had excavated caves around a fine white house, the home of the Shirley family, who had abandoned the house and were now within the fortifications of Vicksburg, surviving the conflict themselves in a dark, damp cave. The rolling green grass and flower beds on the southern exposure of their beautiful home were no longer there. Mounds of dirt were piled high from the shelters and the network of caves created by over a month of determined digging by the Yankees.

Inside the house General John E. Smith and Sergeant Crummer of the Forty-Fifth Illinois awaited the arrival of General Grant and Captain Hickenlooper, chief engineer of the Seventeenth Corps. The parlor had good light. Chairs that had not been broken for firewood were pushed to the walls to make room for a center table that was used during high-level strategy meetings with the generals. Smith had placed a large topographical map in the center of it.

"Sergeant Crummer, I must commend you for your actions during the charge on the redan last month."

"Thank you, General. I did what I had to do," replied Crummer respectfully.

"Did you see Cowan fall?"

"Yes, he was a brave officer. The boys miss him dearly."

"I sent a letter to his wife, Harriet, and their three children a few weeks ago. I let them know what a wonderful and kind leader he was and how dearly he loved his family." added Smith. "It was one of the hardest things I've had to do yet. Especially so, as he was leading my old command." Smith looked down at the map and pointed to the Third Louisiana Redan where Cowan fell.

"We call it Fort Hell, now, General."

Hearing the sound of men approaching, Crummer and Smith looked at the front door as General Grant and Captain Andrew Hickenlooper stepped into the parlor.

Grant had an unlit cigar in his mouth. "Good afternoon, gentlemen," he said.

"Good afternoon, sir," Crummer replied, snapping a salute.

"Captain, are the preparations in order?" Smith asked.

"Yes, General," he replied. "I must commend the thirty-five men who dug the tunnel for us. They completed it in just two days."

"Very well, captain, and how far under the redan is it?" Grant asked as he looked at the map.

"Sir, we have dug it about forty-five feet, and then it splits off in three smaller tunnels for another fifteen feet." Hickenlooper walked to the map, to the other side of the table from Smith and Grant. He placed his forefinger directly on the location of the Third Louisiana Redan and continued. "The gunpowder will be directly underneath the redan."

"Is it ready to go?" asked Grant as he pulled his watch out of his vest pocket.

"Sir, it is packed with over twenty-two hundred pounds of gunpowder."

Grant walked to the four-foot section of wall between two parlor windows and pointed with his forefinger at the redan. "We lost over three thousand men trying to take these forts," he said calmly. He then shook his head and repeated, "Three thousand…three thousand killed and wounded trying to take these forts." He looked back out the window as if noticing something in the distance.

After walking back to the table again, he peered at the war map. He then punched his fist at the spot where the Third Louisiana Redan was located. The thud caused Crummer to flinch. "Captain, do you think the explosion will blast enough space to get the men through?"

"Yes, sir, the crater should allow seventy good men to move rapidly into the rebel works."

"General Smith, do you think this will work?" asked Grant solemnly.

"Yes, sir. I have arranged the Lead Mine Regiment to lead the charge again," replied Smith as he looked at Crummer. The sergeant nodded with confidence.

Grant pulled his fist up and placed it in the palm of his other hand holding his cigar between his thumb and forefinger. After gazing at the engineer's map on more time, he looked at the three and walked back to the windows. He pulled out his pocket watch, looked at it. He then lifted his gaze and looked at each officer before saying, "Godspeed, gentlemen. General Smith, may you blast those rebels to kingdom come."

Smith looked at Crummer and said, "Sergeant, inform your command to light the fuse within the hour."

Crummer snapped a smart salute and strode from the room. The front door creaked loudly and then slammed shut with a thud.

In the silence that came over the room now, Smith looked at Grant again. He then turned to Hickenlooper. "Thank you, Captain," he said calmly. "May God help us all."

Chapter 49

General John E. Smith's Headquarters

July 4, 1863

Early Morning

A week had passed since the Fort Hill explosion and ensuing battle in the trenches. Like the earlier attack, it failed to break the Confederate defense. So Grant decided to continue the siege with all its intended and ugly consequences on the citizens and soldiers defending Vicksburg.

General Smith rose to the smell of campfire coffee and stepped outside his field tent. In the distance to the west, he could see the morning sun reflecting off the Vicksburg Courthouse. He looked at the crater where hundreds of Yankee lives had been lost. Turning to the Shirley house, he could see the Lead Mine Regiment shoring up their dugouts.

Today, though, the morning seemed eerily quiet to him. He could, in fact, hear birds chirping, a far cry from the noise near the trenches. *How strangely quiet it is; how quiet indeed.* His mind continued to drift. He could see beyond the courthouse to Galena now. In his mind's eye, the riverboats floated silently to port. *Aimee and the children will be arising soon from their snugly beds up on High Street. Wish I were there to see the morning sun cut through the stately gables. And how, very quickly, the sun rises above the river and casts its warm light upon the shadows below on Main Street. Bet the parade today will be fantastic...with pomp and circumstance and smiles and laughter, especially when "Yankee Doodle Dandy" echoes to the heights!*

Suddenly, a sound broke the silence that quickly pulled him out of his reverie. He looked quickly to the trenches.

A distinct plodding of hooves echoed from the east. Smith turned to the gathering noise. *It is a rider for sure.* The hurried succession of pounding hooves roused his staff out of their slumber and brought them quickly out of their tents. Buttons were quickly pulled through their frock-coat loops. Suspenders snapped and sword belts clinked. Everyone soon gathered around the general.

The rider stomped in, circling his steed, as it high-stepped for a moment before settling to a stop in front of the general and his staff. The meticulously dressed staff lieutenant snapped a quick salute.

"A dispatch from General McPherson, sir! The rebels have surrendered!" Holding the reins in his left hand, the rider reached in his frock coat and handed the dispatch to Smith.

All within earshot were stunned.

After reading it with a smile, Smith nodded gently. "It is true! Let me read it to you, boys," he said.

> *Brig Genl Jno E Smith*
> *Comdg 7th Division*
> *General*
> *The following telegram has just been received.*
> *Hd Qrs 4th July 1863.*
> *Maj Genl McPherson*
> *Circular—Should white flags be displayed upon the enemy's works at ten this morning it will be to signify the acceptance of the terms of capitulation. The enemy will be permitted to move to the front of his works and after stacking flags and arms will then return to his camps. The works will be*

occupied only by such troops as may afterwards be selected.
Those troops not designated for the purpose will not occupy
the enemy's line, but remain in their present camps.

By order of Maj Genl Grant
J. H. Wilson
Lt. Col. And A.I.G.
Official
Wm. T. Clark
A. A. Genl [18]

There was a short pause after Smith read the dispatch, followed by a shout by a soldier just a few feet away. The word carried along the ranks, and the jubilant noise increased to a roaring crescendo in the Yankee lines, rising like a thunderclap.

The Union siege had finally strangled Vicksburg into a complete submission and surrender.

Smith looked at his men. "We can rest for now. Let us go help those boys on the other side. We have fought the good fight. Let us share our rations with them."

Head-Quarters, 17th Army Corps,
DEPARTMENT OF THE TENNESSEE,

Near Vicksburg Miss July 4. 1863.

Brig Genl Jno E Smith
Comdg 7 Div

General

The following
telegram has just been received. "
" Hd Qrs 4 July 1863.
Maj Genl McPherson

"Circular — Should
White flags be displayed upon the enemys
works at ten this morning it will be to
signify the acceptance of the terms of
capitulation — The enemy will be permitted
to move to the front of his works, and after
stacking flags and arms will then return
to this camps the works will be occupied only

Original Dispatch to General John E. Smith

Chapter 50

Vicksburg Courthouse

July 4, 1863
Late Morning

The rebel soldiers had stacked their arms along with their tattered battle flags.

General McPherson, commander of the Seventeenth Army Corps, advanced with the chosen Yankee regiments to the Vicksburg

Courthouse. The Forty-Fifth Lead Mine Regiment was at the head of the column. They were the first to reach the courthouse.

"General Smith," announced McPherson politely from his saddle, "have the colors of the Forty-Fifth delivered to Colonel Coolbaugh. He will see that they are raised above the courthouse. This is a fine day for our country. I commend the sacrifice of the officers and men of your old regiment and of your brigade."

"Thank you, General," replied Smith. "We are honored to stand here with you."

Smith nodded to Sergeant Crummer, who disappeared into the ranks and then reappeared with the two flags, which were perforated with bullet holes. The wooden staffs had been splintered. He handed them to Colonel Coolbaugh who was nearby with other members of McPherson's staff.

As the colonel entered the courthouse, a few men shouted "huzzah" until a chorus of "huzzahs" from thousands of Yankees echoed down the streets. Soon several soldiers could be seen in the cupola with the flags of the Forty-Fifth. The "huzzahs" rose now to a grand crescendo that carried to the Union camps a mile away.

General Smith looked up proudly at the flags of his old regiment. Old Glory was at the highest point in Vicksburg. It snapped freely in the breeze. The fighting was over now. Vicksburg's surrender was complete.

Chapter 51

Wigwam

Pecatonica River
Late Summer, 1863

A rush of wind blew through the willows on the riverbank. The downward branches that touched the flowing water caused ripples as they swayed. An occasional bluegill darted at the water bugs skimming along the surface, snatching its quarry with a flash of silver fin. The air was hot, yet the wigwam was cool. It had served the friends well, always sheltering them from the worst elements.

"Jenny, will you put my hand where the light ray is?" T.J. asked. "I'd like to feel it's warmth."

Jenny moved to his side of the wigwam and grabbed his hand. She lifted his outstretched arm in the direction of the beam, which shone brightly now from the top of the cave. Dust particles swirled a bit as she let go of T.J.'s wrist. "Just push out another foot or so, and you will find it."

Sunlight cut through the darkness of the cave with an almost vertical ray. It was past noon.

"I got it! I can feel it!" he said excitedly.

Overcome with emotion, Jenny quietly sniffled and pulled out a fancy laced kerchief that was tucked in a pocket of her field dress. Though sad about T.J.'s blindness, she was happy that he could feel the heat of the sun's ray, knowing that it brought back vivid memories for him. T.J. paused for a moment and smiled. He then turned to Jenny and asked,

"Can you hand me the tomahawk?" He turned back to where the beam was and felt warmth now on both palms.

Jenny made her way to the other side of the cave where the tomahawk was leaning. She picked it up and placed it carefully in T.J.'s open hands. He gripped it tightly and then pulled it to his chest. He ran his fingers carefully across the iron blade and felt the carvings that were cut into the handle grip. He nodded and smiled. "Wish Trick could see me holdin' this, too," he said. He then fell silent. He held the weapon out so Jenny could place it back on the wigwam wall.

"Jenny, let's go down to Trick's fishin' hole. I wanna feel the water down there where he pulled out those big catfish back before the war. Can you take me down to it?"

"Sure, T.J., just keep your head down. I will lead you out."

"No need, Jenny, I can make it out myself."

The walls of the wigwam were damp and cool. T.J. could feel the wall he was touching get warmer as he got closer to the entrance. He held one hand in front of him to guide him. When he felt the entrance, he bent forward and stepped outside. The air felt like a blast from a furnace. The distance to the fishing hole was only about forty rods away. T.J. remembered well the footpath that led to it, and the distinct smell of the riverbank rose to his nostrils. He caught a slight scent of dark-green milkweed that grew close to the water and heard the double tweet of a cardinal that frequented the holly bushes around the wigwam where the red berries were so prominent in the wintertime. The guttural barking of a big brown-bellied squirrel, as before, challenged their intrusion along the riverbank.

"If only I had my squirrel rifle and my eyes back," he said to Jenny matter of factly. "I'd make dinner out of that critter!"

Jenny remained silent.

The water nearby lapped a little. Though he could not see it, the water continued along as it always had. Two sticks bobbed along as if racing each other, swirled, and then vanished around the little bend by the wigwam.

"We're gettin' close to Trick's fishin' hole, Jenny. I can feel it and hear it," he said with enthusiasm.

"It's right around this next bend. Keep your hold on my arm. We'll be there shortly."

They continued with cautious steps. Before them was a small clearing that allowed a skilled fisherman to cast a pole without dangling the hook in the small bushes and flora that hugged the muddy shore. T.J. smiled as he listened to the gentle lapping of the water. He squeezed Jenny's arm. He felt secure now as he looked within his mind's eye and remembered his river walks before the war started.

A high-pitched, shrieking voice broke the silence.

"Well, lordy, lordy, by jiminy, and the grace of kingdom come! You two got here lickety-split in time for the big one!"

It was Trick, cane pole in hand, battling another big catfish.

"This is a big 'un, T.J.! Might be even bigger than that one we saw down on the Chattahoochee! Remember that southern suckerfish?"

T.J. grinned and nodded.

Trick's cane pole bent into a large arch. The tip of the rod bounced in and out of the water as an occasional fin broke the surface and rolled back under into a cloudy cauldron, causing ripples to flow across to the other side of the Pecatonica.

"This ol'cat is a beauty for sure, Jenny," Trick exclaimed as he dug his heels in the muddy bank. "Best get ready 'cause I will rightly pull him out of his home. Will be a good-eatin' one for sure!"

Trick positioned himself for the final pull. He squared himself to the shoreline and in one quick flick of his wrist pulled the catfish out of the water. The cane pole snapped. The line and tip disappeared. The lapping waves flattened again to the flow of the river. The catfish had slipped away.

Trick quickly looked at Jenny and grinned. He then broke the awkward silence, "Hee, hee...well, by jiminy, looks like that ol' cat will live to fight another day." He fell silent again. His wide grin faded into a slight smile, and then his face grew solemn. *I am alive. How did I survive a wound that caused others to die? And they died quickly, one by one, under the big oak tree at the Champion house.*

He remembered how happy he was when Allie arrived and how she taught him how to get better, and what she had said to him on his cot under the tree: "I'll be patient if you just hang on." He repeated it to himself every day as he thought of her. *I wonder how Will and Aaron are.* Jenny had told T.J. and him earlier that Colonel Putnam, Will, Aaron, and Allie all survived the May 22 charge. But that was three months ago. *Where are they now?*

The sun was dropping in the west, and the friends started back up-river to the wigwam. As they approached it, Trick looked up to a thick branch extending from the Injun oak tree over the river. He cupped his hand over his brow to block the sun. "Well, ain't that strange," he whispered.

"What is it?" T.J. asked.

Jenny looked up quickly to where Trick pointed.

"Well, ain't that a site," exclaimed Trick, his voice rising from the whisper.

"Come on, tell us what it is. What's goin' on?" insisted T.J.

"Well, there is a turtledove perched just a foot from the reddest cardinal I have ever seen. Those two birds don't sit well together, and I'm a wonderin' what happened to the other dove, ya know, its mate for life." Trick scratched his head and wiped his brow with his sleeve.

T.J. was silent. He tried to comprehend the meaning of it all.

"Yep, and they are starin' at each other now. Must be an omen," Trick replied with a confused look.

"Well, as I see it," T.J. gently added, "the omen is that the turtledove has lost her mate, and that male cardinal at her side now stands for ever-lasting love…like the red berries from the holly branches!"

Jenny placed her hands on her mouth. She did not know what to think.

Trick bent down and picked up his broken cane pole. "Strange to see those birds like that. Never seen anythin' like that before. We best be gettin' home now."

Jenny nodded at Trick and then reached for T.J.'s arm. The three started upriver with Trick in the rear. When they got to the bend in the river, Trick glanced back to the Injun oak for one last look.

Chapter 52

Camp of the Ninety-Third Illinois

Near Bridgeport, Alabama
November 15, 1863

Smoke from hundreds of cooking fires hung in the southern pines. The regiment was resting for the day after many miles of marching.

"Sure wish Jenny and Allie coulda' seen that cave," Aaron exclaimed as he handed a piece of hardtack to Will.

Both boys sat down around a small campfire. The timber cracked sending a spark upward.

"Yeah, that cave makes the wigwam look small, doesn't it?" Will replied.

"Sure does. If that cave was up north, it could hold two dozen runaway slaves!"

Will's countenance grew solemn. "Remember when we met Li'l Joe and Blue two years ago?"

"Yeah, it was a special moment," replied Aaron. They both thought we were slave catchers because T.J. had a rifle. Funny, we didn't even know what a slave catcher was back then!"

Will smiled. "Li'l Joe was so young and scared he could barely speak until Blue came up playin' the flute and spoke as grand as a Sunday preacher."

Aaron peered into the fire. "Do ya' think they ever made it to Canada?"

"Sure hope so. They were nice folk," replied Aaron.

"Wonder how long they stayed in the Oscar Taylor basement?"

"I 'spect it was only a week or so," replied Will, holding up his haversack. "I'd bet everything in here they made it safely to Canada and that Li'l Joe is there now. Blue just guided him, so he's probably helping other runaways now."

Will looked at the fire. The flames settled down into a vermillion hue that seemed to dwindle in the night. "Well, I'm glad the friends helped both Li'l Joe and Blue. Our wigwam is a special place. Can't wait to get back there and rest. Sure miss the Pecatonica, too."

Aaron stood up and pulled out his journal from his frock-coat pocket. He held it up and nodded at Will. "Better write down what we saw today in my diary before I forget," he said in earnest. "The girls will want to know about this place, for sure. That little walnut tree over there looks like a good sittin' spot. Let me know when the hish and hash is ready to eat."

Aaron approached the tree, slipped to the ground, and then leaned back comfortably with his haversack braced between his shoulders and the trunk. He pulled out a tiny pencil from his left front pocket. Pausing for a moment to double-check that he was holding his second volume, he flipped to the next blank page and scribbled his notes quickly.

Sun. Nov. 15
After breakfast...went about 100 rods west of our camp
to explore a cave...we soon found ourselves at the entrance
of the cave and there we found the Col. And several of the
other officers. I soon made my way into the cave. I found
several men in there with candles and it wasen't [sic] long
till I had been in every nook and corner of the cave. Where
I first entered there was a small room...then I had to lay
down and roll through a small crivice [sic] into a larger
room that led to another place of entrance and from that

one we made our way through into a smaller room…there was some beautiful crystal stone on top the rooms that was formed by dripping water…After rambling all over the wild mountain we went back to camp—struck tents—and was soon ready to march…Clear and pleasant. [19]

"Hish and hash is ready, Aaron!" Will shouted as he banged his mess pan with his spoon.

Aaron snapped his journal shut, placed it in his haversack, and scurried over to his messmates by the smoldering campfire.

Chapter 53

Camp of the Ninety-Third Illinois

Missionary Ridge
November 24, 1863
Near Midnight

"Do you see the moon up there?" Aaron whispered so he would not disturb his sleeping comrades.

Will rolled over on his blanket to get a better view. He grunted, pushed himself up with both arms, and craned his neck. "It's an eclipse of the moon, he replied. You can see the shadow of the earth covering it so."

"Looks like an omen to me."

"Oh, Aaron, that's as much an omen to them as it is to us. Besides, it may be a good-luck omen for you. Tomorrow is your birthday isn't it?"

Aaron looked up again. "I suspect it's a sign for something. Well, I best get down to bed. Today was a busy one. Best get the whole thing in my journal. Tomorrow will surely be a fight. Hope tomorrow isn't my last birthday."

Will settled back down on his blankets and pulled the corner over his shoulders. "Good night, old friend," he whispered. "Tomorrow will be a happy day for you."

Aaron walked slowly over to his bedding so he wouldn't disturb the others. He grabbed his bayonet, the good old toad-sticker, and flipped the point down. He pulled open the top of his haversack, shuffled his hand around, pulled out a match and candle, and placed them between his feet. He then reached into his pocket and located his pencil again. He forced the tip of his bayonet into the ground, placed the bottom of the candle into the bayonet socket, and then lit the wick. The comrades continued to slumber.

> *Tues. Nov. 24*
> *I was sleeping sweetly last night about 12:00 when the*
> *Capt. came around and in a low tone ordered us to fall in*
> *as soon as we could...we marched down to the river...and*
> *we soon found ourselves embarked on the pontoon boats and*
> *under full headway for the other shore...about 300 boats at*
> *work...the sight was magnificent...it was just light enough*
> *to see them pass to and fro loaded down with bluecoats...the*
> *army marched in three columns...we marched forward...*
> *through thick brush and mud and water half a knee deep...*
> *we came in sight of a big ridge where we supposed there*
> *was a host of Rebels...every man bespoke his determination*
> *of going to the top...we went on a little farther...met a*
> *squad of cavalry...they informed us that...the long lines of*
> *Rebs that we seen happen to be Federal soldiers...This news*
> *brightened every man's countenance and there was a look of*
> *joy on their faces...* [20]

Aaron put down his pencil and looked across the valley toward the slopes of Missionary Ridge. In the dim moonlight, the ridges looked like ominous black silhouettes against a dark-gray sky. He could see thousands of Confederate campfires twinkling like fireflies. He looked at his comrades huddled in deep sleep around him and then gazed down the slope in front of the regiment and mumbled to himself in almost a whisper, "Well, General Bragg, we've got thousands of brighter ones in the valley below."

The clock had ticked far past midnight. He smiled. It was officially his birthday, and he felt good that he was now twenty-one years of age. Looking at Missionary Ridge one more time, he snuffed out the candle. In a few hours, it would be daylight and the army would move again, so he rolled into his thick wool blanket and quickly drifted off into a deep sleep.

Chapter 54

Missionary Ridge

November 25, 1863

The morning mist on the Tennessee River had burned away. The clouds over Lookout Mountain on Missionary Ridge had lifted, too. The day was clear and ripe for battle.

U. S. Grant and his staff had secured a vantage point near Chattanooga just like they had at Vicksburg. The place was called Orchard Knob. It was located almost at the center of a half circle of mountain ridges once called Mission Ridge by the Indians. From his high position on the knob, Grant had deployed the army again in three sectors. To the right was

Major General John Hooker, in the middle was Major General George Thomas, and to the left was his friend, Sherman. General Hooker had taken Lookout Mountain the previous day. It was up to Sherman and Thomas now to attack from the long sweeping ridge where thousands of rebels waited. It was late morning, and the attacks were underway in the Sherman sector where Aaron and Will were located.

"Gentlemen, it looks like the ball has begun on our left flank," announced Grant as he pointed to Tunnel Hill where Sherman's boys were attacking. He placed his field glasses to his eye brows, and paused for about thirty seconds. Keeping his gaze steady, he continued, "Looks like Colonel Loomis and his Twenty-Sixth Illinois are in a fix!"

"Is that the Loomis from Chicago, the Democrat?" asked Parker as he peered through his field glasses.

"Yes, it is, Captain. We call him Old Hindquarters, nicknamed by Lincoln years ago when he ran for senator against Douglas."

"With all due respect, sir, why did Lincoln name him Old Hindquarters?" Parker replied. The other officers turned to Grant, curious to hear his response.

"Well, as Lincoln in his great wisdom could see even back then, Loomis doesn't know his headquarters from his hindquarters!"

The staff erupted in laughter. Grant kept his composure. Every officer now peered to the left flank to see where Loomis had stalled.

Grant lowered his field glasses and calmly stated, "General John E. Smith's division is close to Colonel Loomis." He waved to a mounted orderly nearby who was waiting anxiously to get into the action. The young officer rode his fidgety horse over to Grant and saluted.

"Lieutenant, take this order to General Sherman. It informs him, if practicable, to advance the Second Division to support Colonel Loomis at the white house at the base of Tunnel Hill. Let him know it is called the Glass house."

"Yes, sir!" the rider exclaimed as he snapped a salute. The horse and rider then disappeared into a cloud of dust.

Suddenly, a long rattle of musket fire could be heard in the distance. Puffs of white smoke from the rebel cannons atop Tunnel Hill were followed by loud retorts that echoed across Orchard Knob. Grant trained his field glasses on the action. Lowering them, he turned to his officers and demanded, "Who ordered those men up the hill? These attacks are to be coordinated, and I see two lone regiments stalled at the top of that hill!"

Parker raised his field glasses. "General, they look like Pennsylvania regiments."

"Someone will pay for this," Grant replied. "I will not sacrifice our men like this. They must not advance unless it is by brigade, division, or corps. Do you understand, gentlemen?"

They all nodded.

Grant looked back at the ridge and shook his head. "Well, I hope General Smith can get Loomis out of his fix."

On Sherman's left flank, the Ninety-Third Illinois was in the valley waiting to advance. They were hidden in a small forest of pine trees and scrub that skirted a large meadow between their location and Missionary Ridge.

Colonel Putnam and Black Hawk were ready. Old Put, as the boys now affectionately called him, advanced out of the tree line on his black war-horse and rode slowly down the length of the regiment. He thought that maybe this challenge would be their greatest yet. He rode with his back stiff like a Roman general ready to wage battle on far-off fields. His dark eyes and black beard contrasted smartly with his deep-blue uniform. The boys felt confident looking at him.

"Boys, General Smith has ordered us to advance to the mountain," he announced. "When we mustered in at Fort Douglas, we stood one thousand strong. You have honored our state, wives, sweethearts, and families by your glorious actions on the field of battle. We are less than three hundred now." He paused, noticed Aaron and Will, and nodded to them as he rode by. "Boys, this is our day. We are the remaining ranks of the Ninety-Third and have a duty to those who have fallen before us. We, along with our brother regiments, are proud to be called the Old Ironsides Brigade. It is a right affirmation of what we have done and what we will continue to do." Putnam reached the end of the line and turned Black Hawk back again. He remained silent until he reached the center. He pulled out his sword and pointed to the ridge, and with a rising voice that all could hear, he shouted, "Let's give those rebels hell!"

The Ninety-Third in perfect chorus gave three "huzzahs" and moved out of the tree line.

Putnam and Black Hawk were in the lead. In the distance was the dreaded mountain just one-half mile away. They would get there in quick time.

As they approached, the image of the ridge got clearer. They spied Union soldiers at the base of the ridge, advancing through the passing waves of smoke. The steep ridge immediately to the right looked like a saddle with a hole—the railroad tunnel—in the center. Confederates in butternut and gray swarmed over the depression in the saddlelike mountain. They were moving fast in anticipation of the rush of Yankees.

Confederate batteries boomed from the horn and heel of the saddle, causing missiles to explode randomly over the advancing boys in blue. Slightly to the left was yet another battery positioned on a spur that jutted into the field before them. Near the base of the hill was the white house.

Suddenly, a bouncing cannonball tore a limb off of a soldier, passed through the belly of a comrade behind him, and tore the leg off an unsuspecting boy in the last rank. Blood splattered wildly before the boys. Everyone thought of running back to the forest. Another shot zipped by, causing the Ninety-Third to stop in their tracks.

Putnam turned and pointed to the burning white house.

"To that battery on the double-quick," he shouted. Black Hawk reared up on his hind quarters and dropped into a full gallop. Within minutes the remaining ranks made it to the battery. They advanced to a small depression in the meadow and fell prone, firmly grasping their muskets. The white house was still at a distance but could be plainly seen. They continued to hug the ground as the fury of lead droned above them.

After a few restful minutes, Putnam proceeded ahead to a small thicket to await orders from the commanding officers who he thought were gathered there. He dismounted and tied Black Hawk to a small scrub oak. A staff lieutenant familiar to Putnam approached and saluted.

"Colonel," he said excitedly, "General Matthies reports that there are two regiments up on the ridge already. They are unsupported and are taking heavy casualties. Most of their officers are dead."

"What regiments are they?" asked Putnam directly.

"The Twenty-Seventh and Seventy-Third Pennsylvania, I am told," was the reply.

"And who sent them up there?"

"It was Colonel Loomis, sir!"

"Loomis, Loomis," Putnam said slowly. "I know a Loomis. Is he from Chicago?"

"Yes, sir."

"Where is he now?"

"He is in the shelter of those trees, sir."

Putnam's eyes glared furiously as he remembered his confrontations with Loomis: at the Tremont Hotel where Loomis insulted Lincoln and from the Freeport Christmas ball where he threw him out the front door into the snow. He thought of the insulting remark Loomis had made to General Smith's son, and his temper began to flare. He stepped out of the ravine and walked deliberately toward the trees where the lieutenant had pointed. Within moments he was there.

And there he was, a little slimmer than Putnam remembered, but still the arrogant, little man with side whiskers.

Loomis saw Putnam coming. The memory of the Freeport ball incident flashed in his mind, and he backed himself up against a small pine tree for protection.

"Loomis, I ought to grab you by the collar again!" Putnam shouted as he got closer. Two large sergeants with bayonet muskets in hand quickly stepped in front of him and blocked his path to Loomis.

"Settle down, Colonel," Loomis replied in a cocky tone. "We are in the same army now, and we have to work together today."

Putnam took off his campaign hat, wiped his brow, and placed it squarely back on again. He took a deep breath to settle himself down. "Did you order those Pennsylvania regiments up the ridge?"

"Yes, Colonel," he replied. "As ranking officer on the field, I borrowed them and sent them up."

"Borrowed them! Borrowed them!" replied an agitated Putnam. "What do you mean borrowed them?"

Loomis smiled curtly, stroked his muttonchop whiskers, and then pointed to the mountain. Cannons and muskets were echoing loudly down the slope. "Those boys up there wanted to make the attack, and I did not want to spare my own. Settle down, Colonel. We will support them in good time."

"Good time! Why aren't you supporting them now, you coward?" He stepped toward Loomis who quickly backed toward the tree again. Anticipating Putnam's move, the guards immediately stepped toward Putnam, blocking his path again.

Loomis smiled, and in a very calm voice continued. "Now, Colonel, since you are here, and I am ranking officer on the field, I order *you* to support those Pennsylvanians." He grinned.

"I will not take any orders from you, you coward. I have already received orders from General Matthies that the Ninety-Third support those boys, and he has sanctioned it."

"Well, then, good Colonel," replied Loomis grinning, "be on your way. Please do visit me in Chicago when this cruel war is over."

Putnam stared at Loomis and said nothing. He looked into the eyes of the guards, who showed no emotion and strode away. He looked at the tunnel where the Pennsylvanians were and wondered how he would make it up the steep slope with Black Hawk. There was a dense forest in front of them with felled trees strategically intermingled to obstruct an advance. The rebels cut even more timber at the summit so the batteries would have a clear shot at the Yankees with their deadly canister.

Putnam walked over to his beloved war-horse and stroked his mane. Black Hawk lifted his head abruptly. The reins around his black coat clinked as his pointy ears perked up anticipating the fight to come.

"You didn't like missing out on that action at Vicksburg, did you?" Putnam said, as he ran his hand across the Shiloh scar. Black Hawk snorted and then nodded his head, straining at the reins, as if he understood. "We have to help those boys on the top of the hill." He then placed his boot in the stirrup, rose up on the saddle, and settled. Turning to his regiment, Putnam spurred on Black Hawk and closed the distance with a steady gait.

The boys saw them coming at full gallop. The white house at the base of the ridge was put to the torch by retreating rebels. Red and yellow flames licked upward and jumped quickly to the upper floors, creating a strange panoramic background. Billowing clouds of black and white smoke rose from the fiery frenzy to the clear blue sky. To the boys it looked like Putnam and Black Hawk were riding straight from hell.

"Looks like Old Put's got some orders."

"Happy birthday, Aaron," Will replied nervously.

Aaron could see he was truly afraid of what was to come. "Thanks, Will. We will get through this together. Let's stay close."

Will nodded.

Soon Black Hawk thundered up in front of the boys. "Boys!" shouted Putnam. "There are Pennsylvanians up there that need our help. We will advance at the quick step with the rest of the brigade. Let's give those rebels the cold steel!"

Captain Taggart stood up and commanded, "Front Forward! To the quick step! Charge!" His commands were shouted by the other captains in the line as the regiment surged forth.

Aaron wondered, *How could this be happening on my birthday? Gotta keep moving! Stay close to Will!*

Will and Aaron with the entire Ironsides Brigade moved up the hill at almost a sprint. Cannons boomed from the heights in defiance.

Let's stop at the burning white house. Let's not go up! We're gonna get killed here! Where's Will? I don't see him anymore! Five soldiers from Freeport in one instance dropped dead from an explosion, causing Aaron to stop, stunned in his tracks. They were gone forever. None of them even screamed. Their mangled bodies dropped onto the timber. *Gotta keep movin'! Gotta keep movin'! Where's Will? Where did he go?* The deadly lead rained down on the men as they jumped over fallen timber, inching their way to the top. *Oh, my God! General Matthies is hit! His head is covered with blood! I hope he's not dead!* The boys kept climbing, making their way to the Pennsylvanians and wrapping their ranks around them.

Aaron looked up. They were only twenty paces from the enemy. He dropped to the ground with the others on the slope. Panting heavily at the point of exhaustion, he looked at Private Trimble from Princeton who he had talked to many times in camp. Suddenly, a large rock thrown from the rebel ramparts crashed into Trimble's face. His scream was lost in the cacophony of desperate cries, musket fire and clanking metal.

Where's Will? Where's Will? Is he wounded? Is he dead? Where is he? Aaron picked up his musket, slipped it down so he could easily place in powder and ball, rammed home the ball, placed a cap on the cone, pulled back the hammer one click, and placed the sight bead on a rebel that was loading the cannon above him. The rebel's head would appear at every movement. First he saw head and ramrod, and then he saw head and powder, and he knew next the can of canister would come. He saw the rebel's head and pulled the trigger. It missed.

Suddenly Will appeared and jumped behind the protective log next to Aaron.

"Where the hell have you been?"

"Firing through smoke. Don't know if I'm hittin' any rebs!" Will rubbed his brow with his sleeve. The hot contest for Tunnel Hill was reaching a crescendo as the deafening roar of musketry continued.

Suddenly, the reflection of steel clanked and shimmered across the ridge.

"They're gonna charge us, Will!" screamed Aaron in horror.

Down they came, crashing into the Union ranks, yelling like devils. Aaron picked up a large rock and knocked out a rebel who tried to bayonet him. Will grabbed his musket and clubbed an officer who tried to take out Aaron with his sword. The officer dropped the sword as he fell. Still conscious, the rebel was grabbed by a stout soldier in blue and taken quickly to the rear.

The clang of metal continued along the lines. *What am I doing here, Lord? Why am I here?* Aaron picked up his musket and crashed the butt into a face that suddenly popped up in front of him. The rebel fell back, hitting his head on a stump. *Where's Will? Where's Will?* Aaron turned and saw Will clubbing another soldier. Everything seemed to be in slow motion. Arms and legs flailed. Blue and gray torsos fell in the timber together, lifeless. After what seemed to be an eternity, the desperate hand-to-hand struggle began to fade. There was a pause, then the rebels receded back to the top of the hill.

Aaron wiped his blackened face with his right sleeve then took in several deep breaths. *We did it! We did it! We repulsed their charge!*

Will soon arrived at his side with a face covered in soot and blood too.

"Do you think they're retreating?" Aaron asked, as he gasped for breath.

"They will keep their stand," Will panted.

Suddenly, a cannonball with a lit fuse bounced down the hillside into the ranks about thirty feet away from Will and Aaron. Everyone within sight of it braced themselves. A husky Fifth Iowa private picked up the twelve-pound ball to throw it out of harms way behind a man-made abatis of rock and timber. To no avail. In a split second, a blinding flash shook the ranks. When the smoke cleared away, what was left of the brave Iowan was grotesquely inter-twined with comrades closest to him … mangled, motionless, silent.

"We gotta do something,'" Will interjected in a solemn voice. "We gotta get over that hill!"

Another explosion just to their left caused the earth to shudder again. Aaron grabbed his ears and buried his face deeper into the cool, damp leaves on the hillside. He closed his eyes and thought, *Will and I can just stay here behind these logs for a while. We've killed enough rebels for today. Besides it's my birthday. I shouldn't have to fight.*

Boom! Boom! Two more cannonballs did their deadly work. *I'm goin' back. Will, you and I are goin' back now. We've fought enough rebs today!*

Aaron lifted his head and turned to Will. He wanted to let Will know what he was thinking. But Will was gone. *He must have retreated already. He must be down there talking to Colonel Putnam about reforming back where we were in that nice little forest.*

Aaron hugged the ground again, rolled over on his back, and looked down the hill.

Hundreds of boys in blue were behind him now. *Looks like two brigades maybe.*

But where did Will go? Did he retreat? He kept looking down the hillside and saw soldiers dropping by the minute.

And then he had his answer.

He saw Lance Sergeant Spellman with the national colors raised high. Behind him was Will, and further down the slope was Colonel Putnam on Black Hawk, traveling across the slope in a zigzag fashion through cut timber and fallen soldiers.

The Confederate guns stopped for a moment as the rebels stared at the strange storming party that was approaching with the flag held high. After a pause, a spattering of lead hit the trees again, breaking the silence.

Spellman waved the colors and dodged to and fro as if dancing with the flag. The brass eagle flag tip caught the afternoon sun light that penetrated the green canopy. The wings of the eagle seemed to glow brighter as Spellman approached where Aaron was. He jumped over the log that protected Aaron and continued on. Will dove next to Aaron. They grabbed their muskets and were ready to charge at the command.

Napoleon smoothbore cannons continued to spray canister from the crest of the hill, as more deadly missiles rolled downhill, exploding in the blue ranks. Spellman weaved to within twenty paces of the rebel works, waving the banner furiously so all could see the nearness of his position through the clouds of smoke around them.

Aaron twisted his head low and looked back down the slope to see the gathering reinforcements merging for the push up the hill. He hugged the dirt firmly and then pushed up, face forward, to see how Spellman was doing. Flag pieces separated from the staff and fluttered to the ground like leaves. Then the wooden staff splintered from a direct hit from a minié ball and dipped it down sideways. The weight of another barrage of musket fire finally knocked it to the ground. Spellman, stunned and with terror in his eyes, grabbed his shattered elbow and fell backward, stumbling over the timber.

There was a pause on the Union side. No one fired their muskets.

Will then stood up and jumped over the massive log in front of him.

Aaron was speechless. *Don't grab the flag, Will! Please, Will, don't grab that flag! You'll get killed! You'll get killed! Please don't do it!*

Will, in a flash, grabbed the standard and raised the brass eagle tip back up again. Only half the flag remained now, but its folds could still be seen by the regiment through the smoke. He held the banner high and looked back at the others behind him. "Come on, boys! Come on!" he shouted, advancing a few paces up the slope.

To Aaron the scene was unreal, in slow motion again. There was even a strange silence about it. Will shouted again, but Aaron could not hear him this time. *Will, get down! Will, get down!*

The colors dipped again, this time shattering the eagle tip on the trunk of a fallen tree as Will buckled over. He looked back at Aaron with a hopeless stare. He clutched his breast and fell forward on the slope. The minié balls continued to spatter the trees like a hailstorm around the stalled bluecoats.

Aaron screamed but could not hear himself with the deafening cannon and rally of musket fire. He jumped over the log in front of him and crawled to Will's side, maneuvering so he could be closer to him. The missiles seemed to fly more furiously now. Will was dead. His eyes were open and fixed in death. Aaron did not have time to weep for he thought the rebels were about to charge again. *Why did you have to do it, Will? You can take me, God. You can take me! I don't care anymore! Why did you let him die?* He almost stood up at the moment but caught himself. He decided he had best get Will's body back home somehow to Allie.

Why did you do it, old friend? Why? He took his hand and brushed his palm over Will's eyes to close them. Then he hugged Will's lifeless form as the cheers seemed to echo louder on the Union side. Aaron looked down the slope. The cheers were indeed louder.

Through the cloudy smoke, he could see Colonel Putnam and Black Hawk maneuvering with ease up the slope. As they continued coming in closer view of the rebel batteries, about twenty paces, the firing stopped again. The Confederates were in a sense frozen by the sight. They marveled at how a horse and rider could make it through the mass of timber and men to the crest of Tunnel Hill.

Black Hawk snorted. Putnam held his reins tightly, ready to advance with the kick of a spur. Looking to the rebel batteries at the top of the slope, Putnam held his determined gaze. When he reached the spot where Will had fallen, he looked at Aaron with an expression that Aaron had never seen before.

"Aaron, is Will dead?" Putnam asked.

"Yes, Colonel," Aaron replied as tears welled up in his eyes.

Putnam gazed at the fallen Will and then back at Aaron. He thought about his daughter, Jenny. He thought about Leonora, his wife.

The Confederates kept their pause.

"Give me the flag!" Putnam shouted. Black Hawk held firm. He did not dance.

Adjutant Hicks, who was nearest to the standard, though wounded above his brow, lifted the flag from the ground with a bloody hand.

Black Hawk, in response to the intense tone of his master's voice, began to prance as the tattered stars and stripes rubbed against his dark mane. Putnam looked down at Aaron and nodded in silence. He pulled out his sword with his right hand and shouted in a clear voice, "Never forsake the colors!"

Hearing his cry to advance, the Confederate musketry answered again in its deafening fury spattering trees and rocks around the determined 93rd Illinois ranks.

"Come on, boys!" he shouted. The line began to advance up the hill again like a wave cresting on the beach. In a flash of fire, the flagstaff fluttered once more. Red and white pieces dropped to the ground. Undaunted by the sting of the barrage, Putnam continued to shout his commands.

Within seconds, the colors dropped. Putnam wavered in the saddle and slipped. Falling backward, he hit the ground hard with a bullet wound gaping from his temple. No one moved behind him. Everyone was stunned. The Confederate fire ceased for a moment and then began again. Those around Putnam did not know what to do. The flag remained on the ground. Nobody advanced to pick it up.

Aaron quickly crawled to the colonel's side, pressing his gaping wound with his right hand, but there was no flow of blood. Soon Captain Taggart with the solidiers from Freeport boys hovered around the stricken colonel in stunned silence.

"Captain, he breathes. Can we do nothing for him?" implored Major Hicks as he held a bloody kerchief on his own head wound.

Aaron looked on in silence. He thought of Jenny now and could barely stand the thought of all of it.

"Let's carry him down the slope, boys. We will take him back home to Freeport," Taggart replied solemnly. "Old Put will fight no more."

Aaron grabbed one of the four corners of a thick wool blanket that served as a battlefield stretcher for the good colonel. He looked up at the crest of the hill where the rebels were still stubbornly defending their ground. The sound of war rose up again. *This is no time to cry. I don't have anymore tears anyway.* He looked at the place on the slope where Will had fallen. *I'll come for him tonight after the fight is over!*

Aaron and his party descended slowly down the slope with Putnam's body. Captain Taggart held Black Hawk's reigns. The great war-horse from Shiloh and Vicksburg was not prancing anymore. He continued downhill behind his fallen master as if in a silent, respectful reverance. When the Freeport contingent reached the base of the slope, the piercing rebel yell rose up again as it had on every charge. Everyone looked to the crest. A third wave of gray soldiers rolled over the blue ranks, this time decimating them for good.

The Battle for Tunnel Hill was over.

Chapter 55

Vicksburg

Camp of the Ninety-Fifth Illinois
January, 1864

"Mail Call! Allen!"

"Here!"

"Bacon!"

"Over Here!"

"Bell!"

"Yo!"

"Briggs"

"Here!"

"Cashier!"

"Here!"

Allie stepped forward and grabbed the letter. It was from Freeport. Her messmates who were not as lucky this day hovered around her, anxiously waiting to hear news of interest from their neighboring town.

"Looks like a letter from your sweetheart, Jenny Putnam, again!" said the closest soldier to her.

"Whoa! Best not read us too much of the details," said another.

Allie pored over the letter as best she could. Gramma Lucy had taught her to read and write, but she still had problems. For this reason, Jenny would write to her in the simplest ways and always with short sentences. The message was very clear today.

"Oh, my God," Allie screeched in a high-pitched voice. "My sweetheart has been killed!" She sunk to her knees around the campfire, almost dropping the letter in the fire. Tears clouded her vision, and she read the letter again in hopes that she had made an error.

"Is Jenny Putnam dead? Your sweetheart?" asked another who was close by.

Allie looked up and wiped her tears with her sleeve. She tried to compose herself. She worried that she was not acting manly enough and that she would be exposed.

She quickly corrected herself. "No! My sweetheart's father, Colonel Putnam, and a dear friend from Freeport, Will Erwin, were killed at Missionary Ridge! They both were carryin' the colors!" Allie suddenly sat down on a log and was silent. She placed the letter gently on her lap and stared into the fire. Her face was ghostly white. The messmates grew somber. No one spoke.

It was late afternoon now, and the sun was close to setting. She thought about Will, and the tension built up within her like a raging forest fire. Unable to cry, she continued to morosely stare into the smoldering embers.

Suddenly, she rose up and took off at a dead run through camp. The white tents around her stood in perfect rows, and she ran unobstructed for a hundred yards. Captain Bush was at the end of the row by the colonel's tent and saw her coming. He stopped in front of her.

"Private Cashier! Where are you going?" he demanded.

Allie dodged him and headed for the colonel's horse, which was tied to a sapling nearby.

"Cashier! Come back here!"

Allie made it to the horse, pulled the reins off the tree branch, placed her left foot in the stirrup, and rose up. She looked back. At least fifty soldiers had crowded around Captain Bush to see what the alarm was all about.

"Private Cashier! Dismount and stand at attention! What the hell is going on?" Bush screamed in an even more commanding tone.

Allie turned the mount around and replied in a quick curt voice, "My best friend was killed, cap'n! They couldn' send him home, so they buried him in a mass grave! He and Old Put got killed carryin' the colors at Missionary Ridge. While the Ninety-Fifth was sittin' around here, my friends in the Ninety-Third got killed!"

"Cashier, get down from that horse, now!"

Allie placed the letter between the buttons of her sack coat, pulled down her kepi, and turned the horse away. She looked back at the captain. "I'll bring him back!" she said. "I promise!" She then reined the horse's neck, straightened him, and darted out of camp in a full gallop.

"Get back here, Cashier!" Bush shook his head and placed his hands on his hips. "Albert will be in big trouble for this escapade," he said to the boys around him. "He's gonna wish he hadn't come back once the colonel is finished with him."

Allie continued at a full trot and then a gallop as the sun began to set behind her. Passing the Stone house on the Jackson Road, she continued to where the rebel siege lines had skirted the perimeter of Vicksburg.

"Halt!" screamed two sentries in unison.

She continued at full gallop now. *Zip! Zip!* Two musket balls droned by her ears.

In a few minutes, she sighted the Shirley house, as white and unspoiled as ever in the setting sun. She wondered how it could have survived all the heavy fighting.

The colonel's horse was strong, did not tire, and proceeded at a full gallop. Allie kept her posture forward to keep her balance. She whispered in the horse's ear, "We'll be gittin there soon ol' boy!"

Within minutes she could see Mt. Ararat where she had last met Will in the darkness before the great assaults on the rebel lines. She began to slow the pace of the horse so she could find her way. The last vestige of sunlight now could be seen only at the peak of the mountain. She slowed the horse to a canter pace and then to a slow trot, finally reaching the trail that led to the top of the summit.

Quickly dismounting from the saddle, she gently stroked the horse's sweaty mane and then tied him to a small tree where he could not be seen. Crisscrossing on the path to the top, she made the arduous walk up to where she and Will had made love. Below her, the twinkling campfires around Vicksburg glittered as before, though the fires were fewer.

She walked over to the familiar flat rock where she embraced Will just seven months before and sat down.

Looking to the clear starry constellation above, she sighed. "Why did you have to pick up that flag, my love?"

Shaking uncontrollably, she looked again to the heavens. Her grief was too great to be compared to anything she had felt before, even though she had seen hundreds of dead corpses mangled, contorted, and heaped on battlefields. She felt like a dagger was in her heart, and she could not pull it out. She had loved Will from the day she met him.

Pulling out a large bowie knife from her belt, a prize she received from a tall rebel after the Vicksburg surrender, she gasped for air. She could not breathe at the thought of Will. She pounded the blade tip into the rocky soil between her boots.

"Why? Why? Why?" she cried as she drove the tip of the blade deeper into ground with each quick, rhythmic, and frantic thrust.

Then she stopped.

The multitude of campfires in the distance seemed to grow brighter in the darkness, and the memories of the wigwam came over her.

She remembered how Will always smiled gently and with approval when she kidded Trick, even pushing him on occasion into the Pecatonica. She also remembered the prank she pulled on Will; how he raced to the sandbar thinking she was chasing him. Most of all, she pondered the quiet times together with their feet gently swirling in the river, and when they carved their initials in the sand … always an "A" for Allie and a "W" for Will, intertwined and intermixed.

The memories made her feel better now, and she felt a sense of peace and grace as if Will was with her somehow.

She looked up to the heavens again and stood up. Turning slowly, she walked to a large, flat-faced boulder in front of her. Placing the bowie knife with the point up, and using the pressure of both hands, she began scratching a "W" on the surface. Though the rock sediment was tough, she could clearly make her mark.

The night breezes began to blow across the rocky point. She could feel Will's presence around her. "I will love you forever, Will," she said softly to the wind.

When she finished etching the "W" into the stone, she rubbed it with her left hand. "That should tidy it up," she said. Holding the knife horizontally now, she scratched a line to make the inside of the "W" an "A". She then carved a heart symbol around the two superimposed letters. She smiled and looked pleased, like a sculptor after putting the finishing touches on a masterpiece. Her heart was not heavy anymore.

"There we go, my love," she whispered as she rubbed the flat of the bowie knife on her front sleeve. "This rock will be here forever."

Placing the bowie knife back in her belt, she turned to look once more at the campfires and the constellation of light above her.

"Best be gittin back to camp," she said. "Best be gittin back to the boys."

Chapter 56

Camp of the Twenty-Ninth Regiment Infantry

United States Colored Troops (USCT)
Quincy, Illinois
April 27, 1864

Five companies of soldiers stood in silent formation on the Quincy green. Some were born free; others were runaway slaves. All of them now mustered into service to fight for the Union and freedom.

A bugle cracked the silence as it sounded reveille. The sharp, quick cadence of the tune raised a prideful spirit in the men as Old Glory slowly ascended to the top of the flagpole in front of them. When the bugler blew the final note, the flag rose to the highest point and came to life, snapping in the cool April breeze. The recruits, in their silence, thought of their families. They wondered what the future would hold for them. Today was the day of departure to Chicago and then on to the battlefields of Virginia.

"Attention E Company! Roll call!" commanded Captain Flint as he held his company roster above his head. "Colonel Bross has instructed all companies to take mess immediately after roll call, prepare six days' rations, and present back here on the green at three o'clock for a farewell address from Brigadier General Prentiss. Once you have answered my roll call, you are dismissed to camp. Are there any questions?" Flint asked.

"OK then. Company roll call!"

"Thomas Adams!"

"Present for duty, sir!"

"Moses Alexander!"

"Present for duty, sir!"

"Wait a minute! My God, do we have the entire Arbuckle clan here? I see we have four in our company! All are privates. Company, at ease. Arbuckles, all of you, step forward."

The four stepped to the front of the command.

"Boys, are you all related?"

"Yes, sir," replied the shortest in the family. "My name is Joseph Arbuckle, and my friends call me Li'l Joe!"

"Well, so it is," Captain Flint replied as he shook his head side to side. "And I see you have some spunk, too! Li'l Joe, I have you marked present for duty. You can return to camp. The rest of you Arbuckles sound off!"

"Conrad Arbuckle!"

"Present for duty, sir!"

"Robert Arbuckle!"

"Present for duty, sir!"

"William Arbuckle!"

"Present for duty, sir!"

Captain Flint continued the roll call for the remaining eighty-five members of Company E. As Li'l Joe returned to his Sibley tent on the Quincy green, he looked across the field and saw a sergeant approaching him. He was dressed in a musician's coat much fancier than what the other enlisted men wore. It had sky-blue lace formed in nine V-shaped rows with nine bronze buttons centered within the pattern. He noticed the sergeant had a distinctive limp, and he looked familiar.

As the sergeant neared, Li'l Joe cried out in glee, "Blue! Is that you? I can't believe my eyes. Blue, oh, Blue, it is you!"

Blue picked up his pace, hugged Li'l Joe, who was now five feet six inches tall, and lifted him off the ground.

"Dear God, Li'l Joe, it is you!" Blue exclaimed gleefully as he welled up with tears. "How did you get here? Where have you been? I assumed you headed to Canada after the friends of the wigwam took you to the Oscar Taylor house."

Li'l Joe rubbed his tears in the elbow of his frock coat and looked up. "Well, after you left me in Freeport, the Taylor family got fond of me. I think they felt sorry that I was alone and not wandering with a family. They asked if I would be a paid house servant, and I gladly accepted. During those years, Mrs. Taylor was so kind. She taught me how to read, write, and speak like you, Blue! For this, I will always be grateful."

"I am so happy for you, Li'l Joe. We are back together again. And who are your comrades-in-arms? What company are you in?"

"I am in E Company. I have other Arbuckle relatives in the company, too! We are all from Wood River. My father, Conrad, is with us, too!"

Blue stepped back dropping his flute to his side. "Your father is alive? He made it to shore?"

Li'l Joe beamed. "Yes, Blue, after our rowboat was swamped the second time, he drifted away from me, and by chance, a large oak tree branch floated near him and he held on firm. He floated downstream until daybreak and was discovered by a fisherman who pulled him into his boat and placed a blanket over him. He then traveled back north on the underground railroad to Alton and freedom!"

"God bless!" Blue replied passionately, "I am so happy for you and all the Arbuckles."

"Have you heard anything from our friends of the wigwam?" Li'l Joe asked.

"No, after I left you at the wigwam, I never went back on the underground railroad through Freeport. I went seven other secret ways through Rockford and Chicago."

"Do you think the boys are fighting for Father Abraham?"

"I'm quite sure they are . . . or maybe they're in heaven now," he replied softly.

"Well, I suspect the two misses are praying for the boys to return soon to Freeport. I remember the shorter one who hugged me when I was scared. Remember, Blue?

"Yes, I do. Her name is Allie."

"She was so kind to me," Li'l Joe replied. "I hope she is still by the cave with her other nice lady friend."

"Her name is Jenny Putnam. Her father was a friend of Mr. Taylor, remember?

"Sure do. She was dressed in fancy clothes. Allie was in britches like I was."

Well, I hope those boys are safe," replied Blue as he held his fife to his side.

Li'l Joe nodded and smiled. He then looked over his shoulder at his company campground. He noticed that all the Arbuckles were working diligently, preparing rations and equipment for the trip back east. He turned to Blue and saluted. "Best be getting back to my company. See you on the green, Sergeant!"

As he returned to Company E, a train engine pulled up with twelve coaches of the Chicago, Burlington, and Quincy Railroads. The train whistle shrieked loudly as the hiss of the boilers and the rumble of iron crossed by the green, rolling to rest at the Quincy terminal several hundred yards away. Soldiers from the other four companies stepped away from the tracks and watched in awe. They mixed in and around the green like citizens in a busy city, all of them moving quickly to make the preparations complete.

By three o'clock, they returned to their formations again, in silence.

General Prentiss, arriving by carriage, walked to a small platform that was constructed the previous day to address the soldiers, all of whom were fully equipped now and ready to embark on the train.

Taking three steps up the platform with Old Glory still flapping smartly in the wind, he looked up at the blue sky and then down at his notes. He smiled and nodded his head, pleased at the magnificent columns of men before him.

"Soldiers of the Twenty-Ninth USCT," he called out, raising his hand like a minister over the five companies whose officers stood proudly in front. "We are called upon to co-operate with our brave companions-in-arms, whose proud lot it is to precede us in the noble cause for which we battle: the restoration of the Union and the perpetuity of the institutions bequeathed to us by our forefathers. To those officers before us who fought valiantly with me at Shiloh and across the land from east to west, our citizens will be forever grateful."

Prentiss paused and looked up at the sky again. The sun was beginning to descend behind the tall buildings on the western side of the green, causing shadows to fall onto the soldiers. The wind picked up.

He looked at the crowd and pulled out a folded letter from his frock coat. He placed spectacles on the tip of his nose. The spectators remained silent.

"As my final farewell to you, please allow me to share with you a few choice words written by our beloved president, Abraham Lincoln, who also sends an affectionate farewell. He is eternally grateful for your enlistment in the Twenty-Ninth USCT Infantry."

Prentiss opened the letter and snugged his spectacles on the bridge of his nose and, after a long pause, continued.

Fellow-citizens, we cannot escape history… The fiery trail through which we pass will light us down, in honor or dishonor, to the latest generation. We say we are for the Union. The world will not forget that we say this. We know how to save the Union. The world knows we do know how to save it… We…hold the power and bear the responsibility. In giving freedom to the slave, we assure freedom to the free—honorable alike in what we give and what we preserve.

Solo shouts from the crowd knifed through the air like pistol shots, causing the general to pause. He smiled and continued with a steady rising pitch,

We shall nobly save . . . or . . . lose the last, best hope of earth. Other means may succeed; this could not fail. The way is plain, generous & just—a way which, if followed, the world will forever applaud, and God must forever bless! [21]

Prentiss smiled, nodded his head, and tucked the letter back in his coat.

Colonel Bross then shouted, "Three cheers for Mr. Lincoln's army!"

A soldier chorus of "Huzzah! Huzzah! Huzzah!" mixed with the cheers and shouts of both young and old. The train whistle shrieked again, beckoning the soldiers now to come, to begin their long journey to eastern battlefields.

"Sergeant Blue, strike up the band!" Bross cried out as he unsheathed his sword and raised it high so the entire regiment could see him plainly. "Soldiers, prepare to march!"

Blue stepped forward with the musicians, who were positioned to the front and side of the troops. Raising his wooden fife to his lips, he nodded his head, and the band played the popular song "We Are Coming, Father Abraham" whose lyrics were familiar to all.

Each captain of the five companies shouted, "Company...march!" as the proud soldiers moved in perfect columns successively. As the fifth company in order, Captain Flint and Company E fell in to the procession last. When Company E approached the musicians, Li'l Joe, while keeping his shoulders straight and his step in sync with the march, turned his head to the regimental band. As he passed, he looked directly into Blue's eyes, smiled, and saluted him with a quick snap of his right hand. Blue's countenance beamed with appreciation as he nodded back, fife at his fingertips.

The train whistle shrieked again as the boiler steam rose and then dropped onto the iron wheels that would carry the railroad cars on the first leg of the journey from Quincy to Chicago.

A chorus of ladies with fancy bonnets that flapped in the breeze hurried to the front of the regiment with colorful bouquets. They handed a flower to every soldier they could reach. As the cheers and shouts for victory rose up, the women began to sing the lyrics of the marching song. More citizens joined in as the troops began to sing in perfect chorus with determined conviction in their eyes.

We are coming, Father Abraham, 300,000 more,
From Mississippi's winding stream and from New England's shore.
We leave our plows and workshops, our wives and children dear,
With hearts too full for utterance, with but a silent tear.
We dare not look behind us but steadfastly before.
We are coming, Father Abraham, 300,000 more!

General Prentiss and his contigent remained on the green as the joyful singing of the soldiers faded away, their dusty boots enveloped in the billowing clouds of steam that rose and then fell to the railroad tracks. As the Twenty-Ninth USCT Infantry disappeared in the shadow-laced steam, a cavalcade of horses and buggies closed in behind them.

Prentiss looked up again to the heavens and turned to his admirers. "Let us bow our heads and pray in silence for victory and the safe return of our boys. God bless Mr. Lincoln's army."

In the distance the haunting moan of the train whistle signaled the celebration and festivities were over, as the new soldiers on the train thought about their families and what the future would hold for them as soldiers in the Union army. Many of them fell silent as they listened to the rapid, comforting click-clack of the train wheels that steadily rolled eastward over the long iron rails.

They knew there was much more work to do.

Chapter 57

Wigwam

Pecatonica River
Early Summer, 1864

The color in the trees was majestic, like it had always been this time of year on the Pecatonica. Turtledoves, two by two, still pecked at seed that drifted from the high grass on the riverbank to the pebbled sand-bars. Gray squirrels with brown bellies chattered in the branches above as they prepared their nests for the winter. Now and then a red cardinal darted through the holly branches by the wigwam, and the tall Injun oak was almost touching the water now, its heavy weight cheated by years of soil erosion at its roots.

The friends were still apart. Allie was fighting west of Vicksburg now. Aaron and Trick were in Georgia about ready to make a march to the sea with General Sherman. T.J. was home in Buda, blind, but able to manage a bookstore somehow. Will rested in a mass grave on the slope of Missionary Ridge.

"Jenny, where are you taking me?"

"To a special place, Charlie."

"Why is it so special?"

"You will see in just a minute."

Jenny held Charlie's hand so he would not slip. He was nine years old and had never been this far down the river. This was a stretch for the both of them, and Jenny knew it, but she continued on, knowing that their mother would not approve. Mrs. Putnam had been very protective of Charlie since the death of his father.

"Now, Charlie, we are almost there. This is a secret place, and you must not bring anyone here. It is too special."

"All right, Jenny," he replied. His faced beamed with excitement.

Jenny reached up and pushed the holly branches away from the entrance. Soon they were in the darkness. The beam of light from the ceiling was almost vertical to the floor.

"Wow, Jenny! What is this place?"

"This is a secret Indian wigwam. There were two Winnegabo Indian lovers who came here before the white men settled. Now only friends of the wigwam come here."

"Aaron?"

"Yes, Aaron is one of the friends."

"Who else is a friend?"

"The others I will tell you about later."

"What are those things by the wall?"

"They are all special things that I will let you hold next time we come. We can only stay here a little while and must get back home now before mother gets worried."

Jenny grabbed Charlie's hand again. She pushed through the holly branches and abruptly went outside. The brightness caused Charlie to shelter his face in the cradle of his sleeve. They were directly between the Injun oak and the holly branches. She looked fleetingly at her little brother and then turned to the hollies. With a careful hand, she plucked a thorny branch from the bush and then quickly walked over to the Injun oak. Reaching out over the river, she snapped off an oak-leaf branch, somewhat small, but the best she could safely grasp.

Charlie said nothing. He wondered why his sister was acting strangely.

"Charlie, the Winnebago lovers planted these holly bushes to hide the entrance of the wigwam. The big Injun oak tree was planted there sometime later by the squaw after her warrior was killed in battle."

Charlie looked confused but nodded his head anyway.

Jenny looked down at the holly branch in her hand and paused. She stared without blinking as if she were dreaming. She smiled again at Charlie.

"Do you remember those holly branches from Father's funeral?" she asked softly.

"Yes, Jenny," he said. His mind flashed back to a day he would never forget. He remembered how the funeral procession moved slowly to City Cemetery at the top of the hill in Freeport. The snow and sleet caused the slush on the muddy streets to spatter as his father's funeral carriage moved slowly to the place of internment. In the lead of the possession was a riderless horse. Military boots were strapped to the saddle's stirrups with the toes pointing backward, a distinctive but yet strange sign of respect for an officer who had fallen facing the enemy. He remembered the black carriages that carried the old folks too, and how the family with Captain Taggart at their side walked the long muddy roads through Freeport from the Presbyterian Church to the cemetery knoll.

"These holly branches are evergreens, and they stand for eternal love." Jenny's eyes welled up. Her voice cracked a little. She continued. "Remember, Charlie, we placed these on Father's coffin before we buried him?" She pulled out a kerchief and wiped her eyes and then quickly placed it back in the front pocket of her country dress.

Charlie nodded again. He could not speak for fear that he would cry. He wanted to be a man. He looked down at his tiny boots, also muddy from his walk to the wigwam.

Jenny tossed the holly branch into the Pecatonica. It floated slowly, swirled once by Trick's fishing hole, and then continued downriver. She held up the oak-leaf branch, paused for a moment, and then continued.

"An oak leaf, Charlie, stands for courage. Allie and I gave these to the boys the day they left Freeport for the war. We placed them in their hats so they would be good soldiers and stand strong and firm in battle."

Charlie reached for the branch and smiled. Jenny handed it to him.

He peered at the Injun oak and studied it for a minute, and then he looked back at Jenny. "If that Injun oak is still there when I go off to war," he asked excitedly, "will you give me an oak leaf, too?"

Jenny looked deeply into his eyes. She felt the innocence of the question like a dagger to her heart, and she started to weep. Her shoulders shook as she tried to compose herself and hide her tears by turning and facing downriver. She thought of the boys and what had happened to them—how innocent they were during the wigwam days, how proud they stood in their new uniforms, and what the terrible war had done to them. She blanked the horror from her mind and turned back to Charlie. She reached over for the oak-leaf branch. He handed it to her gently. She looked at the river again and noticed another colored patchwork of leaves drifting along. Timing her toss, she flipped the branch so it would land in the middle of the mix. Charlie watched with wonder as the green oak branch and collection of autumn leaves bobbed for a moment and then disappeared.

"Did I say something to hurt your feelings?" he asked.

Jenny caught herself and then smiled. She cocked her head and said, "No, my brother, I was just thinking of Allie and the boys."

She looked at Charlie and gazed into his eager eyes. Happy memories of the wigwam rose up as she saw in her little brother's eyes, the same unspoiled innocence that the friends once saw in each other. She could see his little world was all wonder for now.

Jenny reached out for his hand again. "Let's go home to Mother," she said softly.

Placing her other hand on the trunk of the Injun oak, she looked at the Pecatonica one last time. Her memory raced back like a flash to the time when Aaron gave her a first kiss. She thought of T.J. and Trick, opposite in size and stature yet always together with a rifle and cane pole at their side. She also thought of Allie and Will walking in the shallows hand in hand with their trousers rolled to their knees.

She held Charlie's hand a little tighter now as they continued upriver. She looked down at him and smiled.

He smiled back.

Soon they approached the favorite bend that rose up to the Putnam farm. They quietly waded across, and after reaching the other side, they could see the Putnam home on a rise a short distance away. Between the Pecatonica and the house was a small knoll that protruded like a knob in the pasture. Since it was not yet suppertime, Jenny decided to take a rest. She sat down with Charlie and faced the river again.

As she looked to the distance, a feeling of contentment came over her as the sun penetrated the tree branches, causing a multitude of yellow and light-green hues. She looked up. Gray clouds floated in the distance. The setting sun cast rays of orange that streaked the pale-blue panorama. Her thoughts drifted. She felt sad but did not know exactly why. She'd missed all the friends dearly since they had headed off to war, especially Aaron. She knew that she could never turn back the clock. But she also knew that the wigwam would always be there…whenever the friends would meet again. Gazing to the bend in the river, she suddenly saw movement by the trees. She stood up to get a closer look.

"Charlie, do you see it?"

"What?" exclaimed Charlie in a high-pitched tone.

"There is something moving along the river. We best get back to the house!"

"Yeah, I see it…it's a man with a horse coming our way!"

About two hundred yards distant, a silhouette of a soldier with a horse at his side contrasted sharply against the green shadows along the riverbank. Jenny could clearly see that it was a man in a blue uniform. The horse and the man seemed to bob up and down at the same pace. Their walk was not rushed, but steady. Disappearing for a moment behind a small grove of saplings, they seemed to move directly to the knoll where Charlie and she stood. Jenny, slightly alarmed by the stranger, turned towards the house; cupped her hands around her mouth; and shouted, "Mother! Come out here! There's a Union soldier coming up the pasture!"

Her voice echoed across the Putnam farm, and within a moment a short *thud* followed as Leonora firmly shut the door and stepped out on the porch to get a closer look. She peered for a moment with her hand above her brow and then scurried the distance to the knoll where Jenny was.

"Well, my Lord, Jenny, it looks like a soldier to me, too! I don't know a Yankee up here that would harm anyone. Let's just see what this stranger wants from us. Perhaps he's hungry after a long day in the saddle."

The soldier and horse continued toward the knoll, advancing now to about one hundred yards. Charlie looked up at his mother and moved closer to her and Jenny, feeling the need to protect the women now that his father was gone.

"Goodness gracious," said Jenny with excitement rising in her voice. "Could it be? Oh, please, could it be?"

"What, Jenny, what do you see?"

"It's Black Hawk! It's father's war-horse, Mother! I know it is him!"

Leonora was stunned. It had been over seven months since the colonel's death. She could not fathom why Black Hawk would be coming up the pasture. Could it be true?

Jenny took off at a full run down the sloping pasture with Charlie close at her heels. Leonora stayed where she was and placed both her hands on her mouth. She hoped that Jenny's vision was true.

Jenny's laced boots crunched through the cockleburs and high grass as she descended quickly from the knoll. She felt that she was flying across the pasture. She caught good sight of the soldier and then stopped suddenly, catching her breath. Tears of astonishment welled up. She blinked. A tear stream wetted both cheeks. She gasped again for air.

The soldier kept his deliberate pace until he stood abruptly in front of her.

"Did you miss me, Jenny?" Aaron said calmly as he stood almost at attention.

Black Hawk snorted.

Jenny gasped; ran quickly toward him; and hugged him, lifting herself off her heels.

"Aaron, my love, I thought you were dead, and now you are home!" They kissed. Aaron picked Jenny up from the ground as he hugged her. He twirled her around as if in a waltz. Charlie looked up in wonder and grinned.

Aaron smiled at Charlie, winked, and then cupped his hand over his mouth as he whispered in Jenny's ear, "I will always love you, Jenny. I'm home now."

Jenny looked at Aaron, and her tears continued to flow freely. She held Aaron's hand firmly, like when they walked the Pecatonica. She did not want to let go.

Turning, she quickly looked up the slope to the farmhouse. Cupping her hands over her mouth in an awkward yet dainty fashion, she shouted, "Mother, come down! Aaron is home!"

Hearing the announcement, Leonora did not hesitate and, within a minute, had rushed up to greet him. She hugged Aaron, almost pulling him off his feet.

And then everyone quickly moved to Black Hawk, who whinnied excitedly with the commotion around him. After calming Black Hawk down, Jenny and Leonora rubbed his mane while Charlie deftly patted his soft, supple nose.

"What a beauty he is!" Leonora said softly.

Aaron looked at Jenny. He smiled and nodded. "You should have seen him in the fight at Missionary Ridge!" Aaron proudly interjected. Realizing the connection to the fallen Colonel Putnam, he immediately felt an awkward silence as he looked fleetingly over at Leonora.

"It's all right, Aaron," Leonora replied. "Our colonel was brave, too. Black Hawk is safe now."

In the distance a train whistle from the Illinois Central blew across the valley. Two turtledoves took to the wind, causing Black Hawk to jump. His ears were perched. Aaron reined him in.

"Whoa, boy, whoa," he said. "Let's get this military stuff off you now!"

"Is he here to stay?" Jenny asked.

Charlie looked up inquisitively at Aaron.

"Yes, he is here to stay. General Smith and his officers thought you would like to have him home, Mrs. Putnam, so they pooled some money, and we took the fastest train we could! I've been with him in the boxcar for over a week now. Black Hawk even shared some oats with me!" Aaron smiled.

Charlie chuckled loudly. Jenny and Leonora laughed, too.

Leonora looked down at her apron and then looked up. "I best be up to the house now, Jenny…lots to do. Aaron, can you stay for supper tonight?"

"Yes ma'am. Haven't had anything but hish and hash and a few hard crackers since I can remember…and, of course, the oats!"

Charlie smiled again.

Leonora approached Aaron again and hugged him. She turned to Black Hawk and rubbed her hand across Black Hawk's mane again. "I will write a letter thanking General Smith and his gallant officers." She turned to Jenny and Aaron. Tears welled up, so she pulled out her kerchief and dabbed her eyes.

She left the knoll and proceeded slowly up the slope to the Putnam farmhouse. When she arrived there, she continued into the cool parlor room to her writing desk, which was tucked away in a corner by the window. She looked out the window into the distance. After taking in several deep breaths, she sat down and picked up her quill with her right hand. Dabbing her eyes with the kerchief again, she placed the tip into her rosewood inkwell, shook it once, and began to write.

> *Gen. John E. Smith*
> *I received…at the hand of your prompt and faithful orderly, the horse which my dear husband rode and from which he fell at the battle of Mission Ridge. I need not tell you that I am <u>gratified</u>…this word can give but a faint expression of my feelings for your generous act, in placing me in possession of an object I shall so much prize.*
> *Believe me, my dear sir, that nothing in this world can*

go farther towards reconciling me to my present condition
of loneliness and bereavement than the thought that my
husband fell faithfully and bravely fighting to preserve
his Country, and that living and dying he was well
beloved and rightly appreciated by his <u>fellow</u> <u>Officers</u> and
<u>Companions</u> in arms, who shared his hope and dangers.
Your kindness and that of the Officers of the 93d Illinois
Regiment, to me in this regard I assure you, dear Sir, will
never be forgotten…

I remain with high regard
yours very truly
Mrs. Holden Putnam [22]

There was a rustle in the wind.

Leonora put down her quill and walked through the parlor room to the back porch. She could still see Jenny, Aaron, and Charlie sitting on the little knoll, looking toward the river. The shrill whistle of the Illinois Central echoed again somewhere to the west. She paused for a moment as she looked to the sky and then peered across the pasture. A movement along the river caused her to smile.

There was Black Hawk in his storied magnificence, racing at full gallop…like a deep-black undulating mass that seemed to float atop the meadow. His dark mane flapped gently across the deep Shiloh scar, which would forever be prominent on his front left flank. The summer breeze picked up with the setting of the sun, blowing his mane upward, which seemed to accelerate his speed even more.

Black Hawk's blue-and-gold military saddle was gone now. It would never again encumber him on the march. His shiny brass bridle and leather reins that urged him forward in battle were gone, too. Never again would he experience the misty fog of war…or climb mountains touched with fire. He was home now. And like the friends of the wigwam, who shared his journeys, he was free to play again—free to roam along the lazy Pecatonica.

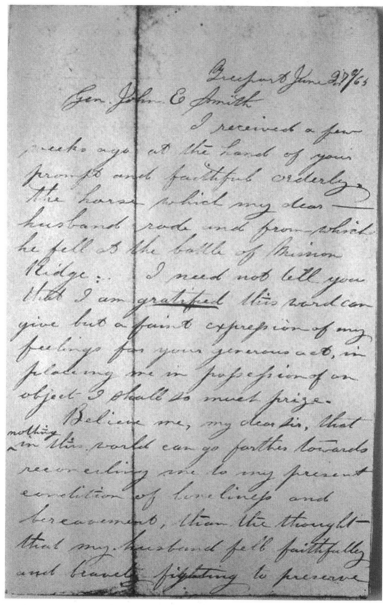

**Copy of Original Letter from
Leonora Putnam to General John E. Smith**

his Country; and that living
and dying he was well beloved
and rightly appreciated by his
fellow Officers and Companions
in arms, who shared his hopes and
his dangers. Your kindness and
that of the Officers of the 93d ——
Regiment, to me in this regard
I assure you, dear Sir, will never
be forgotten or be lightly esteemed,
and my earnest prayer to the
God of battles will ever be, that he
will guard the brave, generous, and
loyal associates of my lamented
husband in safety and honor
through the perils and dangers
of Camp and field. Please
give my kindest thanks to the
Subaltern Officers by whose generous liberality the transportation
of the horse was paid, and also
for the kind assurances contained
in your letter of condolence; please

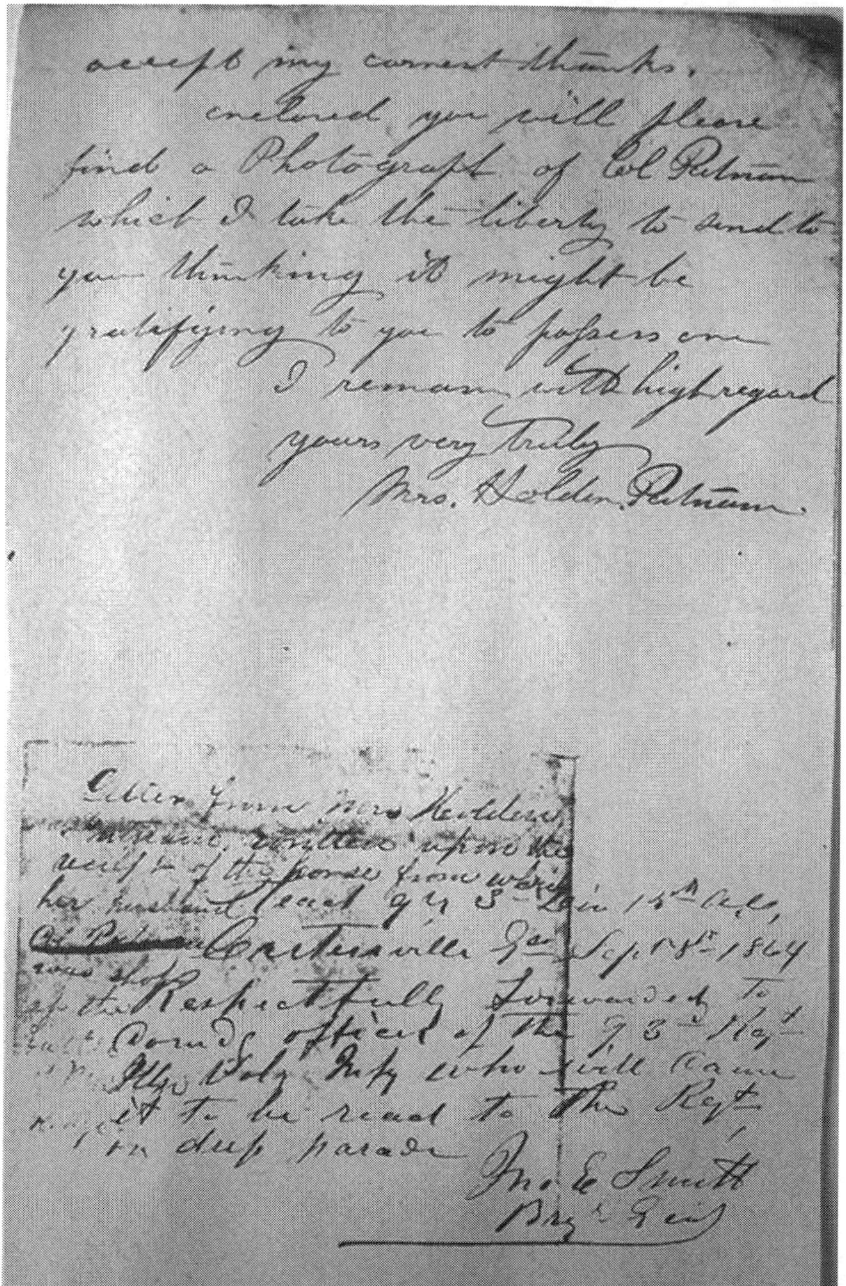

Afterword

Characters by Order of Appearance

Will (William P. Erwin)

Will was buried in a mass grave on the slopes of Missionary Ridge on November 25, 1863. On November 27, 1989, 126 years later, retired marine colonel Ray Erwin, great-grandnephew of William P. Erwin, placed a corrected headstone on his fallen ancestor's grave, thus officially "promoting" Will to sergeant, a promotion received just weeks before his death. On that day a multitude of reporters from two newspapers and a local television station attended the rededication ceremony.

Aaron Dunbar

After the war, Aaron taught school during the winter months and engaged in farming during the summer. His journals written during the war were used to complete the *History of the Ninety-Third Regiment, Illinois Volunteer Infantry* published October 5, 1898.

U. S. Grant

After the Battle of Missionary Ridge, Grant was promoted to general in chief of the entire Union army. By executing aggressive strategy and tactics that he used effectively in the West, he brought General Robert E. Lee to terms at Appomattox Courthouse on April 9, 1865, thus ending the Civil War. In 1868 he was elected to the presidency and finished two terms in the White House. He completed the *Personal Memoirs of U. S. Grant* a few days before his death from throat cancer in 1885. His memoirs are considered by scholars to be one of the great autobiographies in the English language.

Ely Parker

Ely Parker continued as U. S. Grant's military secretary until the end of the Civil War. He was promoted to lieutenant colonel and later became a brevet brigadier general of volunteers. At Appomattox he transcribed in fair hand the official surrender papers for Robert E. Lee. Later in life he became the commissioner of Indian Affairs. He died in 1895, almost ten years after U. S. Grant, his good friend from Galena. His funeral in Buffalo, New York was attended by dignitaries from around the country including Fred Grant, son of General Grant, and leading men and women of the Iroquois nation.

Congressman
Elihu Washburne

After the Civil War, Washburne's most notable assignments were US minister to France and president of the Chicago Historical Society, now the Chicago History Museum. In his retirement he wrote *Recollections of a Minister to France, 1869–1877*. He will always be remembered for his lobbying effort with Lincoln and congress for the promotion of U. S. Grant, his Galena neighbor, to the rank of brigadier general.

Abraham Lincoln

America's greatest president since George Washington, Lincoln kept the Union together for four long years, but was assassinated by John Wilkes Booth just days after Lee's surrender at Appomattox. Illinois's greatest citizen, Lincoln was a man of gentle spirit who rose from the backwoods of Salem to Springfield, Illinois, and then to Washington, DC. His interesting life, history, and contributions to America have filled thousands of volumes since his untimely death on April 14, 1865, at Ford's Theatre. Without question, Lincoln, as subject matter, will continue to fill thousands more volumes for many years to come.

Colonel John M. Loomis

After Missionary Ridge, perhaps due to the disastrous attack and devastating Union losses at the Tunnel Hill fight, Loomis's career in the military was ruined. Letters written to Lincoln and Grant on his behalf requesting promotion to brigadier general were ignored, causing him to resign on April 14, 1864, a little more than one year before Appomattox. In a letter to General Sherman on the same day, he wrote, "The pride and self respect which I cherish is so hurt by the continual promotion over me of my juniors."

Colonel Holden Putnam

Fire Marshal and, later, Colonel Putnam lies buried in City Cemetery, Freeport, Illinois. The epitaph on his memorial reads as follows:

"Thy Name be thy Epitaph"

E. Elmer Ellsworth

Elmer was the North's first casualty of the Civil War, and he became an instant martyr for the Union cause. The devastating news of his death saddened thousands of admirers across America. The Lincoln family openly mourned him as his body lay in state at the White House.

General John E. Smith

After Missionary Ridge, John E. Smith marched with Sherman to the sea. During this time, he was promoted to major general and eventually commanded the District of West Tennessee. After being mustered out of volunteer service in April, 1866, he accepted the colonelcy of the Twenty-Seventh Infantry—regular army—serving during the Indian wars until retiring in May of 1881. He died in Chicago, Illinois, on January 29, 1897.

"Allie" (Jennie Hodgers) a.k.a. Albert D. J. Cashier -Seated to the Right-

Private Cashier (seated on the right) continued through the war unsuspected of being a woman. After Vicksburg, she fought with the Ninety-Fifth Illinois during the Red River Campaign, and Brice's Cross Roads, and at the horrific battles of Franklin and Nashville where there were record casualties. After the war she returned to a hero's welcome at Belvidere, Illinois, and then worked as a handyman and farmhand in Saunemin. She never married and continued to disguise her gender until 1911 when her leg was fractured in an automobile accident and during medical inspection, the attending physician was shocked to notice her true gender. Her secret was kept for a while, but was exposed two years later, causing a sensation in Northern Illinois and across America. She lived another two years in the limelight and then passed away on October 11, 1915. She was buried with full military honors at the Saunemin Cemetery, leaving her legacy as the only documented woman in the Civil War to fulfill an army enlistment. (*Author's note*: In order to avoid any confusion with Jenny Putnam, the name "Allie" was substituted for the first name "Jennie" of Jennie Hodgers legend. According to conflicting historical accounts, Cashier [sometimes recorded as "Cashire"] referred to herself as "Jennie Hodgers" prior to enlistment. Legend has it that Hodgers was a teenage stowaway from Belfast, Ireland, who arrived in America, eventually settling in Northern Illinois near the Rock River in the 1850s.—*jwh*)

Jenny Putnam

After the Civil War, Jenny moved to Chicago with her mother, Leonora, and her brother, Charlie. After experiencing the Chicago Fire firsthand in 1871, she moved to San Francisco where she also survived the devastating 1906 earthquake. It is not known whether she ever married.

T.J. Lockwood

T.J. returned to his hometown, and despite his blindness, he prospered. Aaron Dunbar's *History of the Ninety-Third Regiment* records the following: "He is one of the leading business men of Buda, Ill, and does many marvelous things, in the way of business, for a blind person."

Trick, a.k.a. Patrick Kane

Trick survived his wound and continued with the Ninety-Third Illinois, participating in Sherman's March to the Sea. He returned to Buda after mustering out with the rest of the regiment in June, 1865. Margaret Schmitt, Trick's granddaughter and past curator of the Sheffield Museum in Illinois, remembered well how he would hold his grandchildren on his lap and tell the story of his boyhood friend T.J. who carried him off the Champion Hill battlefield.

Willie Lincoln

Willie died in the White House in 1862.

Tad Lincoln with Father

Tad died nine years after Willie.

Mary Todd Lincoln

Four years after Tad's death, Mary Todd was committed to an insane asylum by her oldest and only living son, Robert. She was released several months later and traveled abroad for seven years. She died in Springfield, where her fondest memories were, in July 1882.

Major Luther Cowan

After his courageous charge at Vicksburg, Luther (seated) was buried in his hometown of Warren, Illinois. The local newspaper, *Warren Independent*, wrote on May 31, 1864, "The funeral of Maj. Cowan took place yesterday and was largely attended. Notwithstanding the inclemency of the weather, the church was full and overflowing."

Elliott N. Bush
Captain Company G
Ninety-Fifth Illinois Volunteers

Killed June 10, 1864, at Guntown, Mississippi.

Lieutenant Colonel Maltby
Forty-Fifth Illinois Lead Mine Regiment

Promoted to brigadier general, he became the military governor of Vicksburg in September 1867. He remained in that position until his death the following March.

Captain
Charles F. Taggart

Captain Taggart, good friend of Colonel Putnam, participated in Sherman's March to the Sea. He resigned in January 1865 due to health. After returning to Freeport, he became a postal clerk and lived fifteen more years. His obituary in the Freeport Bulletin read, "Capt. Taggart enjoyed the fruits of a well spent life surrounded by the blessings vouchsafed to him in a happy home and children of whom any father might be proud."

Charlie (Charles Flint Putnam)

A few years after his father's death at Missionary Ridge, Charlie moved with his sister, Jenny, and his mother, Leonora, to Chicago. Following in his father's footsteps, he chose a military career and accepted an appointment to the US Naval Academy at the tender age of fourteen. After graduation from the academy in 1873, at his request, he served in the Asiatic Squadron in the Far East and then later conducted rescue missions for stranded expeditions to the North Pole. Just one month after his twenty-seventh birthday, he followed his father's fate and perished in the line of duty. A monument today stands as a tribute to Charlie on the US Naval Academy grounds that reads: *To the Memory of Charles Flint Putnam, Master, U.S.N., who volunteered for duty on board the U.S. Steamer Rogers, a vessel dispatched to the Arctic Ocean for the relief of the Jeannette Exploring Expedition. After having gallantly succored his shipwrecked companions while returning to his station of Cape Serdze-Kamen, Siberia, he drifted out to sea and perished alone on the ice in St. Lawrence Bay. Behring Straits, about Jan. 11, 1882. This tablet is erected by his friends and brother officers in loving remembrance and as a memorial of his heroic sacrifice.*

Photo credits and primary source documents courtesy of the Chicago History Museum, Chicago, IL; National Archives, Washington, DC; Galena Historical Society and U.S. Grant Museum, Galena, IL; Bureau County Historical Society and Museum, Princeton, IL; Stephenson County Historical Society, Freeport, IL; and private collections.

Notes

Original Letters & Primary Source Documents

❦

1   Elmer E. Ellsworth diary (manuscript copy) by Mrs. Edgar B. Barton, stepdaughter of Private Francis E. Brownell. Minnesota Historical Society, 1921.

2   Ibid.

3   National Archives Collections, Washington, DC.

4   Chicago History Museum Archives, Chicago, Illinois.

5   Letters of General John E. Smith. Collection of Kirby Smith (descendant of General John E. Smith), Barrington, Illinois.

6   Ibid.

7   Civil War Letters and Diary of L.H. Cowan, Galena Historical Society and U. S. Grant Museum, Galena, Illinois.

8   National Archives Collections, Washington, DC.

9   Civil War Letters and Diary of L.H. Cowan, Galena Historical Society and U. S. Grant Museum, Galena, Illinois.

10   Ibid.

11   Letters of General John E. Smith. Collection of Kirby Smith (descendant of General John E. Smith), Barrington, Illinois.

12   Civil War Letters and Diary of L.H. Cowan), Galena Historical Society and U. S. Grant Museum, Galena, Illinois.

13   Ibid.

14   Ibid.

15   Letters of General John E. Smith. Collection of Kirby Smith (descendant of General John E. Smith), Barrington, Illinois.

16 Civil War Letters and Diary of L.H. Cowan, Galena Historical Society and U. S. Grant Museum, Galena, Illinois.

17 Ibid.

18 Letters of General John E. Smith. Collection of Kirby Smith (descendant of General John E. Smith), Barrington, Illinois.

19 Aaron Dunbar, *Civil War Journals of Aaron Dunbar*, vol. 2, p.3. Bureau County Historical Society and Museum, Princeton, Illinois.

20 Ibid. pp. 23–24.

21 National Archives Collections, Record Group 233, Records of the US House of Representatives (December 1, 1862).

22 National Archives Collections, Washington, DC.